Behold the unicorn ...

It was no longer only a beast of bone. It had grown flesh and form. It was black as night, black as every night of the world together, and it shone as the night shines with a comet. On this burning blackness, the mane and the flaunting tail of it were like an acid, golden-silver fire off the sea, and it was bearded in this sea-acid-fire, and spikes of it were on the slender fetlocks. Its eyes were red as metal in a forge. It was not simply beauty and strength, it was terror. It rose up and up to a height that was more, it seemed, than the room could hold, and its black shadow curved over it, far less black than itself.

Jaive said, quite steadily, "I greet you. But by the powers I can summon, be careful of me ..."

Black Unicorn

Tanith Lee

Illustrated by
Heather Cooper

A Byron Preiss Book

TOR
fantasy

A TOM DOHERTY ASSOCIATES BOOK
NEW YORK

To Louise Cooper,
Maker of stories, singer of unicorns

BLACK UNICORN

Black Unicorn copyright © 1991 by Byron Preiss Visual Publications, Inc.
Text copyright © 1991 by Tanith Lee.
Interior illustrations © 1991 by Byron Preiss Visual Publications, Inc.

Cover art by Dennis Nolan
Interior art by Heather Cooper

A Tor Book
Published by Tom Doherty Associates, Inc.
175 Fifth Avenue
New York, N.Y. 10010

Tor ® is a registered trademark of Tom Doherty Associates, Inc.

ISBN: 0-812-52459-4

First Tor edition: August 1993

Printed in the United States of America

0 9 8 7 6 5 4 3 2 1

PART
One

The first thing Tanaquil saw almost every morning on waking was her mother's face. But that was because a painting of Tanaquil's mother, the sorceress Jaive, hung opposite the bed. The painting of Jaive had a great bush of scarlet hair in which various jewels, plants, implements, and mice and other small animals she used in her researches were caught. "Good morning, Mother," said Tanaquil to the picture, and the picture vigorously answered: "Rise with the sun, salute the day!" As it always did. Since it was anyway usually mid-morning when Tanaquil woke up, the greeting was completely unsuitable.

Once the business with the picture was over, Tanaquil got out of bed and went to see what had been left for her breakfast. Sometimes nothing had. Today there were some pieces of cold toasted bread without any butter, an orange, and green herbal tea in a glass. Tanaquil tried the tea, then peeled the orange cautiously. As she split the segments a bird flew out.

"This way, this way," said Tanaquil impatiently to the bird as it dashed round the room, sticking its beak into the bed curtains. The bird hurtled to the window and flew into the hard red sunshine. Tanaquil stood at the window, looking away across the roofs and battlements of her mother's fortress,

at the desert. It was the same view she had seen
since she could remember. For nearly sixteen
years this had been her bedroom and that had
been the view. The long tawny sands, with their
glints of minerals, which changed shape after the
wind blew, the march of rock hills half a mile off,
some pointed like cones, some with great natural
archways that ran through them, showing the end-
lessness of the desert beyond. From any part of
Jaive's fortress, if you looked out, this was the
kind of thing you saw, dunes and rocks, and the
hot sky. By day the fortress and the desert baked.
At night it grew cold and a thin snow fell, the sand
turned to silver and the stars burned white.

"Hey," said a high-pitched voice outside, "hey."

Tanaquil glanced and saw one of the peeves was
sitting on the roof below her window. It was about
the size of a large cat, with thick brown fur over a
barrel-shaped body and short muscular legs. It
gripped with three paws and with the fourth
scratched itself busily. It had a long dainty muzzle,
a bushy tail, and ears that would go up in points,
although just now they flopped down. In its big
yellow eyes was an urgent look.

"Want a bone," said the peeve.

"I'm sorry I haven't got one," said Tanaquil.

"No, no, want a *bone*," insisted the peeve. It
hopped up the roof and jumped into the embrasure of the window like a fat fur pig. Tanaquil put
out her hand to stroke the peeve, but it evaded
her and plopped down into the room. It began to
hurry about scratching at things and poking its
long nose under the rug, upsetting the stool. It
pattered across Tanaquil's work table, through her
collection of easily damaged fossils, and over a

small clock lying on its back. The peeve scattered cogs and wheels. It sprang. Now it was in the fire-place.

"There are no bones *here*," said Tanaquil firmly.

The peeve took no notice. "Want a bone," it ex-plained, and knocked over her breakfast. The herbal tea spread across the floor, and the peeve drank it, sneezing and snuffling. A piece of toast had fallen on its head, and it threw it off with an irritated *"Bone, bone."*

Tanaquil sighed. She went into the marble bath alcove and pressed the head of the lion for a foun-tain of cool water to wash in. The water did not come. Instead a stream of sticky berry wine poured out.

"Oh, *Mother*!" shouted Tanaquil, furiously. She ran out, kicked the stool across the room, and then the pieces of bread. The orange had turned into a sort of flower that was growing up the left-hand pillar of the fireplace. The peeve was nibbling this. It turned and watched as Tanaquil dressed herself in yesterday's crumpled dress and ran a comb through her hair, which was a lighter red than Jaive's.

"Got a bone?"

"I haven't got a bone for heaven's sake! Be quiet."

The peeve sat down and washed its stomach, now muttering anxiously, "Flea, flea." Then ab-ruptly it threw itself up the chimney and was gone, although a shower of soot fell down into the hearth.

Tanaquil left the room a moment after, slam-ming the door.

Four flights of wide stone stairs, with wooden

bannisters carved with beasts, fruits, demons and so on, went up from Tanaquil's level to the haunt of her mother. On each landing there was an opening to the roof walks and battlements, and in one place Tanaquil saw three of the soldiers sitting on the wall playing a game of Scorpions and Ladders. They were all drunk, as usual, but, noting Tanaquil passing, one called out: "Don't go up, Lady. The sorceress is busy."

"Unfortunate," said Tanaquil. And she climbed the last flight, out of breath, and reached the big black door that shut off her mother's Sorcerium.

In the center of the door was a head of green jade, which addressed Tanaquil. "Do you seek Jaive?"

"Obviously."

"What is your name, and rank?"

"Tanaquil, her daughter."

The head seemed to purse its lips, but then the door gave a creak and swung massively open.

The chamber beyond was full of oily smoke and pale lightning flashes. Tanaquil was used to this. She walked in and found her way among looming chests and stands cluttered with objects, some of which cheeped and chittered. Suddenly there was a great mirror, and in it Tanaquil caught a glimpse of a burning city, towers and sparks and creatures flying through the air. Then the vision vanished, and the smoke sank. Jaive appeared out of the sinking smoke. She stood behind a table covered with books, globes of glass, instruments, wands, and colored substances that bubbled. In a large cage sat two white mice with rabbit ears and the tails of serpents, eating a sausage. Jaive wore a floor-length gown of black-green silk sewn with golden embroidery. Her flaming hair surrounded her face like the burning city in the mirror. She frowned.

"What do you want?" asked Tanaquil's mother.

"Would you like a list?" said Tanaquil.

"I am engaged—" said Jaive.

"You always are. Did you enjoy your breakfast, mother? Mine had a bird in it and then turned into a flower. One of the peeves spilled the rest. My fountain water was berry wine. Most of my clothes have disappeared. *I'm sick of it!*"

"What is this nonsense?" said Jaive.

"Mother, you know that everything is in an eternal mess here because of your magic, because of leaks of power and side effects of incantations. It's awful."

"I search for knowledge," said Jaive. She added vaguely, "How dare you speak to your mother like this?"

Tanaquil sat down on a large dog of some kind that had temporarily turned into a stool.

"When I was little," said Tanaquil, "I thought it was wonderful. When you made the butterflies come out of the fire, and when you made the garden grow in the desert. But the butterflies went pop and the garden dissolved."

"These childish memories," said Jaive. "I've tried to educate you in the art of sorcery."

"And I wasn't any good at it," said Tanaquil.

"Dreadful," agreed her mother. "You're a mere mechanical, I'm afraid." She made a pass over a beaker and a tiny storm rose into the air. Jaive laughed in pleasure. Tanaquil's stomach rumbled.

"Mother," said Tanaquil, "perhaps I should leave."

"Yes, do, Tanaquil. Let me get on."

"I mean leave the fortress."

"Tiresome girl, where could you go?"

Tanaquil said, warily, "If my father—"

Jaive swelled; her robe billowed and her eyes flashed; small faces, imps perhaps, or only tangles, looked out of her hair.

"I have never told you who your father was. I renounced him. I know nothing of him now. Perhaps he no longer lives."

"After all," said Tanaquil, "I hardly ever see you, you wouldn't miss me. And he—"

"I won't discuss it. I've told you before, your father is nothing to me. You must put him out of your mind."

Tanaquil lost her temper again. She stood up and glared at the mice's sausage.

"Perhaps I'll just go anyway. Anywhere must be better!"

"It would take days to cross the desert, stupid child. Only a sorceress could manage it."

"Then help me."

"I wish you to remain here. You're my daughter."

There was a rattling noise in the wall, and a faint soprano voice came down to them from near the ceiling. ". . . *Bone* . . ." The peeve was passing on its quest through the chimneys.

Jaive took little notice. The peeves, desert animals that had made burrows about her fort, thinking it another rock, had years before been infected by her magic and so begun to speak. To Tanaquil the peeve symbolized everything that was wrong. She said tensely, "Mother, you must let me go."

"No," said Jaive. And with tiger's eyes she smiled on her daughter.

Tanaquil got up from the dog and went back across the room and out of the door. On the green jade head, at the age of twelve, she had once painted a moustache, and the head had blinked a ray at her that threw her down the stairs. Tanaquil closed the black door restrainedly and wondered where to vent her anger and frustration.

Jaive's fortress had been built in the time of her grandmother, also a sorceress and recluse. It was a strange building of rather muddled design, and from a distance on the desert it was not only peeves who thought it only a peculiar formation of rock. To reach the kitchen of the fort, it was necessary to roam through several long and winding corridors and then down a gloomy cavernous stair into the basement. This Tanaquil did.

In the third corridor, a carved gargoyle on a beam, touched by another random breath of Jaive's magic, abruptly flared its wings and crowed, but Tanaquil ignored it. She carried the small clock she had been repairing for the cook. This was something Tanaquil was good at. Since the age of ten, she had found herself able to mend things. And so, while her mother extravagantly summoned and questioned demons in her Sorcerium, Tanaquil worked carefully on broken dolls and clocks, music boxes, and even sometimes some of the soldiers' crossbows, or bits of the cannon, which were never used except by accident and often went wrong.

The kitchen lay six feet below ground, with high windows near the ceiling that let in the light

and the sand. Boys were supposed to be constantly at work, sweeping the floors or brushing off
the surfaces. On approaching the kitchen, though,
it was usually remarkable only for its stillness and
the lazy buzz of talk.

Tanaquil opened the door.

The cook sat on her chair with her feet on the
row of ovens, most of which were cold. Two scullery maids were playing Scorpions and Ladders,
and the third was embroidering. None of the
sweeper boys was present. A large pot of yellow
tea was on the table, and a plate of pancakes.

"Here's your clock," said Tanaquil, delivering it.
She took a pancake and poured herself some tea.

"There now. It goes. Just look. What a clever
lady."

"Is there anything else that wants mending?"
asked Tanaquil. For five years, this was all that
had stopped her from going mad, she thought.
And there always was something. But as if out of
spite the cook shook her shaggy head. "Not a
thing. And that doll you saw to for Pillow's child is
still lovely, moving its arms and going *Mamaa*!"

"And she's tried ever so hard to break it again,"
said Pillow, the embroiderer.

"Well, if there's nothing," said Tanaquil, trying
to sound businesslike. She felt dejected.

"Let's see," said the cook, "would the lady like
to make a cake?"

Tanaquil fought with a blush. "No, thank you."
The cook had comforted Tanaquil when she was
little, letting her make iced biscuits and ginger-
bread camels in the ovens, to keep her from being
bored and lonely. But this was not the answer now.
Even mending something was not, although it

would have helped. "I'll be on my way," said Tanaquil airily.

As she closed the kitchen door, she heard the cook say to Pillow, "Madam really ought to have done something with that girl, it's a waste."

A waste, thought Tanaquil as she went back up the stairs from the kitchen. *I've been wasted.* And she shouted at a large rat that was quietly coming down. The rats had never been infected with magical speech, or never bothered to use it if they had. Nevertheless it looked offended.

Tanaquil climbed again up the fortress. She now seemed to herself to have spent most of her days going up and down and around it. She came out on one of the lower battlements, where the captain of the soldiers had his apartment in a turret. In fact he was out on the wall walk with four of his men, rolling wooden balls at a mark.

"It's the young lady," said one of the soldiers.

They all straightened up and saluted her.

The captain offered her his beer flagon, but she refused.

"Nothing to repair," said the captain. "You may have heard the cannon go off last week—Borrik thought he saw an army coming, but it was that dust storm, of course. Even so, the machine worked a treat, thanks to that hinge you saw to."

"Oh," said Tanaquil. "And the bows?"

"First class. Even Iggel's throw-knife works, after you fixed the balance. I expect something or other will go wrong in a day or so," he added encouragingly.

Tanaquil had a sudden humiliating idea that some of the kinder soldiers might muck up their equipment simply in order to give her something to do.

"What a relief," said Tanaquil. "A free afternoon at last!" And she sauntered off.

The other occasional thing Tanaquil had been doing over the weeks, months, years of her life in Jaive's fortress, had been to go for a Walk. Her first memories of Walks were that her nurse—naturally, Jaive had had little time to spare—took Tanaquil up and down all the corridors, and sometimes out into the inner courtyard, which was quite large, and planted with orange trees, grapevines, laurel hedges, and one dusty dilapidated palm only thirteen feet high. At one end of the yard was a kitchen garden, rather overgrown, some grass where goats were penned, and an ornate stone well on which was a stone eagle. Now and then the eagle changed shape, and it was always the first thing the little Tanaquil ran to see: Once it had looked like an ostrich. Then Tanaquil would play in the courtyard, alone but for the nurse, for there had been no children anywhere near her own age. As Tanaquil grew older, and the nurse more elderly, the Walks wended outside the fortress. In the beginning Tanaquil had been very interested in the desert. She had made sand castles of neater appearance than the fortress. But beyond the shadow of the fortress's walls, the dunes blistered. There was no oasis for miles, no village. The fort contained the only water. When she was older still, Tanaquil used to set out for the rock hills. The nurse never made it so far, and used to stand feebly calling on the sand, under her parasol. Tanaquil was twelve before she managed to get to the rocks. Her triumph was marred because there was absolutely nothing on the other side but more sand exactly the same as the rest, stretching away and away to the lavender horizon.

Now Tanaquil went for a Walk every other day, solely to ease her restlessness with exercise. The Walk was completely boring and purposeless. But to do it she must put on boots against the burning sand and cover her red head with a silk scarf tied with a band of ribbon. She would walk as far as the rock hills, sit in their shade, and drink some water she had brought with her. Sometimes she climbed their sides, and dug out small, frail fossils with her knife. Then perhaps she would walk a mile or so further off, west, across the sands. When she did this she fantasized to herself that she was leaving home. That just out of sight was a mighty city of tiled walls, domes and gardens, fountains, markets and noisy crowds. But she knew from the lessons her mother had given her for an hour every day until she was fourteen, that although there was a city, it was a hundred miles off. Nor in all her life had Tanaquil ever seen a caravan cross the desert near Jaive's fortress. They did not come this way. Strangers were limited to desert traders, herders, and wild dogs and jackals. Near sunset, Tanaquil would face up to facts, turn round, and come back from the desert.

Today Tanaquil went for a Walk.

As she plodded across the sand, skidded down dunes, she was entirely occupied with questions. Had yesterday been so different from all the other days? Had she felt, yesterday, this terrific urge, much more than fantasy, to escape? It was as if, like the eagle, she had changed shape over night. Now she was someone else, another, desperate Tanaquil.

But it was impossible. She must get away—and she could not.

Some peeves were romping near the base of the rock hills. They gave off loud raucous squeaks, and Tanaquil realized they had not caught the magic speech.

She drank the water from her bottle, then got up the hill formed like a bridge, nearly flat at the top, and with the great hollow arch beneath. She sat on the bridge-hill and looked at all the old scrapings her own knife had made. There was one small fossil left, a pale shell, but so delicate it would crack if she cut down for it.

Tanaquil stared out instead over the sand. Gradually a mirage came to be, of a river with trees on its banks.

Once the whole desert had been covered by the sea, which had left behind the shells and skeletons of weird creatures now extinct. One night, Jaive had shown Tanaquil an illusion of the sea on the desert. The waves had swirled about the fortress, frosted at the top with foam, and the moon shone redder than the sun.

"You must remember," said Jaive to the nine-year-old Tanaquil, "that this world is badly made. But we sorcerers believe there are other worlds, some worse, and one the improved model of this. Of this perfect world we may catch glimpses." And she had tried to teach Tanaquil use of the magic mirror, but Tanaquil had made a mistake and the mirror cracked and Jaive had been furious.

"Oh, Mother," said Tanaquil.

She sat on the bridge-rock until the sun began

to wester over the sloping dunes. Then she got up and faced back toward the fortress of the sorceress.

Probably she could find some cold snacks in the kitchen. There was seldom dinner in her mother's hall. Then she must search the library for a readable book—though bursting with volumes, the library had few of these. And then. What was there but to go to bed and sleep as long as she could?

Tanaquil went up to her room from the library, where she had read part of a book on ancient witchcraft and part of a parchment on sorcerer-princes, having located nothing else. She had decided to try to find some of her missing clothes, which usually moved themselves into absurd places, such as up the chimney, or mixed themselves with the furnishings and changed color, so that they blended.

As she was investigating the chimney, Tanaquil recalled the peeve that had rushed up there after a bone. She hoped it had found a way out. Although the nights were icy cold, fires were not often lit. Tanaquil, in passing, pressed the lion's mouth for hot water, but a fountain of paper flowers fell out.

Beyond the window, light snow drifted to the desert. The moon had risen, and the dunes were iced biscuits.

Tanaquil looked at her bed.

On the pillows lay something round and black. Tanaquil approached with caution. "*Oh*, no!" shouted Tanaquil. "You wretched thing!"

The peeve of the morning—covered thick with the black soot it had also sprinkled generously all over the bed and the pillows, which it had also decorated with black paw marks—raised its head.

"What?" asked the peeve.

"Just look what you've done, you pest."

"Done nothing," said the peeve. "What done?" It looked about, surprised.

"All this ghastly mess—"

"Soots," said the peeve. "Wash, wash," and it rolled about, licking itself halfheartedly, spreading the soot further.

Tanaquil grabbed the peeve and bore it to the window. She plumped it in the embrasure and gave its flank a sharp tap. "Get out. Go away."

"Moon," said the peeve, staring rapturously skyward.

"Go *away*."

Tanaquil slammed the shutters on it.

She dreamed she was running over the dunes, in the snow. Her feet were bare, she went like the wind. There were no rocks, no sign of the fortress, she did not know where she was and did not care.

She woke up because of a loud rasping and scratching on the shutters.

"Come in," stated a voice, "come in now."

"Go away," repeated Tanaquil to the peeve.

But the peeve went on scratching and demanding to enter.

"If I come to the window, I'll push you off onto the roof below," threatened Tanaquil.

"Come in," said the peeve. "Now."

Tanaquil got up scowling. She flung the shutters wide. There, in a glistening oval of moonshine, crouched the peeve. "Bone," said the peeve to her intently, "*found* a bone."

And it nosed something on the stone at its paw.

Tanaquil gazed. What she had taken for a bar of moonlight was not. It was a bone. Long and slender, unhuman, not at once identifiable, the material from which it was made glowed like polished milk-crystal. And in the crystal were tiny blazing specks and glints, like diamond—no, like the stars out of the sky.

"A *bone*?" whispered Tanaquil. "Where did you find it?"

"*Found* it," said the peeve.

"But *where*?"

"Sandy," said the peeve, "hot." It blinked and took the bone lightly up again into its mouth.

Tanaquil reached out to touch. The peeve growled around the bone and lashed its tail, making a thumping noise on the shutters. *"Mine."*

"Yes, I know it's yours. But you brought it to show me. Let me—"

"Rrr," said the peeve.

It backed away, the incredible tube of starlight gleaming between its teeth.

"You mustn't—don't *crunch* it—" cried Tanaquil.

The peeve wrinkled its face and abruptly threw itself around, in a kind of horizontal somersault. It fled, fur rippling, tail flapping, scuttling and rolling along the roof below, and vanished over an ornamental weathervane into the confused stages of darkness beneath.

Chapter Two

Morning was still dim in the kitchen. The oil lamps burned and the cook was taking her hair out of its pins, while Pillow bathed her child in the sink.

Tanaquil advanced and, bravely opening the pail for the rubbish heap, began to rummage.

"Why, whatever are you after, Lady?"

"I'm looking for a nice juicy meat bone."

Pillow gave a faint shriek.

The cook said winningly, "Now, Lady. Just you wait, and I'll do you some fried bread—"

"No, it's a bone I want, with some good bits of meat still on it—roasted or raw, I don't mind."

"Poor girl," said Pillow.

"There's been nothing like that for a month," said the cook, "not since the last dinner in hall. Is it the marrow you're after, for soup?"

"It isn't for me," said Tanaquil, irritated. The pail contained peelings and eggshells, moldy crusts and other unpleasant debris. No bones and no remnants of meat. She knew quite well the kitchen usually made itself a huge roast joint once a week, but perhaps they had been too lazy recently. "What have you got? Meat fat? Put that on some toast, thickly, for me—and a bowl of that green tea."

"Green?" The cook shook her hair-knots.

"There's no green tea here. Must have been another leak from Madam's chamber did that."

Tanaquil stayed in the kitchen until the toast and fat was ready. She ate an orange while she waited, and watched Pillow's child trying to break her doll on an oven, but the doll survived and only went *Mamaa*!

Armed with the food, Tanaquil hurried back to the stairs to her room, and put the slimy toast out in the embrasure for the peeve. She had left her shutters ajar all night, but it had not returned. Somewhere it must have its burrow, lined with things it had rooted out or stolen. But she did not know where. And where had the bone come from? Somewhere in the sand, in the hot daytime—

It had occurred to Tanaquil that maybe the peeve's bone was an ordinary bone, only transformed by the magic overspill of the fortress. And yet, it had not looked, or *seemed*, of that order. The changes here tended to be ridiculous or alarming. The bone was only exquisite.

Tanaquil sat at her work table, fiddling with fossils, cleaning her repairer's tools, one of which had coiled itself up like a snail and needed to be straightened. Then she merely sat, with her chin on her hands, staring at the open window.

The peeve did not come back. She had annoyed or upset it. Perhaps it had bitten the bone in half and devoured it—surely that could not happen.

The sun turned hotter and bathed the room in light. The fat smelled, and a golden fly danced on it and feasted.

It was midday. The peeve had not and would not come.

Tanaquil stood up. She had found her divided

skirt, and now tucked its hems into her boots. She swung into the window embrasure and out, and dropped the foot or so onto the sloping roof below.

Out here the sun was scaldingly hot. It was a world of roof hills and drainage gulleys, bushed with crops of weathervanes and old mysterious pipes. The copper roof slates greenly seared, and here and there were copses of chimneys. Above rose the tallest towers and the hedge of the battlements, where two soldiers passed each other with a bleary clack of spears. Was the burrow among the roofs, or had the peeve just decided to run up to her window on a whim?

Tanaquil picked her way along the copper slates, in and out of the shadow of chimney pots. The peeve might even have made a lair in one of the most disused of the chimneys. She peered into crevices, and found red flowers growing from cracks. Further over, under the eave of the library, was a large untidy nest once used by some ravens. They had caught speech and flown away yelling that the fort rubbish heap was not interesting enough. The nest lay in the shadow of a tower, and was protected by juts and slopes of the building.

Tanaquil lowered herself into a dry canal between the roofs and pushed through the flowers. At the canal's end was a cistern full of scummy water—it caught the snow by night and fermented by day. There were black paw marks on the cistern's edge.

To reach the library roof Tanaquil had to jump a narrow gap, through which she saw the kitchen yard below. Pillow and another girl, maybe Sausage, were hanging up some washing. They were small as the child's doll. Tanaquil took a breath and jumped. She landed on the library and heard Pillow say, far below, "Just listen, those ravens must be back."

One of the soldiers looked over from the battlements, too. Tanaquil had a moment's fear he might take her for an invader and fire at her, but he only waved.

The ravens' nest was empty, but beyond it a channel went back under the walls of the tower and the overhanging roof. Tanaquil moved on into deep shade, and stumbled over a pile of rugs and straw. The enclosure smelled of peeve, clean fur and meat and secrets. And there was a hoard of silly things—a small pan from the kitchen, some sequins, probably from one of Jaive's gowns, a spear-head ... and, gleaming like white water in the shadow—"Seven," said Tanaquil aloud, "seven of them." Seven bones like the bone she had seen the previous night: two very little, and one very long, broken, and curved, like a rib, perhaps, and four exactly the same as the first, of which it must be a replica. And all of them like milk-crystal and stars.

"*Bad.*"

Tanaquil started guiltily. She looked round, and up on the ravens' nest the peeve poised in silhouette against the bright sky. Its fur stood on end, its ears pointed, its tail was a brush. Under its forepaws was another of the amazing bones. The eighth.

"In *my* place," said the peeve.

Tanaquil wondered if it would attack her.

Then its fur lay flat and its ears flopped. Its face took on a forlorn and sorry expression.

"Oh look, I'm not stealing from you," said Tanaquil, remorseful. "I waited for you to come back and show me the bone again. And when you didn't, I came here."

"My *place*."

"Yes, to your place. Haven't you got a lot of these bones? Aren't you clever."

The peeve sat down in the nest and scratched behind its ear. "Itch," it explained. It seemed to have perked up at her compliment. "Clever," it repeated.

"Of course they belong to *you*. But won't you let me help you find them—I mean, if there are ... more?"

"More. Lots."

A cold shiver oozed down Tanaquil's spine in the boiling day.

"Will you show me? Can I help you?"

The peeve put its head down and studied the eighth bone it had brought. There was a silence.

Tanaquil said, "You know, the ravens might come back to their nest and steal from you."

The peeve tossed up its head and scanned the sky, its whiskers making fierce arcs.

Tanaquil felt like a villain.

"Let me help," she said. She went over to the peeve and gently stroked its head. The peeve allowed this and looked at her out of topaz eyes. "You are so *clever*. It's a wonderful bone."

They went out in the afternoon, when the worst of the heat was lessening. The peeve had been running back and forth all morning, only pausing to drink from the cistern in the roof gulley. After all, the peeve seemed pleased to have company. It bustled along, sometimes rushing ahead, then playing in the sand until Tanaquil caught up. The direction in which they went was that of the rock hills. Tanaquil accepted this with an odd feeling in her stomach. When the little afternoon shadow of the hills came over them, and the peeve bounded in under the hollow hill shaped like a bridge, Tanaquil nodded. The hoard of fabulous bones lay exactly beneath the spot where she had brooded. Perhaps the dust storm a week ago had uncovered them, or even other playful peeves.

The dark heat under the arch of the hill was solemn and purple. Over among the tendons of the rock, the peeve excavated, sending up sprays of sand.

Tanaquil went to see.

And there, sticking up like crystal plants, were the tops of bones.

They dug together.

"Good, good," said the peeve, thrusting in its nose, and suddenly uprooting—there could be no doubt—a whole ribcage. It was large, daunting. How it shone in the shadow. "Sprr," said the peeve. They pulled out the cage of ribs, and leg bones followed and dropped apart in jewelry bits. It was like the leg of a huge dog, or like a horse's leg.

"Is there a skull?" asked Tanaquil.

The peeve took no notice, only went on digging. It had apparently realized that, with Tanaquil to carry the bones, it could unearth all of them.

They had worked in the hollow hill for maybe an hour when the sand gave way, pouring down and over itself into a big cauldron. Some of the bones just coming visible were folded away into the sand-slip.

The peeve rolled about, kicking. Tanaquil used one of the oaths the soldiers were fond of.

Very likely, the bones lay over a void in the sand; they might tumble down into some hidden abyss, unreachable. The sand might also give way entirely under Tanaquil and the peeve, casting them after.

Tanaquil tried to make the peeve understand this, but it paid no attention, only resumed its digging. Tanaquil shrugged, and threw in her lot with it, bracing herself, if she felt any movement under her, to grab the animal and run.

No more slips occurred, and gradually the new bones came clear again. There were parts of vertebrae, and the segments of a long neck: star flowers.

Then, against her plucking hands, Tanaquil felt a smooth mass. She heaved the object out. The sand shook off.

"No good," said the peeve. "Not a bone."

"It's the *skull*," said Tanaquil.

She held the skull in her hands, astonished, even after what she had seen.

It was a horse skull, or very like one, and it gleamed like an opal, polished finer than the other bones. Colors ran through the crystal of it, fiery, limpid. She imagined the brain inside this case, which must have fed on such colors, or caused them. The teeth were all present, silvery white. A pad of bone rose on the skull, above the sockets of the eyes—layers of opal—indented like another socket to hold some precious gem.

Tanaquil looked about. She was surrounded by the bones. The peeve was still industriously digging, shooting sand into the air, disappearing slowly down a hole.

"I think that's all," said Tanaquil. "Almost all of it's here."

"More," said the peeve.

"Let's go back now."

The peeve kicked and the sand gave. The peeve fell only a foot, but Tanaquil leaned down and took hold of it. It came out pummelling the air, sneezing angrily.

"Want dig."

"No, that's enough."

"Dig, dig."

"Let's take these bones to my room. They'll be safe there. You can share my room. You'd like that. I'll get you some lovely meat fat."

The peeve considered. It sat down and washed itself, leaving the bone hole be.

Tanaquil began to gather up the bones. She took the scarf off her head and folded bones into it, and put bones into the cuffs of her boots, into pockets. The ribcage was difficult; she somehow got it on to her back. She picked up the opal skull, cradling it in her free arm. "You take those." She indicated the last few slender vertebrae she had not managed to stow. The peeve got them into its mouth. Its mouth stood open, glittering.

Suppose someone saw them? Generally, the fortress might as well have been deserted during the afternoon. The soldiers and servants dozed, and Jaive swirled about her Sorcerium impervious to heat. Tanaquil hoped they would keep to their usual schedule; she did not want to share her dis-

covery. Although she could not leave the fort, she
had found a temporary escape—for the bones of
the magical beast made her forget herself. In comparison to them, what did anything else matter?

The blast of the sunlight beyond the hill was
mighty, but the sun was lowering itself westward
and the sky was thick and golden.

Tanaquil and the peeve walked toward the fortress with great shadows before them.

Tanaquil told the peeve about the fat toast, and
roast meat, and other things she thought she
might be able to get for it. It kept pace with her,
not arguing, mouth full of magic.

The peeve made a lair under Tanaquil's bed. It
bundled up her rug and pushed that under, and
took a pillow. Streams of feather stuffing eddied
out from the torn pillow, across the floor.

As she arranged the bones along the floor at the
opposite end of the room, she heard the peeve
snuffling and complaining to itself, fidgeting
about. It had eaten the rancid fat in the window,
and she had brought some fresh from the kitchen,
where only two of the sweeper boys were lying
asleep on a cool stone oven. Now and then the
peeve would emerge and watch Tanaquil's actions
with the bones. "Please don't move them," said
Tanaquil. It came to her that it would be better to
suspend the skeleton in the air, from a ceiling
beam, and she opened her work box, measuring
lengths of fine brass chain, cutting these, and finding clips whereby to attach them—she did not
want to pierce any of the bones, was not sure she
could.

On the floor, the skeleton emerged into its true shape.

Tanaquil straightened up at last to stare at it.

Fragments were chipped, and there were gaps, missing pieces of the long spine, omissions in the ribcage—and below the right foreleg the small sharp toe of the hoof was absent. She could replace all the losses in less beautiful but adequate materials, so that at least the beast of bone was whole.

Without doubt, now she could see it was the skeleton of an extraordinary horse—but a horse also of extreme fineness, longer than was usual in the back and legs, the tail and neck, with the head also longer, and on it the strange pad of bone above the eyes . . .

The skeleton sparkled. It looked almost friendly. And then, by some shift of the sunset light, it altered, and a vague terror touched Tanaquil, like nothing she had felt before. Her mother did not believe in religion or priests, but Tanaquil wondered if she should make some offering to God. For only the God could know what this thing had been.

The light melted; the sun had set. In the deep blue sky the stars began to arrive, and the cold of night breathed at the window.

"You'll be warm here," said Tanaquil to the peeve. It snored in its lair.

Tanaquil climbed on her work table and began to put bronze hooks into the beam above—

The door was knocked. The voice of Bird, one of the girls who still sometimes absentmindedly cleaned the chambers of the fortress, came through its timbers. "Lady Tanaquil?" Tanaquil

did not think she had heard Bird's voice for two
months, had not met her anywhere. And now she
was not glad to hear or see Bird.

"Just a minute!"

Tanaquil ran to the bed, swept off the topmost
quilt, and flung it over the skeleton. Then she
opened the door. Bird bowed, as the kitchen people, who saw Tanaquil most days, never did.

"Your lady mother sent me to fetch you."

"What does she want?"

"She's got a demon sitting in her circle of wax.
I screamed when I saw it."

"She's always having demons in her circle. Why
does she want me?"

"She just said fetch you at once."

"It's not convenient—" Tanaquil checked. If
she did not go to her mother, Jaive might come
sweeping down to find her. A visit from Jaive was
rare, but then, so was a summons. "All right," said
Tanaquil, and she came out, shutting the door.
Bird had not seemed to notice the quilt, nor even
the snow of stuffing from the pillow and smears of
meat fat.

They went up the stone stairs. A wooden fruit
detached itself from the banister and bounced
away; neither girl reacted. The open landings
were chilly, and outside braziers burned along the
wall walks and the soldiers were singing sea chan-
ties.

"Do you seek Jaive?" asked the jade head on
the Sorcerium door.

"Oh, who else?"

"Your name and rank?"

But the door found itself being opened from
within in mid-question, and looked insulted.

Bird gave a tweet and darted back down the stairs.

Jaive's chamber of magic was shrouded at the walls by a curious veiledness, like mist in a forest. The center of the room was clear, and there in the wax circle, lit by the burning tapers, sat a demon with two heads, elephant ears and frog eyes, a huge stomach, and no legs, for it stopped at the pelvis—or perhaps the rest of it was in some other dimension under the floor.

Jaive stood imperiously by. She observed her daughter, shook back her scarlet maze of hair, and said, "What have you been up to, Tanaquil?"

"Nothing," said Tanaquil. "How do you mean?" she added, more casually.

"Epbal Enrax says to me that weird elements have entered my fortress."

Epbal Enrax was the demon. It was called up about once a month. Tanaquil nodded politely. "How are you, Epbal Enrax?" The demon breathed out a mauve puff, which was a sign of contentment. "I don't see why," said Tanaquil, "you should think any weird elements here have anything to do with me."

"Epbal Enrax," said Jaive, "speak!"

Epbal Enrax spoke. The chamber shook, and pestles and parchments plummeted from cabinets—its voice was not loud, only *reverberant*.

"*Below*," said Epbal Enrax, "*close by*."

"Which is you, Tanaquil."

"It's also half your soldiers, the maids—"

"Continue, Epbal Enrax."

"*Red of hair sets fingers to a spark of fire*."

Tanaquil shivered. Luckily the demon brought extra coldness—some of the taper flames had frozen—she had an excuse. She looked at her mother scathingly, and said, "He means *you*, mother. Red hair and sparks and all that. There's some stray spell of yours loose on a landing again. He's trying to catch you out. You told me demons are always prone to do that."

Jaive frowned, and turned to the demon.

"Here's my daughter. What of her?"

Epbal Enrax said: *"Rebellion."*

Tanaquil had an uneasy feeling it was now assisting her deception. Demons would always cause mischief if they could. But she took the cue.

"Yes," she said, "it's that row we had, mother. About my leaving here. And you won't let me."

Jaive lost her powerful look. She was exasperated.

"Do you think I want to hear this nonsense now?"

"You fetched me here."

"What were you doing?" asked Jaive, with a last quiver of suspicion.

"What do I ever do? Mending something, fiddling about. I'm bored. It's infuriating. I want to leave and—"

"Be quiet!" stormed Jaive. She turned on the demon again and cast a bolt of light at him. The demon sizzled and began to whine. "You also be quiet! I'm surrounded by fools. If it's excitement you want, Tanaquil, we shall have a dinner in the hall. Yes, a feast, a party. You may wear one of your best dresses."

"That *will* be fun," said Tanaquil.

"Now go away. As for you—"

Tanaquil shut the door quickly, hearing the demon's cries and apologies all the way down the first flight of steps.

The fortress was in near-blackness now, an occasional lamp left alight over the staircases and at the turnings of corridors, stars in windows, and brazier flicker.

Tanaquil opened her door and hesitated.

Through the darkness and through the cover of the quilt, a faint soft glow floated upward from the floor. The starry bones shone like the stars. Fingers to the spark of fire—had the demon really meant herself and what she did? What *did* she do? What sorcery beyond her grasp might she be unleashing?

She went into her room and stood shut in the night of it.

"Peeve," she called softly, "what are we up to?"

No answer. Tanaquil said, "There's to be a dinner. I'll get you a gorgeous meat bone—" and saw that the shutter had been nudged wide at the window. In the feathers on the floor were the marks of fat-sticky paws. The peeve was gone. Drawn by darkness, it had returned to the hollow hill in the desert.

Tanaquil felt a pang of anxiety. She was responsible for the peeve. They shared this adventure. No, that was silly. Who could control a peeve?

She lit her lamp and the glow of the skeleton faded.

"I'll just get on," she said aloud.

She thought of the sand giving way in the hollow hill and the peeve disappearing. Grimly, she got up on her work table and started once more to arrange the hooks.

How slowly the night passed.

Had she ever had a sleepless night before?

Tanaquil could not remember one. Dissatisfaction and boredom had *made* her sleep. Now she was not bored at all, but alert, eager, very worried.

She had done all she could with the tools at her disposal. Tomorrow she would seek the blacksmith, who was one of the soldiers, hoping he was not too drunk to get the forge going. To her specifications he should be able to create for her those parts she needed to repair the beast of bone. A wild idea had come to her, too. Cogs and wheels, hinges and tiny shafts of bronze and copper might be incorporated into the skeleton, its legs, neck and spine. Perhaps it would be possible to make it move, to trot and leap, paw the ground, shake its head and twitch its slender tail. If she was canny, the blacksmith would only think she was at work on another, more complex, clock.

When she had done all she could, the night had swum out into the black hours of early morning. The moon had come and gone. The snow had fallen and frozen. Still shivering, Tanaquil had set a fire on her hearth and lit it.

She left the shutters ajar. Sometimes they creaked and she looked up—but the peeve was not there.

In the morning she would go and look, along the roofs, in the hill. Hopeless to try now; the cold would be impassable. She could not even find her wool jacket or cloak.

Finally, in the dull firelight, she put another quilt over the skeleton to hide its mysterious glow, doused her lamp, and went to bed.

She lay and looked at the normal glow of the fire on the ceiling.

Then she was out in the desert, hurrying over

the rimy snow towards the fortress, and from above she heard the shouts of the soldiers, and they fired their crossbows at her but missed. Tanaquil half woke then, and heard the soldiers in reality clattering about and calling. But that was not so novel. They were always seeing things that did not exist and shooting at them. She picked up a dim cry: "It's only ghost-light on the snow, you idiot!"

Then she was asleep, and standing on the hollow hill like a bridge. On the western horizon the moon, which had sunk, was rising again. She watched it, and then she opened her eyes.

Some more time had passed. The fire was out. The room should have been in darkness, but it was filled with light. The moon had come in at the window.

And then Tanaquil saw the peeve standing on the foot of her bed. It was almost the scene of the previous night, except that she had left the way open for it. Except that now it held in its mouth a thing too large to have been carried with ease, long, and whorled like a great shell from the ocean, spiralled to a point thinner than a needle. And it shone, this thing, it *flamed*, turning the whole room, the peeve, Tanaquil, the air itself, to silver.

Then the peeve dropped its burden gently on the bed, and the vast light diminished, until it resembled only the starlight of the beast of bones. And so Tanaquil saw properly that what the peeve had brought her, from the sand under the hill, was a horn. And never having seen such a horn, she knew it, as would anyone who ever lived in the world.

"Oh, peeve," said Tanaquil. "By the God. It's a unicorn."

Chapter Three

When Tanaquil opened her eyes five days later, the first thing she saw was not the painting of Jaive. Instinctively, Tanaquil had turned in her sleep, and lay facing her work table. And there above, hanging in space, spangling the sunshine from the window, was the finished skeleton of the unicorn.

It was eerie and beautiful, less like bones than some fey musical instrument. The replacement discs and tubes of burnished copper did not spoil it; they were only sunny patches of warmth against the crystal, and the hoof was a dot of fire. The skull of the unicorn was like a pale rainbow, and the horn, which by daylight seemed only a giant shell made of pearl, had been attached to the forehead with pins of bronze; a coronet.

The unicorn stirred faintly in an early morning breeze. The chains that held it from the beam were a bright rain. It was a sort of exquisite mobile.

In the joints of it were the thin shining levers and the wheels Tanaquil had fastened there at midnight.

Under the skeleton, on the table, sat the peeve.

The soldiers had remarked on the peeve, which had followed Tanaquil on each excursion to the blacksmith's forge. They thought the peeve was a pet. They admired its loyalty as it sat staring at the smithing work. Tanaquil knew the peeve was only interested in the parts for the unicorn. As she labored over it in her room, the peeve had watched her from its lair under the bed, sometimes coming out to paddle across her tools and upset them. It rarely spoke. Yesterday the herders had come to the fort, and large cuts of meat were now being prepared for Jaive's dinner. Tanaquil had brought the peeve several samples, which it had dragged under the bed to eat; a nasty, smelly arrangement that Tanaquil tried to overlook.

"Hallo, peeve," said Tanaquil now, letting it know she could see. The peeve ignored her. It slowly raised one paw, and before she could protest, it tapped the lowest bone of the left hind leg.

A sweet chiming note came from the leg, and echoed away through the skeleton.

Tanaquil sat up. The peeve jumped off the table backwards and shot under the bed.

"You see," said Tanaquil sternly, leaning down to confront the peeve's astonished pointed face, "I *told* you not to touch."

She got out of the bed and went to the suspended skeleton. Light as dust, she flicked at the bones of the forelegs, and other chimes winged over the room. She ran her fingers along the cage of ribs, and there was a rill like silver beads falling down a stair of marble.

She had not been able, last midnight, to bring herself to try if the unicorn would move. She was half afraid it might, and that movement would dislodge some bit of it, which would then come down and break. But also, she was just afraid.

The chimes of the bones filled her with awe. She stepped away. And going to the bed she sat there and only gazed at the skeleton, while the peeve put its head out and gazed too, saucer-eyed.

Bird knocked on the door, bowed, and held out a wave of olive-green silk.

Tanaquil's "best" dresses never went sorcerously missing, for her mother stored them in a closet of her own apartment. Tanaquil accepted the dress, a unity of floor-length, wide, rustling skirt, boned bodice, high neck, and complicated sleeves. It had a sky-blue embroidery of lyres and lilies all over it.

Bird spied past Tanaquil unavoidably.

"Ooh, what's that?"

"What exactly?"

"That dangly glittery thing."

"Just something I found somewhere. It's been there ages."

Bird looked doubtful, but she only said, "Your lady mother says I'm to attend you to the feast."

Tanaquil frowned. As she had feared, her mother was set on making the dinner excessive and full of fussy rituals. "I'm to wear my gray velvet gown," said Bird.

"Oh, *good*," said Tanaquil.

"The gong will be struck just after sunset. Then we're to go down."

Bird was obviously looking forward to the dinner. Perhaps everyone was, except Tanaquil, who felt annoyed and almost embarrassed, for Jaive had suggested the dinner to Tanaquil as the cook had suggested she bake a cake.

When Bird had been persuaded to go, Tanaquil shut her door and tossed the splendid dress onto her bed, where the peeve came to investigate it.

Tanaquil was dissatisfied. She had found she did not want to go near her work table under the beautiful bones.

"This evening," she said to the peeve, "before the stupid feast, I'll see if I can't get it to move."

Then she turned her back on the unicorn skeleton and went to sit in the window. But it seemed to throw a far reflection on the desert, which glittered.

An hour before sunset, Bird came back to tong Tanaquil's hair into corkscrew curls. Something had happened to the tongs on the way. They wriggled and heaved and eventually got out of Bird's hands and strode on their two legs into a corner. The peeve hissed and spat at them from its nest in Tanaquil's dress.

"You shouldn't have let your pet get fur on your gown," said Bird.

They threw water on the fire they had meant to use for the tongs, and hoisted the peeve off the dress—"No, *nice*," it cried, clawing out lengths of embroidery—Bird dressed Tanaquil and exclaimed over her glory.

"I can't breathe for these bones," said Tanaquil.

Everything was bones. The tight bodice, the peeve's stinky snacks under her bed, the glimmer of the skeleton from the beam—at which, now, Bird did not even glance.

The peeve sulked on the pillows.

"Go and put on your velvet," Tanaquil told Bird. "I'll meet you by the gong at sunset."

When Bird had gone again, Tanaquil knotted up the skirt of her gown and climbed on the work table. "*Now.*" Taking up one of the fine tools she kept for the insides of clocks, Tanaquil inserted it carefully into a small bronze screw. Next, using the handle of the tool, she hit the wheel in the foreleg of the beast. The wheel span, became a blur. A hinge shifted, a shaft narrowed as a pin slid backward—

"So you won't do it," said Tanaquil to the unicorn, boldly. "You're meant to paw the ground—the air, if you like. Why won't you?" She tried the same procedure on the right forelimb. The wheel spun, the joints of bronze moved, but nothing happened. "Have I miscalculated the weight?" Less nervously, now that she was disappointed and puzzled, Tanaquil tried to wake the tapering tail, the brilliant head. There was no response.

Gradually the immobile unicorn of bone began to change to ruby. The sun was setting in the window.

"If you won't, you won't."

Tanaquil got off the table. She knew a shameful relief, and at the same moment she was drained, as if she had walked for miles under the midday sun.

The unicorn swayed like a fire.

"I'll have to go down."

"Down," said the peeve. It burrowed under a quilt.

Tanaquil left the room and closed the door. Her hands were full of pins and needles. Then she heard the gong booming below, early, and gritting her teeth, descended to Jaive's dinner.

Jaive rose to her feet in an explosion of sequins. "We salute the savory junket!"

Everyone else clambered up. "The savory junket!"

They all sat down again.

And the two old stewards, a pair of many called from retirement in attics and cellars of the fort for such meals, hobbled round the hall with their silver basins. On every enamel plate they dolloped out the junket, which was sallow, and wobbled.

Despite the three lit fireplaces, racks of torches in demon-shaped sconces, and the rose silk curtains along the walls, Jaive's hall was always draughty. A solitary banquet table stood isolated in the midst of it, facing an enormous round window of emerald and red glass. Outside on this window, new patterns of frost had already formed, ferns and fossil-like things. Beyond it lay the darkening, freezing desert, its rough sand a mere five feet below the glass—but the glass was sorcerous and only another sorcery could breach it. From the carved beams, however, hung ordinary cobwebs. There were holes in the curtains, and in the damask table-cloth. The rats had parties in the hall when Jaive did not.

The painted doors at the south end of the room groaned open for the fourth time.

Jaive rose.

"We salute the soup!"

Everyone else got up. "The soup!"

Everyone sat down.

Jaive sat at the table's center, in a tall ebony chair inlaid with sorcerous symbols of obscure meaning. Her guests had taken their usual positions. Tanaquil was on her mother's right hand; Bird was just behind her, with the other attending maids, Yeefa and Prune. On Jaive's left sat the captain of the soldiers in his dress suit of gilded mail and some battle honors that were possibly real. Down the rest of the table, left and right, were placed the captain's second-in-command and seven elderly retainers of the fortress, including Tanaquil's former nurse. Everyone had on their best, in some instances smelling of mothballs.

"We salute the baked fish!"

There was no fish ever to be had at the fortress, as it was more than a hundred miles from the sea. Instead the cook made a fish of salty pastry and painted it green with limes. It was borne in by a lame female steward of ninety years. The fish was always her task, and Tanaquil always expected the old lady would drop the plate, but somehow she never did.

Served, Tanaquil glowered at the doughy greenish lump before her, while around her the maids and the retainers chattered, and the captain and his second passed two of the wine flagons back and forth between them.

"A magnificent meal, Ma'am," Tanaquil heard the captain murmur to Jaive.

Tanaquil looked sidelong at her mother's face. Jaive wore the sublime expression most common to her. Her mind was always on higher things, the mountaintops of magic. Nothing could compare with those heights, but she conducted the silly dinner with a vague air of generously pleasing everyone.

The doors groaned.

"We salute the fruit ice!"

"The fruit ice!"

The ice was orange, and each scoop had an orange flower perched on it. The flowers neither

changed into lizards nor flew away. Where her
mother was present, the respectful spells stayed
under restraint.

Tanaquil ate her ice. The cold of it entered her
stomach like six cold words: *Those bones are nothing
to me.* And then eleven more: *Nothing has happened.
Nothing has altered. I shall never be free.*

The silver spoons lay in the empty ice dishes.
Jaive spoke. "And now I will make an offering."

The retainers, maids, and soldiers became ponderously quiet, and the stewards straightened as
they leant on their sticks.

Although not religious, at her dinners Jaive the
sorceress always performed some worshipful act.

She left the table and walked into the space before the darkened window. She poured a stream of
wine on the ground and cast some powder. The
wine and powder mingled, fizzed, and bloomed
up like a crimson rose. "We thank you for your
gifts, and ask that you will share our feast, all benign powers. Let us in our lives humbly remember the perfect world, that is not this one."

The rose evaporated with a sweet perfume.
Dazzling wisps trailed off into the ceiling.

The doors groaned.

"We salute the meat!"

"The meat!"

In marched two of the sweeper boys in clean
white clothes, playing pipes and perhaps a tune.
Behind them stepped Pillow and Sausage, strewing strips of golden paper. After the scullery girls
stalked the cook, amazing in a cloth-of-gold apron,
and holding in one hand a golden basting spoon,
in the other an ivory flyswatter.

Following the cook came three black-and-fawn

goats, washed and combed, led by the third white-clad sweeper, and drawing a small chariot on which rested the salver of the meat.

Tanaquil stifled a sigh.

The group of big roasts had been built into a towered fortress, with battlements of fried bread, roofs of crackling, windows of glazed red and yellow vegetables, embedded in dunes of mince.

There was greedy applause.

I might as well take the skeleton down, Tanaquil thought. *Put all those gleaming sticks, that rainbow skull, into a chest. A unicorn. I ought to give it to HER.*

Slices of meat were being served her by a steward of eighty-three. Another, of eighty-six, came up with a spouted golden vessel of gravy. Tanaquil thanked them. She thought: *I shall be here in this place until I'm eighty, as well. Or ninety.*

From somewhere, high up in her cranium, or higher, in the fort of Jaive, came a violent crash. Like a door thrust off its hinges.

A few faces were raised from forkfuls of roast dinner. Prune said, "There goes another of Madam's spells."

The captain said daringly to Jaive, "Better than the cannon, Madam." And Jaive smiled.

No more attention was given to the crash than this.

Tanaquil thought: *Perhaps an enemy has approached and is bombarding us! Some hopes.*

But there was still a feeling in her head, tingling and disturbing. It was like a white bright thought prancing down the levels of her brain, tossing its neck, with hoofs that slithered and struck sparks, landed and clicked forward like knives over a shield.

"Drink up your wine, Tanaquil," said her mother, "It will be good for your headache."

Tanaquil realized she had put her fingers to her forehead. "Mother, something's running down the stairs."

"Really? Just some little drip of magic."

"No, Mother, I think—"

Some obstacle tore open, some barricade of distance or sound. The thing in Tanaquil's mind seemed to leap out of it, and, loud as a trumpet from beyond the hall doors, came a brazen squeal of machinery run amok.

Prune, Yeefa, and Pillow screamed. The nurse, the old stewardess, and the goats of the meat chariot gave quavering bleats. The cook turned to face the doors, her spoon and swat at the ready. The captain and his second were on their feet, wavering slightly, but with drawn swords.

"Fear nothing, Madam."

Jaive was bland. "It will be a demon," she said. "I shall deal with it firmly."

Then the doors shuddered as if they had been rammed. They burst open.

What galloped through was a whirlwind of lights. It seemed to have no substance, only motion and prismatic flame. Colors danced off from it, blindingly. There were no chimes now. But there was the unmistakable whirr of wheels, the sharp striking of hoofs. More fearsome than the soldiers' swords, a savage horn slashed the air in pieces.

The skeleton of the unicorn. After all, it had begun to move. It had erupted into movement with a kind of luminous rage. It had snapped chains, knocked away doors, vaulted stairways.

It rushed along the hall, and Prune, Yeefa, Bird, Pillow, and Sausage jumped from its path squeaking. The boys yelled, the retainers doddered, the cook fell over in a bundle, the soldiers bellowed, jabbed and—missed.

Tanaquil had an impression of long streaks of lightning. In their center were tiny bronze whirlings. She saw a shake of the rainbow skull, and the soldiers flung themselves behind the wine flagons.

Jaive had got up from her chair. She called out some incomprehensible mantra and lifted her arms like sequined wings. Rings of power rolled out of her, but the unicorn was too swift. Nothing could catch it, stop it, slow it down. It leapt upon the table—plates and goblets were hurled away. The gravy in the meat dishes splattered up. Prune, Yeefa, Bird, Pillow, and Sausage rushed howling up the hall; the boys, the nurse and one or two others crawled under the tablecloth. The meat steward threw his stick, which smote the captain on the nose.

"Spirit of air or water, clockwork of fire or earth, take heed of the universal commandment!" declaimed Jaive.

The unicorn of bone splashed through her plate, and there, on the sequins of the sorceress, and in her scarlet hair, glowed gravy drops like sneers.

"It's me that it wants," said Tanaquil. She braced herself for the pain of the perfect horn breaking her heart. There was no margin for fright; she was not afraid.

But the racing framework of the unicorn dived by her. She dropped back into her seat astounded.

"*Stop, I say!*" shouted Jaive. Her face was flushing. She had had to come down from the heights, and she was angry.

Tanaquil watched her mother lose control in a marvelous fascination. Had *she* ever been able to make this happen?

The unicorn of bone pelted round the hall. It ran right to left, somehow sprang over itself and ran left to right, like the mechanism of a clock gone mad.

The goats kicked and butted and upset the meat salver. Everyone huddled at the core of the wild circlings. The captain, his purple sash to his bleeding nose, made rushes without leaving the table. "May the God help us," prayed the nurse complainingly from below.

Jaive clenched her ringed fists. Her body seemed to grow taller and to expand like a storm cloud.

"I call upon the force of iron to bind, of heat to consume—"

Tanaquil saw, across the turmoil of the hall, the peeve sitting in the open doorway. Its fur was all on end, its tail like a chimney brush. Like Jaive, it had made itself twice its proper size.

Tanaquil laughed.

There was a ripping noise. One of the silk curtains had caught the wild horn. The silk tore for several feet and fell down. The unicorn of bone was swathed in rosy silk.

"Do as I tell you!" screeched Jaive. *"Obey me!"*

And she flung some gout, some boulder of her magic, across the hall, at the unpredictable flying bone and silken thing that was chaos.

The air quaked.

"Oh the God," said the cook on the floor, "she's done something now."

Then everyone was silent. Probably they did not even breathe. The big, echoing draughty hall was abruptly choked, *filled*, as if stopped time had been stacked there. No one could move. Tanaquil thought she felt her heartbeat, but miles away beneath her feet. She turned her head, and it went with difficulty, as if she were submerged in thick glue.

And how gluey dark it was. The torches and the fires had changed to a horrible black-red.

Across the length of the room strewn with quivering girls, broken crockery, gravy, and goats, Tanaquil saw the heap of torn curtain brought down where the flying thing had been. Jaive's boulder had hit it. Now the curtain had no shape. No smart of hoofs, scud of wheels, no cosmic gleam and glitter.

"Mother, what have you done?"

But Tanaquil's voice did not leave her mouth, because the glue was also in her throat.

As for Jaive, she had shrunk back, not to her natural dominant size, but somehow smaller. Her hair, in the gloom, was without any color.

And then a spear of pure light lanced across the hall.

Tanaquil gasped. It was as if strings were fastened in her heart, and now someone pulled on them.

The heap of torn silk bubbled; it erected itself like a tent, then suddenly slid over. Something rose up, and the silk ran off from it.

Jaive's hall was now filled by the light of a snow moon.

And in the light, which was of its own making, the radiance of its seashell horn, Tanaquil beheld the unicorn.

The unicorn.

It was no longer only a beast of bone. It had grown flesh and form. It was black as night, black as every night of the world together, and it shone as the night shines with a comet. On this burning blackness, the mane and the flaunting tail of it were like an acid, golden-silver fire off the sea, and it was bearded in this sea-fire-acid, and spikes of it were on the slender fetlocks. Its eyes were red as metal in a forge. It was not simply beauty and strength, it was terror. It rose up and up to a height that was more, it seemed, than the room could hold, and its black shadow curved over it, far less black than itself.

Jaive said, quite steadily, "I greet you. But by the powers I can summon, be careful of me."

And the unicorn snorted, and a fiery gas came out of its nostrils. It scraped the floor with its forehoof, and there was a rocking in the hall, like a mild, threatening earth tremor.

And then the unicorn leapt up into the air. It was like an arc of wind, and passed with a sound of far-off roaring, bells, thunder.

Where it came down, beyond the dinner guests, the mess, and the table, it struck the round sorcerous window with the horn. The window gave like a plate of ice. Fragments sheered off to hit the sky and the cold of the night and the snow blew in. But the unicorn blew out. It soared into the pit of empty darkness and was gone.

Then Tanaquil knew what tugged on her. She knew because it pulled her up and forward in a ridiculous scramble. Before she understood what she did, before anyone could think to grip her, she had bolted over the hall, into the hole of the window, and jumped down onto the snow-crusted sand. She felt the freezing through her silk shoes as she ran, and dimly wished she had not worn them. But really she did not grasp what had happened. The sky was colossal, and the land too. And the unicorn raced. And faintly at her heels she heard the fur barrel of the peeve thump down after her, and the skitter of its paws pursuing her, as she chased the unicorn into the desert waste.

Chapter Four

She was very cold.

Perhaps she should get up and light the fire.

Tanaquil opened her eyes. She was already on her feet, and her room had grown much too large. It had no furniture. There was a carpet of white snow, walls and high ceiling of pale black moonlit night.

A sheet of horror fell down and enveloped her.

She knew what had happened, what she had done. Of course, she had been enchanted or possessed—her meddling with the bones had seen to that. In thrall to the unicorn she had chased after it, in a mad trance. Now, coming to, she found herself on the face of the desert, and, turning slowly round, saw nothing anywhere that was familiar, but only the snow and the sand and the night, which were everywhere the same. Her mother's fortress was not in view. The rock hills were out of sight.

Something gleamed in the moonlight on the snow, coming down from a rise. It was a track created by the narrow hoofmarks of the unicorn. Each had filled with ice and curious greenness. Each shone like a pock of stained glass from Jaive's shattered window. The other way the track led on across the snow into the distance. She must not follow this track. She must retrace the steps

the way they had come. Her own footfalls had left
no imprint.

Tanaquil walked quickly along the glassy trail.
She went up the rise. This must have taken a
quarter of an hour. At the top she looked over and
saw the snow and sand stretching to the edge of
vision, nothing on it, no clue. And the weird trail
of the unicorn had vanished. Some night wind had
blown over and erased it.

Had she really come all this way? She could not
remember it. It was as if she had been asleep, yet
in the midst of an exultant dream, like those she
had had before of running across the snow.

Well, there were no doubts now. She had
emerged from the ensorcellment and would freeze
to death in a matter of hours.

"No," said Tanaquil aloud. There would be rescue. Jaive would send the soldiers after her. They
would catch up to her soon, she had only to wait.

Miles off, a jackal gave a wail at the moon.

Tanaquil listened. Sound carried vast distances.
Yet she could hear nothing of any soldiers. But
then, they would have to come from the fort, they
would be erratic and fuddled ... could they find
her? Probably Jaive would put the magic mirror
into service. But again, there were no landmarks
here. Even if Jaive gained a glimpse of her daughter, could she be sure where she was exactly?

Tanaquil was now too cold to shudder. Her feet
and hands were numb. She jumped up and down
and beat her palms together.

As she was doing this, she saw something
bounding toward her.

Was it a starving dog or antisocial jackal?

Dressed for the dinner, she did not even have her knife. She must use her fists, then.

"Hey!" shrilled the dog or jackal. It was neither. "Peeve—"

"Rock," said the peeve, flinging itself against her legs, "big rock with hole."

"Do you mean the hills?"

"Rock," said the peeve. It took a mouthful of her dress and pulled on her. Tanaquil gave up and ran with it. They hurried over the snow, sometimes slipping or falling. The night had become one large ache of cold and blundering.

The rock seemed to appear from nowhere, looming up out of the dunes. Tanaquil had never seen it before. It was the size of a room and had a low doorway, a cave that pierced into it. Tanaquil and the peeve crowded in. It was a shelter, but felt no warmer than the open ground outside. In a shaft of the westering moonlight, Tanaquil began to see tufts and skeins of thorny plants growing inside the rock. The forlorn idea came that, if she had had her tinderbox, she could have made a fire.

The peeve would survive in the desert, it was a desert animal. Unless it had forgotten how, from living at the fortress.

When she sat down facing the cave entrance, the peeve got into her lap. They pressed close for warmth.

"If my mother's soldiers don't find me . . ." said Tanaquil. She felt exhausted. She would drop asleep, and might not wake up again. She talked on determinedly. "But they will. What a fool I was."

"Gravy," said the peeve, apparently for no reason. It slept.

"How did you know about the bones?" asked Tanaquil. "The unicorn must have ensorcelled you, too. Must have drawn you there to dig them out. And I repaired it. And Jaive's magic bolt brought it back to life. And . . ."

If I don't freeze, and live till morning, thought Tanaquil, *I shall be fried alive by the sun.*

No, they'll find me in the morning, or I'll find my way to the fort.

In the cave entrance the moonlit ice shimmered.

A bright shadow came picking over it.

Tanaquil clutched the sleeping peeve. She watched, rigid, as the unicorn came down across the white dunes, over the silence, to the mouth of the cave. There it lowered its fearful head, and its eyes like coals flamed in at her.

Perhaps it will kill me. Then I won't have to wait to freeze or burn.

Tanaquil's teeth chattered.

The unicorn raised its head. Now she could only see its body, the hard slim greyhound curve of its belly and the long and slender legs. It pawed the stone floor just inside the cave. A shower of silver sparks littered through the air, and came in at the entry. They clustered on one of the dry thorny bushes growing in the floor. For a moment the bush seemed full of silver insects. And then curls of smoke were creeping from it. The bush was alight.

"Oh!" Tanaquil rolled the peeve from her lap. On her knees in the low cave she crawled about, breaking off the twigs of the bushes to feed the blaze.

Like something taking flight, the unicorn lifted

away. It vanished, and only the moon shone on the snow, and the hot fire on the floor of the cave.

Tanaquil dozed through the night by the miraculous fire, attentive so it should not go out. She fed in the sticks sparingly, and the peeve lay luxuriously on a fold of her dress, stomach exposed to the warmth.

Nothing else came near for the remainder of the night, and she might have accused herself of dreaming the unicorn, but for the fire.

When the sky began to lighten, Tanaquil went out of the cave and scraped rime and snow off the top of the dunes, putting the sandy stuff in her mouth. She was not yet thirsty, but once the sun came she soon would be. The peeve did as she did, licking busily and congratulating itself.

Tanaquil tore off a third of her embroidered skirt, leaving the bright blue petticoat to protect her legs. She fashioned a head covering from the skirt, and bound her hands with strips of the material. She cursed her shoes.

The peeve became excitable as the sun rose. It bounded about the cave entrance. "Going? Going?"

"Yes. We'll go and see if we can't meet someone."

The sky was a pale and innocent blue as they set off. It was pleasant at first after the harsh night. But they had to walk with the sun. Tanaquil kept her head down.

The going was hard over the sand, as always.

They went on for about an hour. Gradually the comforting heat of the sand changed. It started to bake and blister. Each step was a punishment.

The gong of the sun blared in Tanaquil's eyes and beat just above her head.

Tanaquil thought ferociously of ice. Mountains of ice, scorching her with cold. They melted.

Another hour passed.

Tanaquil wanted only to lie on the sand. Eventually she had to sit down. There was no shade or cover in any direction. She could hardly swallow.

"Mother," croaked Tanaquil, "what are you doing?"

The thought came that Jaive imagined Tanaquil had rejected her. After all, Tanaquil had threatened to leave. Perhaps Jaive believed Tanaquil and the unicorn were accomplices. In that case, would Jaive renounce Tanaquil? Would Jaive abandon Tanaquil to the desert?

Tanaquil bit her lips. She wanted to cry, but shedding tears would only make her thirst much worse.

Suddenly the peeve went flying off. Tanaquil croaked at it; it took no notice, disappearing over the slope of some dunes to the left. Had the peeve also abandoned her?

"She could have sent one of her demons," whispered Tanaquil from her husk of throat. "She *could* have found me. She's a *sorceress*."

One tear came out of her right eye. She would have pushed it back if she could. Why should she cry at her mother's neglect? Her mother had always neglected her. Tanaquil was a disappointment to Jaive, who had obviously wanted her daughter to be exactly like herself. They had nothing to say to one another.

"Confound her," gasped Tanaquil. "That's that."

The sun was very high; time had moved quickly as she sat there in a stupor, and it would soon be midday. Tanaquil began to scoop the scalding sand aside, making a burrow for herself. It was not deep enough, but she got into it and curled up, scrabbling back the sand. She felt as if she were being cooked, but the direct rays of the sun were now lessened. She doubled the skirt to protect her head and face.

I'll survive. Something will happen.

She tried not to hope the unicorn would return. But she dreamed or hallucinated that it did so, and struck the sand with its horn, whereupon a stream welled out. Instead, it was the peeve licking her forehead and cheeks with a hot, sandy tongue.

Tanaquil attempted to embrace the peeve, but it insisted on thrusting something against her mouth. Tanaquil recoiled. The something was a snake the peeve had hunted and killed over the dunes.

"Meal," said the peeve.

Tanaquil looked at the snake dubiously. It had been attractive before the peeve attacked it. Now it was a broken piece of raw meat she did not want. However, it would be sensible to eat some of it, and ungrateful not to.

"Thank you."

"Welcome," said the peeve. It commenced eating the other end, showing Tanaquil how good the snake was by making noises and screwing up its eyes.

Tanaquil managed to extract, chew and swallow some of the snake. The flesh was cool, soothing her throat. But the fine skin upset her. Mirages swam before her eyes, gardens, and lakes with boats on them, such as Jaive had shown her in the mirror. She thought how Jaive always harped on about how badly made the world was, and that there were others even worse, and one created perfectly. Evidently Tanaquil's world was all wrong, a place where you could only live by murdering other creatures. Every animal preyed on another. Even those who got by through eating herbage destroyed the living fruits and seeds. In the perfect world there was a perfect food which all there ate. It was not alive, did not have to be attacked or slaughtered.

"Just look, there's the sea," said Tanaquil to the peeve.

She lay down on the sand with the green cloth over her face. She was aware of a faint extra shade. She realized the peeve had sat by her head, and the sun as it turned from the zenith began to cast the shadow of the peeve's body onto her.

Tanaquil thought Jaive was combing her hair. She was rough with the comb, and Tanaquil protested. They were in a boat on a lake. The boat bobbed violently, and Tanaquil was slammed up and down against the cushions. The peeve landed on her chest. It looked up past her head, snarling at Jaive, who was still raking Tanaquil's hair with the comb.

"Ow. Mother, please," said Tanaquil.

She raised her heavy gritty lids, and the sun lashed at her eyes. Something was pulling her by the hair. She was bouncing over the dunes, and the peeve was scrambling about on her, spitting and hiccuping in wrath.

Tanaquil squinted. Without surprise, she saw

the night-black shape, the day-flame of the horn pointing exactly over her.

The unicorn dragged her by the hair.

This was a dream.

"What are you?" said Tanaquil to the unicorn. "I mean really what are you? Where do you come from? What do you want?"

She was hauled up a hill of sand, behind which the sun flickered away. And then the sun burst out again, and she was tumbling and cascading through a river of grains and particles, the dusts of the desert's centuries. Choking and coughing, she plummeted twenty-five feet into a hard gray bruise. The peeve revolved past her and fetched up, head down, in a sand drift. From this it emerged without dignity and in great noise.

Tanaquil smiled. Although the bruise she had hit had duly bruised her, she now lay in a long blue bar of shade that seemed cold and lovely as a river.

For some while she let it console her. Then she watched the sun, divided by a tree, making gold among great fans.

Then she rolled over. The bruise was a stone, marking a vertical tunnel in the sand. It was a well-head, with a well beneath. The well had a leather bucket. It had deep, cold, black water in it.

The blue bar of shade stretched from a single palm tree of impressive height. The peeve, recovered, had already climbed the trunk and was bumping about in the coppery leaves. A shower of dates pattered into Tanaquil's lap.

The peace of the oasis was wonderful. It gave no warning that night must return, the well freeze, and the snow come down. At the oasis afternoon stretched out forever.

Tanaquil was not thinking at all. She had given it up. Everything was nonsensical anyway.

The sun swung lower, and the sky congealed in darker light. The shadow of the palm seemed to go on for a mile.

Tanaquil looked along the shadow and saw another image. This time it was of a jogging movement of the land. The sand went up in a burnished cloud. Forms like beasts began to appear out of the cloud, and riders and carts. The mirage was not like the others. It had a sound, too, a rumble and mutter and the clean singing of small bells.

Tanaquil watched the mirage benignly. It came closer and clearer, and grew louder. Tanaquil saw five cream camels, with colored tassels and men up on their hilly backs, swaying forward out of the dust, and then the big wheels of three carts with six mules walking before each one. She saw men in tunics, trousers, and boots, with cloth swathing their heads, and next three more camels of brick red, with rocking silk cages perched on their tops.

She got up. She would have to start thinking again.

"Peeve, listen to me. It's a caravan—it truly is. Of course, this is an oasis. They may be—must be—going to the city. Now, we have to be clever. No mention of my mother—they very sensibly won't trust sorcery. And peeve—don't *talk*."

"What talk?" said the peeve. It was part of the way up the palm trunk again, staring at the approaching caravan.

Tanaquil stood, dizzy and stunned, never having

known before such elation. For these were strangers—people—and they were going to a city.

"Good evening, girl," called out the man with the goad walking beside the first cream camel. "What are you selling?"

Tanaquil blinked. "Nothing."

It occurred to her that persons from villages might gather at an oasis where a caravan was due, in order to offer produce to the travelers.

"Then why are you loitering here?"

Tanaquil was affronted. "I'm here to join your caravan. You're going to the city, presumably?"

The man glanced up at the three riders on the nearest camels. All four men laughed. It was not proper laughter, but more of a sort of threat.

"Yes, we're going to the Sea City. You'll have to ask the caravan leader if you can join us. We don't take any old riffraff, you know. There's the fee, as well. Can you pay it?"

Tanaquil had not thought of this. She spurred her brain. Just as it was no use boasting of a sorceress mother, so it was no use expecting strangers to offer her care.

"I'm from the village of Um," said Tanaquil.

"Never heard of it."

"Few have. It's a very small village. I saved up to buy a place in a caravan, but as I was coming here I was set on and robbed. They took everything, my money, my donkey. I almost never got here. Now I'm afraid I'll have to throw myself on your kindness."

The men regarded her. She was only really used to the soldiers, drunk most of the time, and easygoing, who actually had treated Tanaquil more like a wise elder sister. Now Tanaquil saw how most of the men of the world looked at most females. It irritated her, but she concealed this. She smiled humbly up at them. There was a code in the desert, she knew. You could not leave the lost or needy to perish.

"All right," said the man on the ground, striking the goad against his boot, which was hung with small silver discs. "You'd better see the leader." He turned and raised his arm, calling loudly back into the dust and trample of the arriving caravan: "Night's rest! All stop here!"

The caravan sprawled about the oasis in the sunset. In all, there were seven covered carts, and these had been drawn up to make a wall against the desert. In the gap between each pair of carts burned a fire. Jackals had approached, and howled to each other in the near distance. The palm tree and the well were the center of the camp. Here water was drawn continuously, and dates—and incidentally the peeve—had been shaken down.

"What's that?" the man with the goad said, pointing at the peeve. "Funny-looking thing."

"My animal," said Tanaquil.

The peeve growled, and Tanaquil tapped its head. "Ssh."

"*Bad*," said the peeve.

"Eh?" said the man with the goad, glaring at the peeve.

"Oh," said the Tanaquil, "it's just barking."

The man with the goad was called Gork. His head cloth was secured by a silver band, his dark clothes were sprinkled with ornaments, and across his chest hung a large gold pocket watch. He constantly ticked and clinked, and when he felt he was not making enough noise, he rapped the goad on his boots and whistled.

"This way. The leader's awning is going up over there."

Under his awning, the leader of the caravan sat on a chair in the sand. He had been journeying in one of the silken cages on top of one of the three pinkish camels that had brought up the rear. He was a fat man with a beard.

Gork explained the situation in his special manner. "This bit of a girl's come after us, but let herself get robbed on the way. She hasn't a penny, and expects us to take her on."

"I'm afraid we couldn't do that," said the leader, not bothering to look at either of them, only into a box of candied grapes. "You must pay your way. Food alone is expensive, not to mention our protection."

"You can't," said Tanaquil firmly, "leave me in the desert to die."

"Well of course that would, technically, be against the law," said the leader. He beamed upon the grapes. He said nothing else.

The peeve stirred restively at Tanaquil's side.

Tanaquil said quickly, "My three brothers at Um know I meant to join this caravan. Eventually, if they don't get word from me from the city, they might seek out the caravan's leader."

"She's a nuisance, isn't she?" said the leader to Gork. "Give her that lame mule on Wobbol's cart. And a snack to tide her over. Then she can bundle back to her village."

"I don't want to go back to Um," said Tanaquil.

She clawed at her wits and said, "Isn't there something I can do to earn a passage with you?"

"What on earth *could* you do?" asked the leader, looking at her for the first time, as if she were a rotten grape found in the candy box.

There was a spluttering crash and chorus of yells and oaths. Up on the dunes, the watching jackals cackled.

The leader, Gork, Tanaquil, and the peeve all turned to see. Displayed in the firelight, one of the carts had thrown a wheel. The cart now listed, and the man who had been at the wheels, cleaning them of sand and oiling them, lay feebly struggling under several large bags and sacks that had fallen out. Men ran to rescue him—or the bags and sacks.

"Useless," said the leader. He ate another grape. "Deprive that fellow of rations tomorrow."

"Trouble is, leader," said Gork, beating on his boot, "Wobbol was the only one who was any good at repairing wheels and stuff. And as you remember, Wobbol went off in a huff when you bought his cart and load off him at quarter price—"

"Yes, yes," said the leader. "The goods will have to be put onto the mules."

"The mules won't be able to take it, leader, not for all those miles."

Tanaquil felt light-headed. What had happened to her was crazy, but also it must have been right. For now everything conspired to help her. Surely she would never see the unicorn again, and she would come to disbelieve in it, with time. But still a kind of magic was working about her, because she had taken the risk.

"Don't worry," she said, "I can fix your wheel."

"You?" said Gork.

The leader only grimaced; he had sly, flat eyes. "Don't mock, Gork. Let's see if she can. *If* she can," he added, "she can travel with us, eat with us, no charge. On the other hand, if she *can't*, I'll throw her to those jackals."

Tanaquil shrugged. It was on her tongue to say the jackals would be preferable company anyway to the leader, but she did not. Instead she walked over to the spilled cart, the bristling peeve on her heels.

"Clear these sacks out of the way," said Tanaquil, in the imperious tones of her mother. "Are there any tools?"

Presently she was kneeling by the cart. Since it *was* Wobbol's, she suspected he had engineered the faulty wheel out of revenge. The wheel shaft was set crooked, and the pin in the wheel had snapped. Tanaquil organized one of the fires into a forge. She sent the caravan servants running about to fetch and carry. Herself, she hammered out the new pin from a brooch she was handed. It did not take great strength. Even Gork came to watch the stupid village female who could mend wheels.

When the wheel was soundly back in place, Tanaquil stood up.

"That's a fair job," said Gork grudgingly. "Where'd a girl learn that?"

"My brothers taught me," said Tanaquil prudently, "at Um."

Chapter Five

For almost three weeks Tanaquil traveled in the cara-
van. Every hour she was excited. Every hour she
lived with a sense of insecurity and danger she had
never known before. She was out in the world.

At least once a day, they would pass some
marker in the sand, indicating the route to the
city. Most of these were plain stone posts about
ten or eleven feet in height, often looking much
shorter where the sand had washed against them.
But as they came nearer to the city, there began to
be occasional stone pylons stretched up at the sky,
carved with prayers or quotations. On the ninth
day they reached another waterhole. On the sixteenth day, near sunset, there was a large oasis of
palms, acacias, and fig trees, with a village at its
edge. Tanaquil was nervous; they might put her
off here. Nothing else had had to be mended, and
she added weight to the cart in which she traveled. The peeve, too, had caused problems. Although she had still been able to convince
listeners that its grumblings and exclamations
were an odd type of barking, she had seen various
people, including the merchants who rode in the
silk cages, making superstitious signs against the
peeve. Twice it had gone among these merchants'
shelters at night and used someone's costly rug as
a bathroom. The previous night had been the

worst. The peeve had laid its dung near the head of sleeping Gork, then, in covering it, nearly buried the man alive. However, no sooner were they in the oasis, than frowning Gork's gold pocket watch ceased ticking. Having shaken it, cursed it, and hurled it in the sand, Gork found Tanaquil at his elbow. He gave her the watch with awful threats, but she repaired it in half an hour. Not even a hint was made after this that Tanaquil should leave the caravan.

The leader she seldom saw. He rode by day as the merchants did, in a bulb of silk pulled over a wicker frame, on a camel. The other men in charge of the caravan gave orders, shouted, laid down the law on every topic, discussed chariot races, and played violent gambling games. The male servants treated Tanaquil much as one of themselves, although she was a girl and therefore inferior. She had been given their castoffs to replace her gaudy dress. As far as she could tell from splits in the sacks, smells, and accidents, the caravan carried cakes of soap, sugar, conifer incense, and paper, from a city to the east. Tanaquil had never heard of this city. Her mother, who had given her lessons, had only ever spoken of the city to the west. Was this significant?

Mostly Tanaquil tried not to think of her mother at all.

Also, she tried not to think of the unicorn.

The unicorn was something so bizarre that it could only happen once. If that. Perhaps it had assisted her in the desert, or perhaps she had only made that up. Maybe the bush had caught alight in the cold cave naturally. Maybe she had only crawled by herself towards the well.

It seemed to her now that it was possible she and the peeve had not found anything under the rock hill. That nothing had gone wrong at Jaive's feast except that Tanaquil herself had flung open a door and run away.

One morning she actually said to the peeve, "Do you recall the starry bone you found?"

"Bone?" said the peeve gladly, "where?"

And a merchant going by, fanning himself, glared at the peeve and made the sign against evil spirits.

It was the nineteenth day of Tanaquil's journey with the caravan, and a wonderful sunset inflamed the sky, glowing vermilion and amber, with clouds in the west like furled magenta wings. The general opinion was that they would reach the city the following evening. Everyone was pleased, and the servants had all day given Tanaquil tales of the city that were plainly quite absurd. The city's prince was supposed, for example, to have a palace of white marble fifteen stories high. Tanaquil nodded politely.

In the afternoon they had passed a great obelisk with a brass arrow at its top pointing west. The prayer on the obelisk read: *We give thanks to God, who brings us to Sea City.*

The desert changed. Low rocky cliffs drew up out of the dunes, and then the cliffs had dry brown shrubs on them, and here and there a warped, wild tree. As the light blushed, they came into round hills with stands of green cedar. Flocks were pastured, and little villages lay in every direction, one after another, with their fires and lamps burning up like bits of the red sky.

The leader came down from his cage and mounted a mule. He rode at the head of the caravan, with Gork walking beside him. "We'll spend the night at Horn Spring," said the leader in a ritualistic, syrupy voice.

Tanaquil felt something like a twitch of a curtain inside her mind.

She turned to one of the servants, Foot.

"Why is it called Horn Spring?"

"A sacred legend of the city," said Foot.

"An ignorant villager like me," said Tanaquil, "hasn't heard of it."

"No," sneered Foot. He decided to be nice to her. "They say a prince from the city came there. It was a very sandy year, and he was parched with thirst. He asked the God for water, and a beast with a horn ran up out of the desert and cleft a rock with this horn, and out burst the water."

"How convenient," said Tanaquil. The hair had risen on her scalp.

"Watch it, your funny animal's in the soap again," said Foot.

The sky was wine-red, fading. The caravan wound up a dusty trail and they were on a bare dark hill. Above, the top of the hill ended in a big rock, like a chimney. Under the rock was a grove of trees and another well with a stone curb, which was not spectacular. The leader got off his mule and, going to the well, thanked God for the caravan's safe arrival.

The camp was made below the grove, and water drawn from the well. Foot advised Tanaquil to drink some, as it was very health-giving and said to grant wishes. Tanaquil, though, did not go to look at the well; it was dark now, and growing

cold, the thin snow whipping out on a buffeting
wind that rose soon after the sun set.

Tanaquil sat near one of the fires and ate her rations, sharing them with the peeve. "What shall
we do in Sea City?" she said to it, then hastily,
"Don't say anything, here's Gork."

"Nasty," said the peeve.

"That animal really does have an odd bark,"
said Gork. The peeve snarled and went under a
cart with a salted biscuit. "What will you do in the
city?" Gork asked Tanaquil with unknowing repe-
tition.

"Oh, this and that."

Gork studied his pocket watch, tapped his boots
and whistled. Next he said quietly, "Are you
courting?"

Tanaquil was amazed. Should she be flattered or
laugh? Very seriously she replied, "I'm afraid I am.
My brothers betrothed me to someone in the
city."

"Those brothers don't seem to look after you
properly," said Gork.

"But they're my menfolk, so I have to do as
they say."

"Yes, quite right."

The peeve bit down on the biscuit with a cracking noise, and Gork straightened and whistled up
at the snow. Without another word he went off.
Presumably, thought Tanaquil, he had seen the
value of a lady love who could men his cart wheels
and his watch.

And then the sound began.

She took it for some purer note of the night
wind, at first. It seemed everywhere around,
ebbing and flowing.

She thought, idly, still accustomed to the supernatural things of Jaive's fort, *Perhaps there are demons on the wind.*

"*Aaeeh! Look! Look!*"

A pot dropped and smashed. To the eerie sweetness of the wind's tone was added the din of panic. Three servants, who had been descending from the well, had stuck in their tracks, letting fall water jars and wailing, pointing away above the grove of trees.

The whole camp was suddenly in confusion. Men drew knives and cudgels. The merchants emerged from their awnings with whinnying cries, and one sank to his knees, reminding God he wanted protection. The camels, too, were stamping at their pickets, roaring and snorting, while the mules brayed maddeningly.

"A fiend! a *monster*!"

"*Kill* it!"

"*Run!*"

Tanaquil stared over the hill, up along the chimney of rock. She got to her feet as if raised by cords.

Atop the chimney was a blackness on the night blacker than the night. It seemed to have no form, yet there was a flicker over it like foamy fire. And out of it burned two stars beneath a sword of light.

Slowly it turned, this sword, to east and west, south and north, catching on its spiralled ribs, its pitiless point, the blasting of the wind. And the wind played the sword, the wind made music. The sword of the horn *sang*, and now the camp, even the vocal camels and raucous mules, fell silent.

"You exist," said Tanaquil. And before she

knew what she did—again—she held her hands
out into the air, as if to touch that creature on the
rock some fifty feet above her.

But with a splash of whiteness, of black, the
unicorn had turned and bounded off into space.
The music ended. And over the wind, Tanaquil
heard the voice of the praying merchant.

"Just look at her, the witch. Can't be trusted.
She calls up demons."

Tanaquil left the sky. All the men had moved
up around her. They stood on the hill glaring at
her. The knives and sticks made a forest, and for
a moment she could see nothing else.

Then the fat leader pushed through. He observed her distastefully.

"I took you in, girl. I let you keep that animal,
which my good patron Pudit said was bewitched.
Don't trouble with her, I said. She means no
harm."

"I don't," said Tanaquil.

"Then why did you conjure a demon on the
rock?"

Tanaquil recalled her raised arms, and how it
must have seemed.

"I didn't conjure it. And it wasn't a demon—"
She almost blurted that she knew a demon when
she saw one, and just stopped herself in time.
"Don't you know what it was? It was a unicorn—"

The leader gave a sour laugh. "No such thing."

She thought: *He'll believe in something supernatural and evil, but not in the glamour of a unicorn.*

The merchant Pudit had approached. He said,
"There's only one method with a witch. She must
be stoned."

"Sounds reasonable to me," agreed the leader.

Then he was yodelling, leaping up and down, and kicking in the air his left leg, which had a brown fur trouser.

Men rushed to his assistance. The peeve, detaching its teeth with an annoyed growl, sprang instead at the merchant Pudit. It bit him several times, while Pudit's servants, trying to strike the peeve with their bludgeons, thwacked the merchant on the arms and chest.

Tanaquil was not sure if the peeve had meant to create a diversion so she might escape. If so, it failed, for Foot and one of the others had grabbed her by the arms.

After a few more moments of incredible noise and flurry, the peeve in any case let go and fled. It dashed between legs and flailing sticks and vanished down the hill faster than a falling boulder.

"Bitten to the bone," announced the leader. "The animal's her familiar."

Tanaquil noticed there were plenty of stones on the hill, and some of the men had begun to pick them up.

She watched, stunned.

Then she saw Gork thrusting through the crowd, coming over and standing before his bitten leader, clicking and clinking and with the goad going *clock-clock-clock* on his boot.

"It's no good killing her," said Gork. "That'll be bad luck."

"Rubbish," said the bitten leader. But the men with the stones had hesitated.

"Now don't you remember last year?" asked Gork.

There was a long pause. Whatever had happened last year was obviously being remembered in detail.

"That was," said the leader, cuddling his leg, "a different thing altogether."

"Well I, for one," said Gork loudly, "won't travel with a caravan under a witch's dying curse. Nor my men. Eh, boys?"

There was a cluttering of dropped stones.

"All right," said the leader sullenly.

"We'll drive her out," said Gork. "Let her go and talk to demons in the hills." He was rewarded by hearty amalgamated assent. Gork said to Foot and the other man, "I wouldn't touch her if I were you. Who knows what the slut might do next." Then he came over and put his face near hers. Gork winked. He cried: "Be off, you filthy witch." And gave her a weightless shove.

Tanaquil nodded. She turned and ran down the hill, and the men moved back from her, a few shouting names. A thrown missile burst near her heel, but it was only a clod of earth.

As she ran she thought of the useful small knife and the tinder-box she had bartered away from Foot, in exchange for the torn silk of her dinner dress. She thought Gork had probably saved her life. And that the unicorn, which had saved her in the desert, had somehow played a trick on her to-night, stirring up from the peaceful dark danger and uncertainty.

Tanaquil sheltered that night in a cave of the hills, with as much space as she could manage put between her and the caravan. Bushes shielded the cave mouth, and the fire she lit. Sometimes she would stab the fire with a branch and describe aloud the leader, Pudit, Foot and certain others, in vivid terms. To her muttering and firelight the peeve was guided in the early hours of the morning. It had killed a small rodent, and this she apologetically roasted for them. The peeve seemed indifferent to its own loyalty.

They fell asleep, and were woken by sunrise.

When she walked out of the cave, Tanaquil saw that the hills slipped gently down westward to a great plain. Lit by the rising sun, a golden crescent glittered on the plain's farthest edge, and in the curve of it the sky had swum.in on the land.

"It's the city," Tanaquil told the peeve. The peeve groomed itself, not sparing a glance. "And beyond, there's the sea."

She was very impressed. She had a second of wanting to jump up and down and shout, but she controlled it.

Very likely it would take some days to cross the plain, but Tanaquil was reassured by the landscape as she descended into it. The sand had given way to thin grass, in places to tracts of wild red and purple flowers. Palms and acacias grew, and later there were orchards of palm and fig, olive trees and lemon trees, behind low walls. Villages lay along the plain like stepping stones to the city. Tanaquil entered one boldly, and asked for fruit. They took her for a boy with very long hair, gave her the fruit, and were astonished at the "tame" peeve.

Tanaquil and the peeve walked all day, and Tanaquil had words with her ill-fitting cast-off boots. At sunset the wind rose eagerly. Men appeared in the orchards to cover the younger trees against the cold. Since there was another village in front of her, Tanaquil went into it and inquired of a woman on the street if she might have shelter for the night. "I can mend things," Tanaquil added, enticingly.

The woman gave her use of the barn, and presently the village music box was brought her in pieces. Tanaquil sat on the straw, bootless, working on the box, while the peeve chased real and imaginary mice, and the thinnest snow painted in the rims of the village. When she was finished, they gave her a supper of peppery porridge and olives, and took the music box away. She heard it playing from house to house until midnight.

In the night, *night* passed down the street.

Walking, Tanaquil saw under the barn door four black stems with flags of lighted ocean. She heard the shell of the horn scrape along the door. She felt the terror of it, the magic, and the impossibility that it should be there or that she should go to it.

"What do you *want?*"

But the unicorn only moved through the village like the wind, silent, without music.

Just before dawn, four or five women were staring at pink glass hoof-pocks in the rime by the well.

"What's this?" they said.

"Oh, whatever can it be?" agreed Tanaquil.

The peeve laid seven slain mice, subject to the laws of the cruel, badly made world, at the feet of their hostess.

So Tanaquil, daughter of Jaive the sorceress, finally reached the city she had been vaguely hearing of for nearly sixteen years.

She felt so elated that day at having got there, it was almost as if she had invented and built the city herself.

First of all, coming out of some trees, Tanaquil found one of the stone obelisks. This marked the start of a paved road. It was quite a narrow road, however, and empty; looking to either side over the plain, Tanaquil could see in the distance evidence of much dust and traffic obviously going along wider roadways to the city.

The narrow road, which would have taken a light cart and mule, ambled through groves of lemon trees and lilacs, and in one place there was a stone basin with water and an iron cup connected to it by a chain. The chain settled for Tanaquil an idea that had been bothering her.

"Peeve, do you mind if I put you on a leash?"

The peeve had found a lemon and was trying to eat it. She peeled the lemon for it and, while it investigated the pith, Tanaquil tied 'round its neck the long sash that had secured her headcloth. The leash was rather clumsy, but it would serve for now, and might prevent comment from the city people.

The peeve spat out the lemon and clawed at its neck.

"No, no. I'm sorry, but you must put up with it."

"Off," said the peeve, "off! Off!"

"No. *Please*. Just till we get—wherever we're going."

"Wurr," said the peeve.

It rolled about and became entangled with the leash. Tanaquil patiently disentangled it before it strangled. "Half an hour?"

The peeve sulked as they walked along the road. Every so often it would sit down, and Tanaquil would find herself hauling it over the paving on its bottom. The peeve swore. It had learnt some of the soldiers' oaths.

"Or you can stay outside."

The city was surrounded by houses that had grown up under the wall. There were gardens with cypresses and banks of flowers, blue and white, yellow and mauve and red. The houses had roofs of dragon-colored tiles. The wall stood over them, and it had, as reported, tiled pictures on it of chariots drawn by racing horses, of lions, trees of fruit, and so on. The narrow road ended at a narrow gate, where two soldiers stood to perfect attention, like dolls.

Out of the city came an enormous noise. There seemed to be every sound on earth taking place at once. Tanaquil heard wheels rumbling, engines that toiled, buckets that rattled, and water that swilled; she detected cattle lowing and dogs barking, while trumpets crowed, doors slammed, birds flew, men and women quarrelled and laughed and sang. She was taken aback. *Well, what did you expect?*

The peeve was gazing at the city's noises in disbelief, attempting to snuff out all its smells, including that of the sea.

"Lots of bones and meat and biscuits here," said Tanaquil.

She sauntered toward the gateway, and all at once the two soldiers came alive.

They clashed over the entrance to the city their crossed spears.

"Halt."

Tanaquil halted. What now?

"State your business in Sea City."

"I'm visiting my aunt."

"You will produce her letter inviting you."

"I don't have it."

"Without such a letter or other confirmation, you can't enter the city."

"My aunt with be furious," said Tanaquil.

The soldiers did not seem distressed by this news. They said nothing, their faces were blank, and the spears remained locked.

"What are the grounds for entering?" said Tanaquil.

"An invitation in writing from a citizen. A summons by the Prince or other dignitary. The bringing of merchandise into the city. The desire to practice a legitimate business there. One word of warning," added the soldier. "*Don't* say you *mend things*. We hear that feeble excuse about twice a day."

"I see. I didn't understand." It seemed to her she had never made a plan so swiftly. "I'm an entertainer. I do magic tricks."

"This may be allowable. The bazaar supports entertainers. But you'll have to give proof."

"You mean you want to watch me perform? That's rather awkward. You see, I was robbed in the desert. They took everything—my donkey, my bag of tricks—"

"How can you carry on your business in the city then?"

"I do have one thing left," said Tanaquil. "You see this peeve? Just an ordinary desert creature. But by a clever illusion, I can make it appear to *talk*."

The soldiers turned their mask-like faces on her.

Tanaquil abruptly tugged the peeve's lead.

The peeve kicked. It parted its jaws. "Rrr!" it went.

Tanaquil coughed. "Sorry. Dust in my throat. Try again—"

She toed the peeve mildly in the side.

It spat. "*Bad,*" said the peeve. "Won't. Don't like it. Go desert." And spinning in the sash it managed a short dash and pulled Tanaquil over. As she and the peeve tumbled on the hard paving, she heard the soldiers split their masks, giving off guffaws.

"That's a riot," one choked. "Can you do it again?"

"Once is enough for now," said Tanaquil.

"Bite!" cried the peeve, chomping on the sash. "Wup!"

"Yes, that's really terrific!"

The peeve swore, and the soldiers almost had a fit. They uncrossed their spears and clapped Tanaquil much too heartily on the back as she dragged the squalling peeve into the city. "Good luck, boy. That's a marvelous turn you've got there. We'll tell all the lads."

Chapter Six

Every exaggerated fantasy Tanaquil had ever had of the city was outstripped by the facts. Even Jaive had never demonstrated, in the magic mirror, anything like this. It was like being inside an enormous clock of countless parts and pieces. It seemed at once jumbled and precise, random and ordained. Just like the sound it made, which was a mix of a thousand sounds, so its shape was formed out of all shapes imaginable—lines, angles, bumps, cones, rounds—and its basic colors of brown, yellow and white, were also fired by the noon sun into blooms of paint, fierce blinks of metal, and cracked indigo shadows.

Tanaquil did not try to take it in, she simply marched in *to* it, staring about her wildly, overwhelmed. While the peeve accompanied her in noisy bewilderment—the million scents of the city had entirely taken up its attention, it growled and whined, snuffled, grunted, and sometimes squeaked. Now and then it ran sideways after something or other, and Tanaquil, her concentration scattered, was tugged against the brickwork or into the mouths of lean alleyways. She thought of undoing the leash and allowing the peeve to rush off on its own. Perhaps she would never see it again—something dreadful might happen to it. It knew the desert and was as surprised here as she was.

At first, near the gate, there had been few people, only the small groups you might come on in a village, women in doorways or at a well, or some men going by with spades over their shoulders. Then the streets, winding into and around each other between the walls and under the arches, opened on a broad white avenue. Palm trees of great height grew along the avenue, and there were marble troughs of water, to one of which three polished-looking horses had been led to drink. The sides of the avenue swarmed with people of every description, and at the windows and doorways and on the balconies of the buildings along the road, were crowds thick as grapes on a bunch. Flights of steps went up too high to see, from the avenue, what was at the top, and up and down them strode and ran the citizens, sometimes colliding. Tree branches curled against the sky from gardens on rooftops. Stained-glass windows flashed as they were constantly pushed wide or closed. The road boomed with voices, and with the vehicles that went both ways along it, chariots and carts, silken boxes carried on the shoulders of trotting men, and one stately camel under a burden of green bananas.

Tanaquil stalked up the road, pushing through the human swarm as she had noted everybody else was doing. The peeve, on a very short leash, kept close to her now, its muttering lost in the general uproar.

Soon wonderful shops began to open in the buildings. She saw shelves of cakes like jewels and trays of jewels like flowers and sheaves of flowers like lances and, in an armorer's, lances like nothing but themselves.

She wanted to look at everything, to laugh and to shout. She felt taller than anyone in the crowd. Also she was dizzy. There was too much, and she was drunk on it, as the peeve had got sozzled on smells.

The end of the avenue was an even further astonishment. It expanded into a marketplace, a bazaar, where every single public activity known to the world seemed to go on.

Two pink marble lions guarded the entrance, and Tanaquil and the peeve rested against the plinth of one of these while porters, carts, and the banana camel trundled by.

Tanaquil attempted to view the things of the market individually, but it was impossible. Her eyes slid from the baskets of peaches to the bales of wool to the pen of curly sheep, to the juggler with his fire-work knives and the fortune-teller's tent with the wrong sorcerous signs embroidered over it, and on.

The market went downhill and was terraced to prevent everything tipping over. But Tanaquil's gaze tipped all the way down, and there below, in a rainbow frill of objects and actions, bluer than the sky, bluer than anything, was the sea. Contrasted to the flurry of the shore, slender ships glided slowly across the water, on russet and melon triangles of sail. The fishy, salty scent sparkled like glass in the air, stronger than perfume, sheep, and peaches.

"Oh, Mother," said Tanaquil, "we salute the *fish*!"

"Now then, move along for God's sake," said a beefy man in an apron. He shouldered past.

"Be good," said Tanaquil to the peeve, "and I'll—" she hesitated. She had been going to promise to get the peeve some cooked meat from one of the stalls. But of course, she had no money. Indeed, she had never *seen* money except in Jaive's coffer, and more recently at the dice games of the caravan. "Er, we'll see," said Tanaquil. They would not starve. She had, did she not, her fabulous magic "trick"? Instead of gawping at the bazaar, she should find a pitch and thrill the unsuspecting populace with the talking peeve.

They went into the market, and walked down the terraces through flares of blood-red silk and garlands of woven baskets.

The juggler was encouragingly earning a large pile of coins, tossed by the crowd. In another place a girl danced with bells on her wrists and ankles, and elsewhere boys made a living pyramid, and fire was eaten.

Tanaquil and the peeve came against a side of ox in which the peeve was rather interested. As she tried to separate them, Tanaquil beheld another marble lion ahead. Seated between its feet was a man playing a pipe. As he played, he swayed, and out of the wooden bowl before him rose a swaying snake, itself with a skin like a plait of bright money.

"Just look," said Tanaquil to the peeve, prizing it off the ox carcass. The peeve looked, for once obliging. Tanaquil realized she had made a mistake. "No—"

The leash burned through her fingers and was gone.

Like a flung brown snowball, the peeve demolished the distance between itself and the marble lion. The crowd about the statue's base parted with cries. The peeve skirled through. It rose steeply. It landed.

There was a kind of explosion of tails, paws, bowl, pipe, snake. Fur and scales sprayed up in the air.

The piper stood baying and waving his arms, obviously afraid to intervene in this cyclone. The unsympathetic crowd laughed and jeered.

An awful clattering rebounded on the marble. The snake was gone, instead, a heap of scales and wobbling springs lay on the lion's feet. The peeve, with a silver spine and head in its mouth, galloped at Tanaquil.

She caught it. *"Bad,"* said Tanaquil, inadequately. "You fool, it's not even real—"

The peeve crouched at her feet, worrying the silver backbone of the mechanical snake and growling. It seemed slightly embarrassed.

"I'm so sorry—" Tanaquil hurried to the statue and looked up at the snake charmer, who was picking over the shattered bits of his act.

"Seventy-five weights of copper and three pence this cost me," he moaned. "Made by the finest craftsmen in the city. Now see."

The peeve had followed Tanaquil, trailing its leash. "Give me *that*." She got the spine and head from its teeth, and it seemed glad to forget them in a thorough wash. The head had faceted green glass eyes, and hinged jaws of ivory fangs. Tanaquil began to try the springs back against their slots. "I think I can mend this."

"No, no, just my rotten luck. Ruined."

"Really, I think I can. I *can* mend things."

The snake-charmer glared at her with tearful eyes.

"*You're* an artisan?"

"Well—I suppose so."

"All right. *Do* it then."

"I'll need some tools—"

"An artisan and no tools," scoffed the embittered snake-charmer. He sat on the lion and refused to glance at Tanaquil, the peeve, the crowd, or the snake.

"Over there, Bindat's stall—he'll lend you a few artisan things," said a man who had come across from the meat rack. "Meanwhile, you can pay me for the bite your dog's taken out of my ox."

"I haven't a penny," said Tanaquil.

The man surprisingly answered, "Have it free then. It was worth it for the laugh."

All afternoon, Tanaquil sat under the marble lion and repaired the mechanical snake.

It was quite a difficult job, but the further she went with it the more she got the hang of what needed doing. The scales, which she had feared might be the worst task, merely linked into one another with tiny hooks.

As she worked, people stopped to watch. Ignoring the peeve tied to a post and the snake charmer lurking on the lion, a few inquired what Tanaquil would charge for mending a toy, a clock, a small watering device. Tanaquil said, "I charge half the going rate."

This meant that by the time the sun westered, various items had been left in her care. The bazaar did not shut up shop with sunset; already lamps and torches were being lit.

"Here you are," said Tanaquil raising the renewed snake in the reddening light. "See if it will go."

"Of course it won't. Hair-fine mechanisms—"

"Just *see*."

The snake charmer snatched the snake and cast it in the bowl as if he loathed it. But he blew a trill on the pipe. The snake stirred. To swaying melody, the snake flowed upward from the bowl and danced at the sunset.

The snake charmer took the pipe from his mouth, and the snake hovered upright, gleaming.

"I won't thank you. Your dog broke it in the first place."

"No, *please* don't thank me," said Tanaquil. "After all, it might become a nasty habit."

She flexed her fingers, swallowed her hunger and thirst, and, taking up the two halves of a doll soldier, began again to work.

Four hours later all the left items had been collected, and a pocketful of coins sat gleaming like the snake under the torches.

Somewhere a bell sounded. It was midnight. Looking up, Tanaquil found a ragged man in front of her. An iron cap was over his head and covered his eyes. He probed an invisible void with his stick. A blind beggar.

"Clink, clink," he said. "I heard the coins fall. Spare me a coin."

Tanaquil put a coin into his thin searching hand.

She remembered the unicorn with a shock of the heart. This imperfect world—

* * *

Bindat's wife, Cuckoo, suggested that for the payment of three pennies, Tanaquil might spend the night in their outhouse. Tanaquil was exhausted and accepted. They had a long walk, however, to Bindat's house, which lay behind the great market and far from the beautiful avenue, in an area of slums. Here the dwellings leaned on each other to stay up, and rickety wooden bridges went over the streets, and, washing-lines, from which, even as they passed, thieves were stealing the washing. Bindat and Cuckoo even greeted one of these thieves warmly. They crunched through open drains, frozen by night, and came to Bindat's house. The outhouse was a hut with holes, white with frost. Wood was stacked there, and it was busy with beetles. The peeve, leash off, spent all night chasing and eating these beetles, despite the bowl of thin soup it had shared with Tanaquil. In the morning, very early, Tanaquil learned that, in addition to the three pennies, she must pay for her lovely night by sweeping the yard and milking the goat. As a child, for a treat, she had sometimes milked the goats at her mother's fortress. This was harder, as the goat and the peeve had declared war on each other.

After a breakfast of burnt crusts, Tanaquil and the peeve returned with Bindat and Cuckoo through the hot and reeking drains, and lamenting owners of stolen washing, to the bazaar. Tanaquil was delighted to find a queue of people waiting for her under the marble lion: Word had got around.

At noon, Bindat came over to Tanaquil and told her in a friendly way that he would have half her earnings, as he and Cuckoo had personally sent all her customers to her. As he spoke, Cuckoo might be seen cleaning a large knife at their stall.

Tanaquil did not argue. She gave Bindat half her coins. When he was gone, she told her next customer she would be moving to the tents of the spice-sellers, whose smell had already attracted her.

Once she had returned all the previously mended things to their guardians, she slipped away, and descended the terraces out of Bindat's sight. Among the spice jars, at an obelisk with a stone fish on it, she sat down again with the peeve, and as she resumed her work, she watched the fish market below, and the blue sea that was greener against the harbor.

Once or twice during the night in the outhouse she had dozed. Then she had believed the unicorn poised outside the door, clean as black snow in the slum. But waking as the peeve scampered over her in its hunting, she knew the unicorn could not be there.

Now she felt she was working in a set of condiments—the pepper and ginger, cinnamon and hyssop and anise, with the fishy salt of the sea.

The peeve sneezed and ate the baked joint she had bought it. Then it slept on her foot after its hard night, and her foot also went to sleep.

A shadow fell across Tanaquil as she was fastening the frame of a mechanical board game involving a lot of small porcelain animals. She glanced up. Her new customers were three large men. The central figure wore black and red clothing, and the buckle of his belt was a gilded hammer crossed by a brass chisel.

He said ringingly, "I am Vush."

"Well done," said Tanaquil.

Around her, the chatter and frisk of the spicery had gone quiet. Everyone was staring at Vush and his two burly companions.

"You don't know me?" asked Vush. He had a terrible beard, which lurched at her as he spoke.

"I'm very sorry."

"I am the Master of the Artisans' Guild of Sea City."

Tanaquil received an inkling of alarm. She grabbed the peeve's leash at the neck. It was already practicing a snarl.

"How nice to meet you," said Tanaquil.

"It's a girl," said the companion to the left of Vush. He shifted, and Tanaquil saw his guild apron, and that he too had the hammer and chisel device, and a brass-bound cudgel.

"Then," said Vush, "she should be at home, not here causing trouble.

"Oh dear, have I?" Tanaquil groveled.

Of course it was apparent what had happened. She did not need Vush's right-hand companion to announce: "Bindat reported you to the guild. He says you charge half the going rate for your work. All prices are fixed by us."

"And you're not a member of the guild," said Vush. "Which means you're not allowed to work in the city at all."

"I didn't know," said Tanaquil. "You see, I come from this backward village—Um—and nobody ever said—"

"Give me that," said Vush, pointing at the game.

Tanaquil thought, *He's going to smash it. Perhaps over my head.*

Before she could make up her mind to let loose the peeve, Vush's left-hand crony leaned down and skimmed the game away.

Instead of hitting her with it, all three ponderously examined its mechanism.

"Not a bad bit of work," said Vush at last.

Tanaquil simpered. "*Thank* you."

"We have no women in the guild," said Vush. "You'll have to join as a boy."

"But you'll have to join," added the right-hand crony. "Or it's the harbor for you."

"You mean you'll put me in a boat?"

"We mean we'll drop you in the sea with lead sandals."

"I'll join," said Tanaquil. "An honor."

"The fee is forty weights of silver."

"Oh."

"You'll have to get someone to sponsor you, pay it for you. One of the guild members may do so."

"Then you'll be in his debt."

"You'll have to work extra hard to pay it off."

"You'll need the guild, then."

"Yes."

The peeve reached out and aimed its claws at Vush's expensive boot. They missed.

"Come to the Guild Hall at sunset," said Vush. "Anyone will direct you."

"If you don't come," said the left-hand man, "we'll come looking for *you*."

"Too kind," said Tanaquil.

She longed for one of Jaive's spells, which, ac-

cording to Jaive, would have transformed Vush
and Company into frogs.

It was true that everyone seemed to know
where to find the Guild Hall of the Artisans, or at
least the people Tanaquil asked directed her without hesitation. The building stood on another fine
street, bathed in the sunset, and its gilded pillars
shone, and the symbol of the hammer and chisel
shone above the door. The door, though, was
firmly shut. Tanaquil, with the peeve on a new
strong leash bought that afternoon, knocked politely, and next violently, but without response.
Perhaps the artisans' baleful invitation had been
only a dare, or a joke to make her look foolish.
This hope was destroyed when, from a round ap-
erture above, a fat, frowning male face stuck out.

"Who is there?"

"I was summoned here by Vush the artisan."

"You're the woman from the market. Control
that animal." The peeve was scratching at the gilt
on the pillars.

As Tanaquil tried to control the peeve, a smaller
door in the great door suddenly slid open.
Tanaquil stepped through, pulling the peeve with
her. The small door, a thing of clockwork, snapped
shut again behind them.

They were in a long corridor lighted by hanging
lamps. At the corridor's far end was a second massive door. The only option was to go forward, and
this Tanaquil did. No sooner had she begun to
walk toward the second door than mechanical oddities activated all around her, perhaps triggered by
her footfalls on the floor. Bells chimed, tiny windows flapped open, and wooden birds whizzed

out—the peeve leapt at them—plaster heads turned menacingly, poking out red plaster tongues. Tanaquil thought it all rather crude.

When she reached the door, the peeve struggling beside her, trying to make plain its needs— *"Bird! Bird!"*—Tanaquil knocked once more, and this door flew wide.

The Artisans' Hall—it was labelled in gold lettering on the wall facing the door, above another gold hammer and chisel, some gold saws, braces, measures, and other stuff—was exactly square, washed with black, and lit by torches. On black chairs around it sat thirty men whom Tanaquil took for officers or superiors of the guild. And facing the door, beneath the lettering, was a man who must be Vush, for his chair was the largest, and a fearsome beard escaped beneath the mask he wore. Every man in the room was masked. The masks were all the same, bronze visors with panes of black glass at the eyes. Meant to create a sinister impression of uninvolved ruthlessness, the masks had succeeded. Tanaquil wavered between scorn and extreme uneasiness. And catching her mood, the peeve crouched, speechless and bristling, at her feet.

A voice came abruptly from the air. Another device, but startling.

"Here is the boy Tanaquil. He is able to mend games and toys, and seeks admission to our guild. Meanwhile, he has worked without membership and owes the guild a fine of three weights of copper. Also he cannot pay the fee of membership. A sponsor is asked. Say brothers, will any do this service for the boy Tanaquil?"

One of the masked men, thin and bony, cranked

to his feet. Sourly, he said, "Vush the Master has proposed that I do so. I'll therefore pay the silver for the boy Tanaquil, which he will then owe me as a debt, plus interest to me of one half-weight of bronze, all cash to be returned to me during the next year, before next year's Festival of the Blessing." He sat down.

"We heed," said the voice in the air, "the generosity of our brother, Jope. Does the boy Tanaquil hear and comprehend? Does he owe that he will honor this loan, and repay it at the proper time?"

Tanaquil shrugged. "If I must. If I *can*. Do I have a choice?"

"No," said the mask with Vush's beard. "Answer correctly."

"I'll repay the loan," said Tanaquil. "What if I can't?"

"You will be whipped through the city by the guild, as a defaulter," said Vush's mask, annoyed.

"Wait," said Tanaquil. "I'll give it up. I won't mend anything. I can find different work."

A loud murmur came from the room, and she picked out another of the masks saying, "I told you, it's that girl I heard of with the animal that talks."

Vush cleared his throat, and the hall was silenced.

He said, "Too late. It has been decided." And then he thundered: "Bring forth the Fish of Judgement."

With a slight rumble of hidden wheels, part of the floor moved sedately backwards, drawing twenty-nine of the chairs up to the walls, while Vush's chair ran in a graceful arc to the right.

The peeve growled.

The wall with the gold symbols and lettering split on a high rectangular door.

Tanaquil had a glimpse of trees in some yard or garden behind the Guild Hall, of peacock-blue evening sky sewn with stars—escape—but something came instead into the hall, and the door closed.

The voice in the air droned:

"From the sea comes the wealth of the city. To the sea we give homage. Let the sea be our judge."

An iron table was sliding from the wall and up to Tanaquil. On it rested a bronze balance, the two cups of which swung as it advanced. There was a strong, now-recognized, odor.

The brotherhood of the guild arose. "The Fish!"

Tanaquil thought of her mother's dinner.

In the left-hand cup of the balance lay a silver-scaled fish. It was artisan's work, and beautifully made, like the snake in the bazaar. In the other cup of the balance was another fish. This was greenish gray and smelled to high heaven. A real fish, from the fish market.

The guild brothers were raising their masked heads and arms.

Vush said, face to the ceiling, arms upheld, "Choose now, boy Tanaquil, which fish is it to be?"

Not having had the ceremony explained to her, Tanaquil assumed she was to choose the made fish, which anyway would be more pleasant. On the other hand, perhaps the reeking real fish represented honest toil? If she chose wrongly, what ridiculous and ghastly punishment would be inflicted?

She thought, irresistibly, *The last idiotic ceremony was my mother's dinner. The unicorn got me out of that.*

She pictured one of the doors that led into the hall crashing open and darkness flying in behind the seashell moon of the horn.

Then she looked down again at the two fish.

There was only one.

Was this divine intervention? The fish that was left was the nice example, which had been made.

"Well I suppose," said Tanaquil. She stopped because the artisans had also lowered their heads, and even through the masks she guessed they were gawking at the empty cup on the balance.

"Where's that fish?" said the sour voice of Jope.

"It was here," said another one. "I *smelled* it."

"Without the fish the ceremony is null—"

"Where, oh, where—?"

"*There's* the fish," tolled Vush.

Tanaquil became aware that something hot and furry sat by her leg, and from its pointed face, out of its motionless jaws, drooped three inches of silvery green tail.

Tanaquil snatched the made fish from the other cup.

"Behold!" cried Tanaquil. "I choose the fish that is made. But my peeve has chosen the fish which may be eaten."

"Sacrilege!" moaned Jope. "The ancient ritual has been mocked. Am I to put up all that fee for her now?"

"This is certainly very grave," said Vush.

Tanaquil confronted the ring of wicked-looking masks, the laughable dangerous darkness of these men, who were probably even madder than her mother, and much more unjust.

"What punishment for eating the fish?" moaned the wretched Jope.

"The fish," muttered Tanaquil, "the meat, the soup, the stairs, the door—I put you together out of bones and clockwork and you came alive—Is this a spell I'm making? Where *are* you?"

"She's seen our hall," said Vush, "and the ritual of membership. But she can't join. It would be bad luck on us all."

"It's the harbor for her," said a voice she recalled.

Chapter Seven

The wall under the letters, hammer, and chisel changed. Then, quite easily, it parted. There again were treetops and a darker, bluer sky of wilder stars. Pernickety as a cat, the unicorn came, as if on shoes of glass, in through the opening, down across the hall. There was no violence, no speed. It moved to the rhythm of an elder dance, putting all the rituals of the world to shame. Black, silver, gold, and moon-opal, night and sea, fire, earth, air, and water.

This time I did *call it. Or every time I did.*

At her feet Tanaquil heard the peeve swallowing the whole fish in one gulp. And the unmuffled drum of her own heart.

Then one of the artisans shrieked.

"It's the Sacred Beast! Fly! Save your lives! The city's lost!"

And somehow the mechanical chairs were knocked over, and the shut door to the corridor was wrenched open, and out of it the artisans sprang and sprawled with masked shouts and frightened thumps.

The unicorn, mild-mannered as a deer, trotted lightly after them. It went by Tanaquil like a wave of stars. She thought she heard the music of its bones and of a night wind wrapped about the horn.

As the unicorn passed through the door and along the corridor toward the outer exit, the peeve tugged on its lead to follow. And once more Tanaquil was propelled to chase the night-dream thing.

In the corridor the plaster heads turned and poked out their tongues irrelevantly, and then there was the street beyond the opened pillared door. And down the street rushed the artisans in their secret regalia, revealed, speechless now in the single-mindedness of panic. With the unicorn dancing after.

Tanaquil hauled on the leash. "No—let it go—I shouldn't have—no—no—" And the leash snapped and the peeve bounced out into the street, pursuing maybe only its old fantasy of a meal or a treasure—the bone—and Tanaquil *walked* after. She forced her mind to do some work, while her feet tried not to run.

How had the unicorn entered the city? She saw it leap from the sky like a falling planet. But no, the event had been more simple. She seemed to see the narrow gate through which she had come in, and one soldier asleep by a wine flask, and the other standing idle, regarding something come quietly up out of the groves and orchards of the plain. A horse? Yes, a fine horse lost by some noble. And the horse came to the gate, and the soldier who was not drunk enough to be asleep smiled on it, and tried to pet it, and somehow could not. But he undid the entry to the city, and like a vapor the unicorn went in. "Horse-horse," said the soldier fondly. "One day, I'll have a horse."

* * *

There were torches burning along the street at intervals, and here and there a lamp hung in a porch or a lit window gave its stained glass brilliance.

Through cold arches of shadow and cold blasts of light the fleeing artisans milled. They panted like rusty bellows now, and sometimes groaned or cursed. One or two craned over their shoulders, now and then, and, seeing the slender blackness of their terror still nimbly prancing after, made fresh rushes of flight that soon broke down.

Nobody looked out to see what went on. The city was full of noises day and night. They met with no one, either.

However, at its end, the street was crossed by another, a wide avenue of special splendor. It was lined by lions of gilded iron, and had lamp standards with lanterns of sapphire, green, and crimson glass. People were passing under these, and there was something of a crowd at the road's edges, standing and looking along the street with mild concern.

The artisans had no charity for this barrier. They plunged into it, hitting out and blustering advice to run or at least to get out of the way. But the crowd rounded on them intrigued, gesturing at the masks: "Look, it's the Artisans' Guild! They've all gone crazy." And when the artisans, breathlessly blaspheming, laid about them with sticks and fists, the crowd responded in kind. A spectacular fight began.

Tanaquil, about eighty feet behind, took her eyes from the upheaval. She saw the unicorn had stopped, clear as the statues in the lights of the avenue. The surging crowd seemed not to see it there. "No," said Tanaquil again, "don't." And the unicorn, as if it heard and would tease her in its sublime unearthly way, turned to the side with a little flaunting, horse-like gambol. There was a garden or an alley there, and into it the unicorn minced.

Tanaquil ran. She caught up to the peeve, who was running still. And at a gap between tall houses, both came to a halt. They peered down a tunnel of dark, and nothing was in it. Once more. Vanished.

The peeve sat on the road and washed vigorously, as if it had just been running for exercise, not *chasing* anything. Tanaquil got its leash.

The racket from the crowd was now extraordinary. Tanaquil grasped that not only could she hear the fight, but the notes of cheers and whistles up the street, and drawing nearer. Citizens uninvolved in battle pointed. She made out an orderly movement and the glint of lanterns on spears. Soldiers were approaching to correct the disorderly crowd. And beyond the soldiers came other lights, drums, the roll of wheels.

"It's a procession," said Tanaquil.

She went forward cautiously.

The flailing artisans and their assailants were now mixed up with scolding soldiers in burnished mail and plumed helmets. The riot had spilled out into the avenue. Suddenly the whole mob unravelled and flooded right across the roadway.

Tanaquil pulled herself up onto the plinth of a lamp, while the peeve scurried up the pole.

Artisans and crowd members were rolling on the road, soldiers were ladling out blows with spear butts, and an entire row of drummers was falling

over them with shrieks, while horses reared and
chariots upended, and flowers and fires whirled
through the air.

"It's not a procession any more," remarked
Tanaquil.

She was gazing with wonder at the chaotic muddle, which seemed unlikely ever to be sorted out,
when a surprisingly intact chariot shot straight out
of the mess and pulled up smartly close beneath
Tanaquil's plinth.

The chariot was small, painted and gilded and
garlanded with flowers, and drawn by two small
white horses. The driver was a girl perhaps a year
younger than Tanaquil. She had long ropes of very
black hair, and a cloak of red velvet and pure gold
tissue that seemed to be embroidered with rubies.

"What," shouted the girl in a penetrating, high,
and regal voice, "is this disgusting silliness?"

At once there was a hush. The fighting on the
roadway ceased. The combatants, where able, detached themselves. Removing masks, holding
cloths to bleeding noses, they stood about looking
cowed.

She's that important, then, thought Tanaquil. And
staring down at the girl, Tanaquil had the most curious feeling she had seen her before.

"Well?" said the girl, still theatrically, but more
quietly, now there was silence. "What are your ex-
cuses?"

"Ma'am, these rowdies just rushed out in front
of us," said a stylish officer of the soldiers.

"Obviously," said the girl. On her head was a
goldwork cap with a red feather. "You," she added
to Vush. Vush got up, his mask half off and a black

eye glaring above his beard. "You're the Master Artisan, aren't you?"

"Yuff," admitted Vush through a split lip.

"What was the meaning of this affray?"

An expression of despair crossed Vush's swelling face. He squared his big shoulders.

"We were chafed by a uniborn, your highnuff."

"A what?"

"A uniborn."

"He means a unicorn, madam," said the officer. He gave a stagey laugh. "Really!"

"Where is it?" said the girl. She looked round with genuine fascination. "Are you making this up?"

"*No*, your highnuff. The Fabred Beaft manifufted among uff." Vush said in a dreadful voice, "Doom. It meanf the end."

A sigh passed over the crowd. Tanaquil saw here and there the making of signs against evil and ill fortune.

"The Sacred Beast," said the girl, "*if* ever it were to return to us, would offer its loyalty to my father, Prince Zorander. We've nothing to fear. As for you, I believe you were all drunk at some artisans' rite. You scared yourselves into seeing things and then ran out here and caused this disturbance. My father will doubtless fine your guild. Look forward to *that*, and stop spreading unwise rumors of unicorns."

The artisans drooped. They had been atrociously embarrassed. Hints of doubt were murmuring between them. *Had* they imagined the unicorn?

Then a thin, cranky artisan stamped his foot on

the road, and thrust a skinny finger at the lamp standard, the perch of Tanaquil and the peeve.

"*She's* the trouble maker. She's a witch. She made us see things," howled Jope.

Every head turned. Every face for a mile, it felt to her, was raised to Tanaquil's own. Including the face of the Prince's daughter below.

The Princess frowned. For a minute she might have been puzzled, possibly by the apparition of the peeve, hanging by one paw and its tail from the lantern hook.

"This girl?" asked the Princess.

Vush said heavily, "Fhe fneabed into our hall difguifed af a boy. Fhe profaned a ritual—"

The Princess interrupted. She said directly to Tanaquil: "What have you got to say?"

"I'm not a witch," said Tanaquil promptly. She stared at the girl and caught herself back. "Of course there wasn't a unicorn. Because I can mend things they tried to force me to join their guild. They threatened to drown me if I didn't."

"Oh, yes," said the Princess. "Father *will* be interested."

The artisans muttered. The officer glanced at them and they stopped.

"Then," said Tanaquil, "they went quite mad and ran out into the street screaming about sacred beasts. I'm a stranger to this city. I'm not impressed."

"Of course not," said the girl. She looked at the soldiers. "Clear the road, please."

Order came after all. The other vehicles were righting themselves, the soldiers herding artisans and citizens out of the way. As Vush was deposited at the roadside there were jibes and laughter.

The Princess said to Tanaquil, "Come down and get into my chariot. You can bring your animal."

Tanaquil said, "I'm sure I don't merit the honor."

"It's not an honor," said the Princess. "It's an invitation."

Tanaquil got down from the lion, and the peeve slithered after her. They climbed into the chariot of flowers, and the Princess flared her reins. The small white horses darted off, straight through the loiterers on the road, who tumbled aside.

A few flakes of snow, unusual in the city, spotted the air.

"By the way, I'm sorry, but Father won't fine the artisans. It would be useless trying to persuade him. It talks, doesn't it?" said the Princess. "The animal."

"I can, er, *make* it seem to."

"Good. I thought you'd be all right."

They sped out of the avenue of lions into an avenue lined by gilded, lantern-lit dolphins. Then they raced to the foot of a hill and roared up it. The peeve wrapped itself round Tanaquil's leg and clawed her. "Too fast. Want get off."

"That's excellent," congratulated the Princess.

"Ow. Thank you."

Over the top of the hill, where the road was lined by lantern-lit gilded octopuses and camels alternately, appeared a peculiar white, lighted mountain.

"My father's palace," said the Princess, faintly bored.

As the chariot slowed, Tanaquil tried and succeeded in counting the lines of windows, balconies. There were fifteen stories.

"You can use that room, if you like it," said the Princess. Her name was Lizra, she had revealed. "Have a bath and choose one of those dresses in the cedarwood closet. Then we'll go down to dinner. It goes on for hours. Won't matter if we're late."

She had thrown off her cloak, and sat about in a red gown with gold buttons.

On their entering her bedchamber, Tanaquil had been half affronted, half delighted. It was a colossal room, and every wall was painted like a beautiful garden of fruit trees and flowers, with a flamingo lake whose water was inlaid lapis lazuli that seemed to reflect and ripple. On the blue ceiling were a gold sun and a silver moon and some copper and platinum planets that moved about in appropriate positions. When Lizra pulled a golden handle by the bed, three white clockwork doves flew over. The bed itself was in the shape of a conch shell, plated in mother-of-pearl. There were no fireplaces. Pipes of hot water, it seemed, ran under the floor and behind the walls from furnaces in the basement.

The peeve, too, was overwhelmed, It immediately laid some dung on a woven-gold rug, then folded the rug over the misdemeanor like a nasty pancake.

Tanaquil expected death at once, but Lizra only took the rug and dropped it out of the window ten stories down to the gardens below. "Someone will find it, put the dung on the flowers, clean the rug, then bring it back."

Nevertheless, she showed Tanaquil and the peeve a marble bathroom, to which a large tray of earth had already been brought.

The other room led from the bedchamber. It was colored like a rose, and in it were a fireplace and a bed, both with columns of cinnabar. "It's where my visitors stay," said Lizra airily, "friends."

Tanaquil raised her eyebrows. "You're too kind. Surely you don't honor me by thinking of me as a friend?"

"Are you an enemy then?" asked Lizra, with a knife-like glance.

Tanaquil said, "I only meant—"

"Don't mind me," said Lizra. She watched the peeve in the bathroom, in a delayed reaction, scraping dirt out of the tray all over the floor. "Make it say something," said Lizra. "I think it wants to."

"Buried it," said the peeve. "Clever me."

"Yes," said Lizra. "I thought so."

Tanaquil bathed in a bath where she could have swum, had she known how. There were jade ducks that floated full of soap, and a fish, when you tilted it, sluiced you with warm water.

From her closet Lizra chose for Tanaquil a gown of lion-yellow silk. It was ornate and boned, like the red gown. "We're the same size. Just as well. You have to be formal here, particularly for dinner. So many rules, like the procession."

Lizra had been driving through the city to "inspire the people." "Father says it does," said Lizra, "but half of them don't take any notice. Why should they? I have to go round once a month. *He* only bothers with the festivals. It makes you sick."

"What does your mother say?"

"My mother's dead," said Lizra briskly. "Don't tell me you're sorry or how awful, because you never knew her, and neither did I, properly. It happened when I was only five."

But Tanaquil had actually paused to visualize a life from the age of five without a mother—or without the only mother she could imagine, Jaive.

"We'll go down then, Tanaquil," said Lizra.

"Will your father want to know who I am?"

"He'll assume, if he notices either of us, that you're some royal person from another city he's agreed to allow on a visit. It happens a lot. I usually find those girls stuck-up or stupid. On the other hand, I was once friends with a road-sweeper's daughter, Yilli, and she came here often. I really liked her. Then she tried to cut my throat one morning. She wanted to steal some of my jewelry, which I hate anyway. She could have had it. I've avoided friends since then."

Tanaquil was shocked into weird sympathy. She could see it all, the sweeper's daughter's painful jealousy, Lizra's bold, blind trust, her own shock, the emotional wound she thought she should be casual about.

"I still sometimes catch sight of her," said Lizra bleakly. "She bakes pies in the Lion Market."

Tanaquil realized she might have eaten one of these pies. She said, "You mean you let her go?"

"I held her upside down out of the window first."

Tanaquil said, "Are you in fact warning me to be careful? Since you don't know anything about me—"

"So what?" said Lizra. "I just think I might like

to *know* you, not *about* you. Yes, poor Yilli was my mistake. But you have to take risks."

"Yes," said Tanaquil.

"Bring your peeve. It'll like dinner."

They went down to the dining hall in the Flying Chair. The peeve did not enjoy this, as it had not enjoyed coming up in it.

Several flights of marble stairs, with vast landings, ran up and down through the fifteen stories of the palace. For each flight there was also a Flying Chair. It was like a birdcage with bars of gilded iron, and inside was a bench with cushions. You entered, sat, and rang a golden bell in the floor of the cage. This communicated to gangs of servants at the bottom and top of the palace, and they began to haul on the gilded ropes. The cage worked against a counterweight, which was gently released to bring the carriage down and gently lowered to lift it. Should you wish to alight at the twelfth story, the bell was rung twelve times, and so on. Sometimes, the bell was misheard, but never by very much.

Tanaquil herself did not completely like the flying up and down through the air of the staircase wells, with carved pillars, balustrades, and windows sliding by in the other direction. The gang of Chair servants could sometimes be seen far below or above, leaning over banisters and grinning. All of them looked quite insane.

"Have the Chairs ever had an accident?" she had inquired, on having the method first explained to her.

"Once or twice," said Lizra. She added, philosophically, "They never fall far. Father's Chief

Counselor, Gasb, once got a broken leg. Rats had gnawed the ropes. The rope-checker was beheaded."

They reached the fifth floor, that of dining, and got out to a chorus of pleased whoops from the lower Chair gang.

The doors to the hall were covered in gold. Two servants flung them open. At once a boy playing a flute and a girl strewing flower petals jumped into their path and preceded them into the room. If anyone of the hundreds of people there looked round, it was unlikely. The din was deafening. Scores of musicians played on a gallery that encircled the chamber, pipes and drums, harps and tambourines. Nobody listened, or tried to.

Ranks of tables, high-legged and low, laden with food and drink, had attracted sitters like hungry gulls. Servants glided about with enormous platters of vegetables, fruits, breads, roasts, and cakes, and vessels of wine, water, tea, and brandy. The meal did not apparently have courses. Everything was served at once and continuously. On the mosaic floor, flowers lay crushed. Sleek dogs, cats, and monkeys, with collars of silver and jewels, roamed the area, while on several of the great golden chandeliers, pet parrots swung, eating something or singeing themselves on the candles. A pink bird dived overhead, trailing a leash of crystals. The peeve made to spring, and Tanaquil held it down. The bird settled in a cut-glass tureen of presumably cool soup, and began to splash and preen.

The Prince's table was at the end of the endless chamber, amid an indoor arbor of vines and potted trees, the branches hung with small gems, glittering. The table itself was of gold, and of an odd coiling and twisting shape, like the beds of a river. About seventy people were seated at it in one curve or another. They were all dressed in incredible clothing, many flamboyant styles, armored by precious metal and stones.

"There's father," said Lizra. "And that's Gasb, with the hat like an owl."

Tanaquil saw the hat first. It was made of feathers, the spread wings extending over the Counsellor's head to either side, the savage face coming down to mask his eyes and shield his nose with a beak of gold. Whatever he truly was, the contraption made him look both absurd and rapaciously cruel. Of the Prince, Tanaquil had only a fleeting glimpse before Lizra had turned her aside into one of the bends of the table: a man with very black, long, curled hair, a diadem with diamonds, patchwork clothes of silk, cloth-of-gold, and the hides and furs of a great many animals, which might otherwise have been living their own lives.

"Have some of this," said Lizra. "Let the peeve on the table if it wants. Look, there's Lady Orchid's marmoset in the pie."

Tanaquil began to eat. The food was good, though some of it highly spiced. The nobles of the Prince's court were also constantly shaking out clouds of pepper, salt, and cinnamon onto their plates, and dipping sugars and essences into their cups. Occasionally, Tanaquil got another look at Lizra's father. He was a handsome man. He never smiled. And though he paid no heed to the general antics, when the clean, dainty marmoset pattered close, he pushed it roughly away, and Lady

Orchid might be seen creasing her glorious gown in bows of apology.

Lizra seemed to have no connection to her father. She glanced about and spoke of several people at the table. She pointed out a lord who had invented a strain of rose that would shrink into the soil at sunset, and thereby not need to be protectively covered every night by gardeners against the frosts, and a lady who had won a chariot race, and a general in golden mail who was said to have eaten a crocodile. But of Prince Zorander Lizra said nothing. *There's nothing between them,* thought Tanaquil. *As I had nothing with Jaive.* Then she and Lizra started to laugh again at something, and Tanaquil heard herself with surprise. *Who does she remind me of?*

"Do you know," Lady Orchid's voice broke out in loud, self-conscious tones, as she tied the marmoset's emerald leash to her chair, "a unicorn has been seen again in the city."

Tanaquil felt as if a stream of boiling cold water were being poured down her spine.

"A unicorn? Some foolishness—"

"No, there were various reports on Lion and Lynx Streets. About midnight a ghostly shape went by with a blazing silver horn."

"I heard the creature was scarlet and had fiery eyes," said a noble to Lady Orchid's left.

"The fishermen said they saw the Sacred Beast of the city swimming in the ocean near dawn."

"There are always these lying rumors," said Gasb suddenly, in a harsh, owl-cruel voice that carried over all the table's coils.

Everyone hastened to agree. "Oh, true, Lord Gasb."

Somewhere above, in the vault of the palace, a huge bell rang out. It tolled for midnight, and the whole hall sank into abrupt and utter silence.

Prince Zorander rose to his feet. He was tall and commanding in his robe of dead things. He raised a goblet cut apparently from a single amethyst. Every person in the hall also got up and raised a drinking vessel. Tanaquil rose too, as Lizra did. The Prince's cold, calm voice rang like the bell. "The city salutes midnight and the Sacred Beast."

"Midnight. The Beast."

They drank and sat down. The peeve, which had speechlessly devoured pieces of meat on the table and spilled gravy, climbed into Tanaquil's lap and ruined Lizra's yellow dress.

Chapter Eight

In the sunrise, Lizra took Tanaquil round the mile of palace gardens.

Tanaquil was not sure she liked going to bed so late and then getting up again so early. The fire lit in her cinnabar fireplace for the night was still glowing when she woke to Lizra standing by the bed with a tray of food, already clad in a wild white gown with feathered sleeves. "Salute the day!" said Lizra, just as Jaive had made her sorcerous portrait do.

However, the sun rising on the many different trees and statues, and over the limpid pools of the garden, was a marvelous sight.

The gardeners were going about uncovering the plants and shrubs. Some had been left to brave the cold; their blooms were frostbitten and black, but already new buds were breaking, and by noon everything would be in flower. Wading birds fished in the ponds.

"Do you think there could be such a thing as a unicorn?" asked Lizra.

"Do you?"

"I don't know where you come from," said Lizra, "no, I don't want to know. But probably you haven't heard the city legends. There are two. One says the unicorn founded the city. It was carried ashore on a great wave, and where it touched the earth with its horn a magic well was formed that became the source of all the waters of the city. Then, from time to time the Beast returned, to greet the princes of the city. One day it will come back and, approaching the prince, touch him and endow him with mighty powers—make him immortal, impervious to harm, that sort of thing. And then the city will flourish as never before."

"What's the other legend?" said Tanaquil, remembering the yelps of the artisans.

"The other legend is that we offended the unicorn—I don't know how. And so when it comes back it will kill and maim, and maybe the sea will wash in and destroy the city altogether."

Tanaquil stood in thought. She pictured the ancient sea covering the desert, the fossils, and the star-bones found beneath the hollow hill.

The peeve fell into a pond. They fished it out.

"Spuff. Bad," said the peeve. *"Wet."*

"It's really brilliant how you do that," said Lizra. "Your lips don't move at all."

Tanaquil wanted to tell Lizra the facts, but once again held herself back. Like Lizra, perhaps she too had never had a friendship. Certainly she had tried to make friends with the maids in the fortress, but resolutely they had kept Tanaquil in her "proper place": Madam's daughter.

The day was warm, and the peeve shook and fluffed itself beside them as they went to see the mechanical waterwheel that drew up water for the gardens.

As they were standing watching the wheel, which revolved the full buckets high, tipped them sideways into a canal, and then swung them on down again into a cistern, a palace servant jogged up to Lizra.

"Highness, your father invites you to his library."

"Thank you," said Lizra, "I obey." The servant went off and Lizra swore. "I know what it is, it's about the Festival of the Blessing at the end of the week—tomorrow. There's just so much ritual," she said, as they entered the palace and walked toward a Flying Chair. As the gang hauled them up with cries of hilarity, Tanaquil clutched her knees and the peeve clawed the cushions, bristled, and looked as if it might be sick. Lizra added, "By the way, I'm afraid the last three floors will be in father's private Chair. It's worse than this."

"Worse?"

They alighted on the twelfth landing, and walked down a corridor lined with saluting golden soldiers. At its end was a carved door, and going through they found a landing of green onyx. On a flight of stairs a band of terrible-looking people were rushing unsafely about, cartwheeling and swinging from the banisters, hanging upside down, and giving awful raucous screams and giggles. They were dressed in beautiful clothes, but were barefoot. Their hair stood on end.

Lizra said sternly, "Chair *down*."

At once the crazed activity was transformed into a thundering, screeching race up the stairs. From three floors up presently there were calls and howls, and then a burst of song—the words sounded nonsensical.

Down the stairwell came a Flying Chair of stupefying magnificence on a rope bound with silver. It stopped at the landing.

"They untie it above," said Lizra. "We'd better get in. They aren't able to stay still for long."

Tanaquil followed Lizra uneasily into the Chair, sat, and held the peeve between her arms in an iron lock.

Lizra kicked a gold thing in the floor and a trumpet pealed overhead.

The noises became a gale; the cage juddered and began to rise.

As they went up, they encountered and passed the Chair gang, who were plunging down the stairs with the other end of the silver rope, shrieking and singing something like "Heave ho, rope and woe—" their feet never missing the treads, their eyes red, foaming at the mouth.

"Oh, the God!" cried Tanaquil.

They reached the upper landing and the chair stopped rock-still.

"They'll tie it up at the bottom now," said Lizra. "Then they must wait for the next one going up or down. When father's busy, sometimes they run up and down every ten minutes. They're the counterweight, you see. It was Gasb's idea. My father thought it was unusual. They all go off their heads. They can't keep still. They have to sleep in clockwork hammocks that sway."

Tanaquil felt sick, and not only from the Chair.

Two gold soldiers now stood with spears crossed over a gold door.

"This is the door to the apartments of the Prince."

"I, the daughter of the Prince, will enter with my companion, the Princess Tanaquil."

"Enter!"

Beyond the door was a thing of which Tanaquil had heard, but never seen: daytime winter.

"Don't take any notice," said Lizra.

They walked up ten steps that seemed made of the sheerest ice, but somehow did not slip. On either side long plains of snow extended to bluish distance, where white snow mountains stabbed into a royal blue sky. On the snow plains great cats of white, spotted fur stalked each other.

Tanaquil grimaced. She made herself recognize the panes of glass between herself and the snows.

They reached the top of the stair, and an open arch. Into the space came a snow leopard treading on taloned feet. It turned its wicked head to them and snarled, and the fur rose along its back.

The peeve lay flat, waggling its rump and grumbling.

"It's only clockwork," said Lizra. "It's all clockwork."

The peeve got up again. The snow leopard had no smell, and now indeed had retreated into a wall.

They walked through the arch and out of the snows into a great library of golden books. The sunlight gushed over the polished floor from a doorway to the roof outside. Butterflies had come in; white and silver and palest blue, they flew about the room and lit upon the books.

"Clockwork," said Lizra. She glanced at Tanaquil. "My father likes things that aren't real."

Along the roof, which was paved with dragon tiles, a painted boat was sailing, drawn by a balloon of sail wind-catching up in the air. The boat came to the doorway, and the balloon deflated and sank down. The Prince and his Chief Counselor stepped into the library. Today Zorander wore a tunic of beetle wings, and Gasb a hat like a vulture.

"Who is this?" said the Prince. For a moment Tanaquil thought he meant his own daughter, and was strangely unsurprised. But it was Tanaquil he referred to.

"Oh, Princess Tanaquil. Of . . . Erm," said Lizra.

"And *that?*"

"Her pet peeve. It can talk."

"Is it house-trained?"

"*Yes*, Father."

"Shorten the leash, please," said Zorander to Tanaquil.

Their eyes met. His were cold, like his snows, and like the clockwork. He seemed not to like her hair, her borrowed dress. She bowed, and he looked away from her. She was glad.

"The Festival of the Blessing," said the Prince to Lizra.

"Yes, Father?"

"This year you'll be a credit to me. The people expect it. Your gown is even now being prepared. Tonight you shall have it. There are seven layers of golden lace."

Lizra winced. The Prince did not see. He stared across the library to where, on a frame, a suit of male clothing was displayed.

Tanaquil observed velvets in purple and a breastplate of gold and jewels. It would be even hotter, though perhaps not so scratchy as lace.

"Go and look at it, if you wish," said the Prince. He was speaking to Tanaquil. Cold as snow, but also a showoff. She went across the room politely and stopped before the frame. "The city offers respect to the sea. And so the cloak is made of the skins of seventeen sharks," he said. "And fringed with the teeth of twenty dolphins." What a pity they could not bite him! Tanaquil glared at the clothes. And saw that at each shoulder, the cloak was fastened to the breastplate by a gleaming, milk-white whorl. Fossils—and of such size and perfection she ached to prize them loose.

"Nice," said the peeve. It stared where she did, intensely. *"Snails."*

"No," said Tanaquil. She pulled the peeve round and went over to a wall of books. The peeve, superior, ignored the fluttering of the clockwork butterflies.

Zorander stood with his daughter at a table, speaking to her in a low, horribly serious voice. She beamed and twittered at him. Each was plainly disgusted by the personality of the other. Tanaquil felt again a type of sickness—for Lizra, for herself.

Then Gasb came sidling up. He limped, perhaps from the old break in his leg, but it made him seem more nauseating then ever.

"Well, well. Princess Tanaquil, of Erm. How remiss. I don't recall Erm. Where is it?"

"A town of the desert," said Tanaquil.

"Ah. Now that reminds me, there was once a Princess Yilli of Roadsweeping. Have you heard of her?"

Tanaquil was soft and slightly witless. "No, I'm ever so afraid not."

"Just as well, maybe. I'd only suggest you bear in mind, *princess*, that many things are tolerated, except nuisance."

The peeve gargled vigorously.

"Talks, does it?" asked the Counselor.

"Wurrupy," said the peeve, and chattered its fangs.

"Naughty little animal," said Gasb. "Perhaps we should skin you for a brown fur muff."

"We have a saying in Erm," said Tanaquil before she could help herself, "never kick a man who wears iron boots."

Gasb straightened. "And who's in the boots? You?"

"*Me?*" twittered Tanaquil.

"Gasb," called the Prince. "We'll go now and shoot birds."

Gasb the vulture went sidling off across the room, eager for more feathers.

Lizra, pale and pouting, came to Tanaquil. She whispered: "We can go down the terrace stair to the stables on the middle roof. If we dress as grooms we can take a chariot out riding."

"What did he *tell* you to do?"

"Go and pray for the good of the Festival."

Prince Zorander and Counselor Gasb had left the room.

The two girls and the peeve remained alone in the sunlit library. The presence of the two men was everywhere still.

Lizra said, "I haven't asked you—just tell me, do you have a mother?"

"Yes."

"You're lucky," said Lizra.

"Lucky to have left her."

"Mine left *me*," said Lizra. "I could kill her for dying."

* * *

Dressed as grooms, Lizra and Tanaquil rode a small plain pony chariot down a ramp, along the edges of the garden, and out into the city. After three or four spectacular streets, they passed into meaner thoroughfares. Tanaquil saw again the sordid huts and shacks, the gaping drains. They came to a section where the city wall was ruinous and low, and went out by an unguarded gateway. Lizra drove the chariot along a road that ran above the beach. Stunted palms grew by the road, and to the right hand the dunes ran out to the ocean. A few houses remained by the road, but they were deserted, their tiles flaked, their roofs fallen in. The city drew away. Despite the sun and the blueness of the water, there was a shadow on the morning.

Tanaquil could think of nothing to ease Lizra's depression, or her own. They, and the peeve—now used to the chariot's motion—stayed silent.

Lizra spoke at last.

"I'm taking you to the spot where the Sacred Beast is supposed to have come out of the sea."

"Oh . . ." said Tanaquil, ". . . good."

"Somehow it seemed right you should see it." Lizra flicked the reins and the ponies went more quickly. "I'm going to ask you another question."

"Yes?"

"I want you to tell me the truth."

"If I can."

"I won't betray you," said Lizra.

Tananquil, who had been thinking of the unicorn, tensed and frowned. She had had the difficult feeling from the start that she could trust Lizra, and this had made her extremely wary.

"What is the question?"

"Are you a witch?"

Tanaquil laughed. "*No!* Good heavens, anything but."

"My father," said Lizra, "told me that witches often have red hair."

"Oh, *did* he?"

"It's a popular belief here."

"Well I can assure you, I have about as much magical ability as an orange."

"That sounds to me," said Lizra astutely, "as if someone tested you, to see." Tanaquil kept quiet. "But what about the peeve?"

"You mean the trick of making it seem to talk? That's just a conjuring act."

"No, I mean the fact that it *does* talk."

Tanaquil stared at the melancholy, sunny view. The stunted palms rattled in a wind off the sea, and sand spurted from the feet of the ponies. A ruined house leaned to the road. The peeve, glaring through under the chariot rail, announced loudly, "Rats there. Let's go house."

Lizra said, and her voice now had some of her father's coldness, "People always lie to me, you see. Or simply don't tell me things. Or they tell me things that are meant to worry me, like the red hair business. Even Yilli, you know, when she caught me by the throat with her knife, said, '*It won't hurt!*' "

"Perhaps it wouldn't have," said Tanaquil. "Or perhaps she did like you enough to wish it wouldn't."

"I hadn't thought of that."

"Rats," said the peeve plaintively.

"You don't want rats. You had an enormous breakfast," Tanaquil said. She said to Lizra, "Everything preys on everything else here. And the elegant city has filthy back streets, and beggars who are blind. Yes, I knew a sorceress. She used to tell me about a perfect world where all things were in harmony. And she showed me a sea in a desert. But she spills magic everywhere like soup. And—the peeve got splashed. That's why it talks."

"My father—" said Lizra, and broke off. "Look there. That's the unicorn place."

The chariot drew up. The peeve leapt out and sprinted back toward the ruin, leash whipping after, unheeded.

It became very silent, and the wind was like the silence given a thin, traveling voice. Heat burned from the sky and off the dazzling sea. A line of rocks rose up out of the water, low platforms that became cliffs as they marched inland. Where the beach met the waves, the cliff was hollowed out, a tunnel, an arch—a bridge. The light made its darkness seemed rimmed with iridescent white, as if fire were cutting it from the sky. It was in shape and look so like the rock hill in the desert near the fort that Tanaquil was not amazed at all.

"Do you want to walk down?"

"Yes," said Tanaquil. She did not, and that made no difference.

"Stand," Lizra said to the ponies.

They left the chariot and started over the dunes of the beach, which scalded their feet like the sands of a desert.

"The city began here," said Lizra, "hundreds of years ago, but then it moved away." They came down to where the arch of the cliff went up, its roots in the sand. "At high tide," said Lizra, "the sea comes in here. There was a well, but it's turned to salt." They had stopped before the arch, as if before a great crystal door. They might see beyond it to the beach and sky through the cliff. But could not pass.

"And they say the unicorn came from the sea?" said Tanaquil, but only to interrupt the silence and the silent meowing of the wind.

"Yes. On a wave. It came out of that archway, and struck the sand with its horn for the well. The rock was called the Sacred Gate. Even now it's supposed to be unlucky to walk through, I mean, right through the hole and out the other side."

They waited on the hot sand, looking at the beach and sea and sky on the far side of the archway.

"Do you dare it?" said Tanaquil.

"People are always going in and out, for the dare. There's a story though of three young men going in who never came out again. And of an old fisher-wife who went in one end and came out the other as a dolphin!"

They grinned at each other. Then they clasped hands, and ran shrieking instantly in under the rock.

The violet shade washed over them, like a wave. The sand was cooler, clammy and clinging; it seemed as if it might suddenly give way and drag them down into an abyss—and Tanaquil remembered how she had dug out the white bones and the sand shifted—and then there was a curious, indescribable moment. It was as if she had shut her eyes; more, as if she had fallen asleep for three heartbeats or five. And then they were running out on to the scorch of the beach, and the sun hammered down on them.

"Did you feel that?"

"It was strange."

"But—just for a moment—*something*."

"Aah!" cried Lizra, "You've changed into a dolphin."

They really did laugh then. And suddenly flung their arms round each other. And as suddenly let go, stood away.

Tanaquil said, "There is a piece of air under the rock that's like running through torn ribbons."

"I didn't notice that." Lizra said, without coldness or demand, "I think you *are* a witch. A sort of witch—of some kind. After all, not all witches can be bad. It's just my father. He told me once how he met this dreadful witch in the desert. A demoness, he said." And Tanaquil, in the blaze of the sun, experienced an arch greater, darker, deeper, more mysterious, more terrible than any gate of a unicorn, yawning up to snatch her in. "It was just before he came to rule, just before he married mother. He went hunting in the desert, got lost, separated from his attendants. He came on a sort of castle or fort. There was a red-headed sorceress, and she made him her prisoner for days, before he outwitted her and escaped her clutches. She had snakes in her hair, he said. She was quite mad." Lizra hesitated. "But I wish I could think who *you* remind me of."

Tanaquil took a breath down to the soles of her feet.

"I remind you of yourself, Lizra, just as you remind me of *me*. And that's quite reasonable. We're sisters."

They stood on the sand, the other side of the arch.

"I believe you," said Lizra. "But tell me why."

"My mother," said Tanaquil. She felt tears, and dire amusement, and hard anger. "She's the red-haired sorceress. She doesn't have snakes in her hair. Actually, she's rather beautiful. She said she renounced my father, but obviously he simply discarded *her*. It explains why she went on so much about this city, and at the same time refused to show me the city properly, or let me *near* the city. How ever did she make him *see* her? Even for a minute? They're like fire and frozen stone. Of course, he knew nothing about me. And I—well, I expect I hoped for something one day. When I found him. My father. Lizra, I'm sorry, I don't like him. He's nothing to me."

"He wouldn't want to be," said Lizra. "I know. It wouldn't, doesn't matter, to him. You'd only be another unnecessary daughter."

Chapter Nine

Tanaquil and Lizra sat on the seashell bed and studied the monstrous green-and-golden thing that balanced on a frame before them. It was twilight. Palace servants would soon come to light the lamps. Light would make the dress much worse. It had its seven layers of stiff gilt lace in flounces down the skirt. The underskirt was cloth-of-gold, stitched into stiff pleats. The bodice was a mail coat of golden scales over lime silk. The lime sleeves were skin-tight and banded with golden circlets set with emeralds. A collar of gilt lace and malachites stood up behind the dress, with a train of green silk and medallions. There was a golden diadem with emerald stars. Just to look at the outfit made Tanaquil too hot, and gave her a headache.

"How will you move?" she asked. "How will you *breathe*?"

"I shan't," said Lizra, resigned. "Last year was quite bad, but not so bad as this. I'll have to wear it. There's no choice. And the Festival's tomorrow. Oh well, the sooner here, the sooner over. You'll come with me, will you?"

"Of course. What," Tanaquil added, "will *I* have to wear?"

"Just something flashy, and some jewels."

They sat and watched the dress, and the servants knocked and came in, and the lamps were lit, and the dress roared bright like a green tiger.

They had not, earlier, talked of the Festival. They had gone back through the arch—shrieking, running—and spent the day riding along the beach or sitting under palm trees eating the food Lizra had had put in the chariot. The peeve emerged from the ruin ratless, and darted about, and once or twice it dashed at the sea aggressively, each time thinking better of it and scuttling back. In the afternoon they made a sand castle. It was a tremendous architecture, all their adult skills brought to bear on it. When the sun westered, waves began to steal up along the beach. They knew the castle would be destroyed before night fell, and drove away so as not to see.

They had spoken to each other of their childhoods, of their adventures and boredoms. They had managed, both, to say very little of the Prince and the sorceress. Probably Lizra kept certain secrets. Tanaquil did not mention the unicorn. It was not that she thought Lizra would disbelieve her. For the first time, Tanaquil had met someone who fully accepted her ideas, credited her experience, did not try to placate or compress her spirit. Rather, it was *because* Lizra would not challenge or dismiss the unicorn that Tanaquil did not tell her. The unicorn was chaos and unsafety, capricious, almost humorous, and terrible. It had rescued, and played jokes. But the horn was sharper than a sword. Its eyes were fire. And she had conjured it, sorceress or not. *It's mine, for good or ill.* When would it appear again? The pre-cast reflection of it seemed to be here in this room. At what unsuitable, ridiculous, or deadly dangerous moment?

Later they went down to the dinner, to almost exactly the same scene as on the previous night. Gasb wore a raven hat. The Prince wore his dead skins. Neither looked at Lizra or Tanaquil. But Tanaquil looked at the Prince and tried to convince herself that this was her father. The harder she tried to take it in, the more uncomfortable she became, the more irritated.

Lizra and she ate very little, although the peeve made a hearty meal. Tonight Lady Orchid's marmoset had not been brought to dine. They returned to Lizra's room long before midnight, and sat at her silver table playing Scorpions and Ladders, Ships and Chariots, or merely going on with their earlier talk—what they had done at five, and ten, and thirteen, and *I did that too*, or *I never did that*. The peeve had made a lair under Tanaquil's bed, and retired early. Squinting in as it slept, by the light of a candle, they saw a pair of silver scissors stolen from Lizra's room, and a small glass bottle, a string of pearls, and two or three other objects she did not recognize. "Whoever do they belong to? It must get out through your window at night."

Finally they heard the midnight bell. Lizra said, offhandedly, "Salute the Sacred Beast."

They parted with strange unexpressed feelings, each as if the other one might vanish in the night, Tanaquil thought. Tanaquil could not sleep. She began to have doubts. Should she not have told Lizra that they were sisters? What obligation did it put upon them? It had seemed wonderful one minute, and awkward the next. The peeve slunk up onto the bed with one of Lizra's jade pawns from the Ships and Chariots, which it laid under Tanaquil's chin. It had brought her a present. She thanked it warmly, and slept after all, with her head against its side.

The Festival Procession of Prince Zorander zigzagged through the city like a jewelled snake.

It was the second hour of the afternoon, and furnace hot.

The heat laid a glaze on everything. It brought out a million smells, delicious and vile. It caught gems and metal and sent blinding rays in all directions.

But the heat did not subdue the crowds, who had been up and about since sunrise.

They jostled and pranced, indulged in games and tussles. They clotted at the edges of the roads, and watched the snake of the procession slide by from avenue to avenue.

There were musicians in lynx skins, and dancing girls in rainbow gauze, great squadrons of soldiers in flaming mail, plumed, and carrying lances, bows, swords, and battle honors on gilded poles trimmed by flowers. There were standards of purple, magenta, and scarlet. There were gold chariots drawn by horses glassily shining, with brilliants on their reins and silver hoofs. There were deafening trumpeters, and clowns dressed as wild animals and sea things, lions and porpoises, squid and jackals, who bounced and rolled, played at attacking each other, or pulling colored ribbons out of the noses of the crowd. There were girls in white strewing poppies, and girls in red strewing

lilies. There were terracotta camels with fierce
men clad for the desert on their humped tops.

Then there came the tableaux. In one was a
great ship with a spread turquoise sail, rocking
gently on the backs of twenty blue and silver people being the sea. In another there was a replica of
the city in gilded wood, with even the fifteen-
story palace depicted, and dolls guarding it, and
moving up and down on the streets with choppy
doll movements, representing the citizens. There
were others of historical moments, and myth. Last
of the tableaux was an image of mythic history. In
crimson and gold, a former prince was shown, and
before him stood an enormous unicorn. It was of
purest white alabaster with mane and tail fluted
by sparkles. Its clockwork head raised and bowed
to the prince, raised and bowed, and toward its
horn of chrysolite he extended a garland of flowers.

After the last tableau of the unicorn rode the
current Prince, driven in his chariot, surrounded
by soldiers with crossbows and drawn swords. He
wore the regalia that had been shown in his library, the purple and the breastplate. His face was
icy cool, it seemed he could not feel the heat.
Down his back gleamed the sharkskin cloak, fastened at the shoulders with the two creamy
fossils—old, maybe, as the earth itself. On his
head was the head of a great blue shark.

After the Prince rode his daughter, the Princess,
like a gold and green doll herself, in her chariot.
At her side was a red-haired princess of some foreign city.

Then the nobles rode by, the ladies, and the

counselors, and Chief Counselor Gasb in a hat like a sea eagle.

Following the court came tamers leading the beasts of the Prince's menagerie, some of which were reported to be clockwork, but all of which snarled, strode, and stared.

More musicians rambled after the beasts, playing soft soothing music.

Merchants and dignitaries strutted next, and all the guilds in their public uniforms, with their symbols and banners, the potters and masons, shipwrights and vintners. The Artisans' Guild seemed unhappy, and kept glancing about, and over their shoulders at the salters, who walked behind and had taken exception to it.

Last of all marched further battalions of soldiers, with carts of war machines, carefully oiled and wreathed, cannon in hyacinths, catapults in asphodel, battering rams in roses.

The crowd cheered everything. It enjoyed everything. This was the wealth and power of the city on display. "We own *that*," they said. "That's *ours*," pointing at things they saw over each others' heads once a year, and at cool Prince Zorander, and the alabaster unicorn that bowed.

From her position in Lizra's chariot, in boned silk and topazes, Tanaquil was very conscious of the presence of Prince Zorander before them, in his weapon-spiked hedge of soldiery, and of Gasb the sea eagle five chariots behind.

Lizra she did not distract. The girl stood like a statue, pale and frowning, half stifled by her clothes. Now and then she would say in a flippant voice, "Just look there," and point something out to Tanaquil in a regal manner. Lizra's public stance and face were as composed as her father's.

The sights she indicated were often extremely odd.

Not only did the procession dress up. In the crowd were persons with indigo faces walking on stilts, huge alarming masks, barrels on legs, and men with the heads of fish. There were also two clowns who had gone farther than the clowns of the Prince. They had put on the canvas skin and parchment head that made them into a horse, but the horse had a horn protruding from its forehead. They were the unicorn of the city. To make things worse, the back end of the horse-unicorn was drunk or crazy. While the front stepped along proudly, sometimes tapping at people lightly with the horn, the back end kept sitting down, doing the splits, or curling into a ball.

"Bad luck," said a noble in the chariot behind Lizra's. "What can they be thinking of? An insult to the Sacred Beast."

"There, there, Noble Oppit. The unicorn won't see." Gasb's voice, like a knife ready at your back.

"Oh—quite *so*, Lord Gasb."

"The Festival of the Blessing is to do with the unicorn," said Tanaquil aloud.

"Of course," said Lizra.

Tanaquil wished she had understood this sooner. Somehow she had not. She thought of the peeve in its lair under her bed at the palace. If something happened, as it must, she might never be able to return. Yet Lizra would care for the peeve—

They were coming into the Avenue of the Sea Horse. Up on plinths the marble sea horses stood

under their lanterns, with fins and curled tails—
and each with a little bright horn coming out from
its brow.

At the avenue's end Tanaquil saw, between the
jumble of chariots and marchers, the dark blue
level of the ocean. The avenue opened into a
square above the sea. The square was packed with
people, and the procession flowed against them,
folding to each side, allowing the central chariots
of the Prince and his retinue to pass through. Before them was a high platform. A wide ramp led
up to it, with purple carpet.

Prince Zorander's chariot was driven straight up,
and the rest of his court followed him.

Tanaquil looked back as Lizra's chariot climbed
the ramp. The square was solid now, raised faces
thick as beads in a box. And the wild beasts growling on their leashes, and the soldiers and weapons
of war, the dancing girls, musicians, and clowns, all
piled up among them, everything at a standstill,
yet managing to wave its arms, shouting, throwing
its flowers, and with its sequins firing off the sun.
And there, the white dazzle of the alabaster unicorn, bowing and bowing.

No way of escape, Tanaquil thought, precisely.

Up on the platform, the chariots halted. On the
other side from the square the ocean burned blue
a hundred feet below, and the rest was sky, with
one tiny smut of cloud.

The Prince left his chariot. They all dis-
mounted.

The Prince went out alone into the middle of
the platform. He turned to the ocean and raised
his arms, and the thousands in the square were
dumb, and farther off, the other crowds along the

streets. It was so still Tanaquil heard the clink of golden discs upon the tamers' leashes. She seemed to hear the clockwork ticking in the bowing unicorn's neck.

Zorander lowered his arms. He stood in his dramatic loneliness at the center of the platform, and in the still and time-stopped sunlight, the unicorn came to him from the sea.

There must be a way up from the platform's other side, and the creature had been led to it. Well-trained, it made the ascent itself. It trotted towards Zorander, and the crowd murmured, easily, like people pleasantly asleep.

The unicorn was a fake. It was a slim white horse with opals plaited into mane and tail, and held to its forehead by a harness of white straps, probably invisible from below, was a silver horn.

It came right up to Zorander and the Prince laid one hand on its brow, beneath the horn. The charming fake nodded. And then it kneeled, in the way of a clever theatre horse, and lowering its head, touched the feet of the Prince sweetly, once, twice, with the horn.

The crowd broke into cheers and applause, laughter and whistles. They must know, most of them, this creature was not a unicorn, only the symbol. Yet they were thrilled, overjoyed at the successful rite.

Under the noise, behind her, Tanaquil heard the noble Oppit mumble, "Look at that cloud—how curious."

Whoever else looked, Tanaquil did. It was the cloud she had noted before over the sea. It was not so small now, and it had risen swiftly up the sky, blown by a hot, moist wind that was lifting all at once from the ocean, fluttering the silks of the Prince's courtiers, the mane of the kneeling horned horse.

The cloud had a shape. It was like a long thin hand, with outstretched reaching fingers. It was very dark. There were no other clouds.

Bells and discs rang in the wind. The bright day faded a little.

"Not a good omen," said Oppit.

This time, he was not contradicted.

People in the crowd were pointing at the sky. There was a swell of altered noise, urgent and unhappy.

The horned horse got to its feet and shook its mane. It glanced about, flaring its nostrils.

Tanaquil watched the cloud like a hand blow up the sky, and her hair lashed her face, and Lizra's hair coiled and flew about under the diadem, and the robes of the Prince; the sharkskin beat like wings.

"It's reaching for the sun," breathed Lizra.

Fingers of cloud stretched over the sun's orb, and the whole hand closed on it. The sun disappeared. A curtain of darkness fell from the air.

There were cries out of the crowd, vague far-off rumbles and screams along the avenues.

"Fools," said Gasb's harsh voice. "It's only weather."

Nails of rain drove down. The ran was hot and salt.

The horned horse tossed its head, it rolled its eyes and neighed. The Prince stepped slowly back from it, dignified and remote, and two handlers scrambled up on the platform, seizing the horse by its harness, pulling it to one side.

The cloud did not pass. The darkness mysteriously thickened. The city seemed inside a shadow-jar. Beyond, the sky was blue and clear . . .

And then, from the hidden ramp, up from the sea, the unicorn came a second time. And now it was as real as the coming of the darkness.

It stood on the platform, a thing of ebony, blazed with light. And in the shadow, the horn was a white lightning.

Now a dreadful silence smothered the crowd. There were only the gusts of the wind, the chinking of objects, the tapping of the nails of rain.

Then the trained horse kicked and plunged, and struck its fake horn against the platform, and the fake snapped off and clattered away.

The unicorn turned to see. The unicorn moved. It was only like a horse as a hilt is like a sword. It lifted its forehoof, poised dainty, like a figurine. And then it pawed the ground, the carpet. It pawed out purple dust, then purple fire. The carpet burst into flame, and the unicorn reared up. No, not like a horse. It was a tower, and the horn swept across heaven. The sky must crack and fall— And in the square the crowd pushed, roaring, against itself, fighting to be gone.

"Oh," said Lizra.

Prince Zorander had picked up the skirts of his robe; the sharkskin head slipped sideways from his own. He cantered. He thrust aside his soldiers and blundered into the royal chariot. His face was no longer cool and distant. It was a stupid face that seemed to have no bones. "Away!" he yelled.

The charioteer faltered. "The people, your Highness—"

"Use your whip on them. Ride them down. You—" to the soldiers—"kill that beast."

The square was, remarkably, already clearing. The crowd, the procession, had forced back in panic not only into the avenue, but also between buildings, and through alleys and gardens on all sides of the square. Herds of people poured over walls, shinned up trees, and dropped away.

Zorander's chariot churned forward.

The soldiers armed their bows.

The black unicorn descended, and as it regained its four feet, a howl of arrow-bolts crashed against it.

The bolts struck the unicorn. They skidded on its blackness, and streaks of fire resulted, and the bolts sheered away, they splintered like brittle twigs. All about the unicorn the bolts lay, and in its mane and tail they hung like evil flowers.

All the world was running now.

Tanaquil and Lizra clutched each other and were knocked down as one. Armored feet jumped over them, lightly bruised them, wheels missed them by inches; heavy silk and ornaments of gold slapped their faces. They covered their heads sobbing and cursing with fright and astonishment, until the stampede had gone by and left them there, like flotsam on the beach.

They sat up, white-faced, and angrily smeared the childish tears from their eyes, cursing worse than the soldiers.

They were alone on the platform in the rain.

Debris scattered the carpet. Arrow-bolts, bracelets, cloaks, and Counselor Gasb's sea eagle hat. One chariot stood abandoned and horseless.

Below, the shattered crowd still struggled

through the square, but the chariots had cleaved a passage and were gone. There was no unicorn. No unicorn at all.

"My father was afraid," said Lizra. "And he left me here."

"Yes," Tanaquil said. She recalled how Jaive had left her to die in the desert. But Jaive had had some excuse.

They stood up. All the sky was now purple as the carpet. Thunder beat its drums, and the rain thickened like oil.

"It was real?" said Lizra.

"It was real."

"Not another horse with a silver horn tied to its head." Tanaquil said nothing. "And the arrow-bolts didn't hurt it. Perhaps the men fired wide—how could they dare to shoot at the Sacred Beast?"

"You *saw* what happened," said Tanaquil.

Lizra said, "Then it's true we've wronged it. It has a score to settle. Did it go after the chariots?"

"Maybe."

But Tanaquil visualized the unicorn moving like smoke through the dark of the day, through the torrential rain. The flying people glimpsed their Beast and cowered in terror. In the highest wall there must be a door. Soldiers would shoot and run away. The point of the horn could burst timbers like glass. Then up the palace ramps, across the mountain of dragon-tiled roofs. Lightning and unicorn together dancing atop Zorander's palace.

"Look at this idiot hat," said Lizra, and kicked the sea eagle.

The tableaux stayed stupidly in the square as

the last of the crowd ran round them. The nodding white beast had fallen over.

After a while, when the square was empty, the two girls left the platform. Incongruous as they were in their drowned jewelry and silk, no one bothered with them, noticed them. The rain and thunder made nonsense of everything. People on the avenues were running, or sheltering under porticos. They heard wailing. Presently, on Lynx Street, a party of soldiers met them and made them out. "It's the two princesses!" Then they had an escort to the palace.

Had the knocking been less loud, they might have taken it for thunder. But then also, they had heard the clank of swords, the thump of spears along the corridor.

They had been sitting in the rose room by the cinnabar fireplace, which had been lit for warmth and cheerfulness. The miserable tension had to be fractured by some ominous act. Here it was.

"Only Gasb would bring a guard with him."

"It will be for me."

"*Why?*"

"This witch thing. It follows me around. And the unicorn—somehow the unicorn is linked to me."

The peeve, in Tanaquil's lap, dropped a piece of cake from its mouth and growled.

Lizra got up. "Stay here. I'll make him go away."

Tanaquil doubted this, but she did not protest. Lizra went out and shut the door. Tanaquil shifted the peeve, went to the door, and listened at the panels. She heard the outer door opened.

"Ah," said Gasb's unmistakably foul voice, "your pardon. I'm looking for the girl from, er, *Erm*."

"Princess Tanaquil," said Lizra in her public voice, "isn't here. What do you mean, anyway, by coming here like this with—three, four, five, *six* soldiers?"

"Tanapattle, or whatever she's called, is a sorceress. She's a danger to us all, yourself, madam, included. Which, of course, you are too young to realize. Her trick of conjuring an illusory unicorn has reduced the city to havoc—"

"I've told you, Counselor," snapped Lizra, "Tanaquil isn't here. Go and bother someone else." There was a pause. Lizra said: "Oh no you d—" and then: "How *dare* you?"

Soldiers' boots marched into the great painted bedroom, and Gasb's slippers lisped after.

"In there?" said Gasb.

"My father will be very angry," said Lizra.

"Your father agrees that the witch should be apprehended."

Tanaquil stepped back, so that the soldiers, when they threw open her door, did not knock her over again. She stationed herself near the fireplace, and the peeve crouched before her like a snarling, back-combed mop.

The door was thrown wide, and six soldiers rushed in, their spears leveled at her heart. Tanaquil's head swam. She thought: *If they knew what they looked like, they'd never* ever *do it.*

Gasb slithered in behind them. He did not wear a hat. He was quite bald, and his features were still those of a bird of prey.

"Courage, men," he said.

Tanaquil gently toed the peeve. "I'll unfasten the window. Jump out to the lower roof and run."

"Stay and bite," said the peeve.

"Proof of her sorcery," said Gasb to the nervous soldiers. "You hear the animal talk. A familiar. We must take her now, before she can summon demons to her assistance."

Lizra said in her put-on, penetrating regal tone, "Before you lay a finger on her, remember she's the princess of a foreign town. Do we want a war with them?"

"*Princess.*" Gasb smiled. "She's no more a princess than that road-sweeper slut."

Tanaquil had been edging from the fire towards the window, the peeve wriggling along beside her. Then there was a soldier in front of her. "No, lady," he said, crossly.

"Don't trouble with calling her *lady*. Surround her. We'll take her somewhere more . . . quiet."

Tanaquil stared at Gasb's bald malevolence. She was afraid of him and felt demeaned to be so. The soldiers had swords; she grabbed the rocking peeve. And in that instant a lawless and unearthly cry, like nothing she had heard in her life, pierced through the arteries of the palace, down through every floor. She knew what it was even as she knew that to hear it in this way could not be possible.

"The Prince!"

The soldiers were transfixed. Even Gasb gaped. Lizra said, "Has it killed my father?"

And Tanaquil saw, somehow, somewhere in her mind, Zorander in his library above the snows, where the clockwork butterflies alighted on the unread books. She saw him turned to the stone of terror. And on the threshold, come from the rain and thunder and lightning country of the roof, black night and murderous horn and eyes like molten lava.

"Seize the witch; she must die at once!" shrilled Gasb. The soldiers started forward again.

There came a rushing whistling through the air. It was a thunderbolt crashing on the palace, on this very room—the soldiers whirled away. Tanaquil dropped flat over the peeve and rolled them aside against the bed. The chimney croaked and bellowed. And the leaping fire—*froze*. The flames were points of yellow ice—

Everyone screamed. The thunderbolt landed in the hearth, and ice and soot and bricks and coal flew out, while the room tottered, and plaster left the ceiling.

"Demons!"

There was only one. Tanaquil looked up and beheld that a thing with two heads and elephant ears and the eyes of frogs sat on its huge stomach and obese tail in the fireplace.

"Come," said Epbal Enrax the cold demon, and cracks slid up the walls. It put out arms like elephant trunks and lifted Tanaquil, and the claw-attached peeve, from the floor. *"Red-Hair, we go,"* said Epbal Enrax. And they went.

PART
✦ Three

Under the stormy sky, the sea bubbled and lashed like liquid mauvish copper. The colors of everything were wrong. The sand looked like cinders from some awful fire. The palms were black, and groaned in the wind. The beach did not seem to be any place in the world, but some sort of other world that was a kind of Hell. And out of the cinders and the copper waves, the rocks rose up like the carcass of something petrified.

From the dune where she had arrived, Tanaquil surveyed the scene. She had been told of demon flights before, though never experienced any. The breath had been knocked out of her, but she was flustered rather than shocked. She understood quite well that she had been rescued from probable death at the hands of Gasb's soldiers. There was a confused memory of a chimney, thousands of roofs below, lightning casts like spears, and descending in a whirlwind. She grasped that this dreadful spot was the sea beach, and through the explosions of brown and puce foam, she made out the unicorn arch, the Sacred Gate. The peeve was seated nearby, washing itself over-thoroughly. Tanaquil glanced behind her. Epbal Enrax balanced on the dunes, apparently up to the pelvis in sand. It seemed pleased—mauve, of course, was the demon's favorite shade.

"Who sent you to fetch me?" said Tanaquil. A demon was at the beck and call of anyone powerful enough to summon it. Disquieting visions of Vush and the artisans hiring a sorcerer went through her mind.

But Epbal Enrax said, *"Lady other Red of Hair. Yonder."*

There was something standing on the sea.

Tanaquil had taken it for a figment of the weather, a cloud, a water spout. Now she got up slowly and started to walk toward the violent edges of the water. The peeve rose to follow, decided against it, and began to burrow into the sand.

The thing on the sea wavered like a flame. It had a flamy red top. The ocean had come further in, and now the thing drifted inland too. It stopped about ten feet from the shore, and from Tanaquil. It hardened, took shape. After half a minute, Jaive the sorceress stood on the water. Her hair blew madly, like a scarlet blizzard in miniature. She was wrapped in a theatrical black mantle sewn with silver and jasper locusts. Her face was fierce. She was silent.

"Mother," said Tanaquil.

Jaive spoke. "Yes, that's right, I'm your mother."

After this unsensible exchange, they braved the storm and stared at each other.

Finally Tanaquil said, stiffly, "So you decided to search me out after all. I thought you wouldn't bother. I mean, after you left me in the desert and so on."

Jaive frowned. Her eyes flashed. "Stupid child! If you knew the difficulties I've had."

"Poor you."

"The unicorn—if I had realized—the magic, the

mystery—I thought it was some toy of yours, made up out of bits of clever crystal, bone, wheels and cogs, your usual paraphernalia."

"I don't make things, I repair them," said Tanaquil. Jaive flapped her hands dismissively. The sea ruffled and spat at her feet. "And *must* you stand on the water?"

"Am I?" Jaive looked about. "This isn't myself. It's a *projection* of my image. I can't manage anything more. My sorcery is in disarray. Had I known—would I, a practiced mistress of the magical arts, have flung my power at a real *unicorn*? The damage to my ability was very great. Only now have I begun to recover my skills."

"I see," said Tanaquil. "You mean you didn't search for me sooner because you couldn't. It wasn't merely uninterest or pique?"

"How dare you doubt your mother?"

"It's easy."

Jaive's face wrinkled up, and a flickering went all over her. Tanaquil was not sure if this was due to faulty magic, rage, or something else.

"I say nothing," shouted Jaive, "of your coming to this city. I say nothing about the palace in which I located you."

"Zorander's palace," said Tanaquil. Jaive's image pleated, twirled. "I'm sorry. If you'd trusted me . . . I know, I mean I know—"

"That man is your father," shouted Jaive. In the pleats and twirls, all of her seemed now to flame. "I renounced him."

"Yes, mother."

Jaive stopped shouting, and the pleats and twirls gradually smoothed out.

"I can overlook your behavior," said Jaive, "because I comprehend that it was the unicorn that brought you here, and the unicorn that needs and demands your service."

Tanaquil's mixture of feelings spun off and left only one question. "Why? What does it want? Mother, do you really know?"

Jaive smiled. It was not like any smile Tanaquil had ever seen before on her mother's face. *She is beautiful, the awful woman.*

"I thought all along you were *his* daughter," said Jaive. "Obsessed with things, mechanical gadgets. But you're mine. Tanaquil, you're a sorceress."

"Here we go," said Tanaquil, impatient. "Of course I'm not."

"Your sorcery," went on Jaive relentlessly, "lies in your ability to *mend*. You can mend anything at all. And once mended by you, it never breaks again. Since you were a little child, I've seen you do this, and it never came to me that it wasn't some cold artisan's knack, but a true magic."

"Mother!"

Jaive held up her imperious hand. "Think, and tell me honestly. When you repair a thing—a clock, a bow, a doll—what do you do?"

"I—look at it. And then I pick up the proper tools—and I—"

"How do you find the fault? How do you know which tool will correct it? Who, Tanaquil, taught you?"

"No one. I can just do it, mother."

"When I was ten," said Jaive, "I summoned a small sprite out of a kettle. They said: 'How did you do it, who taught you?' I said, 'No one. I just can.' "

"Mother—"

"Enough time's been wasted," said Jaive. "The unicorn came to you because it scented your magic and how it would serve. It came as a bone, a broken skeleton, and you mended it, and made it go. It was my own thoughtless blow that fully revived it—a miraculous accident. Or did the unicorn also use me? I'd rejoice to think so. Nothing can destroy a unicorn, Tanaquil, and only despair can kill it. Once it did despair—yet even then its bones remained, and the life in them. Now it waits. For your help."

"My help. What can I do?"

Jaive smiled again. Warmer than her fiery hair, her smile.

"Do you think unicorns can ever really have lived on this earth? No, their country is the perfect world. The world for which this one was a model that failed. For some reason the unicorn strayed, or was enticed, out of a breach in the wall of its world. And then the gate was closed behind it. It couldn't return. It lived here and it pined. It died the only death it could, sleeping in the desert. Until you found it."

"Actually, a peeve found it."

"The peeve has given itself to you, as your familiar."

Exasperated, believing, Tanaquil said again, "Yes, mother."

"Doubtless," said Jaive, "the one who worked the crime against the unicorn, bringing it from its perfect home, shutting the door on it, was the first ruler of the city. To correct the balance, his descendant must set it free. And you, Tanaquil, are the Prince's daughter." Jaive bridled. Anger and pain went over her face, and she crushed them away while Tanaquil watched. Jaive said, "Accomplish your task."

"I think you mean that the archway in the rock is the gate to the other world—that it's broken, so nothing can go back through it. But I can repair the gate. Yes?"

"Yes, Tanaquil."

"But, mother, there's just air and rock—it isn't bronze and iron. There aren't any pins or cogs or springs or hinges—"

"There are. Only a sorceress of your particular powers could find them."

"Oh, Mother—"

"Don't dare contradict me. I was terrified of the unicorn. *I*. But you have never been. And now, look and *see*." Jaive pointed along the beach. Another new expression was on her face. No longer terror, certainly. It was awe, it was youth and laughing delight. "Look and see and don't make it wait *any longer*!"

The unicorn was on the beach below the rock. Its blackness shamed the shadows, its horn brought back the light. The rain had ended and the sea was growing still.

Torn ribbons . . .

Did you feel that? . . . It was strange . . . Just for a moment—something . . .

This time Tanaquil did not shriek, or run. She was alone. The murky milk of the foam swilled through beneath the arch, and she walked up to her ankles in water. The storm was over, but the day was dying quickly in thick cloud. In an hour it would be night.

She had looked back once, and the flame of Jaive

was still there on the darkling sea. It raised its arm and waved to her, as once or twice when she was a child the form of Jaive had waved to her from the high windows of the fortress. But the projected image was faltering, and like the daylight, going out. Epbal Enrax had already vanished. The peeve had hidden in the sand. Tanaquil did not know what she felt or thought of what had happened. Lizra and Zorander and Gasb also had faded. It was the Gate that counted. The unicorn.

The unicorn had drawn away as she approached. Not shy, but precautionary, as if testing her again. She remembered how it had chased the artisans, the moment when it reared upwards on the platform. The unicorn could kill her far more efficiently than Gasb. But it had poised, away up the line of the cliffs, as she entered in under the arch.

Tanaquil moved forward one slow step at a time. The sense of the abyss below the sand was strong. She picked her path, searching after the indescribable sensation that had assailed her, like falling asleep for three heartbeats or five ... For *that* had been when she had passed across the gate, a gate that led now to nowhere because it was broken.

Going so alertly, so slowly, she touched the rim of its weirdness and jumped back at once. *There*. Unmistakable.

But—what now?

There was nothing to see, save the dim rocks going up from the water, and, the other side of the arch, sand and gathering darkness.

Torn ribbons. She had felt them fluttering round her as she and Lizra ran, going through, coming back.

With enormous care, as if not to snap a spider's web, Tanaquil pushed her arms forward into empty air.

And something brushed her, like a ghost.

She did not like it. She pulled back her arms.

She thought: *Jaive is still a sorceress before she's my mother. She put the unicorn first.* She thought: *I can help a unicorn.*

Tanaquil slid her arms back into the invisible something that stretched between the rocks. The brushing came, and she reached in turn and took hold of it.

Her fingers tingled, but not uncomfortably. The elements inside the air were not like anything she had ever touched or handled.

That doesn't matter. She tried to think what happened when she looked into the workings of a lock, a music box, the caravan's cartwheel, the dismembered snake in the bazaar. Then she gave it up. Still holding on to the first unnamable strangeness, she groped after another along the net of the air. She closed her eyes, and behind her lids she saw a shape like a silver rod, and she swung it deftly over and hung it from a golden ring.

Her hands moved with trance-like symmetry. Objects, or illusions, floated toward her, and she plucked them and gave them to each other.

She did not need any implements—only her hands. Perhaps her thoughts.

Not like a clock or engine. Here everything drifted, like leaves on a pool.

She seemed to see their shapes, yet did not believe she saw what actually was there—and yet what was there was certainly as bizarre as her pictures of rods and slender pins, rings and discs and coils and curves, like letters of an unknown alphabet.

Probably I'm doing it wrong.

She opened her eyes and saw no change in anything, except the darkness came hurriedly now.

The unicorn glowed black against the rock a hundred feet away. The fans of the sea were pale with a choked moonrise.

She shut her eyes and saw again the drifting gold and silver chaos of the Gate like a half-made necklace.

Suddenly she knew what she did. It was not wrong. It was unlike all things, yet it was right. She seized a meandering star and pressed it home—

She had half wondered if she would know, dealing in such strangeness, when the work was finished. Complete, would the Gate seem mended—or would it only have formed some other fantastic pattern, which might be played with and rearranged for ever.

It was like waking from sleep, gently and totally, without disorientation.

She stepped away and lowered her arms, eyes still closed.

The Gate was whole. It was like a galaxy—like jewelry—like—like nothing on earth. But its entirety was obvious. It was a smashed window where every pane of glass was back in place. There was no doubt.

Then Tanaquil opened her eyes, and after all, she *saw* the Gate. Saw it as now it appeared, visibly, in her world.

You could no longer look through the arch. A dark, glowing membrane filled it, that might have been water standing on end, and in the stuff of it were spangles, electrically coming and going.

Tanaquil was not afraid of it, but she was prudent.. She moved back a few more steps. And frowned.

What was it? Something, even now—not incomplete, yet missing.

She turned round and walked out of the arch.

The sea had drawn off again, as the tide of night came in. As she moved out on the sand beyond the rock she heard the huge midnight bell from the palace in the city borne on silence, thin as a thread.

She remembered Lizra, Zorander. She remembered Jaive. But in front of her was the unicorn. It had walked down almost to the arch. It was all darkness. The horn did not blaze; even the pale cloudy moon was brighter.

"I've done what I can," said Tanaquil. "Only there's some other thing—I don't know what."

The unicorn paced by her, to the entrance. It gazed in at the sequined shadow. She saw its eyes blink, once, garnet red. Then it lowered its head to the ground, opened its mouth—she caught the glint of the strong silver teeth she recollected from its skull. But two other items glimmered on the wet sand.

Tanaquil went across, keeping her respectful distance from the beast, although it had once dragged her by the hair, to see what had been dropped.

"Did you kill him for these?"

The unicorn lifted its head again. It gave to her one oblique sideways look. She had never confronted such a face. Not human, not animal, not demonic. Unique.

Then it dipped the horn and pointed it down, at

the base of the cliff. The horn hovered, and swung up. It pointed now toward the clifftop twenty feet above Tanaquil's head. After a second, the unicorn sprang off up the sand. It returned to its place of waiting. It waited there.

Tanaquil bent down and took up the two cream-white whorled fossils the unicorn had dropped from its mouth: the Festival cloak pins of the Prince. Which it must have ripped from the sharkskin. And long ago, had they been ripped from this cliffside? These then, the last components of the Gate.

Tanaquil knelt where the horn of the unicorn had first pointed. Old, wet, porous, no longer the proper shape, a wound showed in the cliff that might once have held a circling whorled shell.

"What do I have?" Tanaquil searched herself, Lizra's silk dress lent for the procession. It had no pockets or pouches for a knife, its pendant topazes unsuitable, its goldwork too soft. Finally she rent the bodice and forced out one of the corset bones—as she had hoped, it was made of bronze. With this she began to scrape at the rotted rock, using now and then a handful of the rougher sand for a file.

"One day I shall tell someone about this, and they won't believe me."

She had managed to get the fossil back again into its setting in the rock base. The fit was not marvelously secure, but it was the best she could do. She had studied the Gate. The liquid shadow had not altered. Spangles came and went.

Tanaquil sighed. She stared up the stony limb of the cliff, toward its arched top like a bridge. It had been plain, the gesture of the unicorn. If one fossil was to be set here, the other had its origin aloft.

So, in her awkward dress and useless palace shoes, Tanaquil started to climb the rock.

She was glad the wind and storm had finished, for the rock was slippery and difficult, much harder to ascend than the hills beyond her mother's fort.

As she climbed, she thought of the unicorn dying there beneath the arch in the desert that so exactly resembled the arch of the Gate. Perhaps the likeness had soothed it, or made worse its pain, trapped in the alien world. Maybe it had scented, with its supernatural nostrils, the old sea that once had covered the desert. Or maybe, wilder yet more reasonable than anything else, everything had been preordained—that the unicorn would lie down for death under the hill, and she come to be born half a mile from its grave, a descendant of the city princes, its savior.

"I hope I am. After all this, I'd better be, for heaven's sake."

Her skirt in shreds, her feet cut and hands grazed, she reached the summit of the cliff.

She thought of the shell she had seen in the rock, in the desert, held firm in the stone. Would the situation of this fossil be the same?

No. It would lie to the left of the arch, near the opening, diagonally across from the fossil below. *How do I know? Don't bother.*

Tanaquil crawled to see. She discovered beds of seaweed rooted obstreperously in the rock. With cries of outrage she pulled them up. And found the old wound of the fossil, obvious, exact, incredibly needing nothing.

She pressed the shell into it. It fitted immediately.

She was not prepared—

For the cliff shook. It shivered. And out of it, from the arch below, there came a wave of furling, curling light, and a sound like one note of a song, a song of stone and water, sand and night, and conceivably the stars.

Tanaquil clung onto the cliff. She expected it to collapse, to be thrown off, but the shivering calmed and ceased, and light below melted to a faint clear shine. She looked then away at the unicorn. She supposed it would dart suddenly towards the cliffs and under and in, and away. But the unicorn did not move.

"What is it? Go on!" Tanaquil called. "Before anything else happens—anyone comes—or isn't it right?"

Yes, yes. It was right. The Gate was there, was there. And yet the unicorn lingered, still as a creature of the stone.

Tanaquil hoisted herself over the bridge, and began to let herself down the cliff again. She was urgent now, and not careful enough. She lost her grip once, twice, and eventually fell thirteen feet into a featherbed of sand.

The unicorn was digging her out. She swam through the smother and emerged, spitting like a cat. It was not the unicorn.

"Pnff," said the peeve. "*Bad.*"

"Yes, thank you. Very bad." She pulled herself upright and scattered sand grains from hair and ears. The peeve ticklingly licked her cuts, so she lugged it away. "Why is it standing there? The Gate is—" And she saw the Gate as now it was.

Open. Waiting. In the spangled dark, an oval of light. It was the light of the sun of another dimension. Warm and pure, both brighter and softer than any light she had seen in the world. In *her* world. And through the light it was possible to glimpse—no, it was impossible. Only a kind of dream was there, like a mirage, color and beauty, radiance and vague sweet sound.

Tanaquil rose. She shouted at the unicorn. "Go *on*!"

Then the unicorn tossed its head. It leapt upward like an arrow from a bow. All its four feet were high in the air. It flew. In flight it spun forward, like thistledown, ran like wind along the sea.

It passed under the cliff. And Tanaquil saw it breach the glowing oval of the Gate and go through. She saw it there inside, within the beauty and shining.

And then the peeve shot from between her hands.

"*Nice! Nice!*" squealed the peeve, as it hurtled toward Paradise.

"No—you mustn't—come back you fool, oh, God, you *fool*!"

She saw the unicorn had turned, there in the dream. Its head moved slowly. There was no denial. Was it beckoning?

The peeve squawked and dove through the gate of light.

With a sickening misgiving, with a cruel desire, Tanaquil also ran, over the sand, under the arch. She felt the Gate, like a sheet of heavy water, resisting her, and making way. And she too rushed into the perfect world.

Chapter Eleven

To the sea's edge the flowers came. Some grew, it seemed, in the water. Their color was like quenching thirst. Blue flowers of the same blueness as the ocean, and of a darker blue passing into violet. And after those, banks of flowers of peach pink, and carmine, and flowers yellow as lemon wine. Trees rose from the flowers. They were very tall and tented with translucent foliage of a deep golden green. Glittering things slipped in and out of the leaves. The plain of flowers and trees stretched far away, and miles off were mountains dissolving in the blue of the sky. A single slender path of blossomy clouds crossed this sky, like feathers left behind. The sun burned high. Its warmth bathed everything, like honey, and its gentle light that was clear as glass. Even the waves did not flash, and yet they shone as if another sun were in the depths of the sea. And all about the sun of the sky, great day stars gleamed like a diamond net.

One of the birds slid from a tree that overhung the ocean. It wriggled down into the water. It was a fish. It circled Tanaquil once, where she stood in the shallows, then swam incuriously away.

She looked behind her. The shining sea returned to the horizon. Sea things were playing there, and spouts of water sparkled. A few inches above the surface of the waves, not three feet from her, a leaden egg floated in the air. It was the Gate.

I should close it. No. I shouldn't be here—I have to go back—

The Gate was blank and uninviting. It did not seem to her anything would want to go near it. Even the fish, now plopping like silver pennies from the trees, swam wide of the place.

She looked forward again. The peeve, which somehow itself knew how to swim, had followed its pointed nose to the shore, emerged, and now rolled about in the flowers. They were not crushed. They gave way before it and danced upright when it had passed.

On the plain, the unicorn galloped, swerved, leapt and seemed to fly, a streak of golden-silver blackness, while the sun unwound rainbows from its horn.

"This water can't be salt," said Tanaquil, "or else it's a harmless salt. The flowers don't die."

She waded out of the shallows and stood among the flowers. Their perfume was fresh and clear, like the light. She moved her feet, and the flowers she had stood upon coiled springily upright.

"We should go back," Tanaquil said to the peeve.

The peeve rolled in the flowers.

Tanaquil did not want to go back. If this was the perfect world, she wanted to see it.

Birds sang from the trees. It was not that their songs were more beautiful than the beautiful songs of earth, yet they had a clarity without distraction. The air was full of a sort of happiness, or some other benign power having no name. To breathe it made you glad. Nothing need worry you. No pain of the past, no fear for the future. No self-doubt. No lack of trust. Everything would be well, now and for always. Here.

The unicorn had used up its bounds and leaps for the present. It moved in a tender measure through the flowers, going away now, inland. And once, it glanced toward the shore.

They went after it, without haste, or reluctance.

Not only birds sang.

As they walked over the plain through the silk of the flowers, a murmuring like bees ... There were orchards on the plain, apple and damson, fig and orange, quince and olive. The fragrant trees rose to giant size, garlanded with leaves and fruit. And the fruit burned like suns and jewels. Not thinking, Tanaquil reached her hand towards a ruby apple, and it quivered against her fingers. It lived. Never disturbed, never plucked, never devoured. It *sang*.

"Oh, listen, peeve. *Listen*."

And the peeve looked up in inquisitive surprise. "Insect."

"No, it's the apple. It's singing."

No fruit had fallen. Perhaps it never would. As they went in among the trees, the whispering thrumming notes increased. Each species had a different melody; each blended with the others.

When they came out of the great fragrant orchard, there were deer cavorting on the plain. The unicorn had moved by them, and from Tanaquil they did not run away. Birds flew overhead, sporting on the air currents in the sun.

"What do they eat? Perhaps the air feeds them, and the scents, they're so good."

The peeve stalked the deer, who whirled and cantered back, playing, but the peeve took fright and raced to Tanaquil.

"They won't hurt you."

"Big," said the peeve, with belated respect.

The sun and the day stars crossed the sky above them.

They must have walked for three or four hours, and Tanaquil was not tired. She was not hungry. The peeve showed signs only of vast interest in everything. She had been nervous that it might try to dig something up, nibble something, or lift its leg among the flowers. But none of these needs apparently occurred to it.

In what was probably the fifth hour, the plain reached its brink and unfolded over, down toward a lake of blue tourmaline. A forest lay beyond, and in and out went the flaming needles of parrots. Tanaquil saw animals basking at the lakeside. The unicorn, a quarter of a mile ahead, stepped peacefully among them. They turned to see, flicked their tails and yawned. They knew unicorns, evidently.

"Are they—? Yes, they're lions. And look, peeve."

The peeve looked. Tanaquil was not sure it realized what the picture meant. The pride of tawny lions had mingled and lazily lain down with a small flock of sheep. Some had adopted the same position, forelegs tucked under and heads raised. Others slept against each other's flanks. Some lambs chased lion cubs along the lakeshore, bleating sternly. They all fell over in a heap, pelt and fleece, and started to wash each other.

Tanaquil felt no misgiving as she and the peeve

also descended among the lions. And they paid her no special attention. The sheep bleated softly, and one of the sleeping cats snored. The sheep were not grazing on anything. She saw how alike were the faces of the lions and the sheep, their high-set eyes and long noses.

The unicorn walked on, circling the shore.

A leopard stretched over the bough of a huge cedar. It stared at them from calm lighted eyes.

Swans swam across the lake mirror.

They passed a solitary apple tree, singing, its trunk growing from the water.

"Insect," said the peeve.

In the forest were massive cypresses, ilexes, magnolias. In sun-bathed clearings orchids grew in mosaic colors. Deer moved like shadows, and lynxes sat in the shade while mice ambled about between their paws. The parrots screamed with laughter. Monkeys hung overhead like brown fruit. Ferns of drinkable green burst from the mouths of wild fountains. Water lilies paved the pools. There were butterflies in the forest, and bees spiraled the red-amber trunk of a pine. *Do they have a sting?* Snakes like trickles of liquid metal poured through the undergrowth.

The unicorn might be seen walking before them down the aisles of the forest. It no longer appeared fantastic. Here, it was only right.

When they came from the forest they were high up again, and turning, Tanaquil saw the country she had traveled flowing away behind them. The mountains had drawn nearer, and the sun and its attendant stars were lower in the sky. A rose-gold light, like that of a flawless late summer afternoon, held the world as though inside a gem. Again, as with everything, it was not that she had never seen such light the other side of the Gate. It was that here nothing threatened or came between her and the light. In Tanaquil's world, the best of things might have a tinge of sadness or unease. Nothing was sure, or quite safe. The light of the perfect world was the light of absolute truth. And Tanaquil, who had yearned in Jaive's fortress for order, adventure, and change, knew that here there were other things. To be happy would not become sickly. To be at peace would not bore. Happiness and peace allowed the mind to seek for different challenges. She could not guess what they were, but she sensed them in the very air. Would she come to know them? Would they be hers?

Above, on a hilltop, the unicorn stood against the luminous sky. A soft wind blew, and scarfed about the horn, and the horn sang, lilting and pure. But it was not the savage music she had heard in the desert. The unicorn was no longer terrible. It was only . . . perfect.

Soon they went on, climbing up the hills with no effort. Far off, on another slope, Tanaquil saw a creature glide out of some white rocks into the westering day. It was as large as a house of her world, and scaled like a great blue snake. Its crested head turned to and fro, and the wings opened like leaves of sapphire over its spine. "Peeve, it's a dragon." The peeve looked anxious. She stroked its head. Pale fire came from the dragon's nostrils and mouth, but scorched nothing on the hill. Like the salt of the sea, fire was harmless. The peeve got behind Tanaquil. She shook her head at it as it went on its belly through the grass. And so they continued after the unicorn, which now and then, still, seemed to glance back at them, and which had not attempted to leave them behind.

The sun set. All of the sky became rose red, and the disc of the sun itself was visible, a shade of red it seemed to Tanaquil she had never seen, but perhaps she had. After the sun had gone under the world, the cluster of diamond day stars stayed on the hem of the sky, growing steadily more brilliant. The east lightened and turned a flaming green.

Miles off, a hill or mountain sent a plume of sparks into the air, and something lifted out of them. It flew on wide flashing wings, passing over, not to be mistaken. A phoenix.

"Poor Mother," said Tanaquil. "Wouldn't she love this? Why did she never try to find a way in?"

Nightingales began. The hills were a music box.

The last slope came, and not knowing, Tanaquil mounted it, the peeve bustling along at her side. At the hill's peak, the land opened below, enormous as the sky. It was like a garden of forests and waters, all blurred and glimmered now by the flower red and emerald of dusk. And floating over it, distant and oddly shaped, was a single broad cloud.

Tanaquil thought there were stars in the cloud. They were not stars.

"Peeve—"

The peeve sat staring on the hill with her. If it knew what it was looking at, it did not say.

But Tanaquil knew.

The cloud was not a cloud, either. There were banks and terraces, although perhaps no outer walls. Tapering towers with caps like pearl, and buildings ruled straight by pillars, and statues of giants—and the lamps were being kindled. There, in that city floating in the air, the windows of silver and gold let out their light.

"There had to be," said Tanaquil, "I knew there had to be—people—but—*people*?"

And then in the green-apple rose of the sky, she saw dim shining figures, with a smoke of hair, and wings. Around and around they flew, a sort of dance, and faintly on the wind she heard that they had music, too.

There could be no unhappiness and no fear in that place, and yet, somewhere in the depth of her, were both. Such emotions had become strangers. She felt them in her heart and mind, and was puzzled. But she turned from the winged people and the castles in the air, and looked back again, the way she had come.

She had not seen before. Or had not wanted to see.

The grass and flowers over which she and the peeve had trodden, having sprung up, had dropped down again. The stems were squashed or broken, and in the softness and color, a harsh withering had commenced, the mark of death.

"This world isn't ours. Even invited, we shouldn't have come in. Look, look what we've done."

The peeve put its paw on her foot. "Sorry."

Tanaquil knelt and stared into its yellow eyes. They were comrades, they were, it and she, from an imperfect world.

"It's not your fault. It's mine."

"Sorry," said the peeve again, and, experimentally: "Bad?"

"I must carry you," said Tanaquil. "You'll have to let me. Over my shoulders. And I'll tread only where I've already—it's so terrible, like a *burn*."

Just then, she noticed the unicorn. It had gone some way down the other side of the hill, toward the enormous garden under the floating city. Its horn burned bright.

Should she shout after it? Probably it had forgotten them. Now and then it had glanced back only at some noise they made, or maybe it had seen the ruin of the flowers and grass, had wished them away. But here it would not attack, it could not chase them off as they deserved.

They had been so careful, she, and the peeve also, not to spoil. But their presence was enough. The very steps they took.

She picked up the peeve, and it allowed this. It let itself be arranged, warm and heavy, about her neck. Its back legs dangled, and its tail thumped her shoulder. It fixed its claws into her dress and glared at everything, its face beside her own.

Tanaquil descended the hill, her back to the city. She put her feet exactly into the ruin they had already made. She did not examine it closely, and the light of dusk was merciful.

She had gone about two hundred steps when she heard the drumming of hoofs pursuing her. She stopped at once, not in alarm, for you could not feel alarm here. Yet she was amazed. She swung round, with the peeve, and confronted the unicorn, which ran at her, and halted less than two feet away. Now its horn had faded to a shadow.

In the gathering dark, therefore, she could not see the unicorn well, the gleam of an eye, the mask of ebony—

"Unicorn," said Tanaquil. That was all she could say.

The fierce head flung up. The stars on the horizon threw diamonds to the seashell of the horn. It burst alight like white fires. It wheeled and the sky toppled. What had happened? Had she been impaled? Without terror, Tanaquil tried to understand. For the moon-fire horn had touched her forehead, for half a second, the needle tip, gentle as snow.

"Hey," said the peeve, "good, nice." And it lifted its face.

And the burning sword of the horn went over Tanaquil's shoulder as the unicorn put down its head. Black velvet, the tongue came from its mouth. It licked the peeve, quickly, thoroughly, roughly, once, from head to tail.

The scent of the unicorn's breath was like water, and like light. Of course.

Tanaquil and the peeve hung on the hill in space, breathing, as if lost, and found. And the black unicorn jumped aside and flew up the slope behind the shaft of light, and at the top leapt out, out into the air, and the last of the green sky. Became a star. Was gone. The final vanishment.

"That was goodbye," said Tanaquil.

"Mrrr," said the peeve. It fell suddenly asleep.

And, alone responsible, Tanaquil resumed their retreat from Heaven.

During the night of the perfect world, two moons rose in the east together. One was a golden moon at full, the other a slim, bluish crescent. Their radiance was sheer, and with the stars the landscape showed bright as day.

And the stars came in constellations. And they formed images, not as they were said to do in Tanaquil's world, but exactly. First a woman, drawn from east to west as if in zircons and beryls, holding a balance. And as she went over and began to sink, a chariot rose in quartz and opals. It had no horses in the shafts. No shafts. For each hour, it seemed to Tanaquil as she walked, another constellation came into the sky. After the chariot, a lion, and after the lion, two dolphins, a tree, a bird, a crowned man, a snake that crossed the sky like a river of silver fires.

"You see," Tanaquil muttered, as each came up, "how could we manage *here*?"

The moons and the stars showed her the burnt grass, the blackened flowers. Never had any path been made so easy.

Under the cool-warm lamps of the night, panthers gamboled on the shore of the lake. In the forest foxes upbraided her. Would she have shed tears if it had been possible? Surely she would have been angry.

She came at last back to the orchards above the sea. In the moonlight, under the sinking starry hand of the king, the line of water was like mercury. The star serpent coiled over the orchards, and their song went on by night as by day.

Tanaquil walked through the orchards, and came under one silent tree. She had expected this. It was the tree where she had touched the apple.

The peeve woke. It interrogated the apple tree. "No insect."

"No insect. My fault."

They walked from the orchards through the flowers. Like blackened bones, the snapped stalks where they had trodden before.

They reached the shore. She was not fatigued. Fast and grim, the egg of darkness hung on the light-rinsed sky. The Gate. Theirs.

Tanaquil gazed across the land of trees and flowers and beauty.

"Forgive me."

The peeve shook itself. Its ears went up in points and its whiskers flickered at her cheek.

"Insect."

A weird motion was on the ground. The flowers were rising up again, the black husks crumbling from them. Like a fire along the earth the healing ran up from the shore and away across the plain. She could not hear the silent apple tree begin to sing, but the sharp ears of the peeve had caught it.

A response to apology? Because she was removing them from the world and, like some unbearable weight, as they were taken from it, it might breathe again?

Tanaquil did not know. A pang of ordinary rage went through her. Was it their fault that they had been polluted by being made second best?

"Hold tight!"

She ran into the sea and the mercury water splashed up; nearing the dark Gate she catapulted herself into the air and dived forward. The peeve clawed her shoulder. There was a different sort of night, and perfection was gone for good.

Chapter Twelve

Outside, it was daylight. Imperfect daylight that glared, and ripped blinding slashes in the sea. The sea was also darkly in the arch under the cliff, piled up somehow, though the tide elsewhere had drawn away.

Tanaquil, up to her knees in harsh salt water, ploughed to the arch mouth and let the peeve jump free onto the dry beach.

She spared one look for her world. She was not ready for it yet. But there were things to be done.

She tried to feel nothing, though all the normal feelings—anger, dismay, grief, disbelief, mere muddle—were swarming in on her. She stood in the tide pool before the shimmer, the glowing oval, so like an invitation—as the Gate on the other side was a warning—and, thrusting in her arms up to the elbow, like a furious washerwoman, she pulled the Gate apart.

She tore it in pieces and cast the pieces adrift. And as she did so the light of the Gate crinkled and went out, and only smears of luminescence like the trails of sorcerous snails, remained.

Tanaquil sensed two tears on her face, and blinked them off into the salty sea.

She kneeled in the water and fumbled at the base of the cliff. The fossil came to her hand. She wrenched it out. And standing up again, sopping

wet, she beheld all the sheen of the Gate was
gone. She could see through to the far side of the
cliff, the glare of the sun, and the barrenness of
the sand.

"I'll do it properly," she said.

She pushed out of the arch and sneered at the
cliff top.

Tanaquil had known no tiredness in the other
world. Now she was worn out, as if she had gone
days and nights without rest. Nevertheless, she
must scramble up the slippery rock and get the
second fossil out. There must be no chance again
that anyone might enter Paradise. Or anything
wander out of it.

She climbed the cliff. It was murderous. She
hated it and told it so.

The glaring sun, which burnt you if it could,
had risen further toward noon when she achieved
the top. She lay there, put her hand on the second
fossil, and prized it loose. With both of them, the
primal keys to the Gate of the unicorn, in her fist,
she fell asleep facedown on the rock.

Boom, went the surf, *accept our offering.*

Boom. Give over your rage at us.

"Stupid," said Tanaquil, in her sleep, "I'll never
forgive any of you."

Oh Sacred Beast, trouble us no more.

"It won't, it won't."

The stone of the cliff top was hot, and Tanaquil
was roasting. She shifted, and saw what went on,
on the beach below. She had seen something like
this before. A congregation of people very over-
dressed and in too many ornaments; horses and
chariots up on the road among the palms; soldiers
in golden mail. There was a sort of chorus of

women in white dresses, waving tambourines and moaning. And quite near, a girl, with very black hair and a collar of rubies, was poised by the sea and throwing garlands on to it. The flowers were roses, and would die. "Stop it; what a waste," mumbled Tanaquil.

"Trouble us no more. We regret any hurt or insult," cried the girl to the sea, and to the arch mouth. She tossed the last garland proudly, and came on toward the cliff. No one kept up with her. She hesitated by the limb of the arch and said quietly, "May God protect us from the horn of the unicorn. And may God watch for the safety of my father, the Prince Zorander. And for my lost friend and sister, Tanaquil, carried off by demons."

"Lizra," Tanaquil called softly, "Don't jump. I'm alive. I'm up here."

Lizra raised her head. She was white and blank, like paper without writing. What would be written in?

"It was a demon of my mother's," said Tanaquil. "It saved me from Gasb and brought me here. The unicorn's gone now. But I thought it—I mean, the Prince is well, is he?"

There was still no writing on Lizra's face.

"Yes, my father the Prince is well. Are you Tanaquil?"

"Definitely. And this is the wreckage of your dress. What can I say? I've got a lot to tell you."

"We came to placate the unicorn," said Lizra, like a sleepwalker.

"Well, as I said, it's gone. Back through the Sacred Gate."

"If that's true, my father will rejoice."

"I'll bet. By the way, if you want proof of me, look down there."

Lizra turned. The peeve was snorting and sneezing its exit from a burrow in the sand. Catching sight of Lizra, it pounced forward. Lizra dropped to her knees and embraced it. The peeve seemed startled but not offended; it licked Lizra's cheek.

Tanaquil had moved her attention to the crowd on the beach. The courtiers only stood there, glittering and gaping. But among the chariots on the road there was a flurry of unpromising movement.

Lizra got up. "Gasb's here. Father sent him with the escort."

"Lovely," said Tanaquil.

Men were running, gleaming military gold, from the road. The sun described faultlessly spears, lances, crossbows, and swords. And Gasb, who strode after in a hawk hat.

Over the sand, like memory, she heard his ghastly voice.

"The witch has returned. She haunts the Gate of the Beast! Did the fishermen not tell us weird fires have burned in the Gate for the past three nights, and that they avoided it in fear?"

Three nights, Tanaquil thought, bemusedly. *I was only gone a day.*

She sat up, on the cliff. Something said to her, *Stay flat*. But even now she did not quite credit the weapons. In front of all these people, would Gasb openly kill her? He might.

"The unicorn is—" shouted Tanaquil—

"Don't let her speak a spell!" screeched Gasb. "Silence her!"

And suddenly, as simply as that, Tanaquil beheld the spear that was to be her death arcing toward her through the sunlight. For to a practiced spearman, the distance up the rock was nothing. And she, sitting against the sky, made an excellent target. It was as though she had reasoned all this before and helped them, helped the man and the spear. She saw it come, soaring up, as if rushed by a cord to her heart. She saw it, and imagined swerving sideways, but although the spear came slowly, she moved more slowly still. And in the last instant the point of the spear was there before her, and it blinded her with light.

So she did not see, only heard, a kind of splintering sizzle. She had an impression of fireworks and bits of wood. The courtiers on the beach were screaming.

Then she saw again. The spear, in shreds, was tumbling down the cliff. People who seemed to have recalled an urgent appointment were hurrying toward the road, falling in the sand, and tottering on again.

The spear must have hit something, some obstacle, just before it reached her.

Gasb had backed away. His hat fluttered. He threatened the soldiers, but they only stood there under the cliff goggling at the fallen spear and at Tanaquil. The man who had made the spearcast was gabbling nonsensically. In the middle of this, the peeve pelted from the cliff base and bit him on the leg, right through his boot. The soldier howled and, perhaps instinctively, kicked viciously with the bitten leg at the peeve.

Tanaquil was a witness now. The kicking foot, rather than striking the peeve, met something in the air. It was invisible, but effective. The soldier was dashed away, as if he had been lifted and thrown by an adversary of great strength. He landed in the sand thirty feet from the peeve, with a terrific thump, and did not move.

The peeve spruced itself. It did not bother with questions, merely watched in apparent glee as the other soldiers sprinted off up the beach and plummeted into the chariots, while streams of courtiers ran by them toward the city, wailing and tripping.

Only Gasb was left. He held up his hands, warding off Tanaquil and her power.

"Mighty sorceress, don't harm me, be kind—" And as her vanquishing blow did not smite him, Gasb too turned tail and bolted for the chariots, and as before when he had run away, his hat flew off and dropped to the ground, glad to be rid of him.

"The unicorn," said Tanaquil. Because she was seated, she got up. Not sure what to do, she started to climb down the cliff. As she climbed, she listened to the pandemonium on the road, the rattle of departing chariots.

At the bottom of the cliff, Lizra stood with the peeve. She was still white above the rubies; maybe they made her look worse. If anything was written on her face, it was a strange worried smugness.

"You *are* a witch. I said."

"The unicorn touched me. It touched the peeve. I suppose—"

"The unicorn touched Father," said Lizra. "It raked him across the chest with its horn, when it stole the shells from his cloak. He'll always have the scar." It was her public voice.

"Lizra, I'm sorry, I didn't intend to frighten you.

I didn't know it would happen. I mean, it's extraordinary."

"You're invulnerable," said Lizra. She bowed. "Great sorceress." It was not a joke.

"Bow to the peeve, as well," grated Tanaquil. "This is too much. I've seen something wonderful that didn't want me—that none of us can have. Friend and sister, you said."

"Everything's changed," said Lizra. She had ceased being a princess. She was small and bleak, a frost child. "And you."

"I haven't changed. Something's happened to me, that's all."

Lizra grew a little. Then she was fifteen again. She said, "I'll have to show you. Anyway, you can't go on in that dress."

"What would you suggest instead?"

"The soldier's shortish, and thin. His mail would fit you. Anyway, he's all that's available."

They went over to the fallen soldier. He had come down on his back. His mouth was open and he grunted vaguely. The peeve's toothmarks showed in his boot.

Tanaquil took off his boots and tried them. They were too large, but would do.

While the man lay unconscious they removed his mail, and left him in neat undergarments embroidered by some doting hand. Tanaquil draped the remains of her dress and petticoat over him to shield him from the sun until he woke.

"Keep the topazes," said Lizra. And Tanaquil, hearing the words, heard behind them another phrase: A parting gift. She thought of the unicorn. *That's goodbye.*

Angrily, she let Lizra help her dress in the mail.

She bundled her witch-red hair up into the big helmet.

"Now what?"

"They've left my horses and chariot. How deliriously kind of them. Last time, on the platform, they ran off with those, too."

They walked along the beach. The waves plashed on the shore, hard and bright. The peeve slunk to them, and drew away.

"What happened after my mother's demon came for me?" said Tanaquil.

"Gasb and the soldiers turned somersaults and fled into the palace. I went to my father. I thought the unicorn had killed him."

"It hadn't."

"Only taken the shells and left the scar." Tanaquil held the fossils more tightly in her fist. She had not shown them, she had never let go. What the unicorn had given her was stupendous. She could not accept it as yet; probably there was some mistake. She wanted an ordinary memento. "My father needs me now," said Lizra.

That's goodbye.

"And you still feel vast loyalty to him, do you?" said Tanaquil, acidly.

"He's my father."

"Oh, has he remembered?"

"Yes," said Lizra.

It was the chariot from the avenue, painted and gilded but today without any flowers. The small white horses perched in the shafts, alert, unpanicked. The two girls got in, followed by the peeve, and Lizra drew up the reins. "Gallop." And off they went, back along the beach road toward Zorander's city.

Remember the sand castle. Where is it now?

"Why are we going to the city?" asked Tanaquil.

"Because the palace is there, and I want you to see."

"What?"

"I want to show you, not tell you. That's why we're going."

The hot mail was uncomfortable; it itched. Had the soldier had fleas? Abruptly Tanaquil felt pity for him. It was not his fault he had been driven to cast the spear.

They did not return into the city by the entrance they had used before. Driving the chariot up into some groves above the beach, Lizra brought them to the city wall and a large gateway with large stone lions at either side. Here there was a fuss, and they were provided an escort. "Only this one lad stayed with you, ma'am? I never heard the like. Frightened by a beggar girl on the beach! I never did."

The city did not seem altered. There was the old noise and activity, the masses of people going about, the elegant shops and exotic market. Then, as they turned into the street of octopuses and camels, topped by the fifteen-story palace of the Prince, they were forced to a halt.

A crowd milled over the avenue, and had gone up the lantern poles. In the middle of the roadway, a chariot lay spilled. Its horses were visible inside the crowd, thieved, being led off to new lives.

"Clear the way!" thundered the escort's captain.

A parting appeared. As had happened on other streets, some cheers were loudly raised for Lizra. They moved forward slowly.

"That chariot is Gasb's," said Lizra. She drew on the reins. "Stand." There in the crowd, she turned to a burly man in the apron of the vintners' guild. "What is the meaning of this?" A tangle of voices answered. Lizra said, "One at a time. You. I addressed you first."

"Honored, Highness. Twenty minutes ago, Counselor Gasb rode up, in a hurry. There were several chariots. Most turned back seeing the crowd here, but Gasb drove straight at us."

"We were only waiting," said a silk-clad man behind the vintner, "for news of the Prince, or news of the ceremony of placation that you, Your Highness, were carrying out."

"It's traditional for the people to have use of this road."

"Yes," said Lizra. "So Gasb rode at the crowd. And then?"

"And then, Highness," said the vintner, "not to mislead you, some of us turned the horses and upset the chariot."

The silk man said in satisfaction, "We got him to dismount."

"Dragged him out," added another one, helpfully.

"He was pelted with eggs and ripe fruit from a handy stall," said the vintner. The men paused, looked at each other. The vintner cleared his throat. "Gasb wasn't popular."

The silk man said, "Some of the rougher elements of the crowd took him away, Highness. To reason with him, perhaps."

"My father will be informed of this," said Lizra. There was no resonance to her dramatic displeasure.

"Make way for the Princess!" shouted the escort captain.

"Good fortune smile on her!" cried the vintner, with especial fervor, to demonstrate he was not the right candidate for the soldiers' swords.

The palace gangs of the Flying Chairs were having a celebration. They sang out the name of Gasb, and went into fits of laughter. The Chair rose without other incident, however. In the long corridor the gold guards saluted, and nobody questioned their fellow soldier marching at Lizra's back, nor the animal on an improvised leash.

At the landing of green onyx, the mad gang who acted as the counterweight were just as Tanaquil recollected them. If they had heard of Gasb's fate, they did not dwell on it. Probably the insanity of their existence had erased any idea of its author.

The Chair rose and the gang pounded down the stairs, whooping.

By the Prince's apartment, the soldiers uncrossed their spears at once. They opened the door.

Beyond, Tanaquil and Lizra climbed up through the ice country. On the white plains no clockwork snow leopards prowled, and at the stairhead no animal emerged to threaten them.

Lizra stopped before the archway. "Don't come in," she said. "If you stay by the door, he won't see."

Inside, the library was dark and lamplit. The doorway to the roof was shut and curtains were drawn over. In this light the books looked ancient and false. Not one butterfly flew in the room. *Does he even fear those, now?*

"Lizra . . . Is that Lizra?"

"Yes, Father. It's me."

Tanaquil had not made him out at first. In the darkest corner he hunched in his fine chair. He wore an old gray robe. His black hair, without a diadem, seemed too young for him.

"Do you see?" said Lizra. Her voice was now neutral. Was she afraid to show triumph? "Yesterday, from the roof, he saw the two men in the unicorn-hide—do you remember?—the back half was drunk. And my father screamed in terror. He ordered out the soldiers to hunt the beast and kill it. Of course, they didn't. The city," Lizra looked down, "the city values me because I didn't run away like the Procession, when the black unicorn came from the sea. The Prince is disgraced. Would they have dared attack Gasb otherwise? My father needs me."

"Lizra, I can hear whispering. What is it? Is there someone there?"

"Only a servant, Father."

"Lizra. Come here, Lizra, tell me what happened at the Gate of the Beast."

Tanaquil said swiftly, lightly, "I saw another world. Which wasn't fair. I should have seen this world first. I'm going to travel it now, I'll look at it. All the far cities. The deserts, the forests, the mountains, the seas. It's what I must do. Come with me."

"Lizra," said the Prince, in the tone of a man two hundred years old, "you're my daughter. Be honest with me. *Did you see the Beast?*"

"No, Father. The Beast's gone. We're safe now."

"If I wait," said Tanaquil, "a few days, a week—"

"My answer would have to be the same." Lizra smiled. She was several beings at once as she stood there. A girl who was sorry, a girl who was a sister, a woman who would rule, a child who wanted to be a child. She was sly and arrogant, sad and wistful, proud and immovable, selfish. Lonely.

Like me. Just like me.

"Have this," said Lizra, unfastening the wreath of rubies from her neck.

"I'm not Yilli."

"Of course you're not. I wish I didn't have to lose you. Take the jewelry. It'll buy things that are useful."

"Thank you," said Tanaquil. She held out her empty palm and let the rubies drop into it.

Then Lizra hugged her. Not as she had hugged the peeve, with easy, immediate affection, but in a quick and stony way, afraid to do more. The embrace of farewell.

And then Lizra went into her father's library and across the shiny lamplit floor. And Zorander looked up at her and held out his hand, which she took.

"You're my comfort now," he said.

The peeve growled, a soft sandy sound.

"Goodbye," said Tanaquil. She tugged on the lead.

The peeve bounded ahead down the three flights of stairs. On the green landing they picked their way through people walking precariously on their fingers.

Don't we all?

* * *

Only one caravan was due to set out for the eastern city that day.

As she approached the leader's awning on the edge of the bazaar, Tanaquil found Gork and his men dealing with the camels and baggage.

"Well, aren't you smart?" said Gork, shaking all his discs and adornments, and striking his leg rapidly with the goad. "But still got that animal. And still dressed as a man. That's not right, you know."

"Much better for traveling," said Tanaquil with precautionary sweetness.

"What? Not married?"

"Oh, you know how these things are."

Gork was pleased. "You want to come with us to East City? I can fix it."

"No, I'm afraid not. But I wondered if someone from your caravan could make a detour; I can give exact directions, about half a day's ride. It's to deliver an urgent letter to a fortress in the desert. I'll pay very well."

"How much?" Tanaquil, who had bartered carefully with a small topaz and one of the rubies, suggested a healthy sum. "*I'll* do it. No trouble. You've got a map?"

"Yes, I had it drawn up only an hour ago. Here."

Gork took money, map, and letter. He showed her the gold watch. "It goes, never misses. And you're prosperous now. I suppose you're not still courting?"

"Unluckily, I am. Isn't it a nuisance?"

Gork grinned. "Till we meet again."

Tanaquil sat near the perfume-makers' booths and thought of Gork riding out to her red-haired mother's fort in all his grandeur. What would happen? Anything might.

The peeve began to eat some perfumed soap, and Tanaquil removed it.

The letter would perhaps only annoy Jaive. It told of the resolution of the adventure, and of the perfect world. It asked a respectful question, witch to sorceress: "Do you believe the unicorn will have any trouble there from the additions I had to make to its bones, the copper and other metal I added? Will it always now, because of them, keep some link to this earth?" Tanaquil did not mention the gift of invulnerability—Jaive might grow hysterical. In any case, Tanaquil did not yet quite believe in it. Nor did she speak of the two creamy fossils fashioned to be two ear-rings at a jeweller's on Palm Tree Avenue, and worn in her ears. Not vanity, but the ultimate in common sense. Who would recognize them now? "Mother, I must see this world. Later, one day, I'll come back. I promise that. I'm not my father, not Zorander. I won't leave you . . . that is, I won't let you *renounce* me. When we meet again, we'll have things to talk about. It will be exciting and new. You'll have to trust me, please."

"Leave that soap alone!"

With her own map of the oases and the wells, and the towns of the eastern desert, Tanaquil set out near sunset on the stern old camel she had bought three days before. Learning to ride him had been interesting, but unlike most of his tribe, he had a scathing patience. He did not seem to loathe the peeve. But the peeve sat on him, above the provisions, staring in horror at the lurching ground.

"Lumpy. Bumpy. Want get off."

"Hush."

They left the city by a huge blue gate, enameled with a unicorn that soldiers with picks were busy demolishing.

The road was lined with obelisks and statues, tall trees, and fountains with chained iron cups. A few carts and donkeys were being hastened to the gate before day's end.

The fume on the plain was golden. The hills bloomed. There would be cedar trees and the lights of the villages, and then, beyond, the desert offering its beggar's bowl of dusts.

Bred for the cold as for the heat, the woolly, cynical old camel could journey by night, while the thin snow fell from the stars.

Somewhere between the city and the desert, sunset began.

The sky was apple-red in the west, and in the east the coolness of lilac raised the ceiling of the air to an impossible height. Stars broke out like windows opening. The land below turned purple, sable, and its eastern heights were roses on the stem of shadow.

"It's beautiful," said Tanaquil.

It was beautiful. As beautiful as any beauty of the perfect world.

"Oh, peeve. It wasn't our fault we weren't given the best, but this, and all the things that are wrong. But can't we improve it? Make it better? I don't know how, the odds are all against us. And yet—just to *think* of it, just to *try*—that's a start."

But the peeve had climbed down the patient, scornful foreleg of the camel, and was digging in the dusty earth. It lifted up its pointed face from the darkness and announced in victory: "Found it. Found a *bone.*"

Destined for an Early Grave

B ones had an arm around my waist, locking me next to him. My squirming only ratcheted my dress higher as his hands bunched it up. Then the sudden pierce of his fangs into my neck made me freeze. A low rumble of pleasure came from him.

"Ah, Kitten, you love that almost as much as I do. Sink into me, luv, as I do the same."

The blood leaving me and spilling into him felt like it was replaced by sweet fire. Bones was right; I loved it when he bit me. My skin felt hot, my heartbeat quickened—and then I was rubbing against him and moaning at the delay of him unzipping his pants.

"Bones," I managed. "Yes—"

The building hit me in the face so hard I felt my cheek fracture. It must have been hard enough to knock me unconscious, too. Just for a second. And then the gunfire registered.

It came in staccato bursts from above us, on all sides . . . everywhere but from the building I was mashed against. Bones had me pressed into the brick. His body covered mine and he was draped over me, shuddering in a wracking way while he punched at the wall in front of me, trying to make a door where one didn't exist.

That's when I realized why he was shaking. Bones was being strafed with dozens of bullets.

By Jeaniene Frost

DESTINED FOR AN EARLY GRAVE
AT GRAVE'S END
ONE FOOT IN THE GRAVE
HALFWAY TO THE GRAVE

Coming Soon

FIRST DROP OF CRIMSON

DESTINED
FOR AN
EARLY
GRAVE

A Night Huntress Novel

JEANIENE FROST

AVON

An Imprint of HarperCollinsPublishers

This is a work of fiction. Names, characters, places, and incidents are products of the author's imagination or are used fictitiously and are not to be construed as real. Any resemblance to actual events, locales, organizations, or persons, living or dead, is entirely coincidental.

AVON BOOKS
An Imprint of HarperCollins*Publishers*
10 East 53rd Street
New York, New York 10022-5299

Copyright © 2009 by Jeaniene Frost
Excerpt from *First Drop of Crimson* copyright © 2010 by Jeaniene Frost
Excerpts from *Memoirs of a Scandalous Red Dress* copyright © 2009 by Elizabeth Boyle; *Lord of the Night* copyright © 1993 by Susan Wiggs; *Don't Tempt Me* copyright © 2009 by Loretta Chekani; *Destined for an Early Grave* copyright © 2009 by Jeaniene Frost
ISBN 978-0-06-158321-6
www.avonbooks.com

First Avon Books paperback printing: August 2009

Avon Trademark Reg. U.S. Pat. Off. and in Other Countries, Marca Registrada, Hecho en U.S.A.
HarperCollins® is a registered trademark of HarperCollins Publishers.

Printed in the U.S.A.

10 9 8 7 6 5 4 3 2 1

To my sister Jeanne,
who had the courage to walk away
and the strength not to go back.

Acknowledgments

Once again I have to thank God, for helping me achieve my old dreams while giving me strength to strive for new ones.

If I gave proper credit to everyone who's helped me, encouraged me, or been instrumental in the success of my series this past year, I'd need a separate book. So to save space, I'll mention a few people I couldn't do this without: my editor, Erika Tsang, who continues to amaze me with support and insight that doesn't just stop at making my books better. If I haven't said it lately, I'm so grateful for all you do.

Thanks to Thomas Egner, whose beautiful covers are like reader magnets. Also thanks so much to Amanda Bergeron, Carrie Feron, Liate Stehlik, Karen Davy, Wendy Ho, and the rest of the fabulous team at Avon Books/HarperCollins.

Deepest gratitude to my agent, Nancy Yost, for your professional expertise, the outstanding attention you give your clients, and your invaluable assistance in guiding my career.

Thanks to the fans of the Night Huntress series, for continuing to allow me to share my world and characters with you. My books are only possible because of your enthusiasm and support. Simply put, you rule! Special thanks also go to Tage Shokker, Erin Horn, and Marcy Funderburk, for keeping my fan site such a fun place for readers—and me!—to hang out.

Melissa Marr and Ilona Andrews, I can't thank you enough for your friendship, wisdom, critiques, and general awesomeness. The two of you have kept me steady through all the unexpected twists and turns this past year. "Sorority Sisters" for the win!

As always, to my husband and family . . . I'd be lost without you.

Destined
for an
Early
Grave

Oпe

IF HE CATCHES ME, I'M DEAD.

I ran as fast as I could, darting around trees, tangled roots, and rocks in the forest. The monster snarled as it chased me, the sound closer than before. I wasn't able to outrun it. The monster was picking up speed while I was getting tired.

The forest thinned ahead of me to reveal a blond vampire on a hill in the distance. I recognized him at once. Hope surged through me. If I could reach him, I'd be okay. He loved me. He'd protect me from the monster. Yet I was still so far away.

Fog crept up the hill to surround the vampire, making him appear almost ghostly. I screamed his name as the monster's footsteps got even closer. Panicked, I lunged forward, narrowly avoiding the grasp of bony hands that would pull me down to the grave. With renewed effort, I sprinted toward the vampire. He urged me on, snarling warnings at the monster, which wouldn't stop chasing me.

"Leave me alone," I screamed, as I was seized from behind in a merciless grip. "No!"

"Kitten!"

The shout didn't come from the vampire ahead of me; it came from the monster wrestling me to the ground. I jerked my head toward the vampire in the distance, but his features blurred into nothingness, and the fog covered him. Right before he disappeared, I heard his voice.

"He is not your husband, Catherine."

A hard shake evaporated the last of the dream, and I woke to find Bones, my vampire lover, hovering over me.

"What is it? Are you hurt?"

An odd question, you would think, since it had only been a nightmare. But with the right power and magic, sometimes nightmares could be turned into weapons. A while back, I'd almost been killed by one. This was different, however. No matter how vivid it felt, it had just been a dream.

"I'll be fine if you quit shaking me."

Bones dropped his hands and let out a noise of relief. "You didn't wake up, and you were thrashing on the bed. Brought back rotten memories."

"I'm okay. It was a . . . weird dream."

There was something about the vampire in it that nagged me. Like I should know who he was. That made no sense, however, since he was just a figment of my imagination.

"Odd that I couldn't catch any of your dream," Bones went on. "Normally your dreams are like background music to me."

Bones was a Master vampire, more powerful than most vampires I'd ever met. One of his gifts was the ability to read human minds. Even though I was half-human, half-vampire, there was enough humanity in me that Bones could hear my thoughts unless I worked to block him. Still, this was news to me.

"You can hear my *dreams*? God, you must never get any quiet. I'd be shooting myself in the head if I were you."

Which wouldn't do much to him, actually. Only silver through the heart or decapitation was lethal to a vampire. Getting shot in the head might take care of *my* ills the permanent way, but it would just give Bones a nasty headache.

He settled himself back onto the pillows. "Don't fret, luv. I said it's like background music, so it's rather soothing. As for quiet, out here on this water, it's as quiet as I've experienced without being half-shriveled in the process."

I lay back down, a shiver going through me at the mention of his near miss with death. Bones's hair had turned white from how close he'd come to dying, but now it was back to its usual, rich brown color.

"Is that why we're drifting on a boat out in the Atlantic? So you could have some peace and quiet?"

"I wanted some time alone with you, Kitten. We've had so little of that lately."

An understatement. Even though I'd quit my job leading the secret branch of Homeland Security that hunted rogue vampires and ghouls, life hadn't been dull. First we'd had to deal with our losses from the war with another Master vampire last year. Several of Bones's friends—and my best friend Denise's husband, Randy—had been murdered. Then there had been months of hunting down the remaining perpetrators of that war, so they couldn't live to plot against

us another day. Then training my replacement so that
my uncle Don had someone else to play bait when
his operatives went after the misbehaving members
of undead society. Most vampires and ghouls didn't
kill when they fed, but there were those who killed
for fun. Or stupidity. My uncle made sure those vampires and ghouls were taken care of—and that ordinary citizens weren't aware they existed.

So when Bones told me we were taking a boat trip,
I'd assumed there must be some search-and-destroy
reason behind it. Going somewhere just for relaxation hadn't happened, well, *ever* in our relationship.

"This is a weekend getaway?" I couldn't keep the
disbelief out of my voice.

He traced his finger on my lower lip. "This is our
vacation, Kitten."

I was still dumbfounded at the notion. "What about
my cat?" I'd set him up for enough food for a couple
of days, but not for an extended trip.

"No worries. I've sent someone to our house to
look after him. We can go anywhere in the world and
take our time getting there. So tell me, where shall
we go?"

"Paris."

I surprised myself saying it. I'd never had a burning desire to visit there before, but for some reason, I
did now. Maybe it was because Paris was supposed
to be the city of lovers, although just looking at Bones
was usually enough to get me in a romantic mood.

He must have caught my thought because he
smiled, making his face more breathtaking, in my
opinion. Against the backdrop of the navy sheets,
his skin almost glowed with a silky alabaster paleness that was too perfect to be human. The sheets

were tangled past his stomach, giving me an uninterrupted view of his lean, taut abdomen and hard,
muscled chest. Dark brown eyes began to tinge with
emerald, and fangs peeked under the curve of his
mouth, letting me know I wasn't the only one feeling
warmer all of a sudden.

"Paris it is, then," he whispered, and flung the
sheets off.

". . . we'll be arriving shortly. Yes, she's very well,
Mencheres. Faith, you've rung me nearly every day
. . . right, I'll see you at the dock."

Bones hung up and shook his head. "Either my
grandsire is concealing something, or he's developed
an unhealthy obsession with your every activity."

I stretched out in the hammock on the deck. "Let
me talk to him next time. I'll tell him things have
never been better."

The past three weeks had indeed been wonderful.
If I'd needed a vacation, Bones had needed it more. As
Master of a large line and co-Master of an even bigger
one, Bones was always watched, judged, challenged,
or busy protecting his people. All that responsibility
had taken its toll. Only in the past few days had he
relaxed enough to sleep longer than his usual few
hours.

There was just one black spot on this pleasure
cruise, but I'd kept it to myself. Why ruin our time off
by telling Bones I'd had more of those silly, meaningless dreams?

This time, they went unnoticed by him. Guess I
wasn't kicking in my sleep anymore. I couldn't remember much of them when I woke. All I knew was
they were about the same faceless blond vampire

from the first one. The one who called me by my real name, Catherine, and ended with the same cryptic admonition—*he is not your husband.*

According to human laws, Bones wasn't my husband. We were blood-bound and married vampire-style, though, and the undead didn't do divorce. They weren't kidding about the whole "until death do you part" thing. Maybe my dreams represented a subconscious desire to have a traditional wedding. The last time we'd attempted that, our plans were demolished by a war with a vampire who thought unleashing deadly black magic was fair game.

Mencheres met us on the dock. Even though Bones called him grandsire, since Mencheres was the sire of the vampire who'd turned Bones, he looked as young as Bones. They'd probably been similar in human age when they were turned into vampires. Mencheres was also handsome in an exotic way, with a regal bearing, Egyptian features, and long black hair blowing in the breeze.

But what really caught my attention was how Mencheres was flanked by eight Master vampires. Even before I stepped off the boat, I could feel their combined power crackling the air like static electricity. Sure, Mencheres usually traveled with an entourage, but these looked like guards, not undead groupies.

Bones went up to Mencheres and gave him a brief clasp.

"Hallo, grandsire. They can't be all for show"—he nodded to the waiting vampires—"so I expect there's trouble."

Mencheres nodded. "We should leave. This ship is announcement enough of your presence."

Reaper was painted in scarlet letters across the side

of the boat. It was in homage to my nickname, the
Red Reaper, which I'd earned because of my hair
color and my high undead body count.

Mencheres didn't speak to me beyond a short,
polite hello as we trotted from the pier into a waiting
black van. There was another identical van that six of
the guards got into. When we sped off, that van followed us at a close distance.

"Tell me about your dreams, Cat," Mencheres said
as soon as we were under way.

I gaped at him. "How do you know about that?"

Bones also looked taken aback. "I didn't mention
it, Kitten."

Mencheres ignored both of our questions. "What
was in your dream? Be very specific."

"They're strange," I began, seeing Bones's eyebrows shoot up at the plural. "They're all with the
same vampire. During the dreams, I know who he is.
I can even hear myself saying his name, but when I
wake up, I don't remember him."

If I hadn't known better, I'd have said Mencheres
looked alarmed. Of course, I was no expert on him.
Mencheres was over four thousand years old and a
genius at hiding his emotions, but his mouth might
have stiffened a fraction. Or maybe it was just a trick
of the light.

"How many of these dreams have you had?" Bones
asked. He wasn't happy. The way his lips thinned was
no accident of light.

"Four, and don't start. You'd have set sail for the
nearest fortress if I'd told you about them, then you
would have hovered over me day and night. We were
having a really nice trip, so I didn't mention them. No
big deal."

He snorted. "No big deal, she says. Well, luv, let's find out what the *deal* really is. With luck, it won't result in your losing your reckless life."

Then he turned to Mencheres. "You knew something was wrong. Why the hell didn't you bring it to my attention at once?"

Mencheres leaned forward. "Cat's life is in no danger. However, there is a . . . situation. I'd hoped this conversation would never become necessary."

"Could you just spit it out without a buildup for once?" Mencheres was famous for taking his time beating around the bush. Guess being as old as he was, he'd learned an obscene amount of patience.

"Have you ever heard of a vampire named Gregor?"

Pain shot through my head for an instant, then it was gone so fast, I actually looked around to see if anyone else was affected. Mencheres stared at me like he was trying to scope out the back of my brain. Beside me, Bones ground out a curse.

"I know a few Gregors, but there's only one who's called the bloody Dreamsnatcher." His fist slammed down, snapping the armrest off. "*This* is what you consider acceptable standards of safety for my wife?"

"I'm not your wife."

Bones swung a disbelieving look my way even as my hand flew to my mouth. Where in the hell did *that* come from?

"What did you just say?" Bones asked incredulously.

Stunned, I stammered.

"I-I meant . . . in my dreams, the one thing I can remember is this vampire telling me 'he is not your husband.' And I know he means you, Bones. So that's what I meant."

Bones looked like I'd just stabbed him, and Mencheres had that cool, hooded expression on his face. Giving nothing away.

"You know, it always seems that when things are going really well between us, you come along to fuck it all up!" I burst at Mencheres.

"You chose to come to Paris, of all places," Mencheres replied.

"So what? Got something against the French?" I felt a surge of irrational anger toward him. Inside me, a scream built. *Why can't you just leave us alone!*

Then I shook it off. What was wrong with me? Was I having a crazy case of PMS or something?

Mencheres rubbed his forehead. Those finely molded features were in profile as he looked away.

"Paris is a beautiful city. Enjoy it. See all the sights. But don't go anywhere unaccompanied, and if you dream of Gregor again, Cat, do not let him lay hands on you. If you see him in your dreams, run away."

"Um, no way are you going to get away with that vague, 'have a nice day' crap," I said. "Who is Gregor, why am I dreaming about him, and why is he called the Dreamsnatcher?"

"More importantly, why has he surfaced now to seek *her* out?" Bones's voice was cold as ice. "Gregor hasn't been seen or heard from in over a decade. I thought he might be dead."

"He's not dead," Mencheres said a trifle grimly. "Like me, Gregor has visions of the future. He intended to alter the future based on one of these visions. When I found out about it, I imprisoned him as punishment."

"And what does he want with *my wife*?"

Bones emphasized the words while arching a brow at me, as if daring me to argue. I didn't.

"He saw Cat in one of his visions and decided he had to have her," Mencheres stated in a flat tone. "Then he discovered she'd be blood-bound to you. Around the time of Cat's sixteenth birthday, Gregor intended to find her and take her away. His plan was very simple—if Cat had never met you, then she'd be his, not yours."

"Bloody sneaking bastard," Bones ground out, even as my jaw dropped. "I'll congratulate him on his cleverness—while I'm ripping silver through his heart."

"Don't underestimate Gregor," Mencheres said. "He managed to escape my prison a month ago, and I still don't know how. Gregor seems to be more interested in Cat than in getting revenge against me. She's the only person I know whom Gregor's contacted through dreams since he's been out."

Why do these crazy vampires keep trying to collect me? My being one of the only known half-breeds had been more of a pain than it was worth. Gregor wasn't the first vampire who thought it would be neat to keep me as some sort of exotic toy, but he did win points for cooking up the most original plan to do it.

"And you locked Gregor up for a dozen years just to keep him from altering my future with Bones?" I asked, my skepticism plain. "Why? You didn't do much to stop Bones's sire, Ian, when he tried the same thing."

Mencheres's steel-colored eyes flicked from me to Bones. "There was more at stake," he said at last. "If you'd never met Bones, he might have stayed under Ian's rule longer, not taking Mastership of his own line, and then not being co-Master of mine when I needed him. I couldn't risk that."

So it hadn't been about preserving true love at all. Figures. Vampires seldom did anything with purely altruistic motives.

"What happens if Gregor touches me in my dreams?" I asked, moving on. "What then?"

Bones answered me, and the burning intensity in his gaze could have seared my face.

"If Gregor takes ahold of you in your dreams, when you wake, you'll be wherever he is. That's why he's called the Dreamsnatcher. He can steal people away in their dreams."

Two

I'D ARGUED, OF COURSE. BOTH MEN GAVE ME looks that said how stupid it was to debate something they knew for a fact. Gregor's ability normally just worked with humans, since vampires and ghouls had a supernatural mind control that prevented such subconscious kidnappings. But since I was a half-breed, it was possible that Gregor's trick would work on me, too.

Wait until I told my uncle that there was a vampire who could do this. He'd shit himself.

"Gregor will attempt to coerce you in your dreams," Mencheres said in parting. "You would do well to ignore anything he says and to wake yourself up as quickly as possible."

"You can bet your ass on that," I muttered. "By the way, what's the significance of Paris? You said we'd chosen to come to Paris like that was significant."

"Gregor is French," was Mencheres's reply. "You

chose to visit his home of nearly nine centuries. I doubt that's a coincidence."

I bristled. "What are you implying?"

"The obvious," Bones said, almost yanking on my arm as we walked up to a picturesque chalet partially concealed by clinging vines. "Gregor told you to come here."

We were greeted by a lovely French couple, both vampires, who met us at the entrance with welcoming words I didn't understand. Bones spoke to them in the same language, his accent sounding as authentic as theirs.

"You didn't tell me you knew French," I murmured.

"You didn't tell me you'd had multiple dreams," he shot back in English.

He was still pissed. I sighed. At least we'd had a couple of peaceful weeks between us.

Introductions in English were made. Sonya and her husband, Noel, were our hosts for our stay in Paris.

"You're married?" I asked in surprise, then flushed. "I didn't mean to sound so shocked, I just—"

"You're the first bonded vampire couple she's met, *mes amis*," Bones smoothly filled in. "I think she was starting to believe she had a monopoly on the status."

They both laughed, and the awkward moment passed. Sonya never even batted an eye at the half dozen vampires who took up position around the perimeter of her home.

They showed us to our room, with views of the surrounding gardens. Sonya was a horticulturist. Her gardens could have been used as a blueprint for Eden.

"Diligence and patience, *ma chérie*," she said when I complimented her. "All things can benefit from the proper application of both."

She eyed Bones in a pointed way after she said it, letting me know she hadn't missed his earlier curt comment.

"My dear Sonya, I'll try to remember that," he replied dryly.

"You'll want to refresh yourselves and settle in, of course. Cat, there is fruit, cheese, and chilled wine. Bones, should I send someone up for you now, or later?"

"Later. First I must speak with my wife."

Again, his tone held a note of challenge when he said those two words. Sonya and Noel left. Before their footsteps faded away, Bones started in on me.

"Blast it, Kitten, I believed we were past this, yet once again you've decided what I can and cannot handle without discussing it with me."

Some of my remorse left me at his accusing tone. "I thought it was nothing, that's why I didn't tell you."

"Nothing? That's a fine way to describe a notorious vampire's attempts to steal you straight from our bed."

"I didn't realize that's what was happening!"

"You knew something was off, but you hid it from me. I thought you'd learned six years ago that hiding things from me was a mistake."

That was a low blow. Several months after we met, my inhuman status was blown when I was arrested for killing the governor of Ohio. I didn't know that Don, the FBI agent who interrogated me, was the brother of my deadbeat vampire father, who'd only impregnated my mother because he'd had sex with her so soon after turning. I also hadn't known that Don had been aware since my birth that I was a half-breed. I'd just thought Don was a high-ranking FBI agent who knew about vampires—and who'd kill Bones if I didn't take his offer to join Don's elite secret team.

So I tricked Bones and went away with Don, believing it was the only way to save his life. Bones didn't take being left behind very well. It took him over four years, but he found me, then he showed me how wrong I had been in thinking it was impossible for us to be together. I still had horrible guilt over what I'd done, and here he'd just shoved a hot poker in that old wound.

"How long are you going to punish me for that? If your last comment is any indicator, I guess I'll have this thrown up at me for years."

Some of the anger went out of his face. He ran a hand through his hair, giving me a frustrated—but less damning—look.

"Do you have any idea what I would have gone through, waking up to find you vanished without a trace? It would have driven me mad, Kitten."

I took a deep breath and let it out slowly. If I thought Bones could disappear on me in his sleep, taken by a strange vampire for unknown purposes, I'd lose all semblance of rationality, too. *Get it together, Cat. Now's not the time to keep score on remarks neither of you means.*

"Let's try to get past this, okay? I should have told you about the dreams. If they happen again, I'll tell you as soon as I wake up. Scout's honor."

He came to me, gripping my shoulders. "I couldn't stand to lose you like that, Kitten."

I covered his hands with mine. "You won't. I promise."

The Palais Garnier Opera house was extravagant in every detail, with an antique, old-world architecture that only came from being old-world. Sonya and Noel went with us, as well as our protective entourage. Bones was taking no chances of Gregor's showing up to crash the fun.

This was my first opera. Usually I didn't get to wear a pretty dress without someone to kill, but unless the opera was far more graphic than the brochure detailed, that wasn't happening tonight.

Bones received so many admiring looks on our way to the gilded entrance that my hand tightened on his. Granted, he looked spectacular in his black tuxedo, a white silk scarf draped around his neck, but did women have to *stare*? Most of the time, I pinched myself over his glittering gorgeousness, not quite believing someone so stunning could belong to me. Sometimes, however, the lustful glances thrown his way made me wish he wasn't such a damned bowl of eye candy.

"They're not staring at me, pet," Bones murmured. "They're looking at you. As I am."

I smiled at the leer he gave me. "It's just the dress," I teased. "The way it drapes makes my hips and boobs look bigger."

The vermillion taffeta gown did have extra swaths across my chest, hiding the light boning that held the strapless dress up. Then those swaths gathered at my hips before fanning out in a fishtail at the bottom of the long, narrow skirt. It was the fanciest thing I'd ever worn.

Bones gave a low chuckle. "I can't stop wondering how I'm going to take you whilst you're in it. Right now I've decided on from behind, although that may change by the end of the opera."

"Why did we go to this if you'll just be mentally molesting me and not watching the performance?"

"Because that's right fun in itself," he responded with a wicked grin. "I'll enjoy imagining all the things I'm going to do to you once we're alone."

Then he became more serious, and the gleam left his eyes. "Actually, I thought we'd see the opera, have a late supper, then stretch our legs exploring the city. Although we'll have our escorts following us, they shouldn't need to be strapped to our backsides, I suspect. Would you like that?"

My mouth dropped. Walking around without full body armor and a highly armed squad at my elbow? Just sightseeing, like normal people?

"Oui, sí, any language the word for yes is in. Please tell me you're not about to say 'psyche'."

"I'm not. The performance is about to start; let's find our seats."

"Okay."

"Very agreeable, aren't you?" That sly tone was back in his voice. "I'll take advantage of it later."

When the curtain came down at intermission, I knew three things: I loved the opera, I wanted a drink, and I had to pee.

"I'm going with you," Bones announced, when I voiced my bathroom necessity.

I rolled my eyes. "They have *rules* about that."

"I have to freshen my lipstick, Cat, would you mind if I accompany you?" Sonya asked. "Bones, you could fetch some champagne, I'd love a glass as well. It's across from the facilities, so you'll have no trouble finding us."

The translation was obvious. Bones would be close in case there was trouble of any kind, be it misguided dream suitor or murderous undead opera buff, and I'd have a bodyguard.

He nodded. "I can escort you. That's not being overprotective. It's only mannerly."

"Sure." My lips twitched. "Whatever you say."

There was a long line at the ladies' room. Bones let out an amused snort when he saw my speculative glance at the empty entrance to the men's facilities.

"They have *rules* about that," he mocked.

"I know all these chicks aren't waiting to let out their bladders, they should have a separate makeup room so the rest of us can pee," I grumbled, then turned to Sonya apologetically. "Um, I didn't mean you. Just ignore everything I say, we'll both be better off."

She laughed. "I know what you meant, *chérie*. Often I've thought the same myself, since the latrines have been of no use to me for a long time."

"Bring me some liquor, Bones, fast, to take my foot out of my mouth."

He kissed my hand. "I'll see you back here."

When he walked away, I wasn't the only one who enjoyed the view of him leaving.

"Mmm hmmm."

The low exhalation came from a brunette farther up in line. I gave her an arched brow and tapped my engagement ring for effect.

"Taken, honey."

She was human, or I'd have thrown down at the

second lingering look she gave Bones before shrugging at me.

"Nothing lasts forever."

My teeth ground. "Except death."

Sonya said something in French that made the woman's mouth curl sulkily before she turned away with a last parting shot.

"If you can't stand for your man to be admired, you would do better to keep him at home."

With her heavy French accent, her h's were almost silent. *You can't kill her just because she's a tramp,* I reminded myself. *Even if you* could *have her body discreetly disposed of . . .*

"He fucks even better than he looks," I settled on saying. Several heads turned. I didn't care; I was pissed. "And that beautiful face is going to be clamped between my legs as soon as we get *ooome,* don't you worry."

From the crowd at the bar, I heard Bones laugh. Sonya chuckled. The woman gave me a venomous glare and stepped out of line.

"*Bon,* one less person in front of us, we'll be finished before he has our drinks," Sonya observed when she quit laughing.

"One down." I eyed the line of women, most of whom either smiled or avoided my gaze due to that little scene. "About a dozen more to go."

Ten minutes later when we entered the bathroom, I was trying not to hop on one leg in impatience. It had been all I could do to wait my turn and not have Sonya use vampire mind control to get the other women out of my way, but that wouldn't have been fair.

When I came out, Sonya was putting her lipstick

back in her small clutch bag. I joined her by the mirror to wash my hands.

"Small world," someone said to my right.

I turned, noticing a cute blonde staring at me. "Excuse me?"

"You don't remember me?" She shook her head. "It was a while ago. I wasn't even sure it was you until you snapped at that woman, but your coloring stands out. Plus, you were antsy the first time we met, too."

From her accent, she was American. And I'd never seen her before in my life.

"I'm sorry, you have the wrong person." After all, I was good at placing people. Half-vampire memory skills, and it had come with my old job.

"It was at the Ritz on Place Vendôme, remember?" I still shook my head. She sighed. "No big deal. Sorry it didn't work out with the other guy, but you seem to have traded up, so good for you."

"Huh?"

Now I was wondering if she was crazy. Sonya moved closer to me. The girl dabbed powder on her nose before tucking her compact back in her purse.

"You looked way too young to get married anyway, so I don't blame you—"

"Huh?" With open incredulity.

She sighed. "Never mind. Nice to see you again."

She left the bathroom. Sonya started to grab her when I muttered, "Don't bother. She's just got the wrong person."

Pain went off in my head, like little needles were jabbing at my brain. I rubbed my temples.

"Are you well, *chérie*?" Sonya asked.

"Fine. She had the wrong person," I repeated. "After all, this is my first trip to Paris."

* * *

We walked along the Rue de Clichy with our body-guards trailing several paces behind us. I'd opted against a full dinner and just had a croissant and cappuccino at one of the many charming cafés lining the streets.

Sonya and Noel hadn't joined us, choosing to let us have our quasi privacy. It did seem kind of intimate, escort and hundreds of passersby notwithstanding. We were just another couple, one of countless, strolling the midnight streets of Paris.

Bones narrated along the way about buildings and structures still standing . . . and what they'd been before. He had me laughing at stories about him, his best friend Spade, and his sire Ian. I could just imagine the hell the three of them must have raised.

We stopped at the end of one of the long streets where the buildings were particularly close together. Bones called out something in French, then led me farther down the narrow alley.

"What did you just say?"

He smiled. "You'd rather not know."

Then he covered my mouth in a deep kiss and molded me to him. I gasped when I felt his hands bunching up my dress.

"Are you crazy? There are half a dozen vampires nearby—"

"None within eyesight," he cut me off with a chuckle. "As instructed."

"They can *hear*, Bones," I continued to object, facing the building as he spun me around.

He continued to laugh. "Then do be sure to say flattering things."

Bones had an arm around my waist, locking me

next to him. My squirming only ratcheted my dress
higher as his hands bunched it up. Then the sudden
pierce of his fangs into my neck made me freeze. A
low rumble of pleasure came from him.

"Ah, Kitten, you love that almost as much as I do.
Sink into me, luv, as I do the same."

The blood leaving me and spilling into him felt
like it was replaced by sweet fire. Bones was right; I
loved it when he bit me. My skin felt hot, my heartbeat quickened—and then I was rubbing against him
and moaning at the delay of his unzipping his pants.

"Bones," I managed. "Yes—"

The building hit me in the face so hard I felt my
cheek fracture. And then the gunfire registered.

It came in staccato bursts from above us, on all
sides . . . everywhere but from the building I was
mashed against. Bones had me pressed into the brick.
His body covered mine, and he was draped over me,
shuddering while he punched at the wall in front of
me. Trying to make a door where one didn't exist.

That's when I realized why he was shaking. He
was being strafed with bullets.

It sounded like our guards were taking even worse
treatment. From the intermittent spaces without
Bones jerking in reflex, they must have formed a perimeter around our crouched bodies. When a concentrated burst of gunfire ended with a scream cut off, I
started to struggle in a panic. It was much worse than
I'd thought. Whoever this was, they were firing silver
bullets.

"We have to run, God, this'll kill you!" I screamed,
attempting to unroll myself from the ball Bones had
me stuffed in. With his strength pinning me, I was
flapping uselessly like an upside-down turtle.

"If we run, they could cut you down," he rasped, almost inaudible over the racket of gunfire. "One of them will have called for backup. We'll wait. Mencheres will come."

"You'll be dead by then," I countered. It was hard to kill a vampire by gunfire, even with silver bullets, because it took too long to shred the heart. Bones had taught me that. *No vamp will sit still and pose for you . . .*

His words over six years ago, dismissing the use of guns as effective weapons. Yet Bones might as well be sitting still and posing for them. Backup would arrive too late. He had to know that, even as I did. For once, he was lying to me.

The building's frame gave where his fist hammered away. People inside screamed. Given time, Bones could tear through the structure, and we'd have a shelter from the pitiless firing. But pounding at it one-handed while being riddled with bullets? Bones was already moving slower, his punches taking on an almost drunken quality. God, he'd die crouched over me, right here on this street.

Something savage surged within me. There wasn't even a clear command my brain gave to my body. All I knew was Bones had to get away from those bullets long enough for him to heal.

With that goal in mind, I managed to maneuver around, then shot straight up with my arms locked around him. We made it to the top of the five-story building we'd been huddled against. Once we hit the roof, I rolled with him, but oddly, no bullets whizzed around us.

I didn't bother pondering why the gunmen weren't targeting us at the moment. Not when I felt Bones sag in my grip. Fear fueled me, sent me leaping onto the roof of the neighboring building with him. And then the next one and the next, not even taking the time to be amazed at what I'd just done. When the remaining gunfire sounded fainter, I stopped. With what I had to do, I'd drop like a stone, but Bones needed blood. A lot of it.

We weren't being chased by any flying assassins. Maybe our guards were holding them up for now, but that might not last. I grabbed Bones's slumped head and slashed my wrist on his fangs, letting my blood pour into his mouth.

For a frozen, petrifying second, nothing happened. He didn't swallow, open his eyes, or do anything but let the red liquid stream out of his mouth. Frantic, I used my other hand to work his jaw, forcing the blood down his throat. Tears blurred my eyes, because he had a mass of silver-filled holes all over him, even on his cheeks. *Oh God, please don't let him die . . .*

At last he swallowed. His eyes didn't open, but there was suction on my wrist that hadn't been there before. That suction grew, pulling the blood from my veins, and the relief crashing through me numbed the dizziness that followed. Mesmerized, I watched the holes in Bones start to swell, then the spent silver rounds expelled from his body. It made me smile even as the edges of my vision became fuzzy and faded just as Bones opened his eyes.

THREE

... waking up now ..."

"... will be leaving soon, he'll arrive tomorrow ..."

The snatches of conversation floated above me. I was warm. Well, everything but my arm. Something soft and cool brushed my forehead.

"Are you awake, Kitten?"

That snapped my eyes open, clearing the lethargy. I tried to sit up, but a firm grip prevented me.

"Don't move, luv, give the blood a few minutes to circulate."

Blood? With a few blinks, Bones focused into view. He still had red smears all over him, but his gaze was steady. That calmed me into sinking back where I'd been, which apparently was draped across his lap. Two empty plasma bags, a hypodermic needle, and a catheter were next to him.

"Where are we?"

"In a van on our way to London," he answered. "You remember the attack?"

"I remember seeing enough silver coming out of you to fund someone's college plans," I replied, glancing around to find Mencheres and four other vampires with us. "You could have been killed. Don't ever do that again."

A breath of laughter escaped him. "That's rich, coming from the woman who emptied nearly all of her blood into me."

"You had too much silver in you to heal. What was I supposed to do, sit back and watch you die?"

"And those gunmen might have blown your head off," was his even reply.

"Who were they? Did they get away?"

I touched my cheek. No pain. It hadn't just been human blood Bones had given me. I might heal faster than the average person, but only vampire blood could mend broken bones this fast.

"I'm sorry, luv," Bones murmured. "Almost got you killed, walking into a gauntlet in such a witless manner."

"How many died?"

"Three out of the six were killed."

There was more than self-blame and sadness in his voice, however. I couldn't pinpoint what.

"Ghouls attacked us, and they were bloody well armed, as you know. Right after you left with me, 'round eight other vampires joined into the fight."

"At least help did come." I smiled at Mencheres. "Thank you."

Bones's mouth twisted. "It wasn't Mencheres's people who came to our aid. Our rescuers likely would have attacked me next if Mencheres hadn't finally arrived with backup."

Maybe the new blood hadn't reached my brain yet,

because I didn't understand. "If they weren't your people, whose were they?"

"We were being followed by two sets of people," Bones summed it up. "Those ghouls, and Gregor's people, I suspect. He must have gotten tired of trying to reach you through dreams and decided on the more physical form of a kidnapping."

It didn't escape my notice that Mencheres hadn't said a word. "What's your take on this?"

He glanced at me. "When we arrive at Spade's, we'll be in better surroundings to continue this conversation."

"Now." One word from Bones, spoken with the resolution of a thousand.

"Crispin—"

"And now you address me by my human name, as if I were still that lad," Bones interrupted. "I am your equal under our alliance, so you will tell me everything you know about Gregor."

Bones was daring Mencheres to start a civil war within their ranks by refusing. I hadn't expected Bones to draw a line in the sand like that and practically piss on it, and from Mencheres's startled expression, he hadn't, either.

Then Mencheres gave a thin smile. "All right. I told you I locked Gregor away for planning to interfere with Cat's future so she'd never meet you. What I didn't say was that Gregor had already taken Cat away with him before I captured him."

I jumped up. "I've never met Gregor before in my life!"

"That you *remember*," Mencheres replied. "You feel pains in your head when you hear of Gregor, right? Those are the stabs of your repressed memory. You'd been with Gregor for weeks before we found the two of you in Paris. By then, he'd managed to infatuate you and confuse you with lies. I knew I had to alter your recollection to fix things, which is why you have no memory of your time with him."

"That can't . . . but he can't . . ." There went the hammers in my skull. *He is not your husband . . . Sorry it didn't work out with that other guy . . . it was at the Ritz on Place Vendôme . . .*

"But vampire mind control doesn't work on me," I finally sputtered. "I'm a half-breed; it's never worked on me!"

"That's why I was the only one who could do it," Mencheres said quietly. "It took all my power, plus a spell, to erase that time from your mind. A lesser vampire couldn't have managed it."

Bones appeared stunned as well. "*Partir de la femme de mon maître*," he murmured. "That's what one of Gregor's vampires yelled at me before he ran. So that's why Gregor is so obsessed with her."

Mencheres was silent. Bones glanced at him, then at me.

"I don't care," he said at last. "Gregor can shove his claims straight up his arse."

I still wasn't convinced. "But I hated vampires before Bones. I would never have gone away with one for weeks."

"You hated them because of your mother's influence," Mencheres said. "Gregor dealt with her first, compelling her to tell you he was a friend of hers who would protect you."

Bones growled. "How far has word of Gregor's claim spread?"

Mencheres considered him. "You haven't asked me if it happened yet."

I felt like they were speaking another language. "What?"

"Doesn't matter. He'll only get her over my dried, withered corpse."

"What!" Now I jabbed Bones for emphasis.

"Gregor's claim," Bones said icily. "Now that he's free, he's telling people that sometime during those weeks you were together, he married you."

Contrary to popular belief, there *have* been a few times in my life I've been speechless. At sixteen, when my mother told me all my oddities were due to my father being a vampire, that was one. Seeing Bones again after four years of absence, that was another. This topped both of them, however. For a space of several frozen moments, I couldn't wrap my mind around a vehement enough denial.

I wasn't the only one goggle-eyed. Even in my state, I noticed the other vampires in the van wearing astonished expressions that quickly turned blank after whatever evil glare Bones gave them. Mencheres continued with his same, uncompromising stare, and finally, I voiced the first coherent thought that came to mind.

"No." Just saying it made me feel better, so I repeated it, louder. "No. It's not true."

"Even if it were, it won't last beyond his death," Bones promised.

I gestured to Mencheres. "You were there, right? Tell him it didn't happen!"

Mencheres shrugged. "I didn't see a blood-binding ceremony. Gregor claimed it occurred right before I arrived. A few of his people said they'd witnessed it, but they could have been lying, and Gregor's honesty is not without fault."

"But what did *I* say?"

All at once I was afraid. Had I somehow bound myself to an unknown vampire? I couldn't have, right?

Mencheres's eyes bored into mine. "You were hysterical. Gregor had manipulated your emotions, and he was being taken away to an unknown punishment. You would have said anything, true or not, to prevent it."

In other words . . .

"Bones has stated his position in this matter." Mencheres flicked his gaze around the van. "I support it as his co-ruler. Does anyone have a differing opinion?"

There were instant denials.

"Then this is settled. Gregor has an unsubstantiated claim, and it will be ignored. Cat cannot confirm the binding herself, and she is the only other person who would know if it occurred. Bones?"

A sudden grin flashed across his face, but it was as cold as I felt inside. "Let's see how long someone lasts if they suggest that my wife is not *my wife*."

"As you wish." Mencheres was unperturbed about the potential thinning of the herd. "We will arrive at Spade's before dawn. I, for one, am tired."

That made two of us. But I doubted I could sleep. Finding out that over a month of my life had been ripped from my memory made me feel violated. I stared at Mencheres. *No wonder I've always had a problem with you.* On some subconscious level, my instincts must have remembered that he'd manipulated me against my will, even if the exact memory of that event was lost.

Or was it?

"Why can't you just look into my mind and see what happened for yourself? You erased my memory, can't you bring it back?"

"I buried it beyond even my reach, so as to be sure it stayed forgotten."

Great. If Mega-Master Mencheres couldn't pry it out, then it must *really* be lost.

"I don't care what Gregor or anyone else believes," Bones said in a softer tone to me. "All I care about is what you think, Kitten."

What did I think? That I was even more fucked up than previously believed. Having a month of my life forcibly removed regarding a stranger I might or might not have married? Hell, where did I start?

"I wish people would just leave us alone," I said. "You remember when it was just the two of us in a big dark cave? Who knew that would be the most uncomplicated time of our lives?"

FOUR

Baron Charles DeMortimer, who re-
named himself Spade so he'd never forget how
he'd once been a penal colony prisoner addressed
only by the tool he'd been assigned, had an amazing home. His house was a sweeping estate with im-
maculate lawns and high perimeter hedges. With its
eighteenth-century-style architecture, it looked like
it was built while Spade had been human. Inside,
there were long, grand hallways. Ornate woodwork
along the walls. Painted ceilings. Crystal chandeliers. Handwoven tapestries and antique furnishings. A fireplace you could hold a meeting in.

"Where's the queen?" I muttered irreverently after
a doorman had let us in.

"Not your taste, luv?" Bones asked with a knowing
look.

Not nearly. I'd been brought up in rural Ohio,
where my Sunday best would have been a dishrag in
comparison to the fabric on the settee we just passed.

"Everything is so perfect. I'd feel like I was desecrating something if I sat on it."

"Then perhaps I should rethink your bedchamber, see if we have something more comfortable in the stables," a voice teased.

Spade appeared, his dark, spiky hair tousled as if he'd recently been in bed.

Open mouth, insert foot. "Your home is *lovely*," I said. "Don't mind me. I'll get manners when pigs fly."

Spade hugged Bones and Mencheres in welcome before taking my hand and, oddly, kissing it. He wasn't usually that formal.

"Pigs don't fly." His mouth quirked. "Though I've been informed that you found wings earlier tonight."

The way he said it made me self-conscious. "I didn't fly. I just jumped really high. I don't even know how I did it."

Bones gave me a look I couldn't read. Spade opened his mouth to say something, but Mencheres held up his hand.

"Not now."

Spade clapped Bones on the back. "Quite right. It's nearly dawn. I'll show you to your room. You're pale, Crispin, so I'm sending someone up for you."

"If I'm pale, it has little to do with lack of blood," Bones said in a bleak tone. "When I came to, she'd drained most of her blood into me. If Mencheres hadn't arrived with those plasma bags, she might have changed over before she was ready."

We followed Spade up the stairs. "Hers isn't just human blood, as has been more than evidenced, so I'm still sending someone up."

"I have other things on my mind than feeding."

Spade hadn't heard yet about the cherry on the sundae of our evening. He only knew about the ghoul attack.

The door opened into a spacious bedroom with period pieces of furniture, a canopied bed Cinderella might have slept in, after the Prince carried her away, of course, and another large fireplace. A glance at the wall enclosing the bathroom showed it was made entirely of hand-painted stained glass. Once again I was struck with unease about touching anything. Even the silk-stitched blankets on the bed looked too beautiful to sleep under.

Bones had none of my qualms. He threw off his jacket to reveal the bullet-riddled shirt and pants he still wore, kicked off his shoes, and flopped into a nearby chair.

"You look like a piece of Swiss cheese," Spade commented.

"I'm knackered, yet you need to be informed of something."

Spade cocked his head. "What?"

In a few brief, succinct sentences, Bones outlined the revelation of those lost weeks when I was sixteen . . . and Gregor's claims that I was his wife, not Bones's.

Spade didn't say anything for a minute. His brows drew together until, finally, he let out a low hiss.

"Blimey, Crispin."

"I'm sorry."

I mumbled it while I looked away from Bones in his bullet-pocked, ruined clothes. *All because of you,* my conscience mocked.

"Don't you dare apologize," Bones said at once.

"You didn't ask to be born the way you were, and you didn't ask Gregor to pursue you so ruthlessly. You owe *no one* an apology."

I didn't believe that, but I didn't argue. It would take up more energy than either one of us had.

Instead, I masked my thoughts behind a wall, something I'd perfected in the past year. "Spade's right, more blood would be good for you. I'll take a shower, and you can drink from whatever bar's open."

Spade gave a nod of approval. "Then it's settled. Some items that should fit you have already been placed in here, Cat, and for you, Crispin. Mencheres, I'll show you to your room, then we'll sort out the rest of this kettle later."

Death chased me. It kept tireless pursuit through the narrow streets and cramped alleys I ran along. With every panting breath, I screamed for help, but I knew with horrible certainty that there was no escape.

There was something familiar about these streets, even deserted as they were. Where had everyone gone? Why wouldn't anyone help me? And the fog . . . damn that fog. It had me stumbling on concealed objects and seemed to cling to my feet when I dashed through it.

"Over here . . ."

I knew that voice. I turned in its direction, doubling my efforts to run toward the sound. Behind me, Death muttered curses, keeping pace. Every so often, claws would swipe into my back, making me scream from fear and pain.

"Just a little farther."

The voice urged me toward a shadow-draped figure that appeared at the end of an alley. As soon as I saw him, Death fell behind, dropping back several paces. With every lengthened stride separating me from the evil that chased me, relief spread through me. *Don't worry, I'm almost there. . .*

The shadows fell from the man. Features solidified, revealing thick brows over gray-green eyes, a crooked patrician nose, full lips, and ash-blond hair. A scar ran zigzag from his eyebrow to his temple, and shoulder-length hair blew in the breeze.

"Come to me, *chérie*."

A warning clicked in my mind. All at once, the empty cityscape around us disappeared. There was nothing but the two of us and oblivion on all sides.

"Who are you?"

This didn't feel right. Part of me wanted to fling myself forward, but another piece was cringing back.

"You know me, Catherine."

That voice. Familiar, yet utterly unknown. *Catherine. No one called me that anymore . . .*

"Gregor."

As soon as his name came out of my mouth, my confusion was broken. This must be him, and that meant I was dreaming. And if I was dreaming . . .

I stopped just short of his outstretched hands and backed up. Motherfucker, I'd almost run right into his arms.

His face twisted in frustration, then he took a step toward me. "Come to me, my wife."

"No way. I know what you're trying to do, Dreamsnatcher."

My voice was my own again. Hard. With every word I retreated, mentally railing at myself to wake up. *Open your eyes, Cat! Wakey, wakey!*

"You know only what they've told you."

His accent was French, no surprise there, and the words were resonating. Even dreaming, I had a sense of his power. *Oh, shit, you're not a weak little hallucination, are you? Stay back, Cat. This puppy bites.*

"I know enough."

He laughed in challenge. "Do you, *chérie*? Did they tell you they stole me from your memory because that was the only way they could keep you from me? Did they tell you they dragged you screaming from my arms, pleading that you didn't want to leave?"

He kept coming closer, but I kept backing away. Figures—in this dream, I wasn't armed.

"Something like that. But I'm not your wife."

Gregor stalked nearer. He was a tall man, almost six-five, and there was a beautiful cruelty to his features that was amplified when he smiled.

"Wouldn't you like to know for yourself instead of being told what to believe?"

I regarded him with more than suspicion. "Sorry, buddy, the trash has already been taken to the curb in my mind. Mencheres can't pry back the lid to see what's inside, and it's only your word that says we're married."

"They can't give you back your memories." Gregor stretched out his hands. "I can."

Gregor will attempt to coerce you in your dreams. Mencheres's admonition rang in my mind. He hadn't been wrong.

"Liar."

I spun around, sprinting in the opposite direction, only to have Gregor appear in front of me like he'd been magically transposed.

"I'm not lying."

My gaze flicked around, but there was only useless pale fog. I had to wake up. If this guy got his hand on me, I might find myself waking up in a load of trouble.

"Look, Gregor, I know Mencheres locked you up for a long time, and you're pissed about that, but let's be reasonable. I'm blood-bound to the man I love, and there are plenty of fish in the sea. Let's say *adieu*, then you can go find another girl to dreamsnatch."

His gold head shook sadly. "This isn't you talking. You didn't want to be a killer, to spend your whole life looking over your shoulder. I can take it back, Catherine. You had a choice before. You chose me. Take my hand. I'll return what you've lost."

"No." I heard a noise behind me, like a low snarl. Fear tickled up my spine. Death had come for me again.

Gregor's hands clenched, as if he heard it as well.

"Now, Catherine, you have to come to me now!"

The growls were louder. Death was behind me, Gregor in front of me, and I had to go to one of them. Why couldn't I wake up? What had woken me the last time? I'd been running, then, too, chased by a monster . . .

I whirled, ignoring Gregor's shout, and ran headlong into the horrid figure of Death. Either this would work or—

A slap stung my face, then another. I was being shaken so hard, my teeth should have rattled out. Bones was talking to me, so engrossed in shaking me that it took my third yelp to get his attention.

"Stop it!"

"Kitten?"

He gripped my face, eyes bright green and wild. I batted at his hands, shivering, and realized I was wet. And cold. And sore. With an audience.

"What have you been *doing* to me?"

I was on the floor, Bones was next to me, and from the soaked carpet, various items nearby, and worried spectators, I'd been out for a while. A glance down told me what I already suspected. I was still as naked as I'd been when we fell asleep.

"God, Bones, why don't we just invite everyone in the next time we have sex, that way they can stop seeing things piecemeal!"

Spade, at least, wasn't nude like he'd been the last time I'd wakened from a nightmare to an audience. Next to him stood Mencheres and an unknown human woman.

"Bloody hell, if I never go through this again, it will be too soon," Bones growled, running a weary hand through his hair. "This wasn't like the other ones, Mencheres. What does that mean?"

Bones was totally unconcerned about being naked. Vampires had *no* sense of modesty. I grabbed for the nearest covering, which was the bedspread, and tugged at his hand.

"Find some pants for you and a robe for me. What—?"

Just the act of moving made pain arc on my back, then intensify into a steady throbbing. My mouth tasted like blood, too, and my head was pounding.

Mencheres knelt next to me. "Do you remember anything about the dream, Cat?"

Clothes. Now, I thought at Bones.

He muttered, "Who cares?" but yanked on a pair of pants and fetched me a robe.

"Here," Bones said, slicing open his hand before clapping it over my mouth. "Swallow."

I sucked at the wound, ingesting his blood, and felt immediate relief from the pains in my body. Then I sat on the bed, where the sight of the floor where I'd been lying made me let out a gasp.

"What in the *hell* were you doing to me?"

"Trying to wake you," Bones answered crisply. "I cut you, threw water on you, slapped you, and set a lighter to your legs. For future reference, which one of those do you think worked?"

"Good *God*," I hissed. "No wonder I thought you were Death incarnate in my dream, and that made me run *toward* Gregor at first!"

"Then you remember the dream," Mencheres stated. "That bodes ill."

The fear of that made my reply snappy. "Hey, Walks Like An Egyptian, how about for once you drop the formal stuff and talk like you live in the twenty-first century?"

"The shit's gonna splatter, start buggin', yo," Mencheres responded instantly.

I stared at him, then burst out laughing, which was highly inappropriate considering the very grave warning he'd just conveyed.

"I find nothing funny in this," Bones muttered.

"Oh, neither do I, but that's still hilarious," I managed. "Sorry about the carpet, Spade. Blood, burns, water . . . maybe you *should* have put us in the stable."

"As I was saying," Mencheres continued, "this bodes poorly."

He gave me a look that dared me to comment. I didn't, my lips still twitching. "You remembered the dream, and you weren't susceptible to outside stimulants, which means Gregor is close by. You need to leave at once."

Bones swung a glance at Spade. "Did you tell anyone we were coming?"

Spade shook his head. "Bugger, Crispin, I barely had notice myself. You're my best friend, and my home wasn't that far from you. It could just be a logical assumption."

"Possibly." Bones didn't sound convinced. "Or perhaps we weren't as careful as we thought and were followed."

"I'll have the car brought 'round, mate."

"Three of them." Bones cast a measured look at me. "All traveling in different directions, with a human and at least two vampires in each. Let whoever might be watching figure out which one carries her."

"You'll need more than evasiveness to fix this."

The sarcastic part of me had an idea. *Let Gregor spend some time with me, that'll cure him of wanting me in his life.* Trouble followed me like a bad smell.

But I just smiled with false brightness. "Spade, love your home. Mencheres . . . classic. Bones." The clock showed nine A.M. I'd only had two hours' sleep, but damned if I was going to get any more shut-eye. "Ready when you are."

"Right now, luv." He threw some clothes at me, pulling a shirt over his head without even glancing at it. "As soon as you get dressed."

Five

THE PLANE TOUCHED DOWN JERKILY. It didn't bother me, but I saw Bones compress his lips into a thin line. He didn't like to fly. If he could've managed the distance, I think he would have tried to talk me into flying the *really* friendly skies. The one where I was strapped to his chest with him as my own private airplane. Still, everyone had limits.

We boarded a mere three hours after we left Spade's house. My uncle Don pulled some strings after I called him and informed him that we had to return to the States right away, so the full flight from London to Orlando suddenly had four more seats. Having a family member with high-up government connections came in handy sometimes.

Mencheres and Spade stayed in London, but two vampires named Hopscotch and Band-Aid came along with us. To kill some time, I'd asked them how they'd chosen their nicknames. Hopscotch, an Aborigine who knew Bones over two hundred years, said that it had been his adopted child's favorite game. Band-Aid had grinned and said he'd picked his name because he was ouchless. I didn't press for more details from him on that.

We were the first ones off the plane, ushered outside by the flight attendants. The plane wasn't even hooked up to the terminal yet. Instead, we got off on one of the tall transport ladders usually reserved for service workers. A limousine was parked nearby, and the window rolled down to reveal my uncle.

I hadn't seen him in a couple months. When his lined face curved into a smile, it struck me how much I'd missed him.

"I thought I'd surprise you."

Bones cast a watchful eye around before leading me to the vehicle. Band-Aid and Hopscotch circled, sniffing the air like bloodhounds while we ducked inside. Then they followed after us and took the opposite seats.

On impulse I hugged Don, startling both of us. When I let him go, I heard a familiar voice from the front.

"*Querida*, no kiss for your hombre?"

"Juan?" I laughed. "Don's got you on chauffeur duty?"

"I'd drive a tractor to see you." He grinned, turning around. "I missed your smile, your face, your round luscious—"

"Drive, mate," Bones cut him off. "We're in a hurry."

Don looked taken aback at Bones's brusqueness. Normally Bones and Juan were quite chummy, all hierarchy aside, since Bones had turned Juan into a vampire last year and thus Juan was under Bones's line. Juan also seemed surprised at Bones's curt comment, since he always flirted with me—and any female within a hundred yards—but Juan didn't say anything. With a last, quick grin at me, he drove off.

"I asked you to have a safe car waiting for us in a low-profile manner." Bones started in on my uncle. "Instead, you parked a limousine straight up to a plane. What were you thinking?"

Don tugged his eyebrow. "Wait two minutes, then see if you should criticize."

"We're both just tired," I said, then thought to Bones, *No one even knows we're back in the States. Quit biting people's heads off.* But I squeezed his hand at the same time, promising him silently that we'd both feel better once we got where we were going.

"I'm rather testy, Don, forgive me for barking at you," Bones said, curling his fingers around mine in acknowledgment. "You, too, Juan, but do me a favor. Keep your compliments to a minimum. I'm afraid it's a sore subject at present."

"Bueno, pero cuál es el problema?"

"English," I reminded Juan.

"He wants to know what the problem is, luv." Bones leaned back and tapped my hip. "Seat belt. All I need is for you to be injured in a car accident."

I clipped the buckle into place. "Happy?"

A black limousine whizzed by us. Then another. And another. I looked out the back window in amazement, seeing a line of at least a dozen limousines all on the outbound road we traveled on.

"The cast of the new Miramax movie just got clearance to leave the airport." Don gave a last, satisfied tweak of his brow. "Poor people, they were held up at Security. They've been waiting for hours."

Bones started to smile. "Crafty old spider, aren't you?"

"I've had practice hiding her, if you recall."

A derisive snort came from Bones. "Yeah, I remember it well."

"Play nice," I said. A pissing contest between them was the last thing we needed.

Bones gave my fingers a squeeze. "Don't fret, I've moved past my anger with him. In fact, he might be useful. So tell me, old chap, do any of your barmy scientists have a pill that prevents someone from dreaming?"

Don listened in morbid fascination as I described what was going on with Gregor, my potential past with him, and why he was called the Dreamsnatcher. When I was finished answering all his questions, two hours had gone by, and my uncle almost looked ill.

"Juan, pull off at the next exit, we have another transport waiting for us at the Shell station," Bones directed him. "Kitten, you'll only have a few minutes before we're off again."

"I'll see what I can do about pills for Cat," Don said once he'd recovered. "I should be able to have something made that could help."

Juan exited off the interstate and pulled up to the first gas station on the right, which was a Shell.

"Ah, here we are. Juan, *vaya con dios*, and Don"— Bones held out his hand—"take care of yourself."

Don shook Bones's hand. "I'll have those pills researched immediately."

I gave my uncle a hug goodbye, even though we weren't big on displays of affection for each other. Still, who knew when I'd see him again? Aside from my mother, Don was all the family I had.

"Thanks for coming along for the ride, Don. It must have played hell with your schedule."

"My appointments could wait until later." Don squeezed my shoulder. "Be careful, Cat."

"I promise."

Hopscotch and Band-Aid were the first out of the car. They did a quick perusal of the gas station's perimeter, then indicated with a thumbs-up that it seemed clear. Bones went over to a maroon SUV, exchanging a greeting with the driver. Must be our new ride.

I got out and went around to the driver's side of the limo. "No hug, buddy?"

Juan put the vehicle in park but kept the motor running, climbing out to give me a bear hug devoid of his usual ass-grab. "*Hombre* is in a foul mood," he murmured.

"He just hasn't slept. We'll be fine."

"Kitten." Bones tapped his foot. "Very out in the open here. Let's not linger."

"Right." I gave Juan one last smile. "Stay out of trouble."

"You too, *querida*."

I headed toward the door marked WOMEN on the exterior of the gas station, giving Bones a mental directive that he didn't need to stand guard outside the bathroom. The interior was gross, in a word, but I didn't have much choice. If I really never wanted to grace a public bathroom again, I'd change into a vampire. Since I'd chosen to remain half-human, there was no one but myself to blame for the inconveniences that involved.

By the time we crossed the twenty-two-mile bridge leading to New Orleans, it was evening again. I'd

never been here before since it hadn't been necessary during my tenure with Don. The Big Easy might
not be low on crime, but surprisingly enough, they
seemed to be of the human persuasion, not rogue
vampires or ghouls.

Bones refused to nap during the five-hour drive
from Tallahassee to New Orleans. My guess was he
was afraid I'd nod off if he wasn't watching me like
a hawk. Hopscotch drove, with Band-Aid in the passenger seat. As we crossed the bridge, I finally asked
why we were paying a visit to the famous city.

"I need to speak with the Queen of Orleans," Bones
replied. "She'd be a powerful ally to have on our side
if things escalate with Gregor, but she doesn't fancy
phone calls when someone's asking for her assistance."

"Another queen?" Europe had less royalty than the
undead.

He cast me a sideways look. "New Orleans's queen
is Marie Laveau, though she goes by the name Majestic now. Marie's one of the most powerful ghouls
in the nation. Those rumors of voodoo? They weren't
rumors, pet."

I didn't like the sound of this. The last queen I'd
met with mystical powers had almost killed all of us.
Women were scarier than men, in my opinion.

"Is it safe to see her if she's into the dark arts and
all that?"

"Marie holds herself to a very strict etiquette. If she
grants you a visit, you have safe passage to, during,
and from that visit. She may tell you she'll slaughter
you first chance she gets afterward, but she'll let you
walk out unharmed. Then, of course, it's a right fine
idea to keep walking."

"*She* might be a polite hostess, but what about every other pulseless person in the city? You know, 'Oops, Majestic, I offed some tourists'?"

Bones gave a grim snort. "There is no 'oops' with Marie. If she sides with us, no one will dare attack within the Quarter. Even Gregor."

"Are we staying at a hotel?"

"I have a house here, but I seldom use it anymore. An old friend lives there, keeps things tidy. Not sure how long we'll stay since my meeting with Marie hasn't been scheduled yet. Marie prefers to have people here if she decides to see them."

The streets grew narrower. By the time we approached the French Quarter, they were all one-way. Brick and stone replaced stucco and plaster as the city seemed to age in an instant. Yet the most striking feature had nothing to do with architecture.

"Bones." My head whipped around in amazement. "My God, look at them . . ."

His lip quirked. "Quite something, aren't they? Don't strike up a conversation with any of them; they'll talk your bloody ear off."

The ghosts were everywhere. Hovering over the rooftops, strolling down the sidewalks, sitting on benches next to (or on top of) unwitting tourists. As we stopped at a red light, our car was next to a group of people on a tour, ironically about the haunted history of New Orleans. I watched as three spirits argued over the errors in the guide's narration. One of the ghosts was so incensed, he kept flying through the tour guide's midsection, causing the man to burp over and over. Poor bastard probably thought he had indigestion. What he had was a pissed-off spook in his gut.

I'd seen ghosts before, but never in such magnitude. Somehow, with the vibe the place gave off, apparent even through the car, they seemed to belong here.

"It's beautiful," I said at last. "I love it."

That made Bones smile, easing the strain from his face. "Ah, Kitten, I thought you would."

The SUV stopped at an intersection past the busiest part of the Quarter. Bones leapt out and came to my side of the vehicle, holding the door open.

"We're here."

Rows of what appeared to be town houses dotted the street, but few had front doors.

"It's the way they were designed," Bones replied to my mental questions, as Band-Aid drove away, and Hopscotch stayed with us. "Creole families found them pretentious. You enter through the side."

He went through a gate at the entrance to a narrow alley and opened a door along the wall. I followed Bones inside, struck by how opulent the interior was in comparison to the somewhat grungy exterior.

"Liza," Bones called out. "We're here."

I whirled, polite smile in place, to see a girl coming down the staircase.

"How lovely to meet you, chère," she greeted me in a lightly accented voice.

"Um . . ." I held out my hand, tripping over my reply. Liza was a ghoul, so she probably had socks older than me, but good God, she looked about fourteen in human years.

Her hand was thin and delicate, like the rest of her. Liza was five-two, if I wanted to round up, and had to weigh no more than ninety pounds soaking wet. Black hair that looked too heavy for her swayed when she stepped up to Bones.

"Mon cher . . ."

One glance at her face when she looked at him was all I needed to confirm my suspicion of their former relationship. *You're a pig, Bones. I always suspected it, but this is absolute proof.*

Bones hugged her. Liza practically disappeared in his arms, but I caught a glimpse of her face. A beatific smile lit her features. She was pretty, I realized. I hadn't caught that at first.

He released her, and she backed away, returning her attention to me.

"I have food prepared for you, Cat, and coffee. It was my guess you would prefer caffeine?"

"Yeah, a lot of it." If I hadn't been so tired, I'd have already hit Bones. She didn't even look old enough to see an R-rated movie. "Thank you."

I suppressed an urge to tell Liza to sit down, before the air-conditioning blew her over. Instead of the usual, instant dislike I felt for any woman Bones had slept with, I had a strangely protective feeling about Liza, absurd as that was. One, she was dead, so she didn't need my protection. Two, judging from the discreet flashes of her gaze at Bones, she was in love with him.

Pedophile!

"Liza, would you please inform Cat how old you were when you were changed?" Bones asked, giving me a pointed look. "I'm about to be assaulted because of a misassumption."

She laughed, a shy series of sounds. "I was seventeen. I think if I'd been human, I would have been referred to as a 'late bloomer.'"

"Oh." At least that wasn't a felony in current times, and from Liza's vibe, that would have been legal back when she was alive. "Why didn't you wait to change over, then?"

Something in Liza's face clouded. "I couldn't. I'd been poisoned and was already dead. I'm only here now because I'd drunk vampire blood that same day. My family shipped me home for burial. After my body arrived, Bones broke me out of my grave and raised me as a ghoul."

"Oh!" Now I felt even more like a bitch. "Sorry. Whoever it was, I hope he killed the hell out of them."

She smiled in a sad way. "It was accidental. A doctor gave me the poison, thinking he was treating me. Medicine's come a long way since 1831."

"Speaking of medicine, we should call Don. Maybe he has something for me."

"Are you ill?" Liza looked surprised.

"She's not," Bones stated. "Has rumor of Gregor's claims reached here yet?"

Liza shot a quick glance to me. "Yes."

"Right, then." Bones sounded even wearier. "Means Marie would have heard them as well." He strode to a phone and started punching numbers into the line. After a second, he began speaking in a language that didn't sound French, but close. Creole, maybe?

Of course, that meant I didn't understand a friggin' word.

"He's telling the person who he is, and that he desires a conference with Majestic," Liza translated, guessing my frustration. "He's saying he wants it with all haste . . . they've put him on hold, I think . . ." Made sense, Bones wasn't talking. His fingers drummed on his leg as the seconds ticked by, and then he began again. "Yes . . . yes . . . He's agreeing to wait for a call back."

Bones hung up. "No need for me to reiterate. Now you can ring your uncle, luv. Do it from your cell, I don't want to occupy this line."

He was almost curt. I reminded myself that he was suffering from jet lag, lack of sleep, and no small amount of stress. While Bones filled in Liza on details concerning Gregor, I dialed Don. By the time I hung up, Don had given me instructions on the dosage of a medication and promised to have it sent immediately to me.

"Don made something for me," I said as soon as I hung up. "It's supposed to knock me from consciousness straight into deep sleep, skipping REM. But it only lasts about seven hours, so then you have to counter its effects by giving me blood to wake me. That way I don't go into a lighter, REM sleep when it wears off."

An expression of relief washed over Bones. "Makes me glad I didn't kill that chap when we met like I wanted to. That's excellent news, Kitten. I didn't think I could stand to let you fall asleep, wondering if you'd disappear from my sight even as I held you."

The emotion in his tone dissolved my earlier irritation at him. If the shoe were on the other foot, and it were Bones who could vanish, yeah, I'd be spitting nails, too.

"I'm not going to disappear." I went to him and wrapped my arms around him.

Then Liza's phone rang.

Six

I WANDERED AROUND THE TOWN HOUSE, struck by its size. It had a beautiful interior, wrought-iron balconies, and three levels. The walls were painted in strong hues, with white elaborate crown molding. All the bathrooms I'd seen were marble. In short, it was rich and tasteful without making me afraid to sit on the eighteenth-century chairs.

Pieces of Bones's influence were seen amidst the feminine touches. A collection of silver knives. Couches that cradled instead of cramped. Of course, I had time to notice such things. He'd left to see Marie without me.

His announcement that he was going alone sent me into a sputtering, livid objection that had Liza hurrying from the room. Bones took my anger in silence, waiting until I'd finished to flatly refuse to take me. He said my presence would distract Marie from hearing him out, or some crap like that.

I didn't believe him for a moment. Bones was just trying to protect me again. If I wasn't going, no matter his claims of "safe passage," then it meant his meeting with her was dangerous. Still, it boiled down to either physically wrestling with him when it was time for him to leave or letting him go with promises of payback. I chose the latter.

So, after I wandered around the house, I took a bath in a claw-footed tub. Then I put on a lace robe and began roaming the house again, looking for a washer and dryer. I didn't have clean clothes to wear, and nothing of Liza's would fit me. It was too early to buy something new, either. The only thing still open after three in the morning was the bars.

When Bones returned, it was almost dawn. He came through the door, pausing at the sight of Liza and me. We were on the floor, and I was braiding her hair. While he'd been gone, I'd struck up a conversation with Liza. She seemed to be a truly nice person, and I'd come to like her with surprising quickness. I gave Bones a single, lasered glance even as I melted with relief that he was safe, then resumed my attention to Liza's hair.

"Your hair is gorgeous. So thick. You should grow it until you trip over it."

"I see the two of you are getting on," Bones said with faint astonishment. "Aren't you going to ask me how it went, Kitten?"

"You walked in and took the stairs one at a time," I answered. "And you haven't barked at me to get in the car, so I take it Majestic didn't tell you our asses were trophies for hunting season. Am I wrong?"

His lip curled. "Still brassed off at me, I see. Then

you should enjoy this—Marie wants to meet you, and she refuses to let me be present when she does."

I laughed with a sharp, self-satisfied guffaw.

"God, Bones, you must have argued yourself blue in the face. Hell, I like her already."

"Thought you'd fancy that." His expression told me how unamusing he found it. "Should I leave you to your braiding and take myself to bed? You seem to find Liza's company preferable to mine."

"Really annoying when you have to sit back and twiddle your thumbs while the person you love goes off into danger, isn't it?" I said, not feeling guilty in the least.

"I didn't relish the thought of leaving you behind," he shot back. "Yet you're almost cackling over your chance to do the same to me."

Liza's head swiveled back and forth between the two of us. Since I still had three of her braids in my hands, however, that made it more difficult.

"You didn't care how I felt, as long as I stayed behind," I flared, the tension from the past several days catching up with me. "So yeah, I'm enjoying the payback. Guess that makes me shallow."

"It makes you a spiteful brat," Bones snapped, striding forward until he loomed over me. "What say you to that?"

I dropped Liza's braids and got to my feet. So the gloves were off, huh? "That it takes one to know one. What's the matter? Are you mad that you sauntered in there, swinging your dick at Marie and reminding her about old times, but you didn't get the results you wanted?"

"For your information, I have never shagged

Marie." Bones actually jabbed me in the chest as he spoke. Liza scrambled out of the way.

I gave an incredulous glance down at his finger, still pressed into my chest. "Get that off me or I'll knock it off."

His brow arched in open dare. "Take your best shot, luv."

You asked for it. My fist connected with his jaw. Bones ducked before I could land another one, green flashing out of his eyes.

"Is that all you've got? Not nearly good enough." And he jabbed me in the chest again.

Oh, it's on now, honey!

I grabbed his wrist and yanked, kicking his shin at the same time to throw him off balance. He was too quick, though, leaping over my sweeping leg and using my momentum against me. One light shove in the back had me sprawling into the couch. Liza let out a horrified bleat.

"Please, both of you, stop!"

I ignored her. So did Bones. My pulse sped up in anticipation as I got to my feet. The opportunity to blow off some steam with a full-fledged brawl sounded great to me. From the glittering green in his eyes, he was game, too.

But just to be certain. . . "Sure you want to play rough?" I asked, keeping my mind blank of my intentions.

His smile was smug, taunting, and sexy as he let me draw close. "Why not? I'm winning."

I smiled back. Then I rammed my fist into his stomach. *Take every cheap shot*, Bones had taught me when he trained me years ago. Who said I didn't pay attention?

But instead of doubling over like I'd expected, he flung me straight up over his shoulders. My body cracked against the ceiling, knocking the wind out of me. I had a split second to kick off the crown molding before he flew at me, and he hit empty space instead. I rolled when I hit the floor, knocking over the coffee room table in my scramble to get away.

He was on me in the next moment. A gloating smile met my gaze as Bones pressed his full weight down to hold me. The top of my robe had sagged open, leaving my bare breast rubbing against his shirt as I squirmed under him. He glanced down, tracing the inside of his lip with his tongue.

"Give up now?" he asked.

My heart hammered with excitement even as I wanted to smack the smirk off his face. He'd left my arms free, which was a mistake.

"Not yet." I reached behind me and grabbed the first thing my hands made contact with. Then I heaved it over my head at him.

The marble coffee table split into large pieces when it crashed over Bones. It hit his head, dazing him, which I took advantage of. I'd wiggled out from under him and was about to crow over my victory —when I felt twin iron bands cut into my ankles. I tried to twist away, but he held on, shaking the table remnants from him. The only thing in reach was the pewter serving platter. I grabbed it and brandished it like a weapon.

"I'll use this next!" I warned him.

Still gripping my ankles, Bones blinked up at me. I glanced around, seeing Liza in the far corner with her hand stuffed in her mouth, horrified. Hopscotch and Band-Aid lingered near the doorway, not knowing what to do.

All at once, I started to laugh.

Bones's mouth twitched. Liza's eyes bugged when he let out a chuckle. It grew even as mine did, until he let go of my ankles and we were laughing helplessly together.

Bones shook the marble remains from his head, still laughing. "Bloody hell, Kitten. Never thought to be flogged by my own furniture. Do you know I saw bloomin' stars when that cracked over my nog?"

I knelt next to him, raking my fingers through his hair to get out the last of the table's shards. His eyes were bright green, and the laughter caught in my throat when he yanked me closer and kissed me.

His mouth was hard, demanding a response. The adrenaline inside me changed to something else as I gripped him back with equal urgency. I had time to hear the door shut behind the hasty retreat of our three onlookers before his body flattened mine.

"We haven't sparred together in quite a while," Bones murmured as his mouth slid down my throat. "I'd forgotten how much I enjoy it."

His hand caressed up my thigh without restriction, as I still had nothing on under the robe. A primal sound came from me when his fingers stroked between my legs.

"Seems you enjoyed it, too," he whispered.

I tugged at his shirt, ignored the pieces of the table everywhere, and slid my legs around him.

"I need you."

I wasn't just talking about how much I wanted him. I'd hated the distance between us the past few days. Right now, I was desperate to feel close to him. To believe that everything would work out, no matter how crazy things got.

He pushed me back against the couch, yanking down his pants. I groaned at the deluge of sensations his first thrust caused, biting his shoulder to keep from shouting at how good it felt.

Bones pressed my head closer as he moved deeper inside me. "Harder," he said with a moan.

I sank my teeth in, swallowing his blood when I broke his skin. The small wound healed as soon as I drew away to kiss him.

His mouth covered mine, stealing my breath with the intensity of his kiss. "I love it when you bite me," Bones growled once I broke away to gasp in air.

I held him tighter, my fingernails digging into his back. "Show me how much."

A low laugh escaped him. He began to move faster.

"I intend to."

Bones woke me with beignets and coffee, and we lingered in bed a while afterward. The surliness between us from before was gone, at least for the time being.

Since my meeting with Marie was tonight, we were still under her guest column, so we still had safe passage in the city. To take advantage of that, we toured the French Quarter. I didn't need a jacket with the hot August weather, but I did put on sunscreen.

Bones led me from Bourbon Street to Jackson Square, then to the Saint Louis Cathedral, which looked very similar to some of the churches I'd glimpsed in Paris. After that, we stopped at Lafitte's Blacksmith shop, one of the oldest buildings in the

Quarter. While outside sipping a gin and tonic at one of the tables, I looked up to find a ghost suddenly standing next to us.

"Sod off, mate," Bones told him. "As I was saying, luv, during the Great Fire—"

"It's wretched justice that only the crazies care enough to talk to you when you're dead," the ghost muttered. "No vampire or ghoul will even bid you good day."

Bones made an irritated noise. "Right then, good day, now off you go."

"She'll wonder who you're talking to," the ghost smirked in my direction. "Think you're mad, she will—"

"I can see you," I interrupted.

If someone partially transparent could look baffled, he did. Eyes that might have been blue narrowed.

"You don't feel touched," he accused.

"You mean psychic? I'm many things, but not that. Isn't it a little rude, though, to plop down and start chatting away when we were having a conversation? You didn't even say 'excuse me.'"

"Kitten, I warned you about talking to them." Bones sighed.

"I didn't think you'd speak to me," the ghost replied, starting to smile. "The undead"—he nodded at Bones—"just ignore us. They're among the few who can see us, but they don't even care!"

He spoke with such impassioned resonance, I would have patted him if he had been solid. Instead, I gave him a sympathetic smile.

"What's your name? I'm Cat."

He bowed, his head going through the table. "I am Fabian du Brac. Born 1877, died 1922."

Bones leaned back in his chair. "Fabian, splendid to meet you. Now, if you please, we're rather busy."

"You're Bones," the ghost stated. "I've seen you before. You're always too busy to talk to us."

"Bloody right I am, nosy spectre—"

"Bones." I tugged his arm. "He knows who you are!"

"Kitten, what does that . . ."

His voice trailed off as what I was mentally shouting penetrated. Then he turned his full attention to Fabian and smiled.

"Why, mate, I reckon you're right. Sometimes I need to be reminded of my manners, I do. Born in 1877, you say? I remember 1877. Times were better then, weren't they?"

Bones was right about ghosts being talkative. Fabian blathered on rapturously about bygone days, the sewage of modern culture, favorite presidents, and the changes in Louisiana. He was like a walking encyclopedia. It was amazing how much a phantom could pick up. Like, for example, the recent influx of out-of-town ghouls in New Orleans. Their hushed gatherings. Gregor's name kept popping up, along with whispers about a threat to the ghoul species.

"Gregor and ghouls, eh?" Bones prodded. "What more did they say?"

Fabian gave him a shrewd look. "I don't want to be forgotten any longer."

"Of course not," Bones agreed. "I've got a grand memory, I'll remember you forever."

"That's not what he means."

It was one of the few times I'd spoken in their conversation. Hell, I couldn't swap tales about early-twentieth-century life, the sadness of seeing automobiles replace horses, or what the air smelled like before fossil fuels. But this part I understood.

"Fabian wants companionship," I said. "He's lonely. That's what you mean, isn't it?"

"Yes." Maybe it was the reflection of the sunlight, but there could have been tears in the ghost's eyes. "I want a home. Oh, I know I can't have a real family anymore, but I want to belong to someone again."

Some things never change. The need for companionship transcends mortality or immortality.

Bones had a resigned expression on his face. "Taking in strays, Kitten? Not without rules first. Any deviance from these, Fabian, would result in an immediate exorcism by the most qualified spook-slayer I could find, savvy?"

"I'm listening." Fabian tried to look blasé, but he was almost quivering in excitement.

"First, you do not report any information about me, my wife, or my people to anyone alive, dead, undead, or otherwise. Got it?"

Fabian's head bobbed. "Agreed."

"Privacy is to be respected just as if you were a real boy, mate. If you think being a ghost allows for voyeurism, you're mistaken."

An indignant huff. "I will excuse your misassumption of my character on the basis of current debauchery, which is so common among modern persons."

"Is that a yes?" I asked with a laugh.

"Yes."

"Right." Bones cracked his knuckles. "And lastly, no bragging about your accommodations. I don't want to be chased everywhere by needy spirits. Not a bloody word, understood?"

"Inescapably."

"Then we have an agreement, Fabian du Brac."

The ghost smiled one of the happiest smiles I'd ever seen. Bones rose from his chair. I followed suit, taking a last swallow from my glass.

"All right, Fabian, you're one of mine now. Can't say it's the best arrangement you could aspire to, but I promise if you abide by our accord, you won't ever lack for a home again."

We left the outside patio area and headed back to the house, the ghost trailing behind us with one hand on my shoulder.

Seven

Bones told me to wear boots. At first I thought they were for storing weapons, but nothing beyond my feet went into my new leather boots. My other new clothes consisted of a pair of midnight-blue pants and a white blouse. I didn't have on any jewelry except for my engagement ring. Liza had wanted to do my hair, but I declined. This wasn't a party. It was a polite confrontation.

We left the house on foot after our escort arrived. His name was Jacques, and he was a ghoul. Jacques had skin dark as pitch, and a subdued but resonating power emanated from him. Bones had negotiated beforehand that he would walk with me to a certain point. After that, Jacques would show me the way. I wasn't armed, and my lack of weapons made me feel like I was only half-dressed. I missed my knives. They felt familiar and comforting to me. Guess that in itself marked me as a weirdo.

Bones walked abreast of me, my hand in his. From

the sureness of his steps, he knew where we were going. Jacques didn't chat on the way. I didn't talk, either, not wanting to say anything the ghoul could later use against me. Just like being arrested, I had the right to remain silent. Of course, anything I wanted to say to Bones, I could just think at him. Times like this, his mind-reading skill came in handy.

Fabian hovered about a hundred feet away, flitting in and out of the buildings as if he were minding his own ghostly business. Jacques never once looked in his direction. It was amazing how ignored ghosts were by those who could see them. The age-old prejudice between the undead and the spectral dead was working to our advantage, however. Bones wasn't allowed to accompany me all the way to my appointment, but Fabian wasn't bound by any such agreement. Liza had been stunned when we brought him home with us. It hadn't occurred to her to befriend a ghost either.

We stopped at the gates of Saint Louis Cemetery Number One. Bones let go of my hand. I gave a look inside the locked burial grounds, and my brow went up.

"Here?"

"It's the entranceway to Marie's chamber," Bones replied, as if we were waiting at the front door of a house. "This is where I leave you, Kitten."

Great. At a graveyard. How reassuring. "So I'm meeting her inside the cemetery?"

"Not exactly." Bones had a tone that was both ironic and sympathetic. "Underneath it."

Jacques twisted a key in the gates' lock and gestured at me. "This way, Reaper."

If Marie Laveau wanted to disquiet someone with

her version of home-court advantage, stepping inside the cemetery led by a creepy ghoul while the gates locked behind me was definitely the way to do it.

"Alrighty then. After you, Jacques."

Marie Laveau's crypt was one of the larger ones in the cemetery. It was tall, probably six feet, wider at the base and narrower toward the top. There was voodoo graffiti written on the side of it in the form of black x's. Dried and fresh flowers were laid at the front of the crypt, where a chipped inscription indicated the name of the legendary voodoo queen. All of these things I had a few seconds to notice before Jacques pointed to the dirt in front of the headstone and said something in Creole. Then the ground began to peel back.

From the grating sound, something electronic controlled the movement. Inside the small fenced area around the headstone, a square hole appeared. There was a dripping noise within, which made me wonder how anything could be underground in New Orleans without being flooded. Jacques didn't share my concern. He simply jumped into the black opening and repeated his earlier directive.

"This way, Reaper."

I peered into the complete darkness of the pit to see the shine of his eyes looking up at me. He was about twenty feet down. With a mental shrug, I braced myself and followed, feeling a small splash as I landed.

Jacques reached out to steady me, but I brushed him off. No need to play the helpless female. The opening above us began to close with that same low creaking sound at once, adding to the eeriness.

Over an inch of water covered the floor of what

appeared to be a tunnel. There were no lights, and nowhere to go but forward. As I sloshed through the passageway after Jacques in the near blackness, I realized why Bones had insisted on the boots. They kept out whatever unpleasant squishy things I stepped on as I kept pace. The air was moist and had a moldy smell to it. When I reached a hand out, the wall was also wet. Still, I kept going, grateful that my inhuman vision meant I wasn't completely sightless in the darkness.

"I thought you couldn't build things underground in New Orleans," I remarked. "Doesn't this flood?"

Jacques glanced back at me while still walking. "It's always flooded. Unless you are invited underneath, the waters are released in the tunnel."

Well. Marie apparently used drowning as a deterrent. That was one way to control nosy tourists.

"That would only work on people dependent on breathing. What about the rest of the population?"

Jacques didn't reply. His verbal quota had probably been exceeded. After about thirty yards, we came to a metal door. It opened on well-greased hinges to reveal a lighted landing behind it. Jacques moved to the side to let me pass, then touched my arm as I went by him.

"Look."

There was a whoosh. Suddenly the tunnel we'd just walked through was engulfed in protruding blades. They came out of the walls from all sides, as if we'd just entered inside a demon's mouth. A few feet back, and I'd have been julienned where I stood.

"Neat," I said. I could appreciate a good booby trap as much as the next person. "Must have cost a fortune, all that silver."

"They're not silver."

The woman's voice came from the top of the stairs in front of me. Smooth, buttery. Like crème brûlée for the ears.

"They're steel blades," she continued. "I wouldn't want undead intruders killed. I'd want them alive and brought to me."

Just like before when I jumped into this rabbit hole, I braced myself. Then I walked up the stairs to meet the voodoo queen.

As stated on her headstone some seventy yards away, Marie Laveau had died in 1881. Beyond that, her being a ghoul and her reputation with voodoo was all I knew. Bones hadn't wanted to go into detail in her own backyard, so to speak. His caution spoke volumes about the person coming more clearly into view with my every step. From what I *had* heard about Marie, I half expected her to be seated on a throne, turbaned, with a headless chicken in one hand and a shrunken skull in the other. What I saw made me blink.

Marie was seated in an overstuffed chair, possibly a La-Z-Boy, bent over nothing more threatening than needlework. She had on a black dress with a white shawl thrown over her shoulders. On her feet were smart little heels that could have been Prada. With her shoulder-length dark hair curling around lightly made-up features, I had a weird flashback to a scene in a movie. She could have been bent over cookies, saying, "Smell *good*, don't they?" while I broke a vase that wasn't really there.

"Oracle?"

It came out of my mouth before I could snatch it back. No wonder Bones had wanted to come with me. I'd piss her off before even introducing myself.

Hazelnut eyes that were way too alert raked me from boots to brow. The needlework shifted when a long finger pointed at me.

"Bingo."

That dessert drawl again, Southern Creole and sweet. If ears could digest verbal calories, my ass would've been getting fat just listening to her. And with that single word, she'd just recited the next part of the movie *Matrix*, which I'd quoted.

"Great movie, wasn't it?" I didn't move to sit because I hadn't been invited to. "One of my favorites. The first film, anyway. Didn't care for the other two."

Those penetrating eyes fixed on me. "Do you think you're the One? The future leader for all of us?"

"No." I advanced and held out a hand. "I'm just Cat. Nice to meet you."

Marie shook my hand. Her fingers tightened on mine for an instant but not painfully.

She released me, a tilt of her head indicating the seat next to hers. "Sit, please."

"Thanks."

The small room was bare of any decoration. Its walls were concrete, dry at least, and the only things in it were our two chairs. It reminded me of a prison cell. Stark and bleak.

"Should I just jump right in and say Gregor's full of shit, or do you want to chat first?"

Meaningless banter didn't seem like a productive use of time. Besides, if I could do small talk, I wouldn't have pissed off the vast number of people that I had. Certain talents were beyond me. Okay, many talents.

"What do you want?" Marie asked.

Her matching bluntness made me smile. "You haven't slept with Bones, and you don't beat around the bush. If you weren't considering backing Gregor against Bones, I'd like you tremendously."

She shrugged, resuming her knitting. "Whether I like people or not has little to do with deciding to kill them. It's either necessary, or it isn't."

That caused a grunt to escape me. "You sound like Vlad."

A knitting needle paused. "Another reason to wonder about you. Vlad the Impaler doesn't make friends easily. Nor is the Dreamsnatcher usually so enamored of someone. You have an impressive list of conquests, Reaper."

My brow arched. "When you conquer something, it means you fought for it. I don't know Gregor, Vlad's just a friend, and Bones is the only man I care about, dominatingly speaking."

A throaty laugh came from her. "Either you're a very good actor . . . or very naïve. Gregor wants you back, and he's amassing support for his claim of a blood-binding with you. Vlad Tepesh has named you as a friend. And Bones, who was notorious for his promiscuity, married you and started two wars over you."

"Two? I'm only aware of one."

"Gregor is understandably angry about Mencheres's imprisoning him for over a decade, but he offered not to retaliate if you were returned to him. Bones refused, and as his co-ruler, that means he spoke for Mencheres as well. Technically, that makes them at war with Gregor."

Great. Bones had neglected to mention that.

"If Gregor hadn't been invading my dreams, I wouldn't know him if I hit him with my car," was my even response. "I remember cutting my hand and swearing by my blood that Bones was my husband, in front of hundreds of witnesses. Where are Gregor's witnesses? Or evidence? If he'd really taken the trouble to marry me, you'd think he would've kept a souvenir."

"You could find out the truth for yourself," Marie stated. "I wonder why you haven't."

I sat up straighter. "Mencheres told me my memories can't be retrieved."

"Did he? In those exact words?"

My nails drummed against the edge of the chair. "Kind of."

"Mencheres can't return your memories, but Gregor can," Marie flatly pronounced. "Mencheres knows that. As does Bones."

I didn't say anything for a minute. She stared at me, absorbing my reaction, then she smiled.

"You didn't know. How interesting."

"That doesn't mean anything," I said, covering my obvious surprise. "I don't know Gregor, but he doesn't sound like the type who would come over to return my memories, then leave with a cheery wave when he was proven wrong."

"What if he wasn't proven wrong?"

Be careful. Very careful. "Like I said, why are all his claims hinging on my memory? It could easily be a ploy to get me within snatching range, then it would be may the fastest man win."

Marie set her knitting down. Guess that meant we were getting serious. "Right now, I believe you don't truly know if you bound yourself to Gregor. If it's proven, however, that you are his wife instead of Bones's, I will ally myself with Gregor according to our laws. That's my answer in this matter."

"You asked me before what I wanted, Marie. I want to go home with Bones and be left alone by everyone for about ten years. I don't remember Gregor, but even if I did, it wouldn't change how I feel about Bones. If it's a fight Gregor or you wants by trying to force me to be with him, you'll get it."

Marie's face had an unusual ageless quality about it. She could have been twenty when she was changed into a ghoul. Or fifty.

"I was married once," she remarked. "His name was Jacques. One night, Jacques beat me, and I knew he liked it. The next morning, I gave him a poisoned tonic, then I buried him underneath my porch. Now every time I take a lover, I call him Jacques, to remind me that if I have to, I'll kill him."

Marie tilted her head and gave me a challenging look. "Care for some refreshment?"

Not after that story. But if she thought I was going to tuck my tail between my legs, she was wrong.

"Love some." *Bring it on, Voodoo Queen.*

"Jacques!"

The ghoul appeared. "My love?"

I quelled a snort with difficulty, getting the reason behind his name. *Yeah, you'd better ass-kiss, buddy. I bet you* never *forget an anniversary, huh?*

"Bring some wine for me, Jacques, and I believe we're familiar with our guest's preferences?"

He returned quickly. The glass with red liquid he gave to Marie with a bow, and the round one filled with clear liquid went to me. I hefted it at my host in salute and swallowed in a long gulp. Gin and tonic, no surprise there.

Marie watched me, taking only a sip of her glass.

When I was finished, I extended it toward the hovering Jacques.

"That was great. I'll have another."

Marie set down her drink and flicked a hand at Jacques, who took my glass and left.

"Your bloodline doesn't make you immune to all things, Reaper."

"No, it doesn't. Still, from what I've heard, you have a protocol about killing people, so in that case, I'll have a keg of whatever you're serving. And my name is Cat."

"Do you have any intention of turning into a ghoul?" Marie asked me.

The question was so unexpected, I paused before answering. "No, why?"

Marie gave me another hooded look. "You live with a vampire. Your life is frequently in danger, and you are weaker as a half-breed, yet you haven't chosen to change into a vampire. I've heard it's because you want to combine your half-breed abilities with a ghoul's power, making yourself the first ghoul-vampire hybrid."

What's in the stuff she's drinking? I wondered.

"That thought *never* crossed my mind," I said.

"A vampire can't turn into a ghoul. Only a human can. So no one but you, as a half-breed, could combine all the strength of a vampire with none of their aversion to silver. You might have unlimited power. But you've never thought of it?"

Open challenge was in her words. I thought back to Fabian saying that there had been a recent influx of ghouls in New Orleans, whispering about a possible new threat to their species. Was this it? Did people actually believe I'd do such a thing out of a twisted lust for power?

"After my father ripped my throat, Bones told me he would have brought me back as a ghoul, if I'd died before his blood healed me. That's the only time I ever thought about being a ghoul. If one day I choose to cross over, Majestic, it'll be into a vampire. So you can tell that to whoever's spouting the rumor that I'm looking to be even more of a freak than I already am."

Jacques came back with another full glass, but Marie gave him that authoritative flick of her fingers again.

"Our guest is leaving."

I stood, my mind running through a list of reprimands. *Good one, Cat. Pissed her off in ten minutes. Guess you'll be the one leaping up the stairs, yelling, "In the car! Quick!"*

"Always nice to meet a famed historical figure," I said.

Marie rose as well. She was tall, probably five-ten, and in those heels, over six feet. Her figure was statuesque, and she radiated an odd combination of menace and matronliness.

"You are not what I thought you'd be."

She extended her hand, creamy mocha and soft. I clasped it and fought not to shake mine afterward to get out the numbness from her power.

"Neither are you. I was so sure about the headless chicken."

Why not say it? When someone wanted to kill you, you really couldn't make them angrier.

She smiled. "Of all the things you'd first say to me, quoting a scene from my favorite movie was the last I expected. Go in peace, Cat."

Jacques held open the door to the tunnel for me. Those long, curved knives slid back into their settings with a hiss. I caught a hazy flash at the end of the tunnel. Fabian on sentry duty. He was gone before Jacques fell in step behind me.

My escort didn't talk the rest of the way. When we reached the door to the crypt, the upper covering groaned as it slid open. Jacques put his hands out to help me up, but I brushed him off.

"Don't bother, thanks. I'll do it myself."

A quick bend of the knees and flash of concentration, and I cleared the twenty-foot space. With my increasing ability to jump, at least I was becoming more like my feline namesake. If I shed my pulse, I could do a hell of a lot more than jump high.

Bones was waiting by the cemetery gates. When he smiled, leaning into the bars as the lock opened, I suddenly didn't care about anything but the shape of his mouth. That smooth curve, lips palest pink. The strong jaw and deeply etched cheekbones. Dark brown eyes taking in the surroundings. His hands clasped over mine when the gate opened, vibrating with no less power than Marie's, but they didn't leave me feeling numb. I felt safe.

"We might have to take some beignets to go," I began.

He squeezed my hands. "Don't fret, I suspected the two of you wouldn't get on. We're packed. Liza's waiting with the car."

Traffic whizzed by in a blur of red and white lights as we approached the Quarter. This was a city that woke up instead of sleeping after midnight. Jacques stayed behind, apparently not interested in following us back to Bones's house.

"What was the last thing Marie said to you?" Bones asked, before I could even question him about it.

"'Go in peace.' Does this have a hidden meaning?"

Bones stopped as we were midway in crossing a street. A horn blared at us. He gave the driver a fingered expression of his opinion, then tugged me to the other side.

"You're sure she said that?"

"I'm not deaf." Was it very bad?

His smile turned into a full-throated laugh.

"Exactly *what* did you say to her, luv? I've known Marie a hundred years, and all I got was a 'Be guarded on your journey,' which is a nice way of saying, 'Watch your arse, mate!' 'Go in peace' means she's backing you. You were only down there thirty minutes. What on earth were you talking about?"

Relief washed over me. "Movies. Drinks. Headless chickens. You know, girl stuff."

Up went his brows. "Indeed?"

We rounded the corner. Four more blocks until his house.

"Good thing for us, she's a *Matrix* fan . . ."

My voice trailed off and I froze in midstride. Bones stopped as well, glancing at me in concern before he became absolutely rigid. He must have felt him, even though I'd barely glimpsed the man three blocks ahead. *I wouldn't know him if I hit him with my car . . .*

But I did know Gregor. At a glance. And I wasn't dreaming.

EIGHT

GREGOR'S EYES SEEMED TO BURN INTO MINE.
Even though I couldn't see their color from this
far away, I knew they'd be grayish-green. His golden
hair had darker strands in it, giving it an ash-blond
color. It was as if Gregor had been too bright and
someone had sprinkled him to tone him down.

"Hopscotch, Band-Aid. To me, at once."

Bones didn't raise his voice, so the two vampires
must not have been far. They came out from the
crowd, taking up position, one on either side of us.
Bones jerked his head toward that immobile figure
and muttered a low curse.

"He's almost right outside my home, filthy sod. Did
he think he'd bloody ring the door for you?"

His hand tightened on mine. I gave a small yelp.
Bones loosened his grip, but not by much. Even with
the distance, I saw Gregor's eyes narrow, flash green,
then he started walking toward us.

Bones let go of me. He rolled his head around on

his shoulders and cracked his knuckles while advancing with deadly purpose. I would have followed, but Hopscotch and Band-Aid grabbed me.

"Bones!"

He ignored me and kept moving. So did Gregor. It was clear neither one had talking on his mind. I was seized with a sick fear even as I struggled with the two men holding me. They'd gotten a good grip when I wasn't paying attention.

When Bones and Gregor were less than twenty feet from each other, Jacques stepped between them, holding out his arms.

"Both of you, go no farther."

They ignored him. Jacques probably would have been shoved to the side, but then another voice cracked through the air.

"You shall not fight in my city!"

Bones stopped. Gregor slowed, pausing within touching distance of Jacques's still-spread arms.

Marie didn't walk up so much as glide. Bones gave her what could only be described as a frustrated look.

"For Christ's sake, Majestic, if you didn't want us to fight, then why did you tell him we were here?"

While they were focused on the drama, I managed to throw an elbow into Band-Aid's eye before slipping under Hopscotch's loosened hold.

"Don't do that again," I warned them as I dashed away.

"I didn't tell him," Marie replied. "Nor did any of my people."

A flicker of arrogance passed over Gregor's face. In person, he was even more imposing than in my dreams. There was something about him I found unnerving, even though he stared at me without hostility. If anything, there was a longing in his expression that made me stop where I was. Little pinpricks of pain began going off in my brain.

. . . I'm from a farm as well. In the south of France, but there were no cherries to be found there . . .

My hands flew to my temples. Gregor's nostrils flared. He took in a long, provoking, audible breath.

"*Catherine.*"

"Take your eyes off my wife."

Bones growled it with barely restrained fury. The power seething off him struck me even several feet away. Gregor let out an equally venomous snarl and took a single step forward.

"That's *my* wife I'm looking at."

When Gregor uncurled his power like a peacock displaying its magnificent feathers, I sucked in a gasp.

Gregor had felt strong in my dreams, but that must have been the watered-down version. With the energy spilling from him in ever-increasing waves, he could have fueled the French Quarter's electricity needs. *Oh, shit. He's at least as strong as Bones, if not stronger . . .*

Brakes screeched close by, but neither man took his eyes off the other. I looked, and saw Liza roll down the window of a van. Her eyes bugged, and she made a hasty gesture with her hand.

"Please, Cat, get in."

"Not without Bones."

I said it to Gregor as well as her. It didn't matter that the memory of Gregor's voice had sliced through my subconscious like a knife. Didn't matter that for a split second, as his gaze bored into mine, I'd felt a flicker of yearning. Awake, or asleep, I belonged to Bones, no one else.

"You see? She's made her choice."

Bones said it with luxuriant hatred in every sylla-ble. Even with his back to me, I could just imagine his taunting half smile. Judging from Gregor's livid expression, I was right.

"Despicable whoreson, her choice has been erased by Mencheres. He dragged her screaming from me only an hour after our binding!"

"I don't give a rot if Mencheres yanked her off your throbbing, rigid cock," Bones snarled. "Go dream a little dream, you sod!"

Marie wasn't going to be able to keep them from brawling much longer. Lethal danger to Bones aside, there were also way too many bystanders. People would get hurt or killed if the two of them went at it. Out of the corner of my eye, I saw Fabian streak into the van.

"Bones." I made my voice calm. *Don't startle the rabid beast.* "If he knows we're here, others do, too. We need to leave."

"You're only in danger because of his blind ar-rogance," Gregor said. "Come to me, Catherine. I'll keep you safe."

"Insolent bastard," Bones spat. "I reckon nothing's beneath a man who'd try to steal another man's wife before they even met."

"Bones, leave." Although Marie didn't raise her voice, her tone was dangerous. "Gregor, you will stay here until the following dawn. You came to my city without invitation to provoke violence. No matter our history, you know better."

"Marie—"

"You're in my Quarter." She cut Gregor off. "You of all people know better."

Gregor flexed his hands. For a second, I thought he might hit Marie. *Don't do it, buddy. She'll be burying you under her porch in no time!*

"As you insist," Gregor said tightly.

Bones inclined his head without turning around. "Get in the van, Kitten. Hopscotch, Band-Aid, you, too. Majestic, I hope more of Gregor's ignorant ramblings won't sway your judgment in the future."

I climbed inside the vehicle, avoiding that smoky green gaze.

"And farewell to you, Dreamsnatcher," Bones went on as he got into the van. "I hope you enjoyed tonight, because it's the last you'll see of her."

"Catherine." Even without looking at Gregor, I felt his stare. "Your memories lie in my blood. They're waiting for you, *ma bien-aimée*, and I will keep my oath—"

The door slamming cut off the rest of Gregor's statement. So did Liza's peeling out of the narrow street like a drunken Tony Stewart. I closed my eyes so I wouldn't be tempted to look back.

"How do you think he found us?"

I didn't ask the question until much later. Truth be told, I hadn't felt like talking after seeing Gregor. Neither had Bones, from his grim silence. The sun was up. Liza still drove. Ghouls weren't as susceptible to morning tiredness as vampires were. Hopscotch and Band-Aid slept, dark sunglasses fixed over their eyes.

In this new SUV, at least there was more room than the last two cars. In case we were being followed, we'd switched vehicles three times. Bones glared the unknowing other drivers into submission while we hijacked their ride. It was done so quickly, a tail would have to have been right on top of us to catch it. There had been no sign of Gregor yet, and we were almost to Fort Worth.

Bones made an irritable noise. "Unless one of Marie's people went behind her back—and that's unlikely—or one of mine did, I'm at a loss." His fingers drummed on his leg. "Perhaps Don had a hand in it. What name did he use to have those pills delivered to my home, Kitten?"

"Kathleen Smith." I scoffed at the thought that my uncle would be so stupid as to use my real name. "And if you factor in the time frame, just a day from me telling him where we were, it doesn't fit. We know Gregor was in Paris and London when we were there, so he'd have to have left soon after we did to make it here. That rules out Don."

Bones stared at me. "You're right. Only Charles knew where we were bound to when we left his house. I don't reckon he ran an ad about it. Marie knew after we arrived. That leaves few people who could have informed Gregor, and they're all in this car."

That woke up Band-Aid and Hopscotch. Liza gave a widened glance into the rearview mirror. I tensed, wondering if one of the two vampires would abruptly attack.

Neither did. They looked back at Bones, and he met their gaze, his expression cold and hooded. Without saying it, I knew he was weighing the option of killing them.

"Sire," Band-Aid began.

"Save it." Shortly. "After Rattler, I don't put betrayal past anyone but three people, and you're not one of them. Still, no need to be hasty. Neither of you will leave my sight until we've arrived, and then you're going to be secluded. If Gregor still finds us, we'll know it wasn't you."

Each of them had a slightly stunned look to his face. Hopscotch recovered the fastest and nodded.

"I wouldn't betray you. I welcome the opportunity to prove it."

"As do I." Band-Aid seconded, giving a furtive glance to Liza.

"Whatever you need me to do," she said softly.

"I won't force you." Bones almost sighed. "Yet I would ask, Liza."

She smiled in such a sad way, it even hurt me to see it. "You'll feel safer. It's such a small thing to do for you."

It sucked giving the people around you a suspicious eye. *Big dark cave.* It was sounding better and better.

"I know I only just met her, but somehow, I don't think it was Marie," I said.

Bones raised a brow. "Why not?"

"Well . . . she told me a weird story about poisoning her husband. At first I thought it was just to scare me, but it was after she said if I was married to Gregor, she'd back his side, since vampires can't divorce."

"Really?" Bones mulled it. "That's interesting. Oh, everyone knows Marie killed her husband when she was human. What I've never heard before is how she did it."

"I thought she hit him with an ax," was Liza's response. "That's the story I was told."

"Interesting," Bones repeated. "Why do you believe this makes her sympathetic to our side, luv? Seems she stated whom she'd support."

I'd rather not say.

I shifted on the seat, wishing I'd shut up before.

"You're blocking me." His eyes flashed green.

Yeah, I was keeping him out of my mind with all the mental armor I could muster. *Big mouth. Why can't you just leave well enough alone?*

It wasn't directed to him; I was berating myself. There were a few things I'd wanted to discuss privately with Bones after meeting Majestic. This wasn't private by anyone's standards.

"We agreed not to do this," Bones went on. "Hide any knowledge or speculation. Whatever it is, Kitten, tell me."

I blew out a deep breath. He wasn't going to like this.

"Marie told me Gregor could return my memories, and that you and Mencheres knew it. She wondered why you didn't want me to remember what happened. On the street back there, she had the chance to demand I get my memories back. We were in her backyard, outnumbered; she could have insisted. But she let us go. I think she did it . . . because she believes I *am* bound to Gregor, and she knows she'd have to back him if it was proven."

Bones went absolutely still. His glare intensified until it felt like I was being hit with emerald lasers.

"Do you want to remember your time with him?"

I took another deep breath, longer than the first one.

"It bothers me that there's over a month of my life I don't know about. You should have told me, Bones. You promised you weren't going to hide things from me anymore, either, but I had to find this out from Marie."

"I didn't tell you because I wasn't certain. In any event, I wasn't going to let that filthy cur put his hands on you, have your mouth on him—"

"Are you serious?" I interrupted. "Where in all of this did you think I'd kiss him?"

Bones shot me a harsh glance. "The power to open your mind is in Gregor's blood, as he said. You'd have to bite him."

"I didn't know how it worked."

"Right, but you'd do it if you could," Bones said with such accusation that I clenched my hands to keep from shaking him.

"If someone ripped over a month of memory from your life, you'd want to know what it contained, too." Spoken without shouting. Good for me.

"No, I wouldn't."

His tone wasn't calm. It was almost a snarl.

"If someone took from my memory an event that might unravel our marriage, I wouldn't want to remember it under any circumstances, but perhaps our marriage means more to me than it does to you."

There went my Zen moment of tranquil chi. *Blackout rage, aisle five!*

"The only person who could unravel our marriage is you. Let's say I *did* find out I married Gregor. Does the thought that there might be a chance for you to be single again sound too tempting to you?"

"You're the only one admitting to looking for a loophole," Bones replied with equal fury. "Fancy the look of Gregor? Wonder if you might have preferred shagging him to me? Is that what you want to remember?"

I was so insulted, it made me incensed.

"You've lost your mind!"

I shoved him, but he didn't move. "I bled my first time with Danny, got it? Or do you need me to draw you a picture?"

Under normal circumstances, I would never say something so personal with a crowd, but rage is funny. It makes you oblivious to everything else.

Bones drew his face right up next to mine. "That sod could have shagged you all night, and you'd have still bled with Danny later. All Mencheres would have needed to do was give you his blood once he found you. Heals all wounds, right? If they took you from Gregor shortly after the first time he'd bedded you, you'd have had a simple wound that could have been healed."

"That's . . ." I was so aghast at the idea, I couldn't begin to respond. "That's bullshit!" I finally managed.

"Really?" Bones leaned closer. "I happen to know differently, because I've done it."

The soft way he said the words made them even more emphatic. Fury, denial, and jealousy spat out my words faster than I could think.

"Damn you for being a conscienceless whore."

Bones didn't take his eyes off me, nor was his response any louder.

"That's what you married, Kitten. A conscienceless whore. But if you recall, I never pretended to be anything else."

Yeah, I knew he'd been a gigolo when he was human, but that's not what stung. *If only his screwing around had stopped once he didn't need the money to survive*, I thought bitterly. *But no. After he became a vampire, he did it for fun, as he just reminded me.*

I didn't want him to know how much his past still

had the power to hurt me, so I drew my mental shields around me. They were my only defense to shut him out. Then I looked out the window. I couldn't bear the sight of his beautiful face at the moment.

Bones let go of me and sat back. We didn't speak the rest of the trip.

Πiπε

"Yee-haw!"

The cry made me shake my head. A bar with an inside rodeo. Nope, I wasn't kidding. It even had a live, snorting bull. For the listed price, proof of prior experience, several signed waivers, and a complete lack of common sense, anyone could ride it, too.

Bones and I were still barely speaking. I told him about the rumor of me wanting to turn into a ghoul, but beyond that, we didn't talk much. Nothing else was going on, either, and that may have been mutual. When we reached the Fort Worth motel after a straight day of driving, I swallowed the pills Don had sent to me and passed out. The most intimate moment I'd had with Bones was when he woke me with his wrist against my mouth. I'd swallowed his blood, declared that I needed to shower, and that was that. He was dressed and waiting for me when I came out, coolly detached with nothing but business to discuss. The invisible wall between us was worse than fighting, in my opinion.

Bones was meeting a ghoul contact at this bar. He didn't like the ghoul rumor going around about me and wanted to see how seriously it was being taken. Spade was meeting us here, too, since Hopscotch, Band-Aid, and Liza were being quarantined.

Fabian proved helpful by checking out the bar first, making sure this wasn't a setup with the ghoul. Only two things cheered me from my current depressed mood. My best friend Denise lived in Texas now, so she was coming tonight. The other plus to the evening was that Cooper, my friend and former team member, was coming, too. Spade was picking both of them up.

When they walked into the bar, I was so glad to see them that I almost shoved past people in my way. Denise returned my hug, albeit with less desperate fervor, and Cooper was somewhat taken aback by my fierce embrace.

Spade came in behind them. He cast an appraising glance at Bones and me while he said hello. No doubt mentally weighing our friction.

"I say, Crispin, you'd look better if you were being nailed inside a wooden box," he commented. His gaze flicked around the bar with mild distaste. "No doubt this wretched music's to blame. I don't know why country singers feel the need to set depression to a melody."

Denise smiled. "I think this place is great. Is that a bull?"

"You bet." As if commanded, the animal snorted unhappily. He and I were in perfect agreement.

"Oh, I wish I could ride it," she said.

It was good to see Denise smile. In truth, I hadn't seen her much at all recently, smiling or otherwise.

After her husband Randy was killed, Denise stayed with Bones and me for a few weeks. Then she went back to Virginia, saying she wanted to get away from everything supernatural.

I couldn't blame her. It was a supernatural attack that had killed Randy; why wouldn't Denise want to get away from the reminders of that? Then she moved to Texas about two months ago, remarking it was the only way she could keep her mother from trying to set her up with other men. Denise wasn't ready to come out of mourning yet. I couldn't blame her there, either.

"Cooper, mate, good to have you with us," Bones said. "Stick with the ladies whilst Charles and I go off for a moment. I'm sure Kitten wants to hear all about what's going on with her old team."

With that, he turned away. Spade went with him, leaving the three of us standing on the outskirts of the bull ring.

Son of a bitch.

Not that I didn't want to spend time with Denise and Cooper, but it was my ass they were discussing with the ghoul contact. Seemed only fair that I got to be in on the details.

". . . remodeled the Wreck room to include . . . are you listening, Commander?"

Only then did Cooper's stream of dialogue penetrate. "Ah, sorry, Coop. I need a drink," I said, heading for the nearest bar.

I ordered a gin, no tonic, and drank it before it even hit the wooden counter. The bartender gave me a look as I slid the empty shot glass at him for a refill.

"That'll be nine-fifty, ma'am."

"Of course," I began, reaching into my jeans before

I froze in embarrassment. I didn't have a wallet on me. No, the only currency I carried was about ten pounds of silver under my shirt and in my pants. God, this was the last straw. *Wait, bartender, while I find Bones so I can get my allowance.*

"Here, keep the change. And pour two more just like it."

Cooper threw money on the table. Denise sat next to me, her hazel eyes wide.

"Cat, are you okay? You look like you might blow a fuse."

The bartender filled the drinks and passed them over. Cooper handed me the third one after I gulped the second as quickly as the first.

"I'm fine."

No use articulating the many things that were wrong. Misery might love company, but Denise had had enough of that without me piling on.

"You don't seem fine."

I didn't want to get into it, but I didn't want to tell her that. Instead, I sought for a distraction. "Look, the bull's out!"

With Denise's attention fixed on the amateur cowboy struggling on top of the bull, I was able to avoid her scrutiny. Across the crowd of people, I saw Bones nudge Spade, then they turned their attention to a tall, very thin, very dead man who approached. Must be the ghoul contact. Soon the three of them melted into the crowd.

I sighed, covering it with a smile as Denise turned back to me.

"That's so cool! Let's grab more liquor, Cat. Maybe you can jump on next."

I'd have loved to drink more liquor, but since Bones

and Spade just went off with the contact, I couldn't very well go over to him and demand his wallet.

"Denise, how much money do you have on you?"

She frowned. "Oh crap, I left my purse in Spade's car."

Cooper reached again in his pants. "I should have brought my credit card. This should last . . ." he pulled out a wad of twenties and gave it a critical glance ". . . ten minutes."

Good old Coop. Can't say the man didn't know how the half-dead could pack it away.

"I'll pay you back," I promised, feeling like a poor relation.

Cooper's prediction turned out to be wrong. It was almost half an hour before his cash ran out. Of course, I hadn't counted on the nearby men offering to buy Denise and me drinks. I refused, but Denise took one drink per male offering, thanking the guys but giving a firm "no" to a second. Most of them took it with friendly, mock disappointment, but a large guy with bushy brown hair needed a little more persuading.

"Aw, come on, honey," he said to Denise, "let's dance."

His hand landed on her leg. My brows shot up. Cooper started to stand when I smacked the man's offensive paw aside.

"My friend only dances with me."

Denise smiled. "Sorry."

The guy gave me an evil, disgusted look, and walked away, his three friends in tow. *Too bad, Bushy Hair,* I thought.

"Nicely done, Commander," Cooper commented.

"Stop calling me that."

I didn't mean to sound so sharp. Cooper just didn't realize the title kept reminding me that my position as leader was forever gone. Right now, sitting at a bar trying without success to drown my sorrows, I felt pretty useless.

Denise glanced between the two of us. "I think we should get my purse now," she said.

Cooper and I walked Denise to Spade's car. It was unlocked, to my surprise. When I questioned that, Denise shrugged and said Spade had remarked that locks just kept honest people out. Her purse was still tucked under the passenger seat where she'd left it. Denise had just slung it over her shoulder when the slurred drawl behind us stopped her.

"Well, now, boys, lookie what we found."

I'd heard them approach. Their smell, loud steps, and obvious heartbeats made them far from stealthy, but since they were human, I hadn't been concerned.

"Beat it, guys," I said.

Bushy Hair from the bar didn't stop. Neither did his two pals, who were equally large.

"Now we was just sayin'," Bushy Hair began with a slur that revealed how drunk he was, "that it weren't fair two such pretty gals was only playin' with this here Negro."

"*Negro?*"

Cooper repeated the word with open challenge. God, a trio of bigots. Just what the doctor *didn't* order.

"I'll handle this," I said coldly. These dumb-asses didn't know I was the most dangerous of the group. They kept concentrating on Cooper, seeing only the well-built male as the threat.

"Here's some really good advice: Start walking. I'm

in a bad mood, so get the fuck out of here before you get on my last nerve."

I didn't bother reaching in my clothes to get my silver. On humans, I didn't need weapons. Spade had parked in the far back corner of the lot. These chumps thought that spelled opportunity, but they were wrong.

It did surprise me, though, when Bushy Hair pulled a gun from underneath his shirt. He aimed it at Cooper.

"You." There was an ugly resonation to his voice. "You're gonna sit on that ground while we make nice with your gals."

"Cooper." It came from me in an incensed growl. I wasn't risking him or Denise getting shot. "Do as he says."

Cooper had been following my orders for a long time. He made a furious noise but sat as directed. From the way Bushy Hair handed off the gun to his friend, he was satisfied.

"That's real smart, redhead." He leered. "Now, you just stand by my buds while your friend and I get in this backseat."

I went right to his friends like he said. After all, one of them had the gun. If I quietly coldcocked them, there'd be no nasty scene—

Bushy Hair only got to place his hand on Denise before I felt a whoosh. I had an instant to tense before I realized who it was, and then there was a sickening thump. Or, to be more accurate, a splat.

It was difficult to say who had the most horrified look on their faces—the two men Bones now had dangling from their necks, or Denise as she stared at the remains of Bushy Hair's head. Spade stood next to her, muttering something foul, then he kicked the twitching figure of Bushy Hair hard enough to have him ricochet off her car. Spade had flung the man to the ground so viciously, his head looked like a watermelon dropped from five stories.

"Denise, are you all right?" Spade asked.

"He's. . . . he's . . ." Denise didn't seem to know what to say.

"Really, really dead," I supplied, relieved that two vampires flying at high speeds over a parking lot hadn't attracted attention. "Bones, let them go, you're killing them."

"That's the point," he answered, still holding them by their throats. "I'd break their necks, but that would be too quick."

They kicked and clawed at his wrists while their tongues protruded from their mouths. Denise looked like she was going to throw up.

"Why did you have to kill him?" she whispered to Spade.

"Because of what he intended to do," Spade replied, low and fierce. "No one deserves to live after that."

Cooper gave the body a pitiless glance. "We need to move him, Commander."

I didn't bother to comment about the title. First things first.

"Bones."

He glanced at me as if there weren't two dying men in his hands. Their limbs were moving slower now. One of them urinated, darkening the blue in his jeans. Clearly, he wasn't just trying to scare them.

"At least don't do it here." I stalled. "This is too public, and you're freaking Denise out. Throw them in the trunk, and we'll fight about it on the way out. If you win, you get to strangle them twice."

His lip curled. "I know what you're trying to do, luv, but in this case, you make a valid point."

He dropped them, and they fell like twin bags of bricks. Harsh, gurgling noises came from them as they began to breathe again.

I heard some people approach. They were laughing, minding their own business—and about to stumble onto a messy murder scene and two half-strangled men.

"Spade, take our car and get Denise out of here," I said. "You can meet up with us later. Cooper, open the trunk, let's get him in here."

"Blue Forerunner, mate, other side of the lot," Bones directed, tossing keys to Spade. Another set was passed to him in the same manner. "Ring you on the morrow."

Spade took Denise away, pausing only to stop the people from coming over with a flash of green.

"Get back inside, you're staying longer," he instructed them. They nodded, did a one-eighty, and returned to the bar. Poor folks would probably stay all night.

"Cooper, I don't want you getting bloody, you can't green-eye someone into forgetting about it," I said as I hefted the lifeless man into the trunk. "Grab one of the others and toss him in."

Cooper complied, picking up the nearest guy and shoving him into the trunk.

Bones lifted the remaining man and shook him. "If I hear a single peep out of either of you, I'll shut you up the permanent way. Now, before I lock you in the boot, where's your car?"

"Unngghh," the guy in his grasp said. "Unngghh . . ."

"You damaged his windpipe, he can't talk," I noted.

"Indeed." Bones scored the tip of his finger across a fang, smiled wolfishly into the man's terrified face, and thrust his bloody finger into his mouth. "Now, answer me. Softly. Or I'll rip your tongue out and ask the other bloke."

With even that small drop of Bones's blood, the man could speak again, if not very intelligibly.

". . . white 'ickup 'ruck . . ."

"The white pickup truck with the Confederate flag near the front?" Bones queried with another shake. "That it?"

". . . essss . . ."

"Who's got the keys?"

A wracking cough, then a pained moan followed his response. "Kenny . . . 'ocket . . . 'illed him . . ."

"In the dead bloke's pocket?"

"Unngh."

"Kitten, if you would?"

I began digging inside the pants of the body. Nothing, front or back. Then I patted down the shirt pockets. Bingo.

"Here."

"Cooper, take their ride and drive it to Twenty-eighth and Weber Street. Wait there, we'll pick you up when we're through."

"Keep your cell handy, just in case," I added, not commenting about the irony of a black man driving a truck with a Rebel flag.

"Right then, mate." Bones dropped the man into the trunk and slammed the lid down. "Watch your heads."

Ten

CANDLERIDGE PARK'S SIGN SAID THERE WERE a number of scenic trails and nature paths, but that wasn't why we were there. No, we were there to bury a body. Hopefully, just one.

Fabian floated above the trees, having hitched inside Spade's car without a word. He had to be touching something to travel long distances. The exception was if he was in a ley line, which I still didn't understand. Something about invisible energy currents that acted like spiritual highways. Later, I'd ask him about it in more detail. Right now, I was arguing with Bones. Again.

"Spade acting in the heat of the moment is one thing, but if you kill these guys now, it'll be in cold blood, Bones. They should go to jail, plus get some brainwashing to have them march in every Take Back the Night parade, not to mention civil rights, as soon as they're let out. But they have families who don't deserve to grieve over their sorry dead asses."

"Everyone has someone who cares for them," Bones replied without pity. "Even monsters. It's not fair, but it doesn't change the necessity."

"The gun wasn't loaded," I muttered, switching tactics. "I checked. Besides, it's not like anything would have happened. I had it under control—"

"Is that even the bloody point?"

Exasperated, Bones shut off the engine and turned to face me.

"You can't hear their thoughts. I can. This isn't the first time they've done such a thing, and even if you stopped them and flogged them into hysterical apologies, their *intentions* were the same. If they weren't human, would you be arguing with me over killing them?"

He had me there. From the look in his eyes, he knew it, too.

"Vampires and ghouls have their own rules." I tried again. "They'd know what would happen if they did such a thing. These bozos didn't get a copy of that playbook. They deserve jail time, yes, but not death."

Bones snorted. "Why *didn't* it occur to them that they were doing something so appalling, if they were caught, they'd be executed on the spot? It's not my fault that vampires have a fairer form of punishment for rapists than humans do."

I put my head in my hands. It was aching. Granted, it probably hurt a lot less than Bushy Hair's must have when it hit the parking lot concrete. Logically, Bones was correct. But it still felt wrong.

"You've obviously made up your mind, so do whatever you're going to do. You're too strong for me to stop you."

Bones gave me an unfathomable stare before climbing out of the car and opening the trunk. I listened as he made the two men carry their friend into the woods. Then Bones ordered them to dig with their hands. It was maybe forty minutes before they were done. Then I heard something like a resigned sigh.

"This goes against my better judgment, Kitten . . . Look right here, both of you. You will go to the nearest police station and make a confession of every blasted crime you've ever committed, excluding only this burial tonight. When you are arrested, you will refuse an attorney, and when you are in front of a judge, you will plead guilty. You will spend your allotted time behind bars knowing you deserve every second of it. Now take your worthless lives and go."

When Bones came back to the car, I was still wiping at my eyes. He shut the driver's door and let out a self-deprecating snort.

"Has it been so wretched lately that letting scoundrels escape punishment is the highlight of our time together?"

The words were flippant; the expression on his face wasn't. It was filled with a regret that I caught before he masked it back into composure.

"It's because this shows that you still care, despite how crappy things have been lately."

There was that flash across his face again. "Did you really think I'd ceased to care? Kitten, I care so much it wrecks me."

I hurtled myself across the car, latching my arms around him and feeling the mind-numbing relief of his answering embrace.

"I can't believe I was so pissed before about being unemployed and without a wallet," I choked, realizing how absurd that was compared to what really mattered.

"What?"

"Nothing." I kissed him, a deep, searching kiss that wiped out the estrangement of the past several days. "How fast can you make it back to the motel?"

His gaze lit up with lovely, hungry green.

"Very fast."

"Good." It was almost a moan. "I'll call Cooper and tell him we'll see him in the morning."

Bones rolled down his window. "Fabian," he called out, "get your ghostly arse back in the car, we're leaving."

Bones did make good time back to the Red Roof Inn. The thought of that uncomfortable mattress with those thin blankets sounded sinfully appealing to me now. Yet while we were waiting at a stoplight about a mile away, pain sliced into my skull.

. . . *understand this man will stop at nothing, and you'll never be safe* . . .

"Gregor," I breathed, so low it was barely a sound.

"Where?" Bones whipped his head around.

. . . *ensure your protection, but you must trust me, chérie* . . .

"Oh, Jesus," I whispered. "Bones . . . I think he's at the hotel!"

Bones made a U-turn, then hit the accelerator. Brakes squealed, and other vehicles slammed to a stop while horns blared. He hadn't bothered to wait for the light.

"Fabian," Bones said in a tight voice, "go back to the hotel to check. We'll be at the gates of the park we just left."

"I will be quick." Fabian promised, and he vanished. We didn't even have to slow down.

Bones continued to floor it, checking the rearview mirror. After several miles, he pulled over at a gas station.

"Come on, luv, time to switch cars."

We got out. The man fueling his Honda next to us only had time to say, "What the—?" before Bones hit him with his gaze.

"This is your car now," he said. "And yours is mine."

"My car," the man repeated, eyes glazing.

"Right. Go home and clean it, it's ghastly dirty."

"Wait until he starts on the trunk," I mumbled, getting into the man's vehicle.

Bones drove less aggressively this time, but he still went way above the speed limit. Instead of the direct route to the park, he took side roads. Once we reached the park, Bones pulled under a tree, shutting off the engine and the headlights.

In the quiet, my accelerated breathing sounded too loud. "Do you—do you think—"

"Why do you believe Gregor's at the motel?"

He asked it as nonchalantly as if he were inquiring, paper or plastic? That didn't fool me. His knuckles were almost white on the steering wheel.

How to explain? "I got these sharp pains in my head, and I could hear him, only he wasn't talking to me *now*. I think it was memories of what he'd said before, and the only other time it happened was when he was close, on the street in New Orleans."

A pause. Then, "What did he say?"

"You couldn't hear it?" That surprised me.

"No." The mildness drained from his tone. "Else I wouldn't ask."

"Um, okay. The first one was quick, just a fragment. Something about there not being a cherry farm in France. This time, he was warning me that someone was after me."

Bones grunted. "That sounds very present tense, don't you agree?"

"Yeah, it does," I mused. "But somehow, I still think it was a memory."

Fabian appeared at the windshield. The sudden sight of him made me jump in my seat. He could sure sneak up on someone.

"The yellow-haired vampire was there," he announced. "He was behind the motel with six others. I don't think they saw me."

Bones stared at me. His gaze was filled with something I couldn't name.

"I'm sorry," he said quietly.

"For what?"

"This."

His fist shot out.

When my eyes opened, I saw darkness with slight flickers of light around the edges. I was sitting, but not in the car. It sounded like we were on a plane.

Immediately, I reached for the blindfold, but cool hands stopped me.

"Don't, Kitten."

I turned in the direction of his voice. "Get this off me."

"No. Quit squirming and let me talk."

I froze, remembering. "You knocked me out."

"Yes." Wariness edged his tone. "Are you going to sit still?"

"Depends. Why'd you hit me?" He'd better have a *damn* good reason.

"Remember when I said the only people who could be informing Gregor of our whereabouts were in the car? Liza, Band-Aid, and Hopscotch didn't know where we were staying in Fort Worth, and even if they did, they've been without means to communicate. Denise and Spade didn't know where we were staying. Fabian was with us the entire time, and if somehow he were a traitor, he could have said Gregor wasn't waiting at the hotel. That leaves only you and me. I haven't told Gregor anything, so that leaves . . . you."

I was stunned. "You think *I've* been sneaking behind your back with Gregor?"

"Not on purpose, but in the same way Gregor maneuvered you to Paris, and communicated with you in your dreams; who's to say he hasn't found a way to eavesdrop as well? It's a guess, Kitten, but if I'm wrong, you only lose some time awake."

And if he was right . . .

"What's your plan? Smack me into a coma and wait to see if Gregor goes away?" I'd thought nothing was worse than feeling helpless, but being a potential liability? *That* was worse.

"Of course not. But when we change locations, I want you to take those pills so you'll sleep. If you don't know where we are, but Gregor's still able to track you, we'll know it's not from his picking through your mind while you dream."

God, this sucked. Like waiting to see if an animal was rabid, I'd be penned and quarantined.

"Then why did you bother waking me? We're on a plane. I can hear the engines. Why not wait until we got to where we're going?"

"You need to eat and drink, and I thought you'd like to freshen up."

Once again I reached for the blindfold, and once again he stopped me.

"Leave it on."

"Why? I already know we're on a plane, but I can't navigate by the clouds!"

"You don't know what kind of plane," Bones replied intractably. "Make, model, type; these things could be used to trace you. It's just for a little while, Kitten."

Just for little while if he was wrong. But for how long if he was right?

"Fine. Which is first, the feeding or the cleaning? I don't know whether to open my mouth or take off my clothes."

He didn't say anything for a moment. Then, "I'm sorry."

"Does that mean you're going to hit me? Last time you apologized, my head got dented."

I clung to flippancy to avoid bursting into tears at the thought that somehow I was the one who'd been tipping Gregor off.

"It's your preference, and no, I'm not going to hit you."

I wished I could see his eyes. They'd have told me more about what he was really thinking. But all I had was his voice, and Bones was keeping it carefully controlled.

"Then show me the way to the bathroom. Even I can tell that I stink."

However long I'd been out, it wasn't for only a quick nap. My bladder was squealing, and my mouth tasted filmy. Charming.

His fingers curled around mine. "I'll show you."

Left with no other choice except to stumble around, I let Bones lead me.

I used the tiny bathroom sink to wash my hair. That was interesting to do while keeping my eyes closed, since I'd insisted the blindfold be removed. Bones stayed in the doorway the entire time, handing me whatever I needed. From the sounds, there were others on the plane with us. Even though none of them would peek, I felt exposed with the door open. When I was finished, he gave me new clothes.

Then I got spoon-fed. With every bite of what tasted like chicken, my sense of despair rose. So much for equality in our relationship. I couldn't be more useless right now. When Bones handed me the four caplets, I gulped them down eagerly. Better to be knocked out than this.

Bones woke me again after however long, and we repeated the procedure. The sightless rocking and lolling told me we were still on a plane, but it might have been a different one. The engine sounded throatier. Again I snatched at the pills and washed them down, this time refusing to be spoon-fed. I wasn't going to starve, and keeping hydrated was the only real concern. Bones didn't argue. He just stroked my head while I waited for them to take effect.

The last thing I heard before blackness claimed me was, ". . . landing soon, Crispin." It sounded like Spade. Or maybe I was already dreaming.

ELEVEN

MY EYES OPENED, ADJUSTING TO THE BRIGHT light of the room. I was still swallowing Bones's familiar-tasting blood when I became aware that it was from a glass, not a vein.

"If I had to drink that animal's blood each day, I'd cheerfully starve myself to death."

Oh, dear God. Please let me be dreaming! "Mom?"

She gave me a disapproving frown before setting the glass on a nearby table.

"You've lost weight again. Can't that creature keep you from starving?"

Nope, not dreaming. This was her in the flesh. "What are you doing here? Where's Bones?"

She held up a hand. "He went out somewhere. Even if I knew where, I wouldn't be able to say. You know, in case the other vampire would find out. I must say, Catherine, you have deplorable taste in men."

Jesus, Mary, and Joseph. Any one of the three, help me. "Can we skip the usual Bash Bones game? I'm not in a good mood."

"Nor should you be," she said without sympathy. How typical. "You married the frying pan, and now it looks as though you may have also wed the fire."

What had Bones been thinking, bringing her here? Sure, have my mother spend some time with me. After that, I'd be *begging* to be drugged.

"Don't mention Gregor, or I'll . . ."

I stopped, and her mouth curled. "You'll what, Catherine?"

What indeed? She was my mother. I couldn't threaten to slap, stab, beat, or even name-call her. I tried to think of something to scare her into never mentioning my predicament with the Dreamsnatcher again.

"I'll become a swinger," I said. Her eyes bugged. Uptight rearing made her uncomfortable with alternate lifestyles. "That's right. Threesomes, foursomes, more. Bones knows about a thousand chicks who'd love to hop into bed with us. It'll be kinky, we'll get our freak on—"

She puffed up in outrage. "Catherine!"

Below us, I heard a feminine laugh. One recognizable and just as unexpected.

"What is it you Americans say? I call shotgun!"

Annette, the first vampire Bones ever created, laughed again. It was the knowing chuckle of someone not kidding.

My mother vaulted to her feet. The bedroom was open and Annette had spoken loud enough for even my mother to hear her.

"The day after never, you voracious English tramp!"

Even though I mentally applauded the insult, I was the one who'd started this. "Mom, don't call Annette a tramp. It's none of your business how many people she's banged."

Okay, so I couldn't be entirely magnanimous. What had Bones been thinking, having both of them under the same roof with me? Considering her centuries-long, graphic former relationship with Bones, Annette and I didn't get along very well on the best of days. My mother and I had lots of issues despite her recent softening toward the undead, one ghoul in particular.

"Mom, nice to see you. Now, I'd like to take a real bath."

She rose. "Everyone in the house knows not to mention where we are, so you can do whatever as long as you don't go outside. I brought some clothes for you. They're in the closet. Oh, and don't turn on the television. Or the radio, and needless to say, you can't use the phone."

With that helpful information, she swept out. I paused for a second, then swung my legs out of bed. At least I'd get to bathe without assistance. Baby steps and all that.

After I was thoroughly bathed, groomed, and dressed, I went downstairs, where I could hear all the other voices. Mission accomplished on me not knowing where the hell I was. All I could surmise was that the house was older, though modernly refurbished, and it was on a steep cliff. The outside window had told me that. Green hills and rocks stretched as far as the eye could see, and the air smelled different. It could have been the northern Rockies, but somehow, it didn't feel like America. Maybe Canada. Maybe not.

I decided I shouldn't keep guessing. That would defeat the purpose, after all.

The chatter stopped with almost comical abruptness when I came into the kitchen. Five heads picked up with false nonchalance. In addition to my mother and Annette, Bones's sire Ian was here, along with Spade and Rodney.

"Hi, everyone," I remarked. "Is this the whole crew? Or are there more of you lurking around?"

"Oh, there's more," my mother began before she cried out, "Ouch! Who kicked me?"

An unladylike snort escaped me. "That would be Spade. So, I'm not even allowed to know who's here? Why does that matter?"

"Just a few guards, Cat," Spade replied dismissively, eyeing my mother with warning. "Nothing to bother about."

"Fine." If I demanded to know more, I'd probably get the blindfold again.

Ian was reclined in a chair, legs crossed at the ankles. His turquoise eyes contained a roguish gleam as he slid them to my mother.

"I missed you last night when I arrived. Lovely to see you again, poppet," Ian drawled.

Rodney gave Ian the same warning look I did, but for a different reason. Rodney and my mother were, ah, dating. Or at least, they were the last I'd heard. Dwelling on my mother's romantic life squicked me out, and that had nothing to do with Rodney being a ghoul.

"Leave my mother alone," I said to Ian, glowering at him.

He smiled, unrepentant. Ian wouldn't know how to feel remorse if his afterlife depended on it. Though he'd proven to be a loyal friend to Bones, Ian and I had a murky history. He liked to collect the rare and unusual, be they items or people. That penchant had led Ian to try blackmailing me into a "friends with benefits" relationship once, before Ian knew my whole history with Bones. Now Ian didn't make an inappropriate move toward me, but he did seem to take enjoyment in finding ways to annoy me.

Case in point: Ian cast a leisurely look at my mother, making sure I saw him pause at certain parts. Then he grinned.

"*Truly* a pleasure to see you again, Justina."

All I could hope was that the same revulsion for vampires that had made my childhood hellish would serve my mother now. My mother hated my father, Max, since he'd seduced her, then told her she'd just had sex with an evil demon—all because he thought it was funny. She'd gotten pregnant from that encounter and thought she gave birth to a half-demon baby—me. I'd paid for my father's warped sense of humor all my life, until Bones showed me that there was more to vampires than fangs.

My mother still must not be convinced that fangs didn't equate to evil, judging from the look she gave Ian.

"Don't you have somewhere else you could be?" she asked him in a withering voice.

Ian's smile just broadened. "Certainly. Pull up your skirt, and I'll show you."

"That's it!" I shrieked, lunging at Ian even as Rodney upended his chair and came after him as well. We both were so blinded by fury; all Ian had to do was slide back to watch us clang into each other instead of him.

"Ian, enough," Spade snapped, stepping between me and Rodney when both of us leapt to our feet for another try. "Cat, Rodney—Ian's finished now. Isn't he?"

Spade glared at Ian, who just lifted one shoulder in a shrug.

"For now."

I was trapped indoors with my mother, her pissed-off boyfriend, Bones's ex-lover, his horny sire, and his secretive best friend. Whatever appetite I'd had when I came downstairs was gone. The only thing I wanted to do was get away from all of them, but that meant hiding in my room, and I'd had enough of that, too.

Maybe there was one thing that could help. I went to the cabinets and began to rifle through them with single-minded determination.

"What are you looking for, Catherine?" my mother asked.

"Liquor."

I was into my third bottle of Jack Daniel's when Bones arrived. It was sunset, the dying rays turning his hair reddish as he walked through the door. Even a glimpse of his hard, rippled frame caused my hand to tighten on the whiskey. God, he looked good, but I needed to slam the lid on my dirty mind and seek other things to think about. Farm equipment. Agriculture. The state of the economy.

"Blimey, Kitten, is this what you've been doing all day? Drinking?"

The judgmental tone Bones used doused my momentary ardor. Nope, no need to ponder the national deficit next!

"Your color's good, so who are you to talk," I said. "Is that what took you so long? Did she taste extra yummy?"

I was jealous, as irrational as that might be. Bones picked women to feed from for two reasons—with his looks, they were pathetically easy to get alone, and he liked their flavor more. I hadn't believed Bones could really taste the difference between male and female blood until he proved it to me. The man could flawlessly genderize a whole blood bank. Once he'd commented that he thought it might be an acquired liking of estrogen.

"She didn't taste like a gallon of whiskey, that's for certain," he shot back, coming over and arching a brow at my near-empty bottle. "Is that all you've had today?"

"Certainly is, Crispin," Ian sang out. "She's been drinking with the pluck of an Irishman!"

I had nothing heavy nearby to throw at Ian aside from the whiskey, and I wasn't letting go of that. "Bite me, Ian!"

Bones snatched at my bottle, but I'd been anticipating that. I held on, and it was tug-of-war.

"Put it down," he barked, prying my hand from my prize. "You need solid food, Kitten, and about a keg of water. Crikey, where's your mum? Can't the woman be counted on to at least see that you eat?"

If he had been trying to piss me off, he couldn't have picked a better way. "Oh sure. Have someone feed me, water me, and keep me on a leash. You know what you should have married, Bones? A dog, then you wouldn't have all those pesky problems about it *occasionally* acting on its own."

"This is just what I bloody need," he growled, running a hand through his hair. "Coming home to a drunken harpy, waiting to knock my head off."

This isn't what *he* needed? I was the one who'd been

punched out, drugged, reduced to hand-feedings—all because of a crazy vampire who'd kidnapped me when I was sixteen and didn't want to take no for an answer now. "Being a 'drunken harpy' has been the highlight of my week, so excuse me if I'm not waiting by the door for you with a big red X on my neck to mark the spot where you can get your dessert."

Part of me was horrified at what I'd just said. After all, I wasn't mad at Bones, just the circumstances. But somehow, my mental filter between what I didn't mean and what I'd said, was broken. I couldn't even blame it on the liquor, either. Being half-vampire meant I couldn't get drunk on normal booze.

"Right now I'd say it's what *you* need," Bones shot back. "Is that it? Shall I take you to bed and bite some of the waspishness out of you? Even though I'd rather flog some sense into you instead, as a vampire, I'm up for the task whether I'd want to or not."

My mouth swung open, and my hand actually tingled with the urge to slap him.

And at the same time, I wanted to cry. This was all so wrong. I was falling to pieces and doing it alone, despite the numerous people around me.

Something of this either showed on my face, or he heard it in the whirling chaos of my mind. Bones's features lost their icy callousness, and he sighed.

"Kitten . . ."

"Don't." My breath caught, choking back the sob. I couldn't seem to control how I felt or what came out of my mouth, so it was better if I was alone. Fast, before I said something else I didn't mean.

"I'm, uh, tired."

I walked up the stairs, leaving the whiskey behind on the couch. It hadn't helped. In fact, all I'd done since

I woke up was to make matters worse. I knew this situation wasn't Bones's fault. He was only doing this to keep everyone safe, including me. But somehow, I ended up taking out my frustration on him. At least unconscious, I couldn't fuck things up between us more.

I shut the door behind me. There weren't any glasses in the bedroom, so I cupped my palm and used the sink water to swallow Don's pills. Their quantity was dwindling. I'd have to have him ship more to me—except I didn't know where we were.

That falling sensation began shortly after, like the mattress opened up, and I was being sucked down into it. For a split second, I felt panic, reaching out for anything to hold onto. Yet just as requested, I was alone.

Later, when I felt cool flesh against my mouth, I was relieved. Then I finished swallowing and knew this wasn't Bones, even with my eyes closed and just coming into wakefulness. The blood tasted different.

Spade blinked into view. He removed his hand, but didn't get up from his seated position on the bed. It was still dark out. Sadly, I hadn't slept the whole miserable day away.

"Where's Bones?" I asked.

"He's outside, should be back in shortly."

I didn't say anything, but my anguish at how things had deteriorated to where Bones couldn't even take the time to wake me must have shown on my face. Spade sighed.

"He's not used to this, Cat, and he's handling it quite poorly."

"Not used to what?" *Being married to a psychotic bitch?* my mind supplied.

"Fear." Spade lowered his voice. "Crispin's always prided himself on his emotional control, yet he has none with you. He's never before experienced the fear of losing the person he loves to someone else. Oh, your friend Tate might brass Crispin off, but he knows Tate is no real threat. Gregor's different. He's older than Crispin, more powerful, and no one knows how much you might have cared for him."

I was afraid Spade had underestimated the situation. "I don't think that's the issue. Bones and I can't even be around each other without fighting."

"Both of you are in foul tempers with little to do but lash out at each other, but don't lose sight of priorities. Isn't he what you're fighting for?"

I bit my lip. "What if it *is* me that's giving away our location? What if everything I know gets repeated to Gregor in my sleep somehow? I'd be putting everyone in danger by just waking up! And I can't seem to get a grip on myself."

My voice cracked. The room blurred as my eyes filled up. See? Emotional train wreck, just like I'd described.

"I think I should go to Don," I said finally, wiping my eyes. "He has facilities I don't know about, and they're built to withstand bunker-buster bombs. I could wait there until things calmed down. And then I wouldn't be jeopardizing everyone around me—"

"You're not going anywhere."

Bones filled the doorframe behind Spade. I hadn't even heard him come up the stairs; he'd moved almost as silently as Fabian. Green glinted in his eyes, and his expression was granite.

"In case you weren't paying attention, Kitten, I'll say it again. You're not going anywhere. Not to Don, or to anyone else. You're mine, so don't mention leaving again."

This wasn't a tender declaration of "I need you here with me." No, it was the dispassionate pronouncement of "You're *my* ball and chain, and it's *my* ankle you're shackled to!" Bones turned and walked away after making the statement, not bothering to say anything else.

Spade squeezed my hand before sliding off the bed, looking at me almost pityingly before he left.

"It will be all right."

I didn't argue, but I didn't believe him. Bones hadn't even given me a chance to apologize for earlier before he'd stalked off. Everything that mattered to me—my relationship with Bones, my independence, being there for my friends, taking down murderers—all that was in tatters. Most of that was Gregor's fault. Some of it, however, was mine. At least I could do something about that.

First things first. I had to get my wildly swinging emotions under control so that when I saw Bones later, we could talk things out. I concentrated on my emotional defenses, strong barriers forged from my childhood days when even my mother rejected me, then honed and thickened over the years when I'd left Bones. They were as familiar to me as my skin, and right now, they were the only things that could hold me together.

When I felt grounded enough, I began to plan. I'd start with a long, hot shower, then do some training to blow off steam. If I was lucky, I'd get Ian to spar with me. Tearing into him sounded like a good start, and he'd been spoiling for a rematch since the day I beat him.

Well, Ian, I thought, *today's your lucky day!*

And then after that, I'd talk to Bones. Try to hash things out between us before they got any worse.

†WELVE

Iᴀɴ ɢʟᴏᴡᴇʀᴇᴅ ᴜᴘ ᴀ† ᴍᴇ. "Iꜰ ɪ† ᴡᴇʀᴇɴ'† ꜱᴏ bleedin' close to dawn, I'd make you beg for mercy."

I was on top of him, my legs on either side of his waist. He might have liked it under other circumstances. Right now, though, with a knife sticking out of his chest, he had other things on his mind.

"Sore loser," I responded, yanking the blade out and leaping to my feet. "Come on. Again."

"This is a poor substitute for shagging," he grumbled, rising and frowning at the rent in his shirt. "You've ruined it."

"I told you to just take it off." With a shrug.

Ian grinned at me. "Ah, but I thought you only wanted to enjoy the goods, poppet."

He'd kept up a steady stream of comments and innuendoes designed to throw me off my game. I didn't take it seriously. I knew it was just how he operated.

"Keep talking, pretty boy. It only makes your silent moments better."

That drew a laugh as we circled each other. Ian's eyes glittered with expectation. He loved a nasty brawl. It was one of his admirable qualities.

"Find me pretty, do you? I always knew it. Alas, Reaper, we'd have had a grand time of it before, but you had to marry Crispin. Now you're off-limits forever, but it would have been fun. Very fun."

"You never stood a chance, Ian."

He ducked the knife I flung at him with another dirty chuckle.

"Poor aim, sweet. Missed me by a meter. Still chafing at the thought of how easily I could have bedded you before Crispin came back into your life? Do you really think you could have resisted me for long if I'd set out to have you?"

Arrogant bastard. I charged at him, but Ian sidestepped me at the last instant. Too late I knew I'd made a mistake. His foot swept out, his fists followed, and I was knocked off-balance. An elbow crashed into my back. It dropped me to the floor with him right on top of me. He yanked my arms back, bending them the wrong way, and his mouth latched onto my neck.

"One flick of my fangs and your throat would be torn open," he murmured before releasing me. I flipped over, wincing, to find him staring down at me with objective triumph.

"Temper, temper," he said. "It's both your weakness and your strength."

I scrambled to my feet, moving slower from what had to be broken bones in my rib cage. My rotator cuffs were hyperextended as well. They burned almost as much as my ribs. "One out of three, Ian. I wouldn't be so quick to brag."

"I knew I'd beat you eventually," he countered. "Everyone makes mistakes, given enough time."

I heard footsteps approach, and my mother came into the room. She looked at the haphazardly rearranged furniture, at me, then at Ian.

"Catherine, how long are you going to be bashing around down here?" she asked.

"Aren't you going to say hallo, poppet?"

Ian fairly purred the question. I mouthed wordless dire threats to him over her shoulder. He just grinned at me.

She ignored him, my irregular breathing registering to her. "Are you all right, Catherine?"

Two could play the taunting game over her. For effect, I wheezed noisily.

"No I'm not. Ian broke my ribs."

"Tattletale." He smirked, knowing what I was doing.

Instead of being overcome with concern, she tapped her foot.

"You shouldn't have let him get that close. Maybe since you quit your job, you're losing your edge."

Son of a *bitch*. I puffed up in outrage. Ian stifled a laugh.

Then the television stuffed into the far corner of the room turned on. I glanced around in confusion, expecting to see some newcomer with a remote control, when Ian let out a curse.

"Bollocks."

"Huh?"

He grasped my arm with one hand and my mother's with the other. My protest was cut off with his next muttered words.

"Dawn. Why does every ghoul feel the need to attack at dawn?"

Ian propelled us out of the room and up the basement staircase. From every corner of the house, people were coming out of their rooms and the TVs were on. Not blaring, just set to low volumes. It hit me then what the synchronized powering of the televisions was. An alarm. A subtle one.

"Who's attacking?"

"Can't stay and chat about it," Ian ground out, rounding the next corner to nearly collide into Bones. "Ah, Crispin. Feeling frisky, I trust? It promises to be a busy morning."

"So it does," Bones said, landing a heavy hand on my shoulder. "You're coming with me, Kitten. Ian, take her mum below."

"Wait."

I tugged at one of the knives on Bones's belt. He was wearing several. Maybe this wasn't so unexpected after all. "My ribs are fractured and I've got some torn ligaments. You'll have to give me blood so that doesn't slow me down."

Ian let out a mocking grunt. "I won't wait to hear the rest of this."

"Nor should you," Bones shot back. "Kitten, this way."

He ignored the knife I held up and drew me up to the third level of the house. At first I thought he had weapons waiting for me. Or protective gear, Bones was big on me wearing that. But when we entered the bedroom and he pushed an unseen button in the closet, revealing a small room I hadn't known was there, I understood.

And was furious.

"You're out of your mind if you think I'm hiding in this box."

"I don't have time to argue," Bones cut me off, shoving me inside. "There are monitors, a phone, your cell, and more of your belongings. These are ghouls attacking. With those rumors Majestic said were swirling around, who do you think they'll target? You, and anyone guarding you. If you remain out of sight, it will improve the chances of everyone fighting, so for God's sake, Kitten, stay here."

One glance at Bones's blazing eyes told me that awake or lights out, I would be in this shelter.

"You have a monitor facing this door," he went on, tapping another button on an interior panel. "If anyone you don't recognize tries to get in, you hit this. Now back away."

Without waiting for me to comply, he pushed me farther into the room and hit the exterior device. The door slid shut with a heavy clinking sound of locks settling into place. They quieted with a finality that was appropriate for the settings. I was sealed in.

Something caught my attention farther back in this shoe box. Monitors. There were six of them, all with different angles. One pointed toward the closet exterior, as Bones had said, but the others were aimed at the outer grounds. It startled me to see the exterior of the house, because it spoke volumes about where we were. No wonder I hadn't been allowed to even step outside. From the looks of it, I was in a small castle. I hadn't been able to tell that from the inside, considering how modern the interior was.

Dawn was just breaking. The sparse lightening of the sky made it easier to see the rush of activity outside, since it didn't appear that the cameras had night vision. Most of the angles were fixed at points around the castle, but one was aimed at the sloping hill of the lower yard.

I gasped. There were so *many* of them.

Over a hundred ghouls marched with lethal steadiness up the uneven ground. They were all armed. Some held even more deadly devices than guns or knives, like rocket launchers. How many people were here? Bones, Spade, Rodney, Ian . . . and a few guards, Spade had said. Against such numbers, it would be a slaughter. *Why didn't they land-mine the lawn?* I raged. *Why aren't there more people here? And why are they lining up in front of the house like fucking targets, instead of barricading behind the walls!*

A man strode up from the ranks and approached the castle. He was of medium height, with salt-and-pepper hair and a commanding manner. He was saying something, but the damn monitors didn't have sound. The room was too reinforced for my ears, so I couldn't hear on my own, either. Whatever it was, it didn't appear to be well received. Bones pointed an emphatic finger at the man, and it wasn't his index one. The guy spat at the ground before whirling around and returning to the others.

With or without sound, it was clear that negotiations wouldn't happen.

The first of the machine guns began firing. As one, the vampires took to the air, while Rodney manned a machine gun of his own. I was relieved to see some unfamiliar faces come from the castle to join Bones and the others. The vampires disappeared from the screens for a few seconds, reemerging as they bombarded the ghouls like their bodies were inhuman missiles. When they flew off in bursts of speed, either the ghoul would be headless on the ground, or dazed.

It was an incredible sight to see. From my rapid calculation, there were a dozen vampires guarding the castle, and each one of them struck with the force of a guided tornado.

Except it didn't appear to be enough. The ghouls who survived the fierce one-on-ones didn't stay dazed long. They shook themselves off and began their grim march forward. Step by step, they were covering the distance to the castle. Their numbers were lessening, true, but they had an obvious determination. Bones and the others might be formidable, but math was math. There weren't enough of them.

After about twenty minutes of fierce fighting, the ghoul spokesman fired a flare, illuminating the still-muted sky in a blaze. I tensed, my hand pressed against the unforgiving screen as if that could offer assistance. It didn't, of course. And the others forces began emerging from beneath the cover of the lower hills.

I screamed, vaulting up and tugging at the door to my sealed cage. It didn't even budge. I started searching to find the lever to open this trap. There had to be one.

My heart was pounding so loudly, it seemed to be screaming along with me. Another hundred ghouls had just come from the concealment of the landscape. They had attacked in two waves, a clever, deadly plan. Pick just before dawn when the vampires were weakest. Have them expend their power on the first segment, draining them further. Then, when they were at their weariest, close in for the kill. And here was I, locked in a safe room, utterly helpless to do anything but watch.

A ring shattered my concentration. With my hammering pulse, I actually waited a second to see if it was real or imagined. It sounded again, and I had to wade through the spilled items I'd flung about to find its source. Underneath some clothes was my cell phone. I grabbed at it, hoping against hope that it was Don. Maybe he could help. Send some troops, even if I didn't know where the fuck we were.

"Catherine."

The voice reached me before I'd even had time to gasp hello. It wasn't my uncle.

"Gregor."

I was breathing heavily, a combination of my broken ribs, terror over losing Bones, and my futile search for a way out.

"Don't be afraid, my wife."

His tone was soothing, but it had an undercurrent of something else. What, I didn't know or care.

"I don't have time for this . . ." Spaces were needed to catch my breath. "Have to get out of here . . ."

"You are in no danger."

That made a harsh laugh escape me. "Boy, are you wrong."

"They won't harm you, Catherine."

Now I clutched the phone and recognized what his voice held. Confidence.

"These are your ghouls, aren't they?" I breathed.

On the screen, Bones was regrouping the vampires nearest to him, dodging gunfire with every second. The earlier scene made sense to me now. An envoy had approached and made a demand that Bones refused.

It didn't take a genius to figure out what that demand was. That's why Bones had me under lock and key. He knew I wouldn't have sacrificed everyone if I could help it.

"It doesn't have to end this way, *ma chérie*," Gregor said. "Come to me, and I swear my people will leave without further harm to yours."

"What you don't know is that I'm locked in a panic room," I snapped. "Even if I wanted to, I can't go anywhere."

"You don't have to move from where you are to come to me," he almost purred, "I am the Dreamsnatcher. I can get you if you but sleep."

Sleep? Who could sleep at a time like this? The walls vibrated from the barrage of shooting, and I was going to throw up over what was on the monitors. Short of banging my head against the wall until I passed out, I didn't see sleep happening.

"Easier said than done."

My voice trailed off, losing its desperate scorn. Bones had packed this room with care. There were a few books, snack foods, beverages, writing utensils, and most importantly—pills.

I weighed the decision, glancing between the pill bottle and the desperate scenario playing out on the monitors. *Mencheres said Gregor didn't want to hurt me. All the precautions Bones had taken were to keep Gregor from finding me, but not because Gregor wanted to kill me, because Gregor wanted me with him.*

It might be dangerous to go to him, but Bones and my friends were in far more danger now than I'd be with Gregor later. I couldn't just sit back and hope a miracle would prevent them from being slaughtered before my eyes.

"I'll do it, but not without conditions."

Gregor made a disbelieving noise. "Perhaps you don't know the seriousness of what's happening."

"I've got a bird's-eye view," I corrected him, biting my lip. "But I still have conditions."

Another scoff. "I won't harm you, Catherine."

"That's nice, but it's not what I'm after." God, the new force of ghouls was starting to fire, converging with the remaining first group. I didn't have much time. "As soon as I'm with you, this attack stops. You're responsible to make sure they get called off and stay called off. You want me to remember what happened with us? Fine, I'll do it. But if after I remember everything, I still want to go back to Bones . . . you'll let me leave, immediately, and without exception. It's a gamble, Dreamsnatcher, how confident are you?"

I was deliberately going for his arrogance. There was no doubt in my mind that whatever I discovered, it wouldn't change my feelings toward Bones. Gregor didn't know that, of course. With my open challenge, he'd have to be insecure not to agree, and he didn't strike me as insecure.

"I wouldn't turn you out without protection, if it came to that. I would see you safely escorted," was his careful, measured reply. "Yes, I am confident enough to gamble. Your terms are acceptable."

I wasn't going to let him mince words. "Swear it on your life, Gregor, because that's what I'll take if you're lying."

"You're threatening me?" He sounded amused. "Fine. I swear it on my life."

I released a deep sigh. I didn't really trust Gregor, but I had to take the chance. If I didn't, and everyone here died, I'd never forgive myself. *Lord, please let Gregor be telling the truth, and please, please, let Bones understand.*

"All right. Get ready to do your stuff, because here I come."

I snapped the cell phone shut and picked up the bottle of sleeping pills Bones had stored in case I needed to keep Gregor out. What he hadn't guessed was that I might use them to let Gregor in.

Don had been very specific about the dosage. Four pills all at once. If I took less, they'd make me fall into normal sleep. I unscrewed the cap and popped two in my mouth, washing them down with a bottle of water. Then I grabbed a pen that had been stacked near my books. The pills metabolized quickly; I was already starting to feel dizzy. There wasn't any paper in this cell, so I ripped out a page from one of the books and scribbled on the small blank space.

I'm coming back . . .

The words blurred before I was even done writing them. With my last effort, I stabbed them into place with the pen. Then my vision blackened completely.

I was running, except for once, I wasn't being chased.

"Come closer, Catherine."

I followed his voice and saw him ahead. Gregor was smiling a cool, expectant grin. It made me slow down the last few paces.

"Remember our deal." I warned, feeling his power reach out with its invisible tentacles.

Gregor's gaze glinted. "Come to me."

For a second, I hesitated. I glanced behind my shoulder, hoping Bones would somehow appear. He didn't, of course. He was battling for his life and the lives of those around him. Well, at least now, I could help.

I crossed the space and let Gregor enfold me in his arms. Something that might have been his lips brushed my neck, but aside from that . . .

"Nothing's happening."

I said it into his chest, him being so damn tall. That blurry dreamlike feeling didn't cease even though the air around us seemed to electrify.

"I don't understand," he muttered.

"Of all the luck, now you're having performance issues?" I hissed, growing agitated over the thought of what was happening to Bones. "Come on, Gregor. Get your Dreamsnatcher on."

He held me tighter. "It must be you," he whispered. "You're blocking me."

Shit. Dropping my defenses was about the hardest thing for me to do, especially with a stranger I didn't trust.

"I'm trying not to."

His eyes blazed. "Your delay could be costly."

Damn him, he was right. I had to get into this. Fast.

I wound my arms around his neck and pulled his head down. When his mouth slanted over mine, I kissed him, slightly surprised that it felt familiar. With the distraction of him kissing me with a rough hungriness, I felt my shields waver and crack. *Let go, Cat. Just ease up and relax . . .*

A roaring pain swamped over me, like I was being pulled inside out. Amidst the white noise and confusion, I would have screamed, but I didn't have a throat, a voice, or a body. I felt the indescribable terror of being stripped from my own skin and flung into nothingness. It was the worst feeling of falling, only at sonic speed.

When it culminated, I wasn't reunited with my body; I was splattered back into it. The sensation of being blood, flesh, and bone again had me transfixed by the sound of my own heartbeat, a numbing cadence that was the sweetest thing I'd heard.

"Catherine."

Only then did the rest of my senses kick into gear. Guess a molecular transport will knock the everliving shit out of anyone unlucky enough to experience it. It occurred to me that I wasn't standing anymore, though I was still wrapped up in Gregor's arms. In slow motion, my mind began to take inventory. *Two arms, two legs, check. Wiggle fingers and toes, check. Ribs still hurt, okay. Heart pounding like a jackhammer, right.* But something was missing.

Large hands slid down my bare back. Gregor, solid and very much not a dream, wore a triumphant smile on his face.

And just like me, it was the only thing he had on.

Thirteen

WHERE ARE MY CLOTHES?"

It was a furious demand that earned me a reproving frown. "Don't snarl so, Catherine. I can only transport the organic."

Maybe that was true, but it didn't explain why he was also *au naturel.* I doubted it was an accident. His caressing me sure wasn't accidental.

"Get your hands off me, Gregor, and go call off your men like you promised. Right now."

I didn't say it in the same angry tone. No, this was with a cold, flat insistence.

He stared at me in a way that made me think he was going to refuse. Then, with deliberate slowness, he uncurled himself from me.

"Don't try to get up yet, you'll need time to recover."

I was in a bed. Oh, sure, like this wasn't specifically orchestrated. "I'll be fine as long as you stick to your word."

He didn't respond, just strode to the door and yanked it open. I had enough instinctive modesty to flop onto my stomach, but there was still no coordination to my limbs.

Someone was right outside the room, and Gregor stepped back to let that person in.

"Lucius, observe."

Lucius, a tall blond who might have been Nordic, observed, all right. He caught an eyeful of me glaring daggers at both of them.

"I have my wife. She came of her own volition, so you can instruct Simon to pull back his forces."

"I have yet to learn that I'm your wife, and I came because you blackmailed me," I replied, giving him a look that said I didn't appreciate his play on words.

"Be sure to detail her exact condition for Simon to report," Gregor said, ignoring that. "And do be sure to include mine as well."

God in heaven, Bones was going to flip out. I felt a stirring of unease. Maybe I should have thought this over more.

"*Oui, monsieur.*"

Lucius left without a backward glance, and Gregor shut the door. I didn't care for that, since he was still on the inside.

"Is he going to call this Simon? How close are we to there?" I asked, able to grasp some of the blanket and roll myself into it.

"He'll call." A light gleamed in his eyes. "But we're very far from Bavaria, Catherine."

"Bavaria?" Jeez, no wonder it had seemed remote. "Where are we now? Or I suppose you won't tell me."

It was very awkward having a conversation with a naked stranger. Gregor didn't make any attempt to cover himself, either. I wasn't looking, but I wasn't blind. He was built like a football player, with a whole lot of muscle and intermittent scars on his skin.

"I'll tell you. I'm not like that scavenger who shuttled you back and forth while keeping you sightless and witless."

That last sentence told it all. It had been me after all.

I gave Gregor a level look. "I might not be dreaming of you, but you're still in my head poking around. You must have been doing a pretty thorough job to know details like that."

Gregor sat on the edge of the bed, reaching out to stop me from rolling away. The lack of synchronization in my movements frightened me. I wanted to jump out of the bed, but all I could do was twitch.

"I know what you know," he said, tracing his hand down my arm. "I cannot transport someone, or invade their mind, without their blood having been inside me. Even though it was many years ago, your blood is still a part of me, Catherine."

Another tidbit no one had mentioned before. "If you know what I do, then you're aware I love Bones," I answered.

"You think you do." His hand slid lower, to the bottom of the blanket and slowly up inside it.

Feeling his fingers climb up my calf didn't arouse me. It pissed me off.

"What kind of piece of shit would fondle a woman who can't move to stop him?"

His hand froze on my leg. I managed to flop back around and keep the blanket over me with a shaky grip. At least now I was facing him instead of craning my neck around.

"The only reason I agreed to withdraw my men in

exchange for your compliance is because Bones has saved you from death several times," Gregor ground out. "But now, he gets no more passes from me."

"Is that what you call not murdering him, my mother, and my friends in a dirty ambush at dawn? A *pass*? How'd you find us, anyway? It wasn't from me this time."

Gregor's jaw clenched. "I found you because of Bones's stupidity, and if he'd had me and my men in a similar circumstance, he'd have acted with the same ruthlessness."

I opened my mouth to respond when there was an urgent knock.

"I said no interruptions," Gregor barked, streaking to the door and flinging it open.

It was Lucius again. He almost hopped up and down in nervousness. "Master, you must come with me. I-I have . . . news."

The way his eyes kept flicking to me had me swinging my rubbery legs out of bed and managing to stand.

"What happened? Did what's-his-name not get the message?" I asked, fighting dizziness.

"You need me to come with you now?" Gregor repeated, gesturing to me. "This is the first I've spent with my wife in a dozen years. This can't wait?"

"No, *monsieur*," Lucius whispered, lowering his head.

"Is it Bones?" I demanded, staggering and falling when my legs wouldn't hold. "If he's dead, Gregor—"

"Is that swine still alive?" he interrupted. "Answer so she won't become hysterical."

"Ah, yes, he is." The sweetest of words. "If you would please come this way—"

"My mother?" I cut him off, thinking what else might have gone tragically wrong.

"I have no knowledge of any fatalities among your friends," Lucius said, almost wringing his hands.

"You've heard what you requested," Gregor said, picking me up and depositing me back in bed. "If you don't want to injure yourself, stay there. I won't be long."

With that, he swept out. There was the distinct sound of bolts sliding after he shut the door. Left with few other productive options, I lay there and practiced moving my limbs.

Gregor came back about an hour later, dressed in pants but no shirt. Some clothes were better than none. I sat up with the sheet to my chin and pillows propped behind me. When he met my gaze, something flickered across his hard features. His mouth softened, but he didn't quite smile.

"You remind me of the girl you were. You're not her anymore, but right now, you look like you are."

It was incredibly strange. He was remembering someone I used to be, and I had no idea who that was. A sixteen-year-old Catherine who didn't hate vampires and went to Paris with one? Never met her.

"No, I'm not her anymore," I agreed. "Since there's no turning back the clock, why don't we part in a semifriendly manner now?"

He didn't respond to that. "Your body's also different. You're an inch taller, and you've gained weight."

"Everyone's a critic," I muttered.

That made him smile, creasing the scar on his eyebrow. " 'Twas no insult, *ma femme*. It plumps your breasts and softens your thighs."

Way too much information and in the wrong, wrong direction. "Gregor," I shifted, and a strained breath escaped me. The movement put pressure on my ribs.

In the next instant, he was looming over me. "You're hurt. I thought it was just unease after the transport, but you're in pain."

"It's nothing." I brushed his hands away. "Got banged up sparring with a friend, I'm fine. Where are we? You never said."

"Austria." He sat without being invited, and I scooted back, not liking his proximity.

"And what's this news Lucius doesn't want me to know?" My brow arched as I asked, daring him to tell me.

His shoulder lifted in a half shrug. "No one you hold dear was captured or killed. My men ceased as instructed, and my promise is fulfilled."

"Not all of your promise." Sharply.

"Nor all of yours. It's your turn." From his pants pocket, he withdrew a small silver knife, intricately etched. "Drink from me. Learn what was stolen from you."

Now that it was time for me to discover what had been ripped from my mind, I was uncertain. Was it possible I'd loved the vampire in front of me? I couldn't imagine that, but Gregor seemed so sure. What if learning this piece of my past *did* change things between Bones and me? Could I risk that?

But on the other hand, I didn't have a choice. If Gregor wanted to force me to drink his blood, in my condition, it would be easy. Besides, I refused to let doubt dictate my actions. I loved Bones. Nothing I remembered would change that, no matter what Gregor thought.

I didn't look away as I accepted the knife. When I reached for his hand, however, Gregor stopped me.

"No. Take from my neck, as I once took from yours."

I *really* didn't want to be closer to him, but refusing would be irrational. *At least Bones was wrong,* I thought. He swore Gregor would make me bite him.

Without hesitation, I jabbed the dirk into Gregor's throat and sealed my mouth over the wound, sucking. As I swallowed, I felt his arms go around me, but they didn't fully register. Something exploded in my brain. I wasn't falling this time; I was being propelled forward.

I waited downstairs by the front door as Cannelle, Gregor's housekeeper, had instructed me. She'd muttered something in French I hadn't completely understood, but it didn't sound friendly. Oh, in front of Gregor, Cannelle was polite. But as soon as his back was turned, she was cold and cutting. I didn't know why, but it made me sad. I was a long way from home, and I hadn't seen another soul aside from the few people in this house. A friend would have been so nice.

Gregor's entryway had the coldest design, I'd decided. High ceilings that didn't offer a glimpse of the sky. Harshly done paintings of unsmiling figures glaring at all who dared to enter. A set of hatchets crisscrossed together over a coat of arms. Yeah, comfy. If you were Adolf Hitler.

Gregor walked through the door moments later. He looked very imposing, wearing a long dark coat and shirt over coal-colored pants. Even though he intimidated me, I couldn't help but be dazzled by how gorgeous he was.

It still didn't seem real that Gregor was a vampire. I'd barely come to terms with being a half-breed myself before I was whisked away by a strange vampire that—unbelievably—my mother seemed to trust. Since she didn't trust anyone, Gregor had to be special.

"You're beautiful in your gown," he commented as he looked me over. "Very much a lovely young lady instead of a wandering farm child."

I cringed, but I didn't want him to see that he'd struck a nerve. "Thank Cannelle. She had everything laid out for me."

"I shall thank her, later," he answered with a glint. "Don't you prefer this to stained jeans and twigs in your hair?"

I'd barely spoken at all in the past two days, being too awed by him and my new circumstances, but that stiffened my spine. "It's been good enough for me my entire life," I said. "If you've got such a problem with where I came from, maybe you should put me back on a plane."

Come at me all you want, but don't put down my family. They couldn't help it that we weren't wealthy. My grandparents worked harder than most people and they were up in years.

Gregor spread out his hands. "I meant no offense, *chérie*. I'm from a farm as well, in the south of France, but there were no cherries to be found there. You see? More that we have in common."

I was somewhat mollified. "What else do we have in common?"

"Ah," he smiled, his features changing from their hard planes. "Come. You'll find out."

Gregor and I walked through the Parisian streets.

He took me to the lighted fountains in the square, retelling their history. It would have been a dream evening, if I hadn't had so many unanswered questions he kept changing the subject about.

"Why am I here with you?" I ended up blurting in growing frustration over not knowing why I'd been shuttled out of Ohio in such a hurry. "I mean, my mother said I had to go with you because some bad vampire was after me, but nobody said who."

We were almost at the Eiffel Tower. It was breathtaking, but all the scenery in the world couldn't distract me from finding out what was going on with my future.

Gregor gestured to a nearby bench, and we sat on it. The temperature had been dropping since sundown, and he took off his coat and handed it to me.

The simple gesture touched me and made me feel shy again. It was the way a guy would act on a date, or so I imagined. Gregor sat very close to me as well. Self-consciously, I worried about my breath, or if there was anything in my teeth.

"What you are, Catherine," he began, "is very rare. There are vampires in this world, as well as humans and ghouls, but there has only been one other known half-breed in all of history, and that was centuries ago. Because of your uniqueness, there are those who would exploit you. One man in particular would try to use you."

"Who?" I gasped, feeling so alone at the knowledge that there was no one else like me. "And why?"

"His name is Bones." Gregor almost spat the words. "He will force you to become a killer as he is. Turn you into a whore to lure his victims. Kill your family, so you will have no one but him to protect you. And you'll need protection, Catherine. After the atrocities he'll have you commit, you'll be running from danger for the rest of your life."

"No!"

It was a cry of denial at the fate he'd just predicted. Hearing I'd become a monster who would get my family murdered made me want to run, but Gregor put an arm around my shoulders, keeping me where I was.

"That's why I came, *ma chérie*. He won't find you here. Soon, I'll bind you to me, then no one can take you. If you do what I say, you'll never suffer such an existence."

"My family? My mother? They'll be safe?" I was shaking at the thought of their deaths.

"As long as you are with me, they're safe."

He sounded so confident. *That's why my mom sent me here*, I thought dully. If I didn't leave, they'd all be killed.

He brushed my cheek. "You must heed me, though, *oui*? Else I can't protect you from this."

"Okay." I drew in a deep breath. "I'll do what you say."

"Good." The green left his eyes, and his smile was relaxed. "It's for the best. Now, come to me."

He held open his arms, and I hesitated. He wanted a hug?

"Um," I fidgeted. "What—"

"Already you question?" he interrupted, gaze narrowing.

"No, no." At once I put my arms around him, my heart starting to beat faster. This wasn't a position I was used to.

"Better." It was almost a growl. Gregor tightened

his grip until I blushed. "We'll return home now. You must be weary."

"Well," I began, "A little—*huh?*"

He propelled us upward. My bleat of fright dissolved into a gasp of wonder as I looked down. *Oh, wow.* No wonder they called this the City of Lights.

Gregor glided us above the buildings, too high to be seen from below. It was indescribable to feel the wind whistling by me and the power radiating off him while looking at the stunning visual canvas. My heart wasn't beating; it was thundering. If this is a dream, I thought, I don't want to wake up.

All too soon, he landed at the gray building that was his house. I had to hold on for a second longer while I regained my footing, still overwhelmed with the experience. *Flying.* If that was a vampire perk, being a half-breed couldn't be all bad.

"You enjoyed that," he noted the obvious, smiling. "You see? All you must do is trust me."

"I don't know what to say." It came out breathlessly. He'd let go of me, but he was still very close. "Thank you."

His smiled deepened. That fluttering began in my stomach. No one had ever smiled at me like Gregor did.

"You're welcome, Catherine."

Fourteen

THE NEXT THREE WEEKS PASSED WITH AMAZ-
ing swiftness. Aside from Cannelle's continued
snootiness and worrying about my family, I had to
admit I'd never been happier.

Gregor was wonderful to be around—as long as I
didn't argue with him or challenge him with a differing opinion. I learned that fast. Who was I, a teenager, to argue with a thousand-year-old vampire who
possessed powers and knowledge I couldn't even imagine? That was Gregor's favorite line when he was
ticked. It was a good one, too. I didn't have much to
rebut it with.

But when Gregor was in a good mood, it was heav-
enly. He'd listen for hours as I spoke about my inse-
curities growing up. He encouraged me to show my
nonhuman traits, something I'd tried to hide as much
as possible around my mother. Then he bought me
clothes, shoes, and jewelry, overriding my protests by
saying pretty girls should have pretty things.

No guy had ever called me pretty before. In fact, no one had ever paid attention to me the way Gregor did. I'd gone from being a lonely outcast to feeling very favored and special almost overnight. Here was this attractive, suave, charismatic *man* spending all this time with me, and even though I knew it was stupid, I was getting more infatuated with Gregor every day.

Gregor didn't act like anything but a protector, however. Every day, I tried to talk myself out of my embarrassing crush. *Not only is Gregor about a thousand years too old for you, he's probably got ten girlfriends. Cannelle couldn't be more obvious about how she wants him, but he doesn't give her the time of day even though she's a beautiful woman. So what chance do you have? None, that's what.*

I'd convinced myself to stop secretly mooning over Gregor by the time he took me to see *The English Patient*. After a crash course, my French was good enough that I didn't need to read all the subtitles to know what was going on, and there were certain parts that required no translation.

The heroine's name was Catherine. Hearing my name moaned during the erotic parts of the movie was like a spotlight on my hidden fantasies. I was hyperaware of Gregor's knee grazing mine, his arm resting on the divider, and how very large he was in his chair. I started feeling flushed, and I bolted out of the seat with a hurried excuse about the bathroom.

I didn't make it. In the hall, I was seized and whirled around, crushed against Gregor's body. My mouth opened in surprise only to have his come down over it, shocking me with his invading tongue. He grabbed my hair and held my head as he kissed me.

It felt consuming, terrifying, and good·all at once. I couldn't move with the grip he held me in, and I couldn't breathe from how deeply he was kissing me. Finally, my flapping hands must have registered, because he let me go. I almost stumbled, glad the wall was there to keep me from falling. My heartbeat must have been loud enough to make his head hurt.

"Your first kiss?" Gregor asked thickly, giving a rude glare to a couple who paused to gawk at us.

I didn't want to admit it, but he always seemed to know when I lied.

"Yes." How pathetic. I was sixteen; half my classmates had already had sex.

A smile curled on his lips. " 'Twas the answer I wanted. You take to it very well." He placed each arm around me, caging me against the wall. "I wonder how well you'll take to the other enjoyments I'll show you."

I stared, thinking I must have misunderstood him. This was such a switch from how Gregor normally acted around me, I couldn't keep up. "You're saying you want to, uh, have *sex* with me?"

He responded to my stunned whisper by yanking me to him. "Why do you think you're here? Why do you think I took you into my home, garbed you in lovely clothes, and spent day and night with you? I've been waiting for you to adjust to your new home, and I've been very patient, *oui*? Yet my patience is running thin. You are mine, Catherine, and I will have you soon. Very soon."

I was at a loss for words. Sure, I'd been madly crushing on Gregor, but I hadn't been prepared to jump into bed with him.

Tentatively, I smiled. "You're joking, right?"

At once I knew I'd made a mistake. His brows drew together, stretching the scar, and his face darkened.

"You mock me? I offer you what Cannelle would kill for, yet you smirk and giggle. Perhaps I should spend my time with a woman instead of a foolish child."

Tears sprang to my eyes. I didn't need to look around to know people were staring as they hurried past us in the hall.

"I'm sorry, I didn't mean—" I began.

"No, you didn't *mean*," he cut me off, his voice thick with scorn. "You don't *mean* because you don't *think*. Come along, Catherine. You've been out enough for tonight."

With that, he jerked me by the arm and led me out of the theater. I kept my head down, so that the new people we passed couldn't see I was crying.

Gregor didn't speak to me for two days. I called my mom, only to have her berate me for insulting such a wonderful man. Didn't I know how lucky I was he'd taken me in? Didn't I care that he had my best interests at heart? I didn't mention to her that my heart seemed a little north of what he'd expressed interest in. Maybe I really *was* ungrateful. After all, Gregor had done so much for me. Without him, me and my family would all be in terrible danger. And he was a grown man—a *very* grown man. I couldn't expect someone as old as Gregor just to want to hold hands if he was interested in me.

Properly contrite, I waited until the third day to talk to him. I had a plan; I just had no idea if it would work.

First, I put some makeup on. Gregor seemed to

prefer me wearing it. Then, I fixed my hair. Next the outfit. Pants were my favorite, but Gregor hated those. I flipped through my new clothes while heaping more coals onto my head. *See all these pretty things? He bought them for you. Look at this bedroom. It's almost as big as your grandparents' whole house. No one's ever treated you so well. Sure, Gregor has mood swings, but you're a half-breed freak. Who are you to throw stones?*

I chose a sleeveless white dress and worked myself up into an apologetic frenzy. Then I brushed my teeth one last time and headed to his door.

Once outside his door, however, I stopped. What if he'd already decided to send me back home? God, how could I have been such an idiot?

"Come in, I can hear you," he called out.

Oh, crap. Now or never.

I entered his bedroom, and the interior almost made me forget my purpose. Wow. How barbarically antique.

The bed was about twice the size of the king in my room. Curving up on all four sides were twisted, polished tree trunks. They were carved in various shapes, forms interlapping, and they met at the top to provide a complete canopy of sculptured wood. The whole bed looked like it was from one gigantic, steroid-induced tree. I'd never seen anything like it, and I blushed when I studied some of the forms more clearly. There were figures locked in combat, and other things.

"It's over four hundred years old, modeled after Odysseus's bed, and built for me by a carpenter who grew trees to bend and entwine any way he chose," Gregor answered my silent awe. "It is magnificent, *non*?"

"Yes." I took my riveted gaze from the bed and switched it to him. He was at a desk on the computer. He minimized the screen and sat back with his arms folded. Waiting.

"I'm sorry about the other night," I started. "I've developed a huge crush on you, but I thought it was silly because, because you couldn't possibly be interested in me. So, when you kissed me, then you said . . . well, you know what you said, I was so blown away I thought . . . it couldn't be real, because I could never be so lucky."

In forming my mental apology, I'd thought it would go over better if I outed myself over my crush, no matter how embarrassing that was. And it was true. I *didn't* know why Gregor would want me when there were tons of pretty, gorgeous women who'd be happy to have him. If not for his temper, I'd think he was perfect.

"Come closer."

I breathed a sigh of relief that he didn't sound mad anymore and came toward him, stopping about a foot away.

"Closer."

I advanced until my knees brushed his legs.

"Closer."

It was a purred directive while his eyes started to change. The gray in them gave way to swirls of emerald.

I laid my hands on his shoulders, beginning to tremble. His legs opened, and I stood between them.

"Kiss me."

Nervous about that, but afraid to refuse, I laid my lips on his, wondering if I was even doing it right.

His mouth opened, and his hands came to life. They pressed me to him even as his tongue delved past my closed lips. All the sudden, I was lying on him, the chair tilting backward and Gregor kissing me like my mouth possessed hidden treasures.

I liked kissing Gregor, even though it was overpowering. What had me grunting in protest was him lifting me with one powerful hand and then the mattress flattening against my back.

"Gregor, wait."

It was gasped when his mouth moved to my throat. Cool air fell on my legs, with my dress being shifted up.

Whoa. I'd meant to apologize and be on good speaking terms—maybe even do some kissing—but this wasn't what I intended.

"What did you say?"

He almost snapped the question, pausing as he unzipped my dress. I was trembling at the sight of fangs protruding from his mouth. I'd only seen his fangs once before, on my grandparents' porch the night we met and he'd proved that he was a vampire. His fangs scared me, but they also gave me an idea.

"I want you to bite me," I improvised, my heart pounding in fear of that, too, but I needed an alternative and fast. One that wouldn't throw him into a livid tirade. "Drink from me."

Gregor stared at me. Then he smiled. "*Oui.* Tonight, the blood from your body, and tomorrow, the blood of your innocence."

Oh God. What had I just done?

Gregor sat up and pulled me along with him. His hand swept aside my hair as he tugged the collar of my dress down.

Everything inside me braced. How bad would it would be?

"You're afraid," he murmured. His tongue swirling around my throat made me jump back. His grip tightened to welded steel. " 'Twill sweeten your taste."

I started to say something—and then it only came out as a cry. Fangs pierced me, and I literally felt my blood exploding out from my skin. Gregor sucked, sending a sliver of pain through me, but smothering that was the heat that broke over me. He sucked harder, increasing the dizziness that had taken hold, and I gave myself up to the blackness waiting for me.

Fifteen

"Y ou're awake."

My eyes blinked open to see Cannelle bending over me. She straightened and pointed to a nearby tray.

"Here. Food and an iron pill. You'll need both. You only have a few hours until sundown."

"What?"

That sat me all the way up. A cattle prod would've had the same effect. Even as her words registered, dizziness swept over me. Cannelle watched with no sympathy.

"He drank a lot from you," she said, before muttering something under her breath in French.

Even though I still wasn't proficient, I caught the words for "skinny" and "goat."

"What's up, Cannelle?" I asked, not in a good mood at all. "Don't you know it's rude to insult someone in a different language so they can't answer back?"

She put the tray onto the bed, making the tea slosh

with her lack of care. "I said I don't know why he'd take so much nourishment from a scrawny little goat," she summarized bluntly. "Now, I suggest you eat. Gregor won't be pleased if you're unable to do more than bleed underneath him."

I blanched at this graphic analogy, seized with apprehension and clueless how to extricate myself. Gregor wasn't the type to take an "I've changed my mind" lightly.

And so that left me with the other alternative: going through with it. Maybe it was the better option, my anxiety aside. Gregor wouldn't get mad, I wouldn't be sent away, and according to him, I'd have no pregnancy or disease worries. Yes, I would have preferred to wait longer, *much* longer, before taking such a step, but apparently, my time was up.

"Cannelle." I lowered my voice, gesturing for her to come nearer. She did, her expression quizzical. "I was wondering if you could tell me, ah, what to expect."

I had no one else to ask. What was I going to do, call my mother and ask that? Hardly. I'd never had girlfriends, and the things I'd overheard at school wouldn't help now. Sure, I knew what went where. But details on sex with a *vampire*? Nope.

"What to expect?" she repeated. I gestured for her to keep her voice down, but she ignored that. "Expect to be fucked, you simple little twit!"

Even in my extreme embarrassment, I had a flash of insight. "Gregor told me you've been with him for sixty years. Says he gives you his blood to keep you young, but you're hanging on for the big promotion, aren't you? You want to be a vampire, and you hate me because you know if I asked him, he'd change me into one. And he hasn't offered the same to you."

Her sky blue eyes narrowed. She bent down with an ugly little smile on her lips.

"You know what you can expect, your first time?" Now her voice was soft. Almost inaudible. "A lot of pain. *Bon appétit*."

She left. I stared at the tray of food without the slightest twinge of hunger before pushing it away.

The knock came two hours later. It wasn't at my bedroom door, where I'd been watching the clock like an inmate awaiting sentencing. It was at the front door of the house.

Gregor opened it while I peeked downstairs. We didn't get any visitors. The fact that no fewer than six people entered made me come all the way down the hall. They were talking in French at a speed that made it unintelligible for me.

"Merde!" Gregor swore, and then a string of other words followed that might also have been curses. "Tonight? If he thinks to steal her, he's greatly underestimated me. Catherine. Come down at once!"

I did, wondering how much trouble I was in for eavesdropping. To my relief, Gregor didn't seem to care that I'd been listening. He opened the closet and handed me a coat.

"Put this on. We're leaving."

"Now?" I asked. A part of me was singing at my unexpected respite. "What's wrong?"

"I'll tell you on the way," he answered, taking my arm and almost yanking me out the door. "We don't have time to delay."

Two more vampires were waiting with the back open to a black Mercedes. We climbed inside and instantly sped off. The velocity threw me backward. I didn't even have time to buckle my seat belt. Okay, so we were in a big hurry.

"What's wrong?" I asked again.

Gregor stared at me for a long moment. That freaked me out. It looked like he was making up his mind about something.

"Catherine," he said, "you have been discovered. Even as we speak, Bones's allies are searching the city for you. If they find you, they will turn you into the monster I described."

I was stricken. "Oh, please, don't let them! I don't want to be a killer. I don't want to—to become some kind of whore."

For a split second, I'd have almost sworn he looked triumphant. But then his forehead creased, and he shook his head.

"There is only one way to prevent this, *ma chérie*. You must bind yourself to me. It is the only thing that can't be undone."

"Sure, bind me." Whatever that meant. "Bind the hell out of me, just don't turn me over to those monsters!"

"Lucius, to the Ritz," he barked. The car did a swerve that had my life flashing before my eyes, then it straightened. "Tell the others to assemble there as well. I'm not binding myself in the backseat of a stinking car."

Then he turned to me. "Catherine, if you do this, you'll be protected for all of your days. If you don't, then I can't save you or your family. So when the time comes, don't hesitate."

That sounded ominous. It occurred to me to have him specify what "binding" meant. "Er, what do I have to do?"

He took my hand, drawing his finger down my palm. "You cut yourself here," he outlined simply, "then clasp my hand and declare yourself mine. I cut my hand and do the same."

"That's it?" I was afraid it might have entailed turning me into a vampire. "Jeez, give me a knife, let's do it!"

He smiled and kept my hand in his. "There must be witnesses, and Lucius isn't enough. Furthermore, this isn't the proper place for our first union, and I'm not waiting to claim you once you're mine."

There was no translation needed for that statement. Well, considering the alternative, I'd pay this price.

"So this is like a vampire . . . engagement, if we're saying we belong to each other?" I couldn't look at him as I asked. Everything was moving so fast.

Gregor paused, seeming to choose his words. "There's no such state among vampires. If you must have a human analogy, 'twould be considered a marriage."

Marriage? I had enough sense not to blurt, *But I'm not old enough!* We were talking about undead rules, not human ones.

"So it's not like we sign papers or I change my name, right?" With a nervous laugh. "It's just a vampire thing?"

Lucius glanced back at us. Gregor snapped something, and he averted his attention back to the road. Then Gregor smiled.

"Exactly. In your religion or customs, it has no meaning."

"Oh." Now I was just worried about getting away from the fiend chasing us and losing my virginity. "Okay, then."

Two of Gregor's people checked us in to the opulent hotel. Gregor was with six of the vampires who'd come in with us, and I was sent to browse the dress store nearby. Gregor was talking very low, and they stood close together. With all the background noise, I couldn't hear a word.

I fingered the dress in front of me. It was peacock blue and silky, with etched beading down the side of it. Next to me, a young blonde was also looking at dresses, only she was much more enthusiastic. She knocked a few off their perch as she held one and another up before discarding the selected pieces.

"Whenever you're in a hurry, you can't find a thing to wear," she remarked in English.

I glanced around. "Are you talking to me?"

She laughed. "Of course. I don't speak French, and I heard that guy you were with tell you to stay put in English. I'm American, too. Been in France long?"

She seemed harmless, but I knew Gregor wouldn't want me chatting with a stranger. I was supposed to keep a low profile.

"Not long," I answered, pretending to examine a dress across the other aisle.

She followed me. "Hey, is this orange hideous with my complexion?"

I studied the dress. "Yes," I said truthfully.

"That's what I thought!" She swung an accusing glance at the sales assistant. "The French hate Americans. She'd tell me to wear a garbage bag and charge me a grand for it."

From the corner of my eye, I saw Gregor walking toward me. He didn't look happy. "Um, I gotta go. My fiancé's coming. We're ah, late for our rehearsal dinner."

She gaped. "You're getting married? You look so young!"

I started moving toward him, sputtering, "Oil of Olay. It's like the fountain of youth."

"Come along, Catherine," Gregor directed me with an impatient wave of his hand, giving the girl an annoyed scowl.

I hurried after him, hearing her mutter, "Friggin' rude French," as we headed to the elevators with our guard.

Our room was on the top floor. As soon as we entered it, the guards drew all the drapes, cutting off the amazing view of the Paris skyline. Through the open door across from us, I saw the bedroom and shivered. *End of the line*, my mind mocked me.

"Give me the knife," Gregor ordered, not wasting any time.

A small silver blade, etched with some sort of design along the handle, was passed to him. Gregor sliced into his palm without hesitation and held up his hand.

"By my blood, she is my wife. Catherine." He gave me the blade. "Do as I did. Repeat my words."

For a second, I hesitated. Seven sets of eyes were trained on me. Gregor's mouth tightened ominously. I gave myself a mental shake and cut the inside of my palm, before he exploded.

"By my blood, I am his wife," I parroted, relieved and frightened when Gregor's face relaxed. He clasped my hand, and the tingle when his blood met my wound startled me.

The six men let out a loud cheer. They hugged Gregor and kissed his cheeks before repeating the same gesture with me. He was smiling also, his hand still wrapped around mine, the beginnings of emerald pinpointing in his eyes.

"Enough, *mes amis*," he cut them off. "Etienne, Marcel, Lucius, spread the news of our binding. François and Tomas, watch the lobby for activity. Bernard, you stay on this floor."

With that, they left. Gregor turned to me. I started to back away.

"M-my hand," I stammered. "I should bandage it—"

"No need," he interrupted. " 'Tis healed, Catherine, and you are not stalling me."

The hungry way he spoke froze me. So did him kicking off his shoes and removing his shirt. Gregor never stopped coming toward me, even as he stepped out of his pants, and they dropped to the floor, leaving him naked.

Gregor was big and muscled all the way down to his feet. He was also completely erect, and the sight of that would have staggered me if he hadn't grabbed me. He picked me up, striding into the bedroom and trapping me under his body on the bed.

I tried to wiggle back, but he stopped me. "Don't squirm so, *chérie*," he chided, unfastening the buttons on my dress. "You know you are mine now, why are you resisting?"

"Couldn't we, ah, wait a little bit?"

"Wait?" he repeated, like he'd never heard the word before. "You think to deny me my wedding night?"

He looked like he'd get mad any second. "I'm really nervous," I admitted.

His hand stroked down my side while one thigh rested over my legs. His body seemed to dwarf mine. God, he was so big.

"It's natural to be nervous your first time, *ma femme*. Just relax."

With his strength, it was not like I had a choice. I nodded, closed my eyes, and tried to make myself relax. Gregor kissed me again, undoing more buttons on my dress. Soon I felt him tugging it down until it was off completely.

"Beautiful," he whispered, tracing a hand up my stomach to cup my breast. I trembled, never feeling more vulnerable.

Gregor suddenly snarled a curse and leapt to his feet. I blinked before rolling away with a yelp. Coming through the open bedroom door were two men. One had power radiating off him so profusely, it seemed like it was choking me.

"You foolish child," said the tall, foreign-looking one.

For a moment, I thought he was speaking to me. But he stared at Gregor like I wasn't even in the room.

"Mencheres." Gregor's voice was defiant. "You're too late."

The vampire shook his head even as I scrambled to cover myself. "Gregor, you've interfered where you shouldn't."

"You do it all the time," Gregor barked.

"I use my visions to stop death, not to try and gain more power. You knew this was wrong, else you wouldn't have taken such pains to conceal it."

"You want her for the same reason I do, but she's mine now. I've bound myself to her." Gregor snatched me from my huddled position and shoved me forward. "Look at the blood staining her hand. Her throat also bears my mark."

The other vampire went into the bathroom and

came out holding a robe. He handed it to me with his first words since entering the bedroom.

"Here, put this on."

Still in my bra and underwear, I was glad to have something to cover me, but Gregor flung the robe to the other side of the room. "She'll stay as she is to face the man who would sacrifice her to his murdering, whoring whelp!"

I'd guessed they were associates of the vampire hunting me, but having it confirmed made me feel worse.

"Don't do it," I said fervently. "I want to be with Gregor. Why can't you just leave us alone!"

I clutched Gregor's arm, staring at the two stony faces in front of us. Gregor gave them a triumphant look.

"From her own lips, she denounces your intentions. She's my wife now, and there isn't a thing you can do to change—"

I was thrown backward from the blast of power, landing on the bed. For a stunned minute, I thought it had been aimed at me. Then the sight of Gregor locked in some invisible struggle revealed who it was directed at. His arms moved with unnatural heaviness, like a slow-motion movie. Finally, he was frozen.

"What have you done to him?" I whispered in horror.

Mencheres had one hand out to Gregor. I couldn't see the tunnel of energy unleashing from it, but I could feel it. It was like raw lightning. Gregor could barely even talk.

"You will be punished for your interference," Mencheres said. "She will be returned to her home.

You've failed, Gregor. She was never meant to be yours."

"That's a load of, of bullshit," I swore. "I'm not going to be turned into some homicidal slut, and if I ever meet that murderer, Bones, I'll kill him—or myself. I'd rather be dead than be a toy to some bloodsucking psychotic!"

With sudden inspiration, I sprinted into the other room. Both men watched me almost curiously. That changed when I grabbed the small silver knife Gregor had used earlier and held it to my throat.

"If one of you moves, I'll open my jugular," I vowed.

They exchanged a glance between the two of them. I dug the knife ominously into my neck. I wasn't bluffing. *He'll kill your family, so you will have no one but him to protect you*, Gregor had said about this Bones. Not if I could help it.

And then my arm felt like it was blasted with liquid nitrogen. So did my legs and other arm. The only things I could still control were my neck, head, and torso. That left me pretty much a stump. I could breathe. I could talk. Nothing else.

Mencheres walked toward me, and I spat at him, unable to do more in defense. He took the knife from my paralyzed grip.

"You see?" he said to Gregor. "You can take her from her home, poison her head with lies, convince her you are her savior, try to control her completely . . . and yet she is *still* the same inside. What did she do when threatened? She got a knife. It's my proof, Gregor. Yours is as empty as your intentions."

"I hate you," I spat. "You might take me home, but I know the truth. My mother knows. We'll run away from you and Bones."

Mencheres's face was thoughtful. "I believe you."

"You . . . can't . . ."

Gregor forced the words out. Mencheres gave him an inquiring look and flicked his finger. It was like someone switched Gregor's vocal cords back on.

"You can't manipulate her mind," he announced, the words rushing out with savage triumph. "I've tried, but her bloodline makes it impossible. She won't forget me, no matter what."

Manipulate my mind? Gregor tried to do that?

Mencheres made a sound that was almost a tssk. "Just because you don't know how to do something doesn't mean it can't be done."

He turned away from Gregor, another twitch of his fingers cutting off Gregor's shout of rage in midhowl. Then Mencheres considered me next, like I was a project that needed finishing.

"Get away from me," I hissed.

Those charcoal eyes stared into mine. For a moment, I thought I saw compassion. Then he came forward.

I was terrified. What was he going to do to me? Was he going to take me to the vampire who'd end up killing my family? Would they kill Gregor, too? Was there *anything* I could do to stop this?

I stared at Gregor, speaking my last words before those cool hands wrapped around my forehead.

"If I get away, I'll come back to you. If you get away, promise me you'll come back to me, too."

Then I felt and saw nothing at all.

Sixteen

HIS EYES WERE THE FIRST THING I BECAME aware of, gray-green and lighted with emerald. Next was his face, hazy but discernible, features clarifying with every second. Finally, his body, and being held in his arms as tightly as if I'd never left them. In the fragmented moments of returning consciousness, it didn't even seem like I had.

"Gregor," I breathed, dizzy from the deluge of memories.

"Yes, *chérie*," he whispered. "We are together again."

His mouth sealed over mine. Relief flooded me, and I wrapped my arms around him, kissing him back. Even as he held me tighter and I trembled with the memory of those last horrible moments when I'd thought Gregor was about to be killed, the rest of my life clicked into place.

Bones.

The emotions I felt for Gregor were buried under an avalanche. My memories of Gregor had wormed their way into my heart, true, but Bones already owned all that space.

I turned away, cutting off Gregor's kiss. "No."

His whole body stilled. "No?"

I pushed on his shoulder with firmness. "No."

His brows drew together, that scar stretched warningly, and his next words were a disbelieving bellow.

"You *refuse* me?"

My first reaction was to flinch at his anger. Gregor took that as a sign of surrender and pushed me back onto the pillows. I'd been sitting up when this whole trip down memory lane began, but he'd maneuvered the covers off me at some point and put himself conveniently on top of me.

He started to kiss me again when I struck. I might care for him, but this was *not* going to happen. Too bad Gregor had forgotten I still had a knife.

"Let me tell you something you must have missed these last several hundred years—no means *no*. I suggest you don't try any strenuous moves, Gregor."

The silver knife, the same one I now knew had been used to bind us, was stuck in his back. My hand was wrapped around the etched handle as firmly as I'd ever held a weapon. No way would I betray Bones with Gregor, no matter what residual feelings I might still have for him.

The knife hadn't pierced Gregor's heart, but the blade was close. He must have felt that, because he froze.

"*Ma femme,* why would you hurt me this way?" he said in a much softer tone. "If you truly don't want to make love, of course I will not force you."

"Of course?" I repeated with a snort. "Did you think I'd only remembered certain parts? The blade stays."

"You were needlessly hesitant from your maiden fears, any man would have acted the same," he began to sputter.

"Bullshit. You didn't do what any man would do. You did what you wanted to do, as usual. I don't want to hurt you, Gregor, but I don't trust you enough to take out this knife, so here's the deal. I remember everything, just like you wanted me to . . . and now I want to leave."

Gregor looked shocked. "To go back to that hit man?" he spat. "You want to return to Bones, the dog who made you into this—this Red Reaper?"

He flung the name at me like the foulest insult. Far from being insulted, I laughed.

"Bones didn't *make* me anything. I'd killed sixteen vampires by the time we'd met. Bones just made me better at it, and he never made me his whore, either. You're far more of a tramp than I am; how many people have *you* slept with?"

He gave me an indignant look. "I'm a man. It's different."

"That sums up right there why the two of us would have never worked, regardless of Bones," I muttered. "Call Lucius, have him come in here. Despite the fact that it would take care of a lot of problems, I don't want to kill you, Gregor. But if you try anything, I will do what comes naturally, and we both know what that is."

I should have killed Gregor as soon as I sank that knife into his back. Getting my memories back had proved he'd lied to me, manipulated me, and tricked me into binding myself to him. Plus, he was a threat to me and to Bones, since Gregor didn't take rejection very well. But one, I wasn't in any condition to fight off Gregor's people if I killed him—and I was betting Gregor had more than Lucius here. Two, we'd made a deal that didn't involve me murdering him at the end of it.

And three, the remnant of the infatuated teenager I'd been couldn't bear the thought of killing Gregor, even though the adult in me knew he had it coming. Still, that didn't mean I was taking out the knife. If Gregor attempted a double cross, I'd use it.

Gregor glared at me. I didn't blink. This wasn't the Catherine he knew. I was Cat, and he hadn't met me before.

"Lucius," he belted out finally. "Come to me at once!"

After a few seconds, the door opened. Lucius stopped short when he saw Gregor naked on top of me and a knife sticking out of his back.

"Master?" he began. "What—?"

"Listen up, Lucius." I didn't glance away from Gregor, only seeing the other vampire from my peripheral vision. "You're going to get a speakerphone and bring it in here. Right now. You get any other ideas, and you're the next to die, old pal. Got it?"

"*Monsieur?*"

"Do it," Gregor said silkily. He'd regained his composure. "After all, I made *my wife* a promise."

My lips curled at his emphasis, but that was a pissing contest for a later date.

"Glad to know you're going to keep your word. With luck, you'll have this blade out in a few hours."

"Hours?" His forehead creased in incredulity.

"You said we're in Austria," I replied, thinking. "If he agrees to come, it'll take him a few hours to get here. After he arrives, I'll pull out this knife."

"You're calling Bones?"

Gregor asked it with a gleam in his eyes that reminded me how dangerous he was. *I bet you were figuring that's just what I'd do, and you've got the trap of a lifetime waiting for him.*

"You wish," I said. "But no. Someone else."

Vlad Tepesh didn't contain his laughter when he walked in the room. It came from him in full-bodied peals that had him briefly leaning on the doorframe for support.

"Now *that's* worth the trip right there." He chuckled, pink starting to sparkle in his eyes. "How goes it, Gregor? Forgot your manners, did you? If I'd known you were balanced in such a precarious state, I might have taken even . . . longer."

I'd yanked a sheet between us and made Gregor pick up his hips, but the rest of him stayed where it was so I could keep that knife close to his heart. It left Gregor with his ass sticking up in the air while his face stayed level with mine. I wasn't trying to be funny. Only practical.

"Thanks for coming, Vlad. My arm was getting tired."

I'd only met Vlad last year during that awful war, but he was someone I trusted. He'd saved my life, in fact, and even though I hadn't seen him lately, I'd been right in guessing that he'd come if I asked him to. Plus, when doing a mental rundown of vampires in Eastern Europe who were both strong and feared enough that Gregor wouldn't attempt a double cross, Vlad's was the only name on the list. Dracula's bloody reputation wasn't only made during his days as the infamous prince of Wallachia.

"Okay, Gregor, I'm going to pull this knife out nice

and slow. Once I do, you climb off. No tricks."

Gregor glanced at Vlad, who smiled at him in a predatory way. Then Gregor nodded.

I sighed in relief and began to pull out the knife. Once the silver was out of his back, Gregor got up from the bed. He stood over me for a moment, his expression saying he still didn't believe what had just happened.

"I'll let you leave because I promised, but you are still bound to me, Catherine. You may have a few days to settle things, but then, you must return to me."

"Clothes," I prodded Vlad without answering. Frankly, I didn't know what the hell to do about being bound to Gregor. It was obvious he wasn't giving up just because I'd still picked Bones, even with my memory back. Did Gregor really think a few more days would mean I'd come to my senses and come back to him? God, he *really* didn't know me.

"Another thing that makes this trip worthwhile," Vlad commented, handing me a long dress.

I sat up and put it on without any false modesty. Vlad wasn't leering, but he was a red-blooded male. I didn't take it personally. "You've seen the top before, so I'm sure you're not fighting a blush."

"When has he seen your breasts?" Gregor hissed.

"When a horde of zombies ate most of my arm and all of my bra off," I snapped.

Gregor let out a grunt. "That's what you're return-ing to? How you want to live? Think, Catherine!"

"Hasn't she told you?" Vlad purred. "She doesn't like to be called that name."

I paused at the door next to Vlad. "Goodbye, Gregor. Don't come after me, in person or in my dreams."

Something hardened in Gregor's face. It said loud

and clear that this wasn't over, and Gregor would still be chasing me. *Why?* I wondered. Was it just his pride refusing to accept that I'd chosen someone else?

Vlad smiled, rubbing his hands together. Sparks cascaded from them in blatant warning.

"Not thinking of trying to stop us, are you?" he asked silkily.

Vlad could burn someone to ashes with just his touch, even a powerful vampire like Gregor. So most people didn't want Dracula to start playing with his matches.

"I won't have to," Gregor said, looking at me. "I'll show you what Bones is. Then you'll be begging for my forgiveness."

"Goodbye," I repeated. It summed things up right there.

We walked out of the large house with Vlad's four escorts flanking us. No one attempted to stop us. *Are they this afraid of you?* I asked him. *Or is Gregor up to something?*

Just like Bones and Mencheres, Vlad could read minds. "Both and neither," he answered, his dark brown hair swaying with his strides. "Gregor's in a bad way. He needs his ghouls back."

"Huh?"

Out loud this time. Vlad gave me a sardonic smile.

"You've driven Bones into rare form. It was smart of you not to have him come here. He'd have lost his mind completely if he'd seen Gregor poised naked over you. As it is, Bones will already suffer repercussions for what he's done."

"You told me on the phone that Bones was okay, that you spoke to Spade, and they were all right!" I burst out.

Vlad ushered me onto the waiting small plane, and his men climbed in after us. We taxied down a grass field before lifting off. Gregor had chosen a remote location as well.

"From what I gathered after speaking with Spade, Bones had you secured in a room during the attack?" he queried, continuing after my nod. "And at some point, Gregor called you and offered to stop the assault if you came to him?"

Another nod. "Cat, it was a ruse. Bones wasn't outnumbered, and why you didn't know that, I have no idea. Bones had over a hundred of the foulest undead mercenaries hiding beneath that house, just waiting for Gregor's forces to get arrogant and rush them. By the time you reached Gregor, Bones already had the fight won."

My mind went numb. *Is this the whole crew? Or are there more lurking in the woods?* I'd asked. And my mother's response, instantly shushed, *Oh, there's more . . .*

"Shit," I whispered.

Neither of us said anything for a minute, then Vlad pulled out his cell phone.

"I have her," he announced. "She's fine, and we're in the air."

"Is that Bones?" My stomach churned with nervousness. *He's going to be so pissed at me.*

"It's Spade," Vlad answered with the mouthpiece covered. Then, "Yes . . . I know . . . no, we have the fuel . . . She wants to speak to Bones . . . um hmm, quite. We'll be there in three hours."

He hung up, and I blinked. "He's not there?"

Vlad folded his phone and set it back in his coat. The look he gave me was filled with irony.

"Spade didn't feel it would be a good idea to have you speak with him. He's probably going to spend the next three hours trying to calm Bones down."

"He's really angry, I know, but it looked like they were all going to get killed. What was I supposed to do?"

"You both made your choices," Vlad observed. "Whatever the consequences, it's done. Really, Bones surprised me with this whole endeavor. I didn't think he was so clever, but he's shown his best potential in the last couple years."

"How?" I was feeling ill as I thought of the inevitable confrontation.

"First of all, using mercenaries." Vlad smiled wickedly. "Very enterprising, but I suppose he knew most of them from his hit-man days. If he'd rounded up over a hundred of the strongest members in his line, Gregor would have heard about that and smelled a trap. But paid killers, accountable to no one? Who notices when scores of them go off the radar?"

"Bones has always been smart," I muttered. "His intelligence was just camouflaged under a mountain of pussy."

Vlad laughed before he sobered. "Perhaps, but now he's displaying his ruthlessness as well. He's chopped off a head an hour from Gregor's ghouls since you've been gone, promising to decapitate the lot of them unless he gets you back."

"What?"

That bolted me up in my chair. Granted, the undead didn't play by normal rules of engagement, but they were pretty consistent when it came to battle prisoners. Those were taken hostage and traded or bargained for later. Oh, things might get creative when it came to extracting information, but since no permanent damage could be done to the undead, barring mental trauma, that was just the norm. Bones callously slaughtering his captives? I was shocked.

Vlad wasn't. He looked mildly intrigued. "As I said, rare form, which is why Gregor let you go without a fuss. If he hadn't, he'd have trouble the next time he enlisted other people to fight for him. But enough of that. You don't look well."

I let out a bitter laugh. "You think? My husband can't come to the phone because he's too busy slicing off heads, and here's the punch line! He's not really my—"

"Don't say it."

Vlad cut me off. His expression turned deadly serious.

"Knowing and admitting are two separate things. Gregor still wants your public acknowledgment as proof. Don't give it to him."

"Where do you stand in this?" I asked quietly.

It was more than putting him on the spot, but I couldn't help it. I knew Vlad wouldn't demur in giving me his true position, no matter what it was.

He considered me. Vlad Tepesh wasn't a classically handsome man like some of the hunks who'd played Dracula in the movies. His face was oval; lips thin, with deep-set eyes, a wider forehead, and a tight beard. He was lean, too, and he stood an even six feet tall. But none of those actors had Vlad's presence. What he might have lacked in perfection of features he made up for in sheer magnetism.

At last he took my hand. His were scarred in multiple places, as well as being more dangerous than his fangs, since they were the outlet of Vlad's pyrokinesis, but Vlad didn't frighten me. He should have, but he didn't.

"I feel a connection to you, as I once told you. It's not love, it's not attraction, and I won't sacrifice myself for you, but if you needed me, and it was possible for me to help you, like today, I'd come. Whichever side you called me from."

I squeezed his hand once before letting go. "Thank you."

He settled back more comfortably in his chair. "You're welcome."

Seventeen

WE DIDN'T RETURN TO THE HOUSE IN Bavaria. Granted, from the air I couldn't be sure that we *weren't* in Bavaria, but it wasn't the same place I'd left. Not having my pills, I just shut my eyes as we landed, then took a car the rest of the way. Even if I'd had them, I'd decided not to take the pills anymore. Gregor couldn't pull me out of a dream unless I helped him, and I sure wasn't going to do that again. Besides, I wondered if those pills were making me ill, because as Vlad noticed, I felt like hell. I'd have to call Don and ask if there were side effects from taking them.

Spade was the first person I saw when I opened my eyes after Vlad led me into the house. He stood in the foyer with his arms crossed, wearing a truly resigned expression.

"You shouldn't have left."

"Where's Bones?"

I wasn't about to get into it with Spade. Yeah, I had

it coming, but there was only one person entitled to give it to me. The fact that Bones hadn't come out when he heard me arrive spoke volumes. He must be really pissed.

Spade glanced to his left. "Follow the music."

Piano music played in the general direction Spade indicated. Maybe Bones was listening to a relaxing CD. One could only hope it had improved his temperament.

"Thanks." I headed past the next few rooms toward the sound.

When I entered what appeared to be a large library, I saw the music was coming from a piano, not a CD. Bones was bent over it, his back to me, pale fingers gliding expertly over the keys.

"Hi," I said, after standing there several heartbeats without him even turning around. Going to ignore me, was he? Not if I could help it. I'd rather get this over with than prolong it.

"I didn't know you could play," I tried again, coming closer.

When I got near enough to feel his vibe, I stopped. Bones felt wound enough to explode, though the music coming from his hands was serene. Chopin, maybe. Or Mozart.

"Why are you here?"

He asked it with deceptive gentleness, not missing a note or looking up. The question startled me.

"B-because you are," I said, cursing myself for stuttering like an intimidated teenager. I'd had enough of that.

Bones still didn't look up. "If you've come to say goodbye, you needn't bother. I don't need a tearful explanation. Just walk out the same way you came in."

A lump rocketed up in my throat. "Bones, that's not—"

"Don't touch me!"

I'd been about to smooth my hand across his back when he knocked my arm away so hard, it spun me. *Now* Bones was looking at me, and the rage in his gaze pinned me where I was.

"No. You don't get to stroll in here stinking of Gregor, then lay your hands on me." Each word was a measured, furious growl. "I've endured quite enough of being patronized. You treat me as if I was a feeble human who couldn't survive without your help, but I am a *Master* bloody *vampire*."

That last part was shouted. I flinched. Bones flexed his hands, seeming to get a handle on himself. Then he spoke the next part through gritted teeth.

"If it were my wish, I could rip you apart with my bare hands. Yes, you're strong. You're quick. But not strong enough or fast enough that I couldn't kill you if I had a mind to. Yet despite this, you continue to treat me with the contempt you'd show an inferior. I've brushed it off. Told myself it didn't matter, but no more. Yesterday, you believed in Gregor more than me. *You left me* to go to him, and there is no overlooking that, so I ask you again, why are you here?"

"I'm here because I love you and we're . . ." I was about to say, *we're married*, but the words choked me. No, I'd proven to myself that we weren't, as far as vampires were concerned.

Bones let out a cold snort. "I won't stand for this. I'm not going to hold you in my arms and wonder if I'm the one you're really thinking about."

"Bones, you know that isn't true!" I was anguished at the accusation. "I love you, you know that. And if you didn't know it, God, you could look for yourself and see—"

"Only shadows," he ruthlessly interrupted. "Glimpses when your guard was down, when that bloody wall you hide behind wasn't blocking me. I have been open with you about all of me, even the worst of me, because I thought you deserved no less, but you don't hold me in the same regard. No, you reserved that for Gregor. You trusted *him* enough to leave everything at his word. Well, luv, I bow when I am beaten, and Gregor has defeated me in a grand style. He's the one you respect. He's who you trust, so if you're not leaving, I am."

Cold swept over me, and the lump in my throat grew reinforcements. This wasn't a fight. This was something far worse.

"You're leaving me?"

He sat back down on the piano bench. Almost idly, his fingers flicked the keys.

"I can stand many things."

His voice was harsh in its emotionlessness. I recoiled from it. For a second, I was afraid of him.

"Many things," he continued. "I can stand your affection for Tate, much as I despise him. Your repeated jealousies over other women, even when I have given you no cause, for I'd be the same way in your place. I can stand your insistence to participate in dangerous situations that are way over your head, for again, that is also my nature. All of these things ate at me, but for you, I chose to stand them."

Now he stood. That calm, apathetic tone vanished, and his voice rose with each passing word.

"I also chose to stand the things you didn't admit to, like when you secretly wondered if Gregor had made you happier than I had. I could even tolerate the real reason you didn't want to change over, the *real* reason you clung to your heartbeat. I could stand to know that deep down, there's a part of you that still believes all vampires are evil!"

Roared now. I backed up, never having seen Bones like this. His eyes were electric green, and the emotion in him had him shaking on his feet.

"Don't think I don't know it. Don't think I haven't *always* known it! And I could bear it, yes, even knowing the other reason for your hesitancy. Underneath your claims of devotion, past your love—and I do think you love me, despite it all—you don't want to change over because you don't think we'll last. You believe we are only temporary, and becoming a vampire is such a permanent thing, isn't it? Yes, *I know this*. I've known it since I met you, but I've been patient. I told myself that one day, you wouldn't look at me with those guarded eyes. That one day, you'd love me the same way I loved you . . ."

The piano smashed into the wall across the room. It made a horrible keening noise, like it hurt from being destroyed. My hand pressed to my mouth while the emptiness in my stomach uncurled to fill my whole body.

"I've been a fool."

His simple sentence shattered me more thoroughly than the furniture he'd just demolished. I made a gasp of pain that he ignored.

"But this, this is the one thing I cannot endure— your walking out on me. I would rather have died than seen that note you left me. Would have cheerfully tucked myself *in my grave* than to see that filthy piece of paper!"

"I didn't walk out on you. I was trying to help, and I told you I was coming back—"

"Nothing you say matters."

It struck me like a slap. He looked at me, no tenderness, love, or forgiveness on his face. It was as if he were a statue. My heart beat faster with fear, desperate fear at everything falling apart.

"Bones, wait . . ."

"No. Will it change anything? Will it turn back the clock so you won't have left? It won't, so don't bother. You've only ever learned one way. Only one, and I should have remembered that. Perhaps this will finally penetrate into that armor you so relentlessly polish and shine."

He turned on his heel and began to walk away. I stared in stupid transfixion before racing after him, catching him as he approached the now-deserted front entrance.

"Wait! God, let's talk about this. We can work it out, I swear. Y-you can't just *go!*"

I was sputtering in anguish, tears spilling down my cheeks. They blinded me, but I felt his hand as he reached out and softly touched my face.

"Kitten." His voice was thick with something I couldn't name. "This is the part . . . where you don't have a choice."

The door slamming behind him knocked me off my feet.

Eighteen

Annette let the shade fall back over the window. "It's raining. I told you I could smell it."

I turned my attention to the carton of ice cream in front of me. Pralines and Crème. It was almost empty. Next I'd crack open the Swiss chocolate.

"No fooling you with a bogus weather report."

"We'll watch the movie instead of taking a walk," Annette continued. "I hear it's good."

Good? I couldn't seem to remember what that was. I felt like I was a walking open wound. I couldn't even sleep more than minutes at a time, no matter how exhausted I was, because I was afraid if Bones came back, I might miss an instant with him. The only respite in my current misery was that my mother wasn't here. She was somewhere with Rodney, but for obvious reasons, I didn't know where.

"Crispin needs time," Spade had said after that terrible exchange. "Don't tear off after him. Even I don't know where he is."

So I'd been waiting, dwelling on every awful thing he'd said to me, and worse, how most of it was true. I hadn't meant to keep Bones at a distance. I didn't know why I closed parts of myself off. But more than that, I wished with all of my heart that I hadn't left that morning with Gregor.

And Gregor had been busy. Not content with his role in ruining my relationship, Gregor had been feeding the rumors that without his intervention, I might change myself into a vampire/ghoul hybrid. That's how he'd garnered the two-hundred-plus ghoul army he'd amassed to attack in Bavaria. Gregor had promised the ghouls that once he had me, he'd change me into a vampire. Gregor even had the balls to state that if Mencheres hadn't stolen me away and imprisoned him a dozen years ago, I'd already have been a vampire and wouldn't have risen to such notoriety today.

Yet Gregor had let me go with my pulse intact. Now there were rumbles that I'd influenced him as well. What no one cared to hear was that Gregor hadn't had a choice about changing me. The silver dagger in his back made his decision for him.

Adding to these ghoul/vampire hybrid fears were my high jumps in Paris. Who'd have thought that would have been responsible for so much added paranoia? But since flying was a skill only Master vampires possessed, the fact that I had come close to demonstrating it, even briefly, had people wondering what other powers I could be hiding. It fueled the fears about what would happen if ghoul attributes were added to my repertoire. Would I be invincible? Unkillable? Able to leap tall buildings in a single bound and rerotate the spinning of the globe to turn back time? The theories got wilder and crazier.

Little did anyone know that all I was a danger to currently was anything sweet. Before I'd turn to alcohol for useless comfort. Now I used sugar, but there was a lot of pain and not nearly enough sugar.

"When does Spade get back?" I asked Annette. He'd gone out earlier with a vague statement about business. No one told me anything that could be used against me. We all knew Gregor was still snooping in my mind, even though I'd barely slept, and he'd been able to learn almost nothing. I didn't know where we were. How many people were with us. What day it was. Actually, none of those things meant shit to me. All I knew was this—it had been five days since Bones walked out. That's how I measured time. In the minutes and seconds since I'd last been with him.

"After dark," she answered.

Fabian came downstairs and sat—in a fashion—next to Annette. The ghost was smiling at her in a way that could only be called besotted.

I rolled my eyes. Even phantoms had a thing for Annette, it seemed. She'd probably found a way to have sex with him. Though he was transparent and as solid as a particle cloud, if anyone could do it, Annette could.

"What a charming man," she remarked. "Faith, Cat, you might have started a trend. When I leave, I daresay I'll be trying to sneak him past you."

It took so much willpower not to ask, "And how soon will that be?" After all, I'd been trying to control my *think it, say it* tendencies.

"Annette, I think I'll just skip the movie and read something. Watch it without me."

Halfway up the stairs, I passed Vlad. He'd stayed on, making the comment that he'd leave when things were settled. I bet he hadn't figured on being here this long.

I was nearly to the bedroom when I heard my cell phone ring. The sound made me hurtle through the door, almost diving to get it.

"Bones?" I answered.

A contemptuous scoff filled my ear. "No, *chérie*. Still hoping for your lover's return? How amusing."

Gregor. Just what I needed.

"What's up, dear?" Sarcastically. "Still snooping in my dreams, I see. Are you done apologizing to your ghouls because I'm sucking in air instead of blood? Just when you think you've got the little woman cornered, oops, you forget she has a knife."

"You should have stayed with me and spared yourself the humiliation of being yet another castoff of that peasant whore," he purred. "While you pine for Bones, he ruts with other women."

"Liar. Bones might be pissed at me, but he's a better man than that. Of course, that's something you wouldn't understand."

Gregor just laughed. "Oh, Catherine, soon you will see you're very wrong. Did you really think he'd changed? He saw a way out, and he took it."

I hung up, stopping myself from my stamping on the phone only out of concern that Bones might call next, and I'd have broken the thing. I was breathing heavily, like I'd been running. When Vlad tapped on the doorframe, I whirled around and grabbed him by the shoulders.

"Do you know where Bones is? Tell me the truth!"

Vlad flicked his gaze to his shirt, as if to say, *Do you mind?*

"No, Cat. Going to shake me next?"

I dropped my hands, balling them in frustration. "That bastard is playing games with me. He knows what I'm most afraid of, and he's using it to hurt me!"

"Gregor?" Vlad asked evenly. "Or Bones?"

I stopped pacing and shot him a measured look. "I meant Gregor, but . . . you might have a point."

Vlad smiled. "And what are you going to do about it?"

"When Spade gets back," I said grimly, "I'm going to shake *him*."

Spade just made it through the front door when I grabbed him by the shirt.

"You contact Bones and tell him he's made his point. I might have been wrong, but he's being cruel, and I've had enough."

Spade flicked my hands as if they were lint. "You couldn't relay that without creasing my shirt?"

"An attention-getter," I replied with a glint. "Just in case you needed one."

Vlad was on the other side of the room with Fabian and Annette. All three of them were waiting to see if Spade complied or refused. I'd moved some furniture out of the way, just in case Spade chose the latter. No need to trash the place.

"Cat," Spade began, "give me a few more days."

"Wrong answer," I said with a smile, and hit him.

Maybe it was the smile that put him off his guard. His head jerked to the side from the blow, then he took me seriously. The looseness was gone from his posture, and he took a wary step backward, his hands flexing in readiness.

"It's not so simple, but I can't explain why."

"You'd better find a way."

"I need a little more time," he snapped.

I stopped in sudden understanding and let out a harsh laugh.

"Oh, I get it. You can't reach him, can you? That's why you're hemming and hawing. You don't know where he is!"

Spade ground out a curse. "Good show, Reaper! As soon as you sleep, that fact will now be repeated to Gregor. Want to hang a bloody target around Crispin's neck?"

"How long?" I prodded, the first leaking of fear starting through me. "Do you even know where he went?"

"I won't give more information that could endanger—"

"Yes, you will," I said, anxiety and anger sharpening my tone. "Don't you worry about me, if I have to stay awake until this is squared away, I will. I'll break the world record for going without sleep if I have to, but you're spilling your beans, and you're doing it *now.*"

Spade's mouth tightened. Emerald flashed in his tawny eyes, and he gave me a look filled with steel.

"You'd better be prepared to keep that vow, for I'll hold you to it."

The details Spade outlined had me on an emotional roller coaster. Yes, he'd known how to contact Bones when he left. Before I even returned with Vlad, Bones had tersely given him a number for emergency use, leaving his location undisclosed. Two days ago, Spade had left him a message to find out when he was coming back. His call went unreturned. Since then, Spade had paged him, e-mailed him, and tried a few trusted friends as well. No one had heard from Bones.

"I've been making discreet inquiries, such as today when I was gone, and I think he might have been seeking an audience with Marie," Spade finished. "Rodney says he spoke to Crispin three days ago, and he made a comment about how hot it was in New Orleans. Why else would he be there? I've sent Rodney to investigate. That's all I know."

"Why didn't you just call Liza and ask her instead of waiting for Rodney to get there?"

"I did ring Liza." Spade ground his jaw. "She told me Marie had ordered her out of the Quarter a week ago and that she was refused permission even to communicate with anyone in it. Marie didn't give Liza an explanation; she just said she'd let her know when she could return."

"When did you find this out? How could you not have told me?"

"Crispin's specific instructions were to keep you uninvolved," Spade countered. "The last time you ran off like Henny Penny to shout the sky down, it didn't turn out well, did it? I suggest patience this round. Do you worlds of good."

I was about to scald him when my conscience stopped me. *He's right. You did run off last time, and these are the consequences. Maybe Bones just can't communicate right now. Let them do it their way. Wait until Rodney calls.*

"Fine." I sat down. "We'll wait to hear from Rodney."

Spade regarded me with caution, as if waiting for me to take it back. "I'm sure he'll ring soon."

"Soon" turned out to be five hours later. Rodney's voice was audible to everyone even before Spade put him on speaker. He was shouting.

"The fuck is going on there, but they've shut down the whole Quarter! Majestic's only allowing humans to pass who aren't of any vampire or ghoul's line. I don't know if Bones is there."

"How is she doing this?" Spade looked dumbfounded. I was stunned myself. How could Marie quarantine a whole section of the city?

"They've got ghouls and police on every section of the Quarter, supposedly searching for an abducted child. They make it really simple—turn around or you'll wish you did. I tried scoping out the river, but that's guarded as well. Marie's not playing games. We'll have to try something else."

Annette paled.

"They're using police," I breathed, my mind whirling with ideas. "I could ask some of my old team to go and check it out. They're human, and they have higher credentials . . . but that announces our involvement. It needs to be someone else."

I grabbed my phone. This was a big favor that might turn out to be a waste of time, but I was asking anyway. After all, weren't you supposed to be able to count on your family?

"Don," I said once my uncle answered. "In case you were shopping early for my birthday, I've got the perfect gift for you. I'm going to put Spade on the phone, then plug my ears while he tells you where we are. Then, I'm going to ask that you send a plane right away to ferry a ghost to Louisiana. Just get him within a few cities of New Orleans, and he'll do the rest."

"Cat?" Don waited a second before responding. "Have you been drinking?"

A brittle laugh escaped me. "I wish."

* * *

I was waiting again. It seemed to be all I could do lately. Spade made a few more calls to mutual acquaintances, trying to glean in a roundabout way if they had information on Bones, but no one had. Short of asking, "Seen Crispin 'round?" it was a painstaking and frustrating process.

Therefore, when a car pulled up, I ran to the window, praying that it was Bones. It wasn't, and I couldn't have been more surprised to see who walked up to the house.

Tate, the captain of my former team and my long-time friend, strode into the room and came right up to me like no one else was there. "How could you not have told me any of this?" he demanded.

Both Spade and Vlad were giving Tate hostile looks. Tate might be my friend, but he wasn't theirs. I pulled his hands away before he was impaled through the heart with silver.

"I didn't know Bones was missing, I just thought he was pissed."

Tate made a scornful noise. "Not Crypt Keeper. I don't give a shit about him. I meant you and the vampire Don just told me has been chasing you for weeks."

Oh, jeez. Tate was bent that I didn't tell him about Gregor? As if I needed this on top of everything else.

"Because I've hardly seen you since I quit working for Don. Now, are you here to help? Unlike you, I care very much that Bones is missing."

"He's not missing," Tate stated coldly. "He's just an asshole."

He was on his feet when he said it, staring up from the ground an instant later. Spade glowered over him. The anger emanating from him made me step between them.

"You've made your point."

"Crispin isn't here to counter his insults, and I'll not listen to anyone slander him," Spade retorted, his hand on a silver knife.

"Your boy isn't missing," Tate repeated, getting to his feet. "He's in the French Quarter like you thought, and if he's being held against his will, he's sure making the most of it."

"What are you talking about?"

Tate gave me a pitying but hard glance and pulled some sheets out of his coat.

"Satellite imagery. I printed it from the computer before I got here, so it's a little blurry, but there's no mistaking him. See the time stamp? It's 11:32 P.M. Central Time last night. Bones looks fine to me."

Spade and I spread the pictures onto a nearby table. The first one was a shot along Bourbon Street. Not very distinct, but yes, it was Bones. He was walking in the middle of the street. Even with the usual throngs of people, he stood out.

Thank God, was my initial thought.

I flipped to the second image. Bones was in front of his house, if I recognized the structure. And there was a woman in his arms.

A low growl escaped me. I flipped to the next page. The third image had me belting out a curse and almost flinging it at Spade.

"Needed some time to himself, huh? Funny how he doesn't seem to be doing that alone!"

The last image was only a partial of Bones's face. He was half inside the gate leading to his door. The same tramp was plastered to him, I could tell from her outfit, and his features were blocked because he was kissing her.

"He's a cheating prick," Tate said tonelessly. "He hasn't emerged from his house since that shot, according to the satellite. I don't need to tell you that soon we'll have to point it back where it belongs, Cat. Don's stretching his authority on this one."

"Mother*fucker*," I spat.

"This doesn't prove anything," Spade said, recovering from his astonishment. "We don't know what's going on, or who this woman is. She could be a contact and these actions a ruse."

"Oh, there's contact, all right." I wanted to study the photos and destroy them at the same time. "Full frontal, from what I can see!"

"Damn straight," Tate muttered.

"Quiet," Spade barked at Tate, easing his pitch when he turned to me. "Crispin wouldn't betray you that way, no matter how livid he was. There's an explanation for this. Let Fabian go and find it."

Underneath my fury, there was also piercing hurt. I wanted to believe that this was all a misunderstanding. And yet deep down inside there was an insinuating, slithering fear. What if it wasn't?

"Okay." Forced out while my head started to pound. "Fabian, you get down there and find Bones. Let him explain to you who this chick is. I'll wait to see what Bones says."

"Are you out of your fucking mind?" Tate burst. "Didn't you look at those pictures? What more do you need, live video feed?"

"Sometimes that isn't right either," I yelled back.

My eyes stung, but I didn't cry. "I found that out the hard way, and I'm not making the same mistake twice."

Tate just stared at me with disbelief. Then he said, "You're a fool," before walking away in disgust.

"I'll bring you word," Fabian promised.

"Please do." I glanced at the photos again. "No matter what it is."

Nineteen

Ivan came to pick Fabian up. From Ivan's friendly but cautious greeting, I knew he'd seen the pictures.

"How long before he gets there?" I asked Juan when they were about to leave.

He shuffled. "*Querida*, if I'm specific, it'll tell you too much."

"Approximately," I prodded, hating this necessary secrecy, but Gregor had proved he was still sifting in my dreams. If I somehow fell asleep, damned if I'd give him anything useful.

"Around a day, allowing for contact time and return," he estimated.

That long? I'd wear holes in the floor pacing.

"Fine." Years of faking cool when I was an emotional wreck had its advantages. "Take care of my ghost."

Juan gave a wary glance to his shoulder. Fabian smiled at me, his hand disappearing into Juan's collarbone.

"Good seeing you, *querida*," Juan said, still giving his shoulder a cagey stare. I waved with a forced smile. Mustn't look like the worried, jilted wife.

Out of the corner of my eye, I saw Spade rub his temple. Annette was in the doorway, almost leaning on the frame. It had been a long time since any of us had slept.

"Get some sleep, guys. This isn't a group contest on who can stay awake the longest. Especially you, Spade. You may need to be sharp when we get word, so you don't have a choice."

He nodded. "Just a few hours. That should tide me over."

"If you're worried that I'll nod off, don't. I can safely say there's enough on my mind to keep me up."

Spade gave Tate a condemning glare. "For all we know, those images were doctored. His jealousy of Crispin is boundless. It wouldn't astonish me in the least to have Fabian report back that there was no such woman."

"Yeah, right," Tate scoffed. "I wouldn't do that. Before anything else, I'm Cat's friend. And if Bones has nothing to hide, then why's he hiding?"

"Enough, guys." They were making my head worse.

Spade gave Tate a final glare. "You'll be proven wrong soon enough. I'll enjoy informing Crispin about how you needlessly upset Cat in your futile quest to have her, because I think at last he'll kill you for it."

Tate squared his shoulders. "I'm upsetting her with the truth because I'll be damned if I'll shut up while he runs around behind her back making a fool of her."

Spade stared at Tate in a way that worried me. He looked like he was fighting not to kill him.

"You're very lucky Crispin made me swear never to harm you," Spade settled on. "Else you'd already be missing your head."

"Sleep tight," Tate shot back.

"That better be your last word," I warned Tate. Spade wasn't all bark and no bite. Didn't Tate know that?

Spade tensed like all bets were off. I considered tackling him, but then decided on a different tactic.

I swayed with a gasp and put my hand to my head. Spade was at my side in a blink. His chivalrousness went even deeper than his temper.

"What is it, Cat?"

"All this stress and lack of sleep . . . I feel a little faint."

With a final threatening glance at Tate, Spade touched my arm. "I'll get you some water."

He went inside, and I turned my attention to Tate. "I probably just saved your life," I said quietly.

Vlad had been watching the whole thing with faint amusement. He'd known I was faking since he would have heard it in my head.

"Young man, one day I suspect you'll have a terrible accident," he said to Tate. "Keep provoking people, and it will be one day soon."

Tate rolled his eyes. "Yeah, yeah, I know—you'll kill me something awful. If only I had a dime for every time I heard that."

"If I wanted you dead, you would be. You should mind your speech so when you do piss someone off past his control, you'll be strong enough to have a chance at surviving it."

"Good advice," I added. "You should listen to him."

Tate swung his gaze at me. "Fuck, Cat. I'd be jumping at my own shadow if was scared of every threat directed at me. One day I'm gonna die. Everyone will, even our kind. I'll be damned if I spend what time I have sniveling like a coward, kissing ass so I don't make people angry. All I've got is how I live. How I'll die? That's the problem of the guy who kills me."

"God," I muttered. He just wouldn't listen.

Vlad let out a whistle. "I've wondered what she saw in you. You seem so pitiful most of the time. At least you have some semblance of courage."

"You motherfucker—" Tate began.

His feet caught fire. Then his hands. The forward momentum he'd used to charge at Vlad was abruptly changed into an odd stomping dance while Tate tried to douse the flames.

Vlad tutted. "See? Watch your temper."

"Ahem." I cleared my throat. "You mind?"

The fire slowly extinguished on Tate. I shook my head. Fabian couldn't come back fast enough. Who would have thought I'd be so anxious to see a ghost?

"Can I trust you not to kill him, Vlad, while I go inside and *not* sleep?" I asked.

Vlad smiled. "For a while, you can."

Juan didn't come back. Neither did Fabian, though it wasn't eighteen hours before there was word. It came in the form of a phone call. Funny how terrible news usually came to me by phone.

"Cat."

Juan's voice. As soon as I heard it, I knew it was bad. He sounded so controlled. So forcibly gentle.

"I didn't want to wait to tell you, *querida* . . ."

Vlad was staring at me. Tate was, too. Spade almost had his head on my shoulder to hear the report firsthand.

"When Fabian found him, it was clear that Bones wasn't being held against his will. He, ah, indicated that he wanted Fabian to leave . . . would you pull yourself together, *amigo*?" This was presumably to the ghost, since I hadn't broken down. Yet. "Look, *querida*, Fabian said Bones was very harsh. Told him to sod off, or similar."

I took a deep breath. "So you're saying he wanted to be left alone still. Did—did he say for how long? Did he say anything about me?"

I couldn't help it; my voice cracked at the last question. My heart was racing, and I felt faint, but at least my legs were straight.

"*Sí.*" Juan sounded like he'd swallowed something rancid. "Fabian asked, 'How am I supposed to tell your wife this?' and Bones said . . ."

Juan stopped. "Said what?" I almost screamed.

"He said, 'I have no wife.'"

Spade snatched the cell out of my numb fingers. "That's a bloody lie!"

"Look, I don't like it either," I heard Juan snap. "But he's not lying."

Spade didn't stop fuming. "I've known that man 220 years, and I can tell you—"

"Let it go, Spade."

He quit his ranting at my calm tone and gaped at me. "You don't believe this rot, do you?"

I think I laughed. Hell if I could say for certain. "I guess after seeing satellite imagery and hearing eyewitness accounts, I'm going to side with *yes*. Answer me this—did Bones actually say he was coming back to me? Or did you assume?"

Spade straightened. "He didn't need to write it down for me to know his intentions—"

Now I was sure about the laugh, and it was ugly. "In other words, no, you assumed."

Here Bones had clearly told me it was over, but I still hadn't gotten it. I'd clung to the scrap of hope Spade had dangled right up until the bitter end.

Annette stayed in the far corner of the room, smart. Spade hung up on Juan without another word.

"Cat, let's get out of here," Tate said. "You can go back to Don and the team. You've always got a home there. You don't need this."

I stared at him, cold reality intruding between the searing pain. *That's right, this isn't your home. You don't belong here. You don't belong anywhere.*

"No."

I thought it, but I wasn't the one who said it. Vlad brushed by Tate like he wasn't there.

"Gregor's shown he won't let her go, and you can't protect her from him. You'll only get your soldiers killed, and her as well, in short order. She can come with me until she decides what she wants to do."

"I doubt your intentions are honorable," Spade said, his eyes glinting green.

"If Bones were concerned with my intentions, he'd be here to observe them," Vlad replied. Tate's protest wasn't helping. The mood was quickly turning dangerous. "You're guarding an abandoned lover, not your best friend's wife. Why don't you mind your own love life, since you were lax on that front before."

If it were possible for a vampire to whiten, Spade just had. Vlad's reference to Giselda, Spade's fiancée, who had been murdered, wasn't lost on me. Quickly, before things were beyond salvaging, I moved between Spade and Vlad. It wasn't that I was worried about Vlad getting hurt. I was afraid that if Spade touched him, Vlad would burn him to death.

"Spade, whatever you may think, Bones made it crystal clear that we were over. It's my fault I didn't accept it. Tate . . . I can't go back. There is no going back." *God, if only there were.* "Vlad, what's your price? Vampires always have one, so what do you want if I go with you until I figure things out?"

Vlad seemed to consider it. "I'll take feeding from you as a fair price."

"Agreed." Or, *Sold! to the vampire with the coppery-green eyes.*

Spade crossed his arms. "There's no way I'm allowing you to leave with him."

Don't get physical, I sent to Vlad, seeing his lip curl at the challenge. *Spade is my friend, even if he is wrong. No snack for you if you toast him. That goes for Tate as well, since he looks like he's about to throw himself in our path.*

"Do I smell smoke?" Vlad asked, that little smile never leaving his face.

With that, flames began crawling across the walls. It looked like orange and red snakes magically appeared and grew. And grew.

Spade began cursing and went to the sink, filling the nearest containers with water while shouting for assistance.

"If you're quick, you'll have it out in no time," Vlad assured them, holding out his arm to me. "Shall we?"

To stay would be to cause greater damage. The

three of them would come to blows, I knew, and no amount of intervention would stop them. Tate already wasn't rational. He grabbed Vlad's shoulder—and then went flying up through the ceiling. Both of them, from the sounds of it. Rubble showered down amidst the flames.

Vlad didn't even blink. "That's a warning. The next one won't be."

I gave a last glance at the hole in the ceiling and the burning walls before I took Vlad's arm, still reeling from the past fifteen minutes. "Let's go."

We got into a car that I assumed was Vlad's. As we pulled away, there were four distinct ka-booms, and the vehicles in the driveway exploded.

"So they don't attempt to follow us," Vlad said in response to my stunned look.

Lightning broke across the sky. It was the last thing I saw before I closed my eyes.

Twenty

THERE ARE FIVE STEPS TO THE GRIEVING
process, or so they say. Denial is the first. I'd had
plenty of that since I left Spade's. Then anger, and oh
yeah, I was angry. *Couldn't even take a few days to stop
and think about things, maybe let the dust settle? Oh no,
not you, Bones! Back in the saddle, huh, cowboy?*

Then bargaining, perhaps the most pathetic one
of all, which kept me busy through the flight to our
unknown destination. *Let him come back. I love him so
much, and he did love me. Maybe we can still work things
out . . .*

Fuck him! my anger said. *I always knew Bones would
go back to his old tricks. A leopard can't change his spots,
right? Doesn't have a wife, huh? Who needs you, anyway?*

If the vampire next to me was listening to my
mental schizophrenia, he gave no indication. Vlad
whistled while my emotions played Russian roulette.
By the time he announced we'd arrived, I was into a
state of full-blown depression.

Or, in other words, step Number Four.

The car stopped, and I heard people approach. None of them had heartbeats.

My car door opened. There was a light tug on my hand. "Keep them closed a moment longer. I'll lead you inside."

A minute of careful stepping later, and we stopped.

"You can open your eyes now, Cat."

I did. We were in a long hall of some sort, very old-looking. High, high ceilings. Gothic in the very definition of the word.

Vlad smiled. "Enter freely and of your own will, isn't that what I'm supposed to say?"

I flicked my gaze around the hall. "I'm just staying a few days to get my head on straight." *And staple together my broken heart.*

"Stay as long as you wish. After all, you owe me a debt. It might take me more than a few days to collect on it."

I gave him a tired look. "Don't bet on it."

One thing could be said for staying with the uncrowned Prince of Darkness. He didn't have a lazy, inattentive staff. After I was shown to my room by a vampire named Shrapnel, I asked what kind of plasmaless drinks they had. Shrapnel didn't respond by listing them from memory—he brought me the entire beverage contents of the refrigerator. When I told him I would have gone down myself to see it, he stared at me like I was crazy.

Well, he was right on that one.

Vlad had dinner with me each night even though he didn't eat. He was pretty scarce during the day, tending to his own affairs, I guessed. Not that I knew for sure. I spent most of my time in my room, brooding, my mood swinging wildly from anger at Bones to self-recrimination. Had my relationship been doomed from the start because Bones was incapable of changing his promiscuous ways? Or would everything have been okay if I just hadn't left that day with Gregor? I didn't know, and not knowing festered.

I went to the dining room at nine. Dinner was served late, for obvious reasons. Vlad was already seated. His long brown hair was brushed and loose, and he twirled the stem of his wineglass as I took my usual place next to him.

I started to fill my plate from the selections on the table. Rack of lamb with a rosemary reduction, marinated asparagus with mango salsa and tiny, tender red potatoes. Vlad just watched, drinking his wine. Living with a vampire, I'd gotten used to being the one munching while someone else just watched, so I didn't feel self-conscious.

After a few minutes of silent chewing, I paused. "This lamb is really good. Sure you don't want to try any?"

"I'll eat soon."

Something about his voice made my fork poise over the next bite. Vlad didn't sound like he was referring to the feast spread before him.

"Are you mentioning that in passing, or prepping me?"

"Gauging your reaction." With a tilt of his head. "Your eyes aren't as puffy tonight. And your manner is less downtrodden. Does this mean you've finally resigned yourself to Bones's abandonment?"

It was the first time in four days that he'd mentioned him. Personally, I could have stood to let it go longer.

"Don't worry, you won't have to talk me off a ledge again."

"I'm pleased to hear that."

He leaned back in his chair, twirling his glass again.

"You haven't contacted Spade or anyone else since you've been here. Aren't you curious to know if they've spoken to him?"

That had me setting down my fork. I didn't know where he was going with this, but Vlad did nothing without motivation.

"What's up, buddy? Trying to get my blood pumping? Tenderize me before you dig in? No, I haven't talked to them, and I don't want to. I don't need more gory details."

"Like whether he has his hands on someone this very minute? Squeezing her, kissing her . . . holding her naked against him?"

My plate hurled across the room to shatter against the stone wall. Even as I did it, I cursed myself, Vlad, and most of all, Bones.

"You're just seeing how quickly I'll lose it, aren't you? *Gauging* me? Well, I'm a little testy, as you can tell, so excuse me."

I grabbed my linen napkin and headed toward the broken dish, determined to clean up my own mess, but Vlad was faster. Still seated, he yanked me to him.

"What are you doing?" I snapped.

His hold tightened until he was almost hurting me. "Claiming my blood price."

I had time to tense before Vlad's mouth latched onto my throat, and his fangs bit into it.

A cry came out of me, but it wasn't of pain. Vlad sucked harder, drawing more of my blood into him. Pulsing warmth spread through me with each pull of his mouth. *Vampire venom.* Not harmful, but capable of producing a false, very pleasant sensation of heat.

"Vlad, that's enough . . ."

"No." Muffled. "More."

He pulled me closer. Now I was half-sagged against him while those deep suctions felt like they went going straight through to my spine.

Vlad ran his hands down my arms. I gasped. They were hot, so unlike a vampire's normal temperature. Must be from his pyrokinesis. My blood couldn't warm them that quickly.

Just as fast as he'd grabbed me, Vlad released me. I leaned against the table, my knees far weaker than before.

"That should give you something else to think about," he said.

"No, it won't."

It came from me brokenly. All at once, I started to cry. "I still love him, Vlad! I hate him, too, maybe, but . . . I still love him."

His stare didn't waver. "You'll get over it."

Will I?

I didn't say it out loud, not that it mattered. Vlad could still hear me.

"I'm not hungry anymore," was what I did say, and left the dining room.

Later that night, I'd just fallen asleep when the bed shifted. My eyes opened in alarm, then a finger pressed to my lips.

"It's just me. I want to talk."

I was awake now. People didn't usually talk while climbing into bed, which described what Vlad was doing.

"Really?" With heavy sarcasm.

He made a dismissing motion. "Don't white-knuckle the sheets, Cat. I'm not intending to rape you."

"Where I come from, when people want to talk, they do it while upright." To punctuate my point, I sat up. Yes, I was gripping the sheets pretty good. "This smacks of coercion at best, pal."

Vlad just fluffed a pillow under his head and laughed.

"What a perfect picture of outrage you are, Reaper, yet we both know I could burn these sheets to ashes if I wanted to. Come now, aside from your rigid Midwestern upbringing, do you mind that I'm here with you like this?"

My grip relaxed on the bedclothes. He had several points. Vlad was much stronger than I am, so even if he couldn't torch the sheets, if he'd wanted to force sex, he could. Plus, playing hyperappropriate when he'd sucked over a pint from me seemed a tad hypocritical.

"Fine. What do you want to talk about?"

"Your future."

I tensed. "You want me to leave. Fine. I'll—"

"Do you truly believe I came here to tell you I'm throwing you out?" he interrupted. "You should know me better than that."

"Sorry. It's been, well, a rough week."

"Yes." There wasn't any false pity in his tone. "Your self-esteem has suffered a severe blow, and you're very vulnerable. If I had a mind to, you'd be easy to seduce."

"Full of yourself, aren't you?" I said with a snort. "But you're barking up the wrong tree if you thought I'd be looking for a mercy fuck."

His lips curved. "I already told you, my feelings for you aren't romantic. I'm here because you are a friend, and for me friends are much harder to come by than a fuck."

What I felt for him didn't have to do with attraction either, even though Vlad was certainly attractive. No, I felt an odd sort of kinship with him instead.

"I'm glad you're here," I said. It was true. I couldn't handle this being around Mencheres, or Spade, or anyone else who would have taken me on out of a pitying sense of responsibility.

Vlad squeezed my hand. "You will get through this, but before you can do that, you have to face him."

Him. *Bones.* I looked away.

"I appreciate the sentiment, but for this topic, it's wasted. I'm not going to see him. I don't want to see what he's doing, or with whom."

"Catherine, you're being stupid."

I stiffened at the insult and my real name. "How so, Drac?" I snapped, using the name he never went by as well.

"You haven't truly started getting over him because you're still wondering if he's really gone. It's why you won't let go. It's also why you'll end up getting killed, because you're so distracted over that, you didn't notice a vampire in your room until he crawled into bed with you. Settle things with Bones, once and for all. Then move on, either with him or without him."

"I know it's over," I said with a catch to my voice. "He told me loud and clear that it was."

"And you wonder if he really meant it. You're wondering if he hasn't done this just to hurt you, like you hurt him by leaving with his enemy during a battle. You're making yourself crazy wondering if he's waiting to see if you'll go after him just like all those times he chased after you."

"Stop prying into my mind!" To hear my hidden speculations aloud was like surgery without the anesthesia.

"It's not such an ill-conceived notion," he went on coolly. "He'd be inflicting your worst fears on you as you did to him. It's a fair punishment, in my opinion. I just doubt Bones has the backbone to do it."

"Then why are you telling me to find out if you think I'll only get shot down again?"

"Because if you're right, he'll be knocking on my door soon anyway. If not, then you're devastated but resolute since you're much stronger than you realize."

I chewed my lower lip. Risk getting my heart trampled on again just to see if this was some sort of weird vampire power play? And if it was, could I forgive it? Would I want to?

Either way, I'd know, which I guess was better than driving myself crazier hanging on to that slim thread of wonder.

Vlad must have read it in my mind, because he nodded. "In the morning, call Spade and schedule your meeting with Bones. Bones won't refuse to see you, no matter his intentions toward you. Then you'll know if it's over for good."

This was too much to contemplate with a low iron count and little sleep. I lay back down with a sigh, forgetting to be self-conscious about being in bed with him.

Vlad settled next to me, putting his head on my pillows.

"Ahem." I cleared my throat. "Didn't we just agree that we were only friends?"

"Sex isn't what I'm after. It's just been a long time since I've slept next to a woman who meant something to me."

"Oh. Well." A slumber party with Dracula? All things considered, why not? "Okay, but I snore."

He grinned. "I *have* been under the same roof with you for a week, so I already know that."

I gave him a dirty look but then stretched in bed as I normally would.

Vlad put his arms around me and rested his head on my pillow. I should have been embarrassed to be in bed with him, especially since he was bare-chested, and I only had on a long sleep shirt over my underwear, but I wasn't. It felt nice to fall asleep with someone again, even if he wasn't the someone I'd been missing.

"Good night, Cat," he said, though it was almost dawn.

I yawned and closed my eyes.

"Good night, Vlad."

The knock at the door didn't wake me. Must have been too soft and tentative. Only when Vlad said, "Come in," in a less-than-pleased tone did I wake up. God, he was right. My reflexes were shit.

Shrapnel stuck his head inside. I mentally berated Vlad for not giving me a chance to disappear into the bathroom. How incriminating did this look?

"Forgive me, Master, but the caller says it's urgent. May I give you the phone?"

He held it close to his side, obviously nervous. Maybe Vlad was grumpy when he woke up.

Vlad gestured. "Very well, bring it."

Shrapnel moved like a jackrabbit, then hurried out, closing the door behind him.

"Who's this?" Vlad snapped into the phone.

Spade's voice blared out loud enough to bolt me upright.

"If you don't put Cat on the line this time, I'm going to roast you alive in your own sodding juices—"

I snatched the phone away from him. "What is it? I'm here, what's wrong?"

There was a loaded moment of silence. Too late, I realized what I'd done. Vlad lifted a shoulder as if to say, *You're stuck now.*

"I was told Vlad couldn't be disturbed because he was in bed." Each word was a blistering accusation. "That he was *extremely indisposed*. Lucifer's bloody balls, is this why you haven't returned my calls?"

"I-I-I didn't . . ." Good God, I was stammering.

"Indeed!"

"Look, don't even!" My anger came to the rescue. "If something's wrong, tell me, but if you're just going to play Pussy Police, you should start with your best friend. He's probably nose deep in one right now."

"He's arse deep in danger, if you still care," was Spade's icy reply.

That took all the hostility out of me. Spade wasn't one for hysterical exaggerations. I clutched the phone like it was slippery.

"What happened?"

Maybe I sounded as fearful as I felt, because Spade's voice lost some of its anger.

"Fabian, your helpful ghost, has been in New Orleans trying to speak with him. From what he can deduce, Crispin will be forced to leave the Quarter soon. And Gregor's lying in wait outside the city."

"What do you mean, 'forced to leave'?" My voice couldn't get more shrill. Vlad winced.

"Crispin went to New Orleans to have a meeting with Marie. After it took place, from what I've gathered, Marie closed the Quarter to any more undead visitors, and Gregor's assembled a slew of forces beyond the city's outskirts."

I jumped up and began rummaging for clothes. Vlad scooted into my spot, unperturbed. "Are you there? On your way?"

"We can't, that's the whole bloody problem! Because of you, Gregor has clear rights to take Crispin out under our laws. No vampire can come to his aid over this."

I sat on the floor, my knees weak. For a second, I couldn't even breathe. Then I began to plan.

"He'll need to be airlifted out of there. A helicopter would be best. We can arm it with silver bullets. We'll do a midair transport onto a plane. Did you say you've been leaving messages for me about this?" I gave Vlad a truly menacing glare.

"I've been leaving messages for you to call, but we only found out tonight about Gregor's ambush."

Vlad shrugged, unapologetic. "You said you didn't want to speak to them. This part is news to me. I would have told you had I known."

I didn't bitch at him. After all, it was my own fault for hiding, not Vlad's.

"There's a problem with your plan, Cat," Spade said tightly. "Else we would have already done something similar. No one of any line is allowed in the city, and that means above it, too. It would be sentencing them to death by Marie's decree, and she's too powerful to dismiss. I'd risk it myself, but if one vampire or ghoul crosses the line into the Quarter, Gregor and his people will follow. It has to be humans of no vampire affiliation, do you understand?"

Yeah, I did. Now I knew why Spade was in such a twist to get ahold of me.

"Give me your number. I'll call you right back."

Twenty-one

Testing three, two, one . . . You read me, Geri?"

Lieutenant Geri Hicks, my replacement with Don's team, coughed and muttered, "Affirmative."

She had a receiving line surgically planted under her skin, pumping my voice directly by her eardrum. If I shouted, she'd be in pain. Her microphone was less invasively located in her necklace.

"What's your location, Geri?"

"Crossing St. Ann Street and heading toward Bourbon. The bird still show he's there?"

I checked the satellite imagery of the French Quarter on my borrowed laptop. The plane's turbulence didn't help, but I could still spot Bones. And the woman next to him.

"Affirmative. There's a small time delay, as you know, but he should be there. You doing all right?"

Geri was nervous. I couldn't blame her. She had to bring Bones in without getting him or herself killed. Yeah, I'd have been wigged, too.

"I'm good," Geri said.

"Roger that. Now go get him."

I was the only person Spade knew who had human connections without direct undead affiliations and who could amass airpower and support complete with cutting-edge weapons and technology. Sure, it could be argued that my old team had connections to Bones, but none of them were under his command anymore since I'd quit. I owed my uncle big for this.

Since she was human, Geri couldn't see Fabian. He was there, though, trying to drop hints about our plan while not getting noticed by any of Marie's people. That wasn't an easy task. When this was over, I'd owe Fabian big, too. How does one repay a ghost? That was an issue I'd ponder later.

"Approaching target, going silent," Geri whispered.

On-screen, I saw her nearing Bones. He was at Pat O'Brien's, in the outside area, drinking what I guessed was his usual whiskey. His arm was slung around a pretty brunette, who was almost glued to him. Even now, her hand ran along his hip.

I clenched my fists. *Bitch, you and I are going to have a long, bloody chat after this.*

Cannelle couldn't hear my mental warning, but Vlad could. He lounged in the chair opposite me, the jet's turbulence not bothering him. We were on our way to the rendezvous point if all went well.

"You really don't like her."

I didn't answer out loud. That might confuse Geri, since I was wearing a headset.

No. I really, really don't.

"I know this is forward," Geri purred through my earpiece as the satellite showed her reaching Bones and his companion, Cannelle, "but after seeing the two of you gorgeous creatures, I can't decide who I want to fuck first."

"Attagirl," I whispered. God, cheerleading someone to hit on the man I loved! Why couldn't I have a normal life?

Bones set his drink down. If he was surprised to see Geri, he didn't show it. I sucked in a breath. What would he do? He had to know I'd sent Geri. Would he blow her cover? Or play along and get out of there?

"Easy decision, luv." Her necklace picked up every nuance of his accent. "Ladies first. Isn't that right, Cinnamon?"

Cannelle's knowing laugh pierced me straight in the heart. The plane's armrest lost a chunk.

"She looks very fierce, *chéri*. I was hoping for softer company, *non*?"

Geri didn't let Cannelle's disparagement stumble her. She flicked her fingers in Bones's drink, then made a good show of licking the alcohol off them.

"I'll be as gentle as a lamb, honey."

Geri really had come a long way since the person I'd trained months ago.

Cannelle caught Geri's wrist, put her palm up to her lips, and did some licking of her own.

"We shall see."

Then Cannelle put her arms around Bones and kissed him. Through Geri's microphone, I could almost hear Cannelle grinding against him, her muted moan of enjoyment, and his masculine rumble as he pressed her closer.

A full two minutes later, he lifted his head. By then, I almost *wanted* him dead.

Vlad watched me without pity. "Someone else could be doing this."

He was right. I'd insisted on being the relay. I didn't trust anyone else for something so important, no matter that it was brutal for me.

"Get him moving," I said to Geri, very low.

Geri stepped between them. "I don't need foreplay," she said, her throaty voice almost a purr. "Do we have to get to know each other? I just want to fuck like you can't imagine."

Bones disentangled himself from Cannelle to take Geri's hand. "Hate to keep a lovely girl waiting. Come on, Cinnamon. This is who I want tonight."

"Don't I get to choose?"

I heard the pout in Cannelle's voice. It was all I could do not to scream.

"Not this time, luv."

"*Chéri—*"

"Everyone else has been your choice," he interrupted, leading them through the crowds. "Keep whinging, and I'll make you wait until I'm done before you have her."

"Bastard," I spat, unable to help it. *Everyone else? Wasn't that just great!*

Bones stopped at a curb. I tensed. Had he heard me through Geri's earpiece?

But then they were moving again. I let out my breath. So far, so good. *Bastard.*

"Keep heading toward the church," I said to Geri, almost inaudible.

Then I removed my headset and spoke into my cell phone.

"Okay, Don, deploy. They're on their way. Tell Cooper not to drop the ladder until he's fifty yards away."

"Got it, Cat."

I readjusted the headset. Geri was telling Bones that she wanted to have sex on the church's roof, but Cannelle was protesting.

"*Non*, there could be rats! Why can we not leave here for an evening? I told you I have very beautiful friends in Metairie I want you to meet."

"Tell you what, sweet. We'll go tomorrow. You've wanted me to meet these lasses for days, they must be terribly special."

"*Oui. Très magnifique.*"

So Cannelle's been trying to draw him out of the city, right to Gregor, I thought, anger rising. Maybe Vlad's impalement hobby wasn't such a bad idea. What was the matter with Bones that he hadn't wondered at her insistence? Was he *that* blinded by lust?

"Tomorrow we'll do what you fancy, and tonight shall be my evening," Bones went on. "I promise you'll see a new side of me."

And me, too. I was *really* looking forward to seeing Cannelle in person again.

I couldn't see the three of them anymore. They were off my satellite since they started walking. "Look around, Geri. Are you being followed?"

"You don't think anyone will catch us climbing up onto the roof, do you?" Geri asked, sounding coy.

Bones kissed her. I couldn't see it, but I could hear it. "Not at all."

Okay. It was clear. God, I wanted this to be over soon. Safely, and soon.

"Ah, here's the church. Now, my lovely, look at me for a moment. You don't need to fret about my eyes or my teeth, right? You don't notice anything unusual about them. You're not afraid, because you know I won't hurt you. Say it."

"You won't hurt me," Geri repeated. "I'm not afraid."

So, that's how Bones got around the glowy gaze and pointy teeth when he fucked humans. I'd thought as much but never wanted to ask. I knew more about his past than I already cared to. This scene was for Cannelle's benefit, I guessed, since Bones knew Geri was in on his secret. Just going through the usual motions.

I thought I'd puke.

"Cinnamon, shall we?"

"If we must, *chéri*."

"We must."

After a few moments of noisy rustling sounds, Bones spoke again.

"The roof at last. No rats, *petite*, quit cringing."

Vlad, get the chopper's ETA.

He complied with the mental directive and took my cell, hitting redial.

"They're on the roof," he informed Don briefly. "How long? . . . Yes." He set my cell back down. "Six minutes."

"You've got six minutes, Geri. Remember, Bones has to have both you and Cannelle when he jumps, and she won't want to go."

"Come here, lovelies. That's better."

Bones's voice changed. Became the luxurious purr that used to melt me. Listening to it now only made me pissed. Worse, next there was breathiness and the soft chafing noises of kissing.

Then Geri said, "Hey now, sugar. Ease up a bit."

"Why?" Cannelle's voice was belligerent. "I am ready for you to please me."

I glanced at the time. "Two more minutes. Stall but be cool, Geri."

"Cinnamon, don't be so greedy. I'll sweeten her up for you. You'll like it better for the wait."

I beat my fists against my legs but didn't scream anything. Instead, I watched the seconds tick past and tried to listen with clinical detachment for signs of danger. Unfortunately, most of what I heard wasn't the sounds of danger.

Thirty seconds to go. Even if someone overheard, we couldn't wait any longer. "Tell him the score, Geri," I said.

"Bones, a chopper's going to do a pass over the church about two hundred yards up. He'll have a chain ladder dangling. When you see him coming, you blast your ass up with both of us and grab it. As soon as we're clear of the city, you'll leapfrog onto the back of another plane. Spade will be on it."

"What is this?" Cannelle hissed.

"Ten seconds," I rasped. "Nine, eight, seven . . ."

"Know something, Cinnamon?" Bones lost the seductive timbre to his voice, and it turned into cold steel. "I'm sick of your complaining."

". . . one," I yelled.

Then there were only the sounds of the helicopter before I heard a clanging of metal, a thump, and the words I'd been waiting for from Geri.

"We're in!"

The chopper had special silent blades, which reduced its normal noise. It made Cooper and the two copilots inaudible, however. Geri still wasn't, of course.

"Is she still breathing?" Geri asked. "You hit her pretty hard."

"She's alive."

There was a sliding noise, then Geri said harshly,

"Try to shove *my* head between your legs, huh? Who's happy now, bitch?"

"She can't feel you kicking her," Bones said, no criticism in his voice.

"Yeah, well, I can feel it, and I'm enjoying it!"

More thumping sounds ensued. I didn't want to interrupt. Cannelle being kicked pleased me too much.

"Where is she?" Bones asked.

I froze. Geri let out a final "oof!" that sounded like a grunt from a *coup de grâce* kick and replied.

"When you get on the plane, you'll be flown to her."

Bones didn't say anything, but his silence seemed to say it all. *There's no need to see him face-to-face*, I thought bleakly. *Everyone else has been your choice*, Bones had said to Cannelle. Yeah, that was all I needed to hear to know it was over. Vampires might be able to forgive cheating as an acceptable form of revenge, but I must be too human for that. I'd put up with a lot from Bones and consider it justified payback, but not this.

I waited until Bones had transferred to Spade's plane as planned before unhooking my headpiece. Geri was probably delighted not to have my voice pumping into her eardrum anymore. Only Bones was doing the aerial jump; Geri and Cannelle were staying in the helicopter. Spade's plane was supposed to rendezvous with me at one of Don's locations, but that wasn't necessary now.

I called my uncle. "Change Bones's flight plan," I said. "Don't tell me where to, but don't fly him where I'll be."

My uncle didn't ask unnecessary questions. "All right, Cat."

I hung up. Vlad had been watching me the entire time. I managed to muster what would have been a terrible imitation of a smile.

"That answers that."

"It's not as if his prior habits were unfamiliar to you," Vlad replied, no false sympathy in his voice.

No, they weren't. But I hadn't expected to listen while Bones admitted to numerous affairs. Or had I? He might have told me the same thing to my face had I met with him. God, at least I could avoid that. I'd burst into tears and lose the very small shred of dignity I had left.

Two hours later, we landed at the base, though I didn't know where. From the outside, most military installations looked the same, anyway, not that I was looking. I had my eyes shut and my hand on Vlad's arm as I got off the plane.

"Hello, Commander," a male voice said.

I smiled still with my eyes closed. "Cooper, I'd say nice to see you, but give me a minute."

He grunted, which was his version of a belly laugh, and soon I was inside the facility.

"You can open your eyes now," Cooper said.

His familiar face was the first thing I saw, dark-skinned and with hair even shorter than Tate's. I gave him a brief hug, which seemed to surprise him, but he was smiling when I let go.

"Missed you, freak," he said, still with a smile.

I laughed even though it was hoarse. "You too, Coop. What's the news?"

"Geri's chopper arrived thirty minutes ago. The prisoner was secured and awake. Ian is here. He's been questioning the prisoner."

That made me smile for real. I'd had Ian flown here

because he was a cold-blooded bastard—and right now, I liked that about him.

"You can stay here or come with me, it's up to you," I said to Vlad.

"I'll come," he replied, giving Fabian, who'd just floated up, a cursory glance. The ghost hovered over the ground next to Cooper, who couldn't see him because he was human.

"Fabian, you've been incredible," I said. "No matter what, I'll take care of you. You'll always have a place to stay."

"Thank you," he said, brushing his hand through mine in his form of affection. "I'm sorry, Cat."

He didn't need to say what for. That was obvious.

My smile turned brittle. "Whoever said ignorance was bliss was shortsighted, if you ask me. But what's done is done, and now I have an acquaintance to renew."

The ghost looked momentarily hopeful. "Bones?"

"No. The little bitch inside, and you might not want to follow me for this one. It's going to get ugly."

I didn't have to tell him twice. In a whirl, Fabian vanished. Neat trick. Sucked to have to be a phantom to do it.

My uncle waited for me farther inside the hallway. He looked . . . bad.

"Is something wrong?" I asked, instantly worried. Had Bones's plane been tailed, or attacked, or worse?

"No." He coughed. "I just have a cold."

"Oh." I gave him a hug hello. It surprised me when he squeezed back and held on. We weren't a cuddly family.

Vlad sniffed the air. "A cold?"

Don let me go and gave him an annoyed look.

"That's right. Don't concern yourself. I'm not contagious to your kind."

He said it harshly. Jeez, maybe Don really did feel like shit. My uncle wasn't normally so surly, even though vampires weren't his favorite group of people.

Vlad looked him up and down and shrugged.

Don went right to business. It was his defining characteristic. "I just came from the downstairs cell. The prisoner hasn't been very forthcoming about her role in this."

"Then it's time for me to see my old friend."

Twenty-two

CANNELLE DIDN'T APPEAR TO HAVE AGED A day in the twelve years since I'd seen her. In fact, only her reddish brown hair was different with its new, shorter length. I guessed it was where she got her name. Cannelle. French for cinnamon.

She sat on a steel bench that took up an entire wall in the square, boxlike space. Cannelle wasn't restrained, since Ian and Geri were in the room with her. Even if by some miracle she got past them, there were still three more guards outside the door. Her eye was black, and blood dripped from her mouth and temple, but she wasn't cowed.

When I walked in, she blinked, then laughed.

"*Bonjour,* Catherine! It's been a long time. You finally look like a woman. I am very surprised."

I felt a nasty grin pull my lips. "*Bonjour* yourself, Cannelle. Yep, I grew tits and ass and a whole lot more. What a difference a dozen years makes, huh?"

She went right for the throat. "I must compliment

you on your lover, Bones. *Qu'un animal, non?* In this instance, his reputation was . . . not gracious enough."

Bitch. I wanted to rip the smirk right off her face.

"Too bad he didn't seem bowled over by your bedroom skills. I mean, the fact that you couldn't get him to leave the city for a *ménage à cinq* doesn't speak well, does it?"

Ian chuckled with malevolent humor. "Oh, you two ladies have a history, do you? You might want to start speaking now, poppet. I've been gentle with you, but Cat has a wicked temper. She'll likely kill you before I can reason with her."

"Her?" Cannelle flicked her finger contemptuously at me. "She's a child."

Boy, did she pick the wrong girl in the wrong mood.

"Hand me that knife, Ian."

He passed it over, his turquoise eyes sparkling. Geri looked a little nervous. Cannelle didn't even blink.

"You won't kill me, Catherine. You play the hard woman, but I still see a little girl before me."

Ian regarded Cannelle with amazement. "She's unhinged."

"No, she's just remembering who I used to be. Gregor made that mistake also, at first."

I smiled at Cannelle again while twirling the knife from one hand to the other. Her eyes followed the movement, and for the first time, she looked uncertain.

"Remember that big bad bitch Gregor didn't want me turning into? Well, it happened. Now, I'm in a hurry, so here's what I'm going to do. I'm going to slam this knife through your hand, and the only way you'll stop me is by talking, so please. *Please.* Don't talk."

She didn't believe me. When Ian held Cannelle's

wrist to the bench, forcing her hand flat, she was still giving me that I-dare-you glare. When I held the knife over her hand, giving her one last chance to talk, she still thought I was bluffing. Only after I slammed the blade into her hand between her wrist and her fingers, jerking the blade in a twist, did she get the picture.

And couldn't stop screaming.

"I know that hurts," I remarked. "My father did that to my wrist last year, and damn, it was painful. Crippling, too. When I yanked the blade out, all my tendons were severed. I needed vampire blood to heal the damage. You will, too, Cannelle, or you'll never use this hand again. So you can talk, and a dab of vampire blood'll have you good as new. Or don't talk, and I cripple your right hand next."

"Fix it! Fix it!"

"You'll tell us what we want to know?"

"*Oui!*"

I sighed and yanked the knife out. "Ian?"

Cannelle was still screaming when Ian sliced his palm and cupped it over her mouth.

"Quit wailing and swallow."

She gulped at his hand. In seconds, her bleeding stopped, and the wound in her hand disappeared.

Geri couldn't tear her eyes away from Cannelle's mending hand. She shivered and rubbed her own hands together as if in reflex. I was more concerned with Cannelle's face. Judging whether or not she'd go back on her word.

"Since we've established that I'm in a really foul mood, let's move on to the question-and-answer phase. Oh, and if you make me use this knife again . . . I'm not healing anything I cut. What was your purpose in the French Quarter with Bones?"

Cannelle kept flexing her hand while staring at me in horror. "I was to fuck him, *naturellement,* and once assured that you heard of his infidelity, I was to take him to Gregor. Marie wouldn't let Gregor's people into the Quarter, though she did tell Gregor he could come."

That was news. I'd thought no one was allowed in.

Ian was also interested. "If she'd granted him passage, then why didn't Gregor meet Crispin inside the Quarter and fight him there if he wanted to kill him so badly?"

Cannelle's mouth dipped. "Gregor said Bones wasn't worthy of a fair fight."

"Or Gregor was just chicken shit and wanted to stack the odds," I muttered.

"Gregor is stronger," Cannelle hissed, "but why would he allow his opponent to die with honor, considering his crimes?"

I wasn't about to get into a character fight with Cannelle over Gregor. "So Gregor got Marie, the Queen of Orleans, to side with him. Interesting."

Cannelle shrugged. "Marie said Gregor could only ambush Bones outside her city, which was why she didn't let Gregor come with forces into the Quarter. Marie didn't want to participate in making Bones leave, either, but Gregor made her."

"He forced her?"

"*Non*, you misunderstand. He *made* her. 'Twas his blood that raised her as a ghoul, and Gregor killed Marie's other sire the night he changed her, so her fealty was only to him. Gregor agreed to release Marie in exchange, and Marie's wanted free of Gregor for over a hundred years."

"And Bones would trust Marie because she always

guarantees safe passage in her meetings." *That clever, dirty schmuck.*

Cannelle actually smirked. *"Oui."*

My anger turned to ice. "Is that all, Cannelle?"

"Oui."

I turned to Ian. "Think she's got more?"

He met my gaze with equal coldness. "No, poppet. I think that's it."

I still had the knife in my hand, slick from Cannelle's blood.

"Cannelle," I said in a steady, clear tone. "I'm going to kill you. I'm telling you this so you can take a moment to pray if you choose, or to reflect, whatever. You lured my husband around with the full intention of taking him to his slaughter, and that's just not forgivable to me."

"Cat, no," Geri said.

I didn't answer her. Cannelle gave me a look filled with malicious defiance. "But Bones isn't your husband. Gregor is."

"Semantics. You're wasting time. Get right with God. Fast."

"I am a *human*," she hissed. "A living, breathing person. You may have it in you to wound me, but not to kill me."

I ignored that, too. "Marie got her freedom for her role in this. What did Gregor promise? To change you into a vampire?"

Another hostile glare. *"Oui.* It's my payment for all the years I've served him."

"You backed the wrong horse," I said. "You're not going to be a vampire, Cannelle, but I'll let you die like one."

She stood up. "You wouldn't dare. Gregor would kill you."

Then she looked down. The silver knife was buried in her chest. It even vibrated for a few seconds with her last remaining heartbeats. Cannelle watched with astonishment the handle quiver before her eyes glazed and her knees buckled.

I stood over her and felt more of that awful coldness.

"Maybe Gregor will kill me for this, Cannelle. I'm willing to take that chance."

I went to see Don. He was busy with his own preparations for departure. I didn't know where my former unit was stationed now, and that was good by me. I wouldn't have put it past Gregor to use that information to his advantage. Don wouldn't, either. That's why everyone from our division was clearing out right after I did.

Vlad was in Don's office. As soon as I entered, they both quit speaking. My mouth curled.

"How obvious are you two? Come on, boys, what's the topic? 'Will Cat have a breakdown?' or 'Ten easy steps to talk someone out of suicide'? Both of you can save it. I'm okay."

My uncle coughed. "Don't be so dramatic. I was getting a way to contact you since you can't exactly send me a postcard, and Vlad was informing me that you'll be with him."

I gave Vlad a look that would have been challenging—if I hadn't just spent umpteen hours flying overseas on an empty stomach, lack of sleep, and general hypertension.

"For now."

Vlad smiled, disdainful and amused at the same time. "It's your choice, Cat. I'm not forcing you."

Don looked back and forth between us, his gray eyes narrowing. They were the same smoky color as mine, and right now, they were glinting with suspicion.

"Is there something going on with the two of you that I should be aware of?"

"Isn't there something going on with you that she should?" Vlad responded.

Now it was my turn to glance between them. "What?"

Don coughed and flashed a single glare to Vlad. "Nothing."

Vlad let out a noncommittal grunt. "Then that's all you'll get from me as well, Williams."

I was about to demand to know what the hell the subtext of this was when Don spoke up.

"Cat, you asked me before to find out if those dream-suppression pills had any side effects. I've checked with Pathology, and they said you might experience depression, mood swings, irritability, paranoia, and chronic fatigue. Have you noticed any of that?"

I thought back to my last few times with Bones and couldn't help but burst into demented laughter.

"Yeah. All of the above, and all at once. This information would have been useful a couple weeks ago, but it's kind of irrelevant now."

I wasn't going to use those pills again. I'd rather be ignorant of my whereabouts than subject to the side effects that had helped drive Bones and me apart. Don must have guessed some of my train of thought because he gave me a sad look.

The moment was broken when Cooper came running in. "B4358 is coming in for a landing."

"What?" my uncle snapped. "They didn't get permission!"

My eyes widened. Those were the call numbers to Dave's plane. The one that was carrying Bones and Spade.

"I know, sir. The tower ordered them not to land, but they said an Englishman got on the wire and said to shut it or he'd beat the seven shades of shit out of him."

Bones. "We have to leave," I said to Vlad. "Now."

" 'Run, Forrest, run!' " Vlad mocked.

"Stow it, Drac," I snapped. "With or without you, I'm in the air before he gets off that plane."

"It will be with me. Williams"—Vlad gave a nod at my uncle—"farewell. Few people have your determination to walk their road all the way to its conclusion."

I didn't even spare the time to give my uncle a hug. I was halfway down the hall, tossing a "Thanks, 'bye!" over my shoulder.

"Be safe, Cat," Don called after me.

I'd try my best.

It was so close, I knew I'd be haunted by it, and the ghost on board had nothing to do with that. Cooper had fueled our plane while I'd been dealing with Cannelle, so there was no time wasted there. Vlad strode out, entering it moments behind me, with Fabian clinging to his shoulder. I'd have been all right if I hadn't been compelled to look out the small window of the twin-engine craft as we took off. Our plane hit the skies just as the door to the other Cessna swung open, and an achingly familiar figure came out of it.

For a crazy, heart-stopping moment, I felt like Bones was looking right at me.

"Why do I hear *Casablanca* music playing in my head?" Vlad asked in an ironic voice.

I looked away from the runway. "You're a regular movie encyclopedia, aren't you?"

"And you're the boy who cried wolf. If you say it's over, then let it be over, or quit spouting out false absolutes that you don't believe yourself."

Goddamn merciless Romanian usurper. Why was I on a plane with him, anyway? Why didn't I just go off by myself, trek to a rain forest, and hide there alone until Gregor, the ghouls, and everyone else forgot about me as completely as Bones had?

I gave one more last look out the window. We were up high enough now that I couldn't be sure if he was still staring after us—or if he'd turned his head away, like I had to.

"You're right," I said to Vlad.

His hand reached out. The scars that covered it were mute testament to the decades of battles he'd fought, and those were just when he'd been human.

I took it, glad mine weren't empty anymore and hating myself for feeling that way. How weak I was.

Vlad squeezed once. "I don't want to be alone now either," he said, making it sound very reasonable and not at all like something to be ashamed of.

I sighed. *Right again, buddy. That's two for two.*

Twenty-three

WATER SWIRLED ALL AROUND ME. EVERY-thing was dark and foggy. Where was I? How did I get here? The air had a terrible smell, and the liquid I was struggling in became black and too thick to swim in. Some of it got into my mouth, making me retch. It wasn't water after all. It was tar.

"Help!"

My cry went unanswered. The tar seemed to be pulling me under. I gasped, choking, and felt burning as some of the tar went into my lungs. I was being sucked deeper into it. Drowning. A hazy thought flitted through my mind. *So this is how I'm going to die. Funny, I always thought it would be during a fight . . .*

"Take my hand," an urgent voice said.

Blindly I reached out, unable to see past the inky fluid in my eyes—and then the tar was gone, and I was standing in front of the man I'd been running from.

"Gregor," I spat, trying to will myself awake. *A*

dream, you're just trapped in a dream. "Goddammit, leave me alone!"

Gregor loomed over me. An invisible wind blew his ash-blond hair, and those smoky green eyes were glowing emerald.

"You may have swept your lover beyond my reach this time, but I will have him soon enough. How does it feel, my wife, to be cast aside? Ah, *chérie.* You deserve your pain."

Gregor had a tight grip on my arms. I could feel him try to pull me outside my own skin, and I fought a moment of panic. I'd just arranged for Bones to get away, why hadn't I expected Gregor to be waiting for me to shut my eyes? His power seemed to be seeping into me, slowly filling me up. I wanted to distract him, fast, from coiling that dangerous aura around me.

"You made a mistake sending Cannelle. In case you haven't heard, I killed her. Ian's shipping her body to you with a big red bow. You'll have a harder time getting recruits to do your dirty work when people hear about that."

Gregor nodded, not looking particularly upset. "*Oui,* that was unexpected, and it will cost you, *ma femme.* Return to me, and perhaps I will not make the price too steep."

"Why are you so obsessed with me coming back?" I asked in frustration. "We're clearly not compatible. You don't act like you love me. Half the time, I don't even think you like me."

Something flashed across Gregor's face, too quick for me to determine what it was. "You're mine," he said at last. "Soon you will see you belong with me."

There was more to it, I just knew, but I had bigger concerns at the moment. Gregor's power flexed around me. I tried to pry his hands off, but it was as if they were welded onto me.

"I've got bad news for you then, because going back to walking on eggshells around your every mood swing? Sorry, Gregor. You lost your chance with me when I grew up and developed self-esteem. I'm never coming back to you."

"Why do you do this!" he shouted, giving up his false exterior of calm. "I offer you everything, and you scorn me as though I were lower than that whore of a lover who left you!"

His anger was drawing his power back into himself and away from me. I pressed my advantage.

"Because I'm happier being the castoff of a whore than I'd ever be as your wife."

Gregor shoved me away from him. I landed back in the tar pit, up to my shoulders in that sticky black goo. He stood over me and shook his fist.

"You are mine whether you prefer it or not, and you can think about this as you continue to hide from me. I will find Bones again when he doesn't have his people surrounding him. It's only a matter of time. And then, *chérie*, he will die."

I didn't have a chance to scream out my hatred of him, because the tar closed over my head in the next instant. I was moving downward very fast, like I was being flushed, and then—

I sat bolt upright in bed. The sheets around me were damp, but not from tar. I was covered in a cold sweat. And I was madder than hell.

"I'm going to kill you, Gregor," I growled to the empty room. Whatever leftover positive emotion I'd had for him as a teenager was gone. If I had another chance with a silver knife stuck in Gregor's back, I'd twist it with a smile. *You should have before,* my mind mocked. *No good deed goes unpunished.*

Vlad walked in my room without knocking. "Your rage has been seething in my mind for the past five minutes."

"I hate him," I said, getting up from the bed to pace.

Vlad stared at me without blinking. "I have no cause to war with Gregor, Cat, but it does pain me to see you like this."

"It's so maddening," I went on. "Bones might be able to kill Gregor, if he got him alone in a fair fight, but Gregor won't go for that. And I'm not strong enough to take Gregor down. I breathe, bleed, I don't heal instantly—I'm not tough enough for him. Being half-human was great for my old job. All those things I mentioned lured my targets and made me a more effective hunter. But with really old vampires, like Gregor, it just makes me . . . weak."

Vlad didn't say anything. He didn't have to. We both knew it was true.

"What are you going to do about that?" he asked at last.

I stopped pacing. *That was the million-dollar question, wasn't it?*

The next night, Vlad, Maximus, Shrapnel, and I were upstairs playing poker. Vlad had been winning all night, a feat I attested to his mind-reading skills— though he swore he wasn't using them on me—and the fact that Shrapnel and Maximus were probably afraid to beat Vlad even if they could. It was almost midnight when there was a loud knock downstairs. The three vampires leapt to their feet in a blur of motion. Flames were already shooting out of Vlad's hands.

Vlad hadn't been expecting anyone; that much was clear from his reaction, so I understood the cause for their alarm. Whoever it was had managed to get past Vlad's formidable guards without notice, chosen to knock to show us they didn't need the element of surprise, and had done all this without the very powerful vampire striding out of the room realizing they were even here.

In short, we were in deep shit.

I started after Vlad, but he whirled around with a snarl.

"Stay here."

I responded with a mental roar of how he could go straight to hell if he expected me just to wring my hands and wait, when something moving outside the window caught my attention.

I pointed. "Look."

About three dozen of Vlad's guards were elevated in stark relief against the clear night sky, all twirling in lazy circles about twenty feet off the ground. They were opening and closing their mouths, unable to speak, but apparently trying.

That gave me a pretty good idea who was downstairs knocking on the door. Only one vampire I knew could cloak his power level to avoid detection and twirl hardened undead guards in the air like fireflies.

Vlad must have guessed also, judging from the flames slowly extinguishing from his clenched fists.

"Mencheres," he muttered.

I froze in the hallway, wondering if the mega-Master vampire was alone—or accompanied.

The knock sounded again. Now it seemed even more ominous than when I thought it was enemy forces.

Vlad motioned for Shrapnel and Maximus to lower their weapons. "Stay here," he said to me again, but with none of his prior vehemence. "I'll find out what he wants."

"Mencheres," I heard Vlad say moments later, to the echo of a door flinging open. "You are welcome in my home and may enter. You"—and here my heart skipped a beat, because the venom in that one word confirmed my suspicions—"may not."

A laugh responded to that rude greeting. Hearing Bones so close hit me like a physical blow.

"Tepesh, I've come a long damned way to get here, and pretty as your little dragon door knockers are, I don't fancy spending more time outside admiring them."

Mencheres, more tactful, addressed Vlad with the patience a parent used on an errant child.

"Vlad, you know I cannot allow you to forbid entry to the co-ruler of my line. To do so would insult me as well, and I know you don't mean to do that."

"Let my men down," Vlad said with an edge to his voice.

"Of course." Mencheres actually made it sound like he'd forgotten about elevating over thirty vampires in the air. There were multiple thumps a moment later.

In another mood, I would have found that funny.

"Very well, come in." Vlad's tone was far from gracious. "But you'll abuse my hospitality if you venture even a foot up those stairs, and we both know who I'm talking to."

Bones laughed again, only this time, it sounded closer. They must be inside.

"Really, mate, you're like a hound fretting over his scraps. Careful you don't unwittingly combust, or you'll ruin this fetching imitation Persian rug."

"And I have had enough of your comments about my home!" Vlad barked. I could practically smell the smoke coming from him. "What do you want, not that you stand a fuck-all chance of getting it, *mate*."

Vlad's exaggerated Cockney accent drained away my momentary shock and turned it into alarm. Bones had wasted no time in getting Vlad good and mad. What was he up to?

"I'm here for Cat," Bones replied, all bantering gone.

Such a wave of emotion swept over me that I felt dizzy. Just as quickly, I slammed my mind shut, wishing I could do the same with my heart. This could be about business. I wouldn't humiliate myself by letting Bones know how just the sound of his voice was affecting me. Bones had said how great my shields were at keeping him out. *Here's hoping I hadn't lost my touch.*

"If she doesn't want to see you, then you've wasted your time," Vlad said, each word a dare.

I was still making up my mind whether or not I did want to see Bones when he let out a rude snort.

"You misunderstand, Tepesh. I'm not here to see her. I'm taking her with me."

My jaw dropped. Vlad let out something like a growl. "I'll fry you where you stand."

The unmistakable sound of knives scraping together had me out of the room, shoving Maximus aside with all my inhuman strength even as Bones replied, "Try it."

"Stop!"

Three heads swiveled up toward me. Vlad's hands were still in flames, and Bones had two silver knives in his grip. Mencheres stood a few feet off, watching them like a silent referee. I came down the stairs. Fabian floated after me, darting in and out of the wall.

A glance showed me what was different about Bones since I'd last seen him. His hair was shorter, cropped close to his head and curling at the tips. His eyes were hooded as they met mine. Devoid of any emotion at all. That was the hardest thing to see.

"What do you think you're doing?" I asked him.

"Getting you," he answered, arching a brow.

If he'd said it while holding out roses and apologizing, I might have been moved. But Bones said it like he was talking about a pair of shoes he'd misplaced. I narrowed my eyes.

"And what if I don't want to be *gotten*?"

Bones looked at Vlad, at me, and gave a frightening smile.

"Then as his guest, Tepesh will feel honor-bound to defend you. That means he and I will have to fight, and he's quite brassed off already. I reckon he'll try to burn me to ashes straightaway. Of course, that's if I don't rip his heart open with silver first. So if you refuse to come with me, one of us will be dead in the next few minutes. Or, you can come along and we'll both live."

Vlad let out a foul curse even as I sputtered, "Are you serious? *You* left *me*, remember? Now you want to fight to the death over me? What kind of game is this?"

"No game, luv," Bones replied. "Just retrieving what's mine. You might want to decide soon. Vlad looks as though he's about to explode."

I cast a quick glance at Vlad, who did look like he was moments away from detonation.

"You come into my home to blackmail my friend?" Vlad snarled. Those flames climbed higher on his arms. "I'll—"

"I'm leaving."

Vlad swung his gaze to me. I reached out, ignoring the licking flames on his arm. "Don't. I couldn't . . ."

I hoped only Vlad heard the rest of that sentence. *I couldn't stand it if something happened to him.* I might be pissed at Bones. Hell, I might want to roast him over a few flames myself, but I couldn't risk his life by stubbornness. From the energy rolling off Vlad, he wouldn't strike to wound.

Not to mention, I wasn't about to risk my friend's life; the glint in Bones's eyes said he wouldn't strike to wound, either.

Vlad tugged his beard and gave Bones a chilling glance. "I won't forget this."

Bones smiled in open taunt. "I certainly hope you don't."

Things would get violent any second. I swept past them. Forget my things; it was time to *go*.

"Are you coming or not?" I asked Bones as I went outside.

"Of course," Bones replied. I didn't wait, but took the arm Mencheres politely offered me and stomped over to what I assumed was their car, Fabian trailing behind me.

"Love your home," Bones said to Vlad in parting.

The answer he received made me glad I'd chosen to leave. If the two of them fought, there was no doubt that only one would walk away from it.

I waited a full half hour after we pulled away before

I spoke. Bones had handed me a pair of headphones as soon as we got into the car. I'd blasted them loud enough to be dangerous. Damned if I knew where we were going with all that noise. But finally, I took them off, keeping my eyes closed.

"What the hell do you think you were doing? Vlad might have burned you into nothing more than a smear on his floor if I hadn't decided to go with you."

Bones let out a snort. "I didn't doubt your actions for a moment. You've never been able to turn down playing the hero to rescue me."

Bastard, I thought, and hoped that got through loud and clear. Whatever Bones's motivation in coming tonight, it wasn't for romantic reasons to win me back, that was clear. Was it just vampire territorialism? Even though he didn't want me, Bones didn't want someone else to have me? That was probably it. Well, I wasn't anyone's property, as he and Gregor would learn.

"You'll regret this," I settled on saying.

Another snort. "I don't doubt that either, Kitten."

I didn't reply, just put my headphones back on.

Twenty-four

"You can't be serious."

I eyed the abandoned building with the blown-out windows, crumpled far wall and dilapidated roof with more than a little dismay. To make matters worse, it was surrounded by a junkyard. A smelly junkyard. Even Fabian looked like he wanted to run.

Bones shrugged. "I don't see the problem. It's quite safe."

You vindictive, manipulative—

"Care to see your room?" he interrupted my mental rundown. The look on his face said he was enjoying this.

"Let me guess—it's that smashed-up car right over there," I said, pointing to a flattened old Buick.

"Oh, you're not staying out here," Bones replied, walking over to the shell of the building. "Quasimodo!" he shouted.

There was a loud creaking noise, like what a machine would sound like if it could feel pain. Then from out of the ruined side of the building, two vampires appeared as if sprouted from the ground.

"We thought you'd be here an hour ago," one of them commented. "Her food's cold."

I was about to assure this unknown person that the smell had killed my appetite anyway, when a brunette seemed to levitate from the crumbled concrete next to him.

"Catherine."

I gave Bones a glare promising terrible revenge. He didn't look at me, but his mouth twitched.

"Next time," my mother said, forgoing a hello, "call if you're going to be late."

The building was a front. The section that appeared to have collapsed hid an elevator complete with fake concrete blocks on top of it. At least the structure below had its own air-conditioning system, so the stench from the junkyard was greatly lessened in the underground dwelling. My guess was that it was an old bomb shelter. Don used some of those back in the States for his base of operations. Waste not, want not and all that.

"Welcome to Trash Castle," my mother said as she gave me and Fabian the tour. "They had to drag me in here against my will when I first saw it. I'm sure your scurvy husband chose it just for revenge."

So was I, but I wasn't going there. "Bones isn't my husband, as I'm sure you've been told."

She gave me a shrewd look. "You don't believe that."

Six minutes, ten seconds. That's all it took to make me want to run out of here screaming.

Bones wasn't here. He'd dropped me off with a comment that he had business elsewhere. It had been all I could do not to yell, "Why did you risk your life taking me from Vlad's if you still can't stand to be around me?" But that would let on about how much I cared. So I didn't say a word. I watched Bones leave without once asking when, or if, he intended to come back. Would I rather rot under a huge trash heap than admit how much it hurt to see him again, let alone see him walk away? You bet.

After three days at Trash Castle, I decided it was the perfect place to be if you wanted to go crazy but had a limited amount of time to do it in. Being fifty feet under a dump locked in the equivalent of a cellar with a listless ghost and an outspoken mother, all while thinking about the man who'd left me, was bound to bring on insanity faster than any circumstance I'd experienced before. Soon the idea of banging my head against a wall seemed like a fun way to spend ten minutes, and I fantasized about near-death experiences like they were a chocolaty dessert. Puberty had been an aromatherapy session compared to this.

Despite the smell, I took to going topside and clearing out sections of the junkyard just to *do* something. Fabian had his own way of dealing with the situation. He watched endless TV. My mother read or did crossword puzzles, in between comments about how if I would have listened to her, I wouldn't be here today. Was it any wonder I preferred spending my time around stinky garbage?

I'd been sweeping up the far section of the dump when I heard the thrum of the automobile. Even though I knew it couldn't be a lost tourist, since it was clear that we were on the ass-end of nowhere, I hadn't waited to see if it was friend or foe before climbing to the top of the nearest garbage heap. Death? Didn't scare me. It would be a vacation from Smell Central.

"Who came up with the password *Quasimodo*?" Spade muttered as he got out of his car.

"Hello, Spade," I called out, shaking the debris off the rake I'd made from thin strips of metal and a truck axle.

Spade stared up at me, revulsion and disbelief competing on his handsome face.

"Lucifer's hairy ball sack. You've become a Morlock."

Seeing Spade looking so suave in his white shirt with his shiny black shoes and creased pants reminded me that I was covered head to toe in dirt and probably smelled like a bad case of flatulence.

"I've been buried underneath a junkyard for days, what did you expect?"

Spade slammed the door to his car. Just looking at it, I fought an impulse to jump in and drive until I passed out at the wheel.

"I can't sit back and watch you and Crispin drown in your own stubbornness any longer. Good Christ, Cat, just die already and be done with it."

I blinked. "Fuck you too, pal."

"Move back to your vehicle, you're not expected," Techno, one of the vampires stationed there, said. He'd come around from the side of the building and had an Uzi that was loaded with silver bullets pointed at Spade.

"I'm on the list, you imbecile," Spade barked. "Now turn around before I break that toy off in your arse."

Spade's back was to me. I grabbed a nearby tire and chucked it at him, smiling to see tread marks ruin the perfection of his white shirt. "Don't talk to him that way, he's doing his job."

Spade recovered from the tire beaning him in the back and was in front of me with nosferatu swiftness.

"For God's sake, Cat, take the leap, what are you waiting for?"

For a second, I wondered if I'd really lost it. It sounded like Spade was trying to taunt me into killing myself.

"Did I do something to piss you off?"

Spade spun around, balling his fists. Techno looked at me in confusion, as if questioning whether I was in danger.

"Want me to shoot him?" he inquired.

"Do you want to incite things? You're barely human now; why do you persist in clinging to your last useless, mortal shred?"

"Don't shoot," I said to Techno, who'd raised the Uzi with purpose. "In fact, go away."

"He's not—" Techno began to sputter.

"Not what?" Spade asked. "Not supposed to tell her about it, I'll wager? That's why she's looking at me like I'm barmy, right? Because she doesn't have a clue what I'm talking about."

My jaw clenched. Techno's face confirmed it all. *Son of a bitch.*

"Is it the ghouls again?" I asked, inwardly cursing that I'd been so wrapped up in my own problems, I hadn't been suspicious about the lack of word on that front.

Spade gave Techno one last threatening look before folding his arms.

"Yes, it's the ghouls. Their rhetoric is growing bolder. In certain areas, Masterless vampires have begun to disappear. It could be they're stupid and got shriveled by one of our own kind, but there's reason to believe it might be something more."

I stared at him. Spade's tiger-colored gaze was uncompromising. *Gregor is behind this*, I realized. The more paranoia about me becoming a vampire/ghoul hybrid, the more support he garnered for his cause to get me back so he could control me.

"Why wasn't I told?"

Spade rolled his eyes. "Can't you guess? Crispin doesn't want this to influence your decision whether to turn into a vampire."

"He doesn't care about me," I muttered before I could stop myself.

"You're an idiot."

I could feel my eyes turning angry green. "Excuse me?"

"Idiot," Spade repeated, drawing the word out for emphasis. "Why do you think he fetched you from Vlad's? Crispin knew if it came to a choice between you or Vlad's people, you'd lose. Tepesh might be fond of you, but he's beastly protective of his people."

I had to glance away for a moment. Then I shook my head. "If Bones cared about me, fucking his way up and down New Orleans was a funny way to show it."

Spade regarded me with cynicism. "If you thought Crispin was yours, and you didn't care for his actions, why weren't you waiting for him after New Orleans instead of jetting off with Tepesh?"

My jaw dropped. "Do you hear yourself?"

"You're not thinking like a vampire," Spade muttered. "The sooner you're done with your human perceptions, the better. Look, can we discuss your reasoning inadequacies later? If I have to smell this rancid air a moment longer, I'll dry heave."

"In*ad*equacies? Screw you!"

Spade gave me an arch smile. "You should be less concerned with what I'm saying and more focused on what you'll say to Crispin when you try to convince him to change you into a vampire."

That made my heart skip a beat. Spade heard it and snorted. "Got your attention now, don't I? Crispin's the one who has to do it. I certainly wouldn't dare. He'd kill anyone who changed you, make no mistake."

"How do you know I've decided to cross over, anyway?"

The sarcasm and flippancy were wiped from Spade, and he gave me the most serious look he'd bestowed on me.

"Come now, Reaper. We both know you've been hanging on to your humanity too long. You just needed a push, didn't you?"

So many different things ran through my mind. I remembered all the years of my childhood, hiding my growing inhuman abilities so I didn't upset my mother. Later in school, how out of place I'd felt pretending to be "normal" when nothing about me was normal. And later still, in my teens and early twenties hunting vampires, hadn't my humanity been more of a disguise than how I felt inside? Then there was now, how frustrated I was that I was too weak to take Gregor on myself. With no element of surprise about my dual nature, I'd always be too weak to battle the really old, mega-Master vampires—as long as I stayed part human, that was.

But more than that, even if Bones and I were through, the situation with Gregor magically disappeared, and there were no ghoul rumblings, could I ever go back to living among humans, pretending to be just like them?

No. I couldn't pretend anymore that all the things inside me weren't there. Even if I walked away from the undead world for good, I'd still be more vampire than human. And if I wasn't going to walk away or try to pretend to be human again, then why *was* I still hanging on to my heartbeat? God, was Bones right? Had it really been just my deep-seated prejudice that held me back from taking this step before? There were a lot of reasons to change over. Did I have *even one* to stay the way I was?

"I'll ask Bones to do it," I heard myself say. "But he'll probably say no."

Spade didn't have headphones to keep me from hearing where we were going. No, instead he whacked me a good one to make sure I stayed asleep for the majority of the trip. Spade was a Master vampire, so when I came to, damn, my head hurt.

"You should shower straightaway before you see him," was Spade's comment once I was awake. "You still smell dreadful. Crispin might refuse to sire you just because he won't be able to stand getting close enough."

I mentally cursed Spade up one side and down the other. Something cool brushed over my hand. Without opening my eyes, I knew it was Fabian, giving me his version of a sympathetic pat. He'd tagged along on this trip. Guess even a ghost couldn't stand life at Trash Castle. At least Fabian never commented on my smell, one of the perks of not having a real nose.

"Ah, there it is," Spade said. "No peeking; can't have Gregor seeing a mailbox number in your sleep."

I was so sick of being blinded wherever I went. If Bones refused to sire me, I knew where I was going next—straight to Vlad's. I'd already called him and asked if he'd be willing to do the honors. His response had been an instant yes. I didn't know what about me had inspired Vlad's friendship, but I was grateful for it.

After another minute of driving, the car came to a stop. "Stay here," Spade said. "I'll announce us, then come get you."

"You mean you'll find out if he's even going to let me step foot out of this car," I replied with my eyes still closed.

"No worries about that. You're getting out to wash even if I have to wrestle Crispin to the ground long enough for you to do it."

"Thanks," I said. Spade just shut the door, laughing. As Bones's best friend, all his loyalty was to him, so Spade didn't care about how hard this was for me, even without all his Smelly Cat comments.

Outside the car, I heard many voices, presumably from those in the house. I strained to pick up one in particular. It was hard to filter over the din, however. There were a lot of people here, wherever *here* was.

". . . Crispin . . ." Spade's voice, raised for a second.

". . . brings you . . . ?" Bones, the rest of it snatched away.

". . . outside . . ." Spade was saying. ". . . see you . . ."

Why can't everyone shut up for a minute so I can hear? I thought.

". . . by all means . . ." From Bones.

That settled it. I sighed. "Looks like we're going in after all, Fabian."

"Good," he said at once, then paused. "If that's what you were hoping for, of course."

In fact, a part of me had hoped Bones would refuse to even let me get out of the car. No such luck for my emotional well-being, though.

Moments later Spade opened my door. "Straight into the showers with you, he'll see you afterward. I told him it would be in his best interests to wait."

"Another comment about how I smell, and I'll stab you through the heart," I said, meaning it.

He clucked his tongue. "Vicious girl. Come along, take my arm—not so hard!"

I'd squeezed for all I was worth. Hearing Spade's yelp made me smile. "You'll have to get my clothes out of the trunk so I have something else to wear afterward, or showering will be a waste."

"We're inside," Spade commented. "You can open your eyes."

I did. Fabian floated in front of us as we walked along a very lovely foyer. Not a hint of crushed cars or garbage in sight. So this was where Bones was staying, while I'd been stuck under a trash mountain? *You're so wrong, Spade,* I thought. *Bones could obviously care less about me.*

We walked farther down the hallway. An unknown vampire gave the three of us a curious look as he passed by.

"What's that smell?" he wondered.

Fabian dematerialized, but not before I saw his grin. Spade began to laugh.

"Mind your own business," I snapped, then lashed myself when the vampire blanched. *God, how rude of me!*

"I'm sorry," I said. "Please don't mind me, I've been stuck in an underground garbage can."

Spade was still cracking up, so I elbowed him none too gently in the ribs.

"Can we get on with it?"

"Right away," he agreed, wiping the pink from his eyes. "Carry on, young man," he said to the dumbfounded vampire.

I walked away with as much dignity as I could muster, which in my case, was zero.

Twenty-five

AFTER AN HOUR OF VIGOROUS SCRUBBING, I didn't have any stench left on me. Of course, that was probably because I had hardly any skin left, either. I'd washed my hair no fewer than four times, too, then conditioned it twice. Anyone whose nose was offended now could just kiss my shiny-clean ass.

Spade was in the bedroom attached to this bathroom, lounging in a chair. He gestured to something lying over a nearby chair. "Brought you some togs. Didn't know if you wanted me to borrow a brassiere or knickers, too, or if you'd be skittish about that."

Discussing underwear with Spade wasn't helping my mood. "Where are *my* clothes?"

His grin widened. "Threw them into the furnace. I shouldn't dare bring your reeking suitcase inside Crispin's home."

I took a deep breath. "You didn't have any right to do that," I managed to say in a very calm tone.

Spade got up. "Let's just skip the morality issue and

go onto whether or not you want me to rustle you up some knickers."

"I'm not wearing some unknown chick's panties, thanks. I'd rather go commando."

Spade winked. "That's the spirit. Make Crispin more amenable to whatever you ask, I daresay."

I pointed to the door. "Goodbye."

He just laughed as he left. I wished I were as amused.

I eyed the dress with dread. Once I put this on, there would be no more stalling.

"Fuck it," I announced out loud. I'd present my offer to Bones, probably get turned down, and be on my way to Vlad's. I zipped myself up, put on the matching shoes that were a tad too tight, and marched out of the guest room. My hair was still damp. I gave it a shake and glanced around, not seeing anyone.

"Hello?" I called out. Damned if I'd start peeking in doors. Where was Spade? Or Fabian?

"Downstairs."

It was Bones's voice. I fought a shiver, giving myself a mental slap. *Get a grip.*

"Am I supposed to say 'Marco'?" I asked, going down the stairs.

I heard his amused snort inside the room to the left of the landing. "If you'd like."

Enter freely and of your own will. I squared my shoulders and did just that.

Bones sat on a brown leather sofa that was a few shades lighter than his eyes. The walls were rust-colored, with white crown molding, and the floors were a darkened oak with thick rugs. He almost matched the room with his outfit; a cream shirt that was unbuttoned at the neck, sleeves rolled up, and tan pants. And he was so friggin' gorgeous that it hurt just looking at him.

"I wasn't expecting you, so I don't have any gin," he said, filling a glass. "Care for a whiskey instead?"

"Sure. Thanks," I added as an afterthought, lingering by the door.

He gave me a look as he poured another one. "You didn't come all the way here just to hug the door-frame, did you?"

Left with few options, I sat, choosing the couch opposite him. As soon as I did, however, I stiffened, remembering my lack of underwear. The dress was a few inches north of my knees. What if Bones thought I was trying to flash him?

"Er, do you mind?" I stammered, quickly taking a seat on his couch, but as far away from him as I could scoot.

An eyebrow rose. "Not at all."

He handed me the whiskey. I gulped it down in one swallow.

"Thirsty, are you?" he remarked, taking it and filling it to the top. "You must be. Otherwise, one might think you needed liquor in order to speak with me."

His dry tone told me I was being obvious. I took the glass but only gave it a sip this time.

Bones leaned back, studying me. I felt so self-conscious. If only I had a shield of makeup, some perfectly arranged hair . . . and oh yeah. Some panties.

He didn't say anything. The silence extended. Somehow, I couldn't bring myself to just spill out the reason I'd come. Maybe I hoped he'd pick it from my mind, and I could skip the whole conversation part.

I glanced away, but I could feel his eyes on me. Bones was still half-reclined, sipping his whiskey, watching me until I squirmed. If this was an interrogation technique, it was working. I'd soon be spilling my guts just to break the silent tension.

"Okay, then . . . let's get down to it."

I tried to look at him when I spoke, but I couldn't. It wasn't fair that seeing him was so devastating to me and yet so clearly meaningless to him.

"I'm, uh, ready to become a vampire," I blurted.

Talk about a graceful way to broach the topic. I flicked my gaze to his for a second. Dark brown eyes met mine before I looked away.

The tension made me jumpy. I got up, ready to start pacing, when he set his glass down and his hand shot out to grab me.

I yanked back at once, but his fingers tightened. "Sit down," he said in a quiet, steely tone.

Short of bracing my legs against his chest and pulling, I wasn't getting my arm back. Frustrated, I flopped onto the couch. "I'm sitting, now let go of me."

"I don't think I will," he replied with that same metal undertone. "I'm not hurting you, so quit glaring at me, and if you tug away even *once* more, I'm going to fling myself on top of you until we're finished with this conversation."

That stilled me. Bones never made empty threats. The thought of being pinned under him had me alarmed for several reasons, and none of those was fear.

"That's better." His grip loosened, but he didn't release me. "Right then, I have some questions, and you're going to answer them."

Why hadn't I insisted on discussing this over the phone? I mentally groaned.

"Ask. You've got me anchored. I can't go anywhere."

I wished he'd let go of me. I kept glancing at his hand as if I could make it disappear from my arm.

"You're blocking me again."

He said it casually, but his eyes narrowed. Green began to swirl in their depths, then it blazed forth to swallow the brown.

"Nice try," I barked, "but I thought we'd already established that I have good defenses."

Uh-oh. I'd jerked away while I said it, an instinctive reaction to him trying to pry into my mind. In a flash, I was flattened on the couch, Bones holding my wrists and tangling his legs in mine.

"Get off me," I demanded.

Instead, his hold tightened. I became acutely aware that further thrashing would only ratchet my dress up higher. Considering the position I was in and the fact that it was already well past my knees, not wearing any underwear was about to become a real issue right away.

"Bones." I stopped moving, trying another tactic. "Please get off of me."

"Why do you want to become a vampire?"

Guess he wasn't going to budge from his position. He wasn't balancing his weight, either. He was letting all of it hold me down while flexing to counter my smallest twitch. I was having a hard time trying not to think that it had been, wow, weeks since he'd been on top of me. Furthermore, at this proximity, it was impossible to avoid his gaze.

I cleared my throat. "I'm sick of being a walking transmitter to Gregor, for one. If I'm a full vampire, Gregor gets locked out. No more shutting my eyes and plugging my ears when I travel, no more being bothered while I sleep."

He didn't glance away. "Is that the only reason?"

If I said yes, this conversation was over. Bones would never think that was a good enough reason. Only the truth was, even if saying it made my eyes fill with tears.

"You were right." It was a whisper. "I did still think being a vampire was in some way evil. After all I'd seen, I was still prejudiced. What a fool, huh? You're probably proud now that you shoved it in my face. Who could blame you?"

His fingers weren't biting into my wrists anymore. No, they were doing something worse—stroking them with little circles. His eyes hadn't turned all the way back to brown yet. I hoped it was just residual anger.

"No, I'm not proud for railing at you the way I did." His voice was very low. "It took me fifteen years to come to terms with what I was after Ian turned me. Little wonder you still had mixed feelings over it."

I hadn't expected this. I'd steeled myself to hear a resounding agreement that yes, I had been a total ass over my discrimination. I swallowed, blinking to clear my eyes from the tears.

"Okay . . . so does that mean you'll change me over?"

"Not so fast. The only reason you've listed for wanting to change is to thwart Gregor."

"Do you just not want the responsibility of being my sire?" I asked, getting frustrated by the interrogation. "If so, Vlad already agreed to do it."

Something glittered in his gaze. "I'm sure he did, but if anyone's changing you over, it's me. I daresay I've earned that. And if you think to do it behind my back, I swear right now that I'll kill whoever sires you, no matter who he is."

He'd kill anyone who changed you, Spade had said. Guess he was right. Damn possessive vampires.

"If you take my old prejudice out of the way, there's no reason for me to remain part human," I answered steadily. "As a half-breed, I'm easier to kill, and my abilities have a definite ceiling on them. As a full vampire, my potential is what I make it, not what my pulse and breathing limit it to. Plus, I can never go back to pretending to live a normal, human life. For all intents and purposes, I'm already a vampire. I just don't have fangs yet."

"Do you really believe that?" His voice was silky, but his gaze was rock hard.

"Yes." No hesitation.

"Then prove it. Let me in your mind to see for myself."

Oh *hell* no. No way was I about to drop my mental shields and expose myself like that. It wasn't because I was lying about what I'd said. I was too afraid of everything else he'd see.

"Sorry, Bones, but you'll just have to take my word for it."

He didn't say anything for a long moment. It was all I could do not to hold my breath.

"All right, then," he replied at last. "I'll do it tomorrow."

I'd almost sighed in relief when he spoke again.

"On one condition."

Figures. "What is it?"

"Oh, nothing too taxing. You'll just have to share my bed tonight."

I waited a beat, but he didn't follow it with a punch line.

"You're serious?" I got out.

He looked at me like I was slow. "Very."

"Is this because I'm not wearing any underwear?"

That made him grin. "No, but it doesn't help your cause."

"You're being ridiculous!" I pushed at him, but it was like shoving a brick wall. "What is this, some kind of undead dominance crap?"

"I'm testing your resolve," he said calmly. "You refuse to let me into your mind to see if you're just doing this because of Gregor or the ghouls. If you truly want it for your own reasons, then it would be worth my price. There's always a price with vampires, Kitten. You know that." He shrugged. "Or, let me in your mind to see for myself that you want this only for you."

Strip bare either my emotions or my body. What a choice.

"I'm surprised you'd be able to clear your bedroom schedule on such short notice," I said, hoping to piss him off into changing his mind.

His brow arched. "We all do what we must."

I didn't know how I'd be able to manage either option. Both would leave scars on my heart. "And the fact that I absolutely *don't* want to have sex with you doesn't matter?"

He turned my cheek until his lips brushed my throat. "Well, luv . . . I consider that my job to change your mind."

His voice was filled with promise of pleasure. I couldn't help the shiver that ran through me when he nuzzled my skin. Damn my sensitive neck. It was betraying me even as I fought to appear unmoved.

But the thought of him looking into my mind, seeing how deeply he was still buried inside my every thought, was far more frightening than anything else. *Checkmate, Cat. You lose.*

That didn't mean I was going to be magnanimous, however. I gave him a bitchy glare.

"I hope it's the worst fuck you've ever had, you ruthless, manipulating bastard."

"Pillow talk already?" he replied with a slight grin. "Now you're just trying to switch me on."

I only wished I hadn't showered before this damned meeting—and where was a festering yeast infection when I needed one?

"I have a condition of my own," I said. "I showered in an empty guest room. We can do the deed in there." The last thing I needed was to roll around with Bones in his bed, considering he might have rolled around with another woman in it the night before. Ew.

"Whatever you like." He still had that curl to his lips. Apparently I couldn't antagonize him into changing his mind either. "We can even use this couch, if you prefer."

The way he traced his tongue on the inside of his lower lip told me he was thinking about it. That sent a flush of heat through me even as I cursed him. *This'll be a neat trick. Keeping my emotional distance while having sex with him.*

"The guest room will be fine," I managed.

His eyes glowed. "Right, then. Shall we?"

There was so much more than a simple query in those words. I looked around in futile hope that something would happen to delay this. An earthquake. Fire. Alien attack. Whatever, just bring it!

But there was nothing but him and me and the agreement I'd just made.

"I guess so."

Twenty-six

BONES EASED OFF ME IN A SINGLE LITHE motion, drawing me to a standing position along with him. I couldn't help but flinch as his hands stayed on my waist, and I couldn't have kept my heart from speeding up unless I'd put a bullet in it.

He walked very close next to me, a hand on my back propelling me forward. I didn't drag my feet, but oh, I wanted to. We passed a person or two as we headed up the stairs, but I kept my head lowered, concentrating on everything but what would happen once we got to the room.

How could I possibly keep my cool while getting sweaty with him? What if I screamed out something horrifying, like "I love you"? What if I had an epileptic attack and started drooling or spitting right in the middle of things?

I had worked myself into a state of moderate panic by the time he pulled me inside the same bedroom I'd left just a short time ago. The robe I'd worn was still tossed over the chair. Bones shut the door and, in desperation, I tried to get a handle on things.

"Okay." My voice was higher than usual. "Did you have anything particular in mind, or should I just start with the obvious?"

His mouth twitched. "Trying to make an assignment out of me? Sorry, luv, this is my night. When I want a favor from you, and this is the condition you set, then you can be as controlling as you like. In the meantime, I'll take the lead. Now, kick off those shoes. They look like they're pinching you."

Almost grimly I did. The bed seemed to loom in size while the walls felt like they were shrinking, leaving nothing in this room but that soft, waiting arena.

Bones drew off his shirt. I looked away from the stunning, sculpted flesh it revealed. My nails dug into my palms. Things were coming to a head quickly.

"Turn around."

I was both grateful and reluctant to do it. While it meant I didn't have to stare at the carpet instead of him, I also felt vulnerable. Like I couldn't defend myself if I didn't see what was coming.

Cool fingers pushed my hair aside, making me shiver. A tiny tug on my dress preceded the slow, inexorable sliding of the zipper all the way to its base. Without that support, the dress sagged on my shoulders, slipping, then was flicked aside to fall to my feet.

A slight hiss came from him. Absurdly, I shut my eyes, as if that made me any less naked. I held my breath, shivering again.

"You're chilled, luv. Let's get you into bed."

His voice was thicker, his accent stronger. I walked the short distance to the bed, letting him sweep the covers back, and pulled them over me as soon as I climbed in.

Bones knelt next to the bed, reaching out to touch my hair.

"With those covers up to your chin and your eyes so wide, you look very young."

"I guess that makes you the would-be pedophile."

He inclined his head. "Considering our age difference and all the things I intend to do to you, it does indeed." Then he became serious. "Kitten, underneath your sarcasm, indifference, and outright anger, I think you still want me, else I wouldn't have insisted on this. I admit to being a ruthless, manipulating bastard, just as you said, but I'm not a rapist. If you truly don't want me, I'll let you alone, but tomorrow I'll still change you like I promised."

He paused. Dropped the curl he'd been toying with and cupped my face. "Yet I will do my best to persuade you otherwise. I have absolutely no qualms about that."

Oh no, was my thought. *I'm a goner. Think about the junkyard. That smell. Gregor's sneer. Anything but the fact that he's now undoing his pants.*

There was one thing guaranteed to douse my mood. "Why did you cheat on me, Bones?"

He stopped. His top button was undone, but the zipper stayed up.

"You truly believe I was unfaithful?"

A rude snort came from me. "After seeing pictures, then Fabian's report, Cannelle's reminiscing, and hearing you admit it that night Geri pulled you out of New Orleans, *yeah*. I do."

His gaze felt like it was drilling into the back of my head. "You saw pictures of me entering my home with women, but you didn't see what happened once the door shut. I'd gone to New Orleans under the pretense that I was celebrating my bachelorhood, hoping Gregor would take the bait. He did. Even sent Cannelle there, as if I were too stupid not to smell him on her. It was easy to drink her blood and convince her to report back to Gregor that I was defenseless in my debauchery. By the time Fabian confronted me, several of Gregor's spies were around. What was I supposed to say to him?"

My mind reeled. "But I heard you. You told Cannelle she'd picked all the women the two of you had fucked together!"

"And she believed that," Bones replied. "I let her pick a new human girl each night to take back to my house. Then I drank the pair of them into insensibility and had them wake up naked together. It was a simple deception. I know what it would have looked like to you, Kitten, but you should have let me explain what it *was,* instead of going off with Tepesh."

My emotions warred with my suspicion. I mean, what woman, after everything I'd seen and heard, would believe it was all an elaborate charade, and her lover had been only *fake* cheating?

"But you left me." I couldn't keep the pain out of my voice. "You said you were through."

Bones sighed. "I went mad when I discovered you'd gone to Gregor. Didn't know if you'd choose to stay with him out of love, or you'd be forced to—and neither idea made me rational. By the time you'd returned, I still hadn't gotten control of myself. One of the reasons I left was because if I didn't, I'd have said more things I regretted. Then I went to New Orleans to end this issue with Gregor, intending to sort things

out with you afterward, but you jumped the gun."
Again, his tone implied.

"By *rescuing* you?"

He gave me an exasperated look. "Did you forget
I could fly? Gregor knew that. So did Marie. She
wanted me to slaughter Gregor, so she told Gregor
she intended to force me from the Quarter, knowing
full well Gregor would realize either he had to come
in and get me or I'd fly out to safety. But you sent
your old team after me, which Gregor would have
soon been alerted to no matter how covert they were.
I knew they'd get themselves killed if I resisted and
gave Gregor time to storm in, so I let them take me.
But it ruined my plan."

Bones didn't say the other, obvious word: Again.
Oh *shit*. If a hole had appeared in the ground, I'd have
gladly crawled into it. *Spade's right, you* are *an idiot.
With a capital I.*

My mental flogging must have gotten through to
him, because he said, "You're not an idiot. Charles
told me he dragged you into it, though he of all
people should have known better. Still, he'd have said
trapping Gregor alone was too risky, which is why I
didn't tell him about it."

"You must hate me," I said with a groan. "That's
twice I've fucked things up while thinking I was
helping."

His brow arched. "Three times, actually. You also
left me to go off with Don, thinking you were helping
me. I thought all of these showed your lack of respect
for me by not letting me fight my own battles, but
I've come to realize you can't help yourself. It's who
you are. You will never sit and wait for the outcome
of a fight involving someone you love before throw-

ing yourself into the mix, no matter how you might promise to change."

His words were like a knife in my heart. *This is why he left,* my conscience taunted me. *You'd like to think it was just so he could fuck around, because then it would be his fault, not yours. But it was you. Bones is right; you'll never change. And no one in their right mind would put up with you.*

Saying I was sorry was useless. More than useless—insulting, considering everything that had happened. So I did the only thing I could do to show how much I wished things were different. I dropped my shields, opening my mind to let Bones hear everything I was feeling, stripping myself naked of all the things I normally used to rationalize my actions.

He closed his eyes. A ripple went through him, as if my thoughts struck him like a physical blow. Once freed of the tight restraint I kept on them, everything seemed to tumble out of me, with long-hidden emotions frothing to the surface.

"Kitten," he murmured.

"I just wanted you to know I understand." The lump in my throat made it hard to speak. "You gave it your best, Bones. I'm the one who trashed things."

His eyes opened. "No. It was my insistence in taking Gregor on alone that caused our separation. I could have told you it was a trap before putting you into that panic room. I could have told you about New Orleans and had you take those pills, so Gregor couldn't learn it from your dreams. But I wanted to handle everything myself. My pride and my jealousy drove us apart. Every mistake you've made with me, Kitten, I've made the same with you, but I don't want to talk about that anymore. I don't want to talk at all."

He drew down his zipper even as I blinked in shock. "After all this, you still want to sleep with me?"

Bones slid out of his pants. He didn't have anything on under them, as usual.

"After all this, I still love you."

That stunned me into silence. Then I spoke the first words that came into my mind.

"You must be crazy."

He laughed, soft and wry. "It was your brash bravery that made me fall in love with you in the first place. Even though the same thing drives me mad now, I probably wouldn't love you if you were different than the way you are."

I wanted so badly to believe that love could conquer all. That Bones and I could make things work based on sheer feelings alone, but life wasn't that easy.

"If neither of us can change," I said, my heart squeezing, "sooner or later, we'll drive each other away again."

He put a knee on the bed. "You're right—we won't change. I'll always want to protect you, and I will get insanely brassed off when I can't. You'll always jump into the fire for me, no matter how much I want you to stay safe on the sidelines. We'll have to constantly battle our own natures to make this work. Are you willing to take that chance?"

When I started dating Bones over six years ago, I knew a relationship with him would break my heart. It had, more than once, and Bones wasn't offering assurances that it wouldn't this time, either. Yet just like back then, I couldn't resist him.

"Playing it safe is for chickens," I whispered.

He crouched on the bed, all curved sinews and pale hard flesh. Then he leaned forward, taking the time to drag his mouth from my stomach to my neck. My nipples hardened, need clenched in my belly, and I arched toward him.

His mouth slanted over mine as he gathered me in his arms. Feeling his naked body on top of me blew my control apart. My skin tingled everywhere his flesh made contact. I couldn't get close enough to him, and I kicked the covers away. Bones kissed me like he was drowning, his tongue raking mine while he continued to rub sensually against me, stroking me without entering, touching me everywhere and all at once.

I ran my hands over him as well, moaning into his mouth. My need was almost painful when he pushed his fingers into me, finding my most sensitive spot and rubbing it intensely. I began to claw at his back. Tears leaked from my eyes. The ecstasy built to a tremendous level, straining against my skin, until I tore my mouth from his.

"God, Bones, yes!"

It was a sob and a scream combined. He responded by flipping me on top of him, lifting me in the same motion, and burying his mouth between my legs.

I convulsed at once, the spasms shaking me. His arms clamped around my waist while he tongued my flesh and sucked without fangs, as if he were drinking my pleasure into him. I clutched his head, shuddering, as the last remaining waves rippled over me.

Bones set me back against the mattress without breaking contact with his mouth. I was still panting from the orgasm and now half-sagged on the pillows. He lifted his head, his gaze pinning mine as he crawled upward toward me.

"Look at me," he said, lowering his hips between mine.

I did, opening my thighs and arching to meet his first thrust. Oh God, I'd forgotten how Bones stretched me when I wasn't used to him. His hardness pushed against my walls, filling me so deeply, I felt tears in my eyes. *Yes. Yes. I've needed you like this.*

"Harder."

Moaned when he began to move gently in me, but I didn't want gentleness. I wanted what I knew he had lurking past his concerns for being tender.

He moved with more force and kissed me, his eyes still open. I didn't close mine, either. Seeing his face while he was inside me overwhelmed me. I grabbed his hair, locked my gaze to his, and kissed him until I had to break away to breathe.

"I can taste myself on your mouth," I panted. "I want you to taste yourself on mine. I want to suck you, swallow you when you come—"

"Stop talking like that, or I'm going to come right now." His hands flexed on my hips, holding me tighter. He was close. I could feel it in the way he held me and in those tempered, measured thrusts that devastated me with passion. His nearness to orgasm filled me with erotic purpose, making me want to bring him over the edge.

I ground myself against him, crying out at how good that felt. "More. Take me harder."

He unleashed his restraint, leaving me gasping at the blinding concentration of sensations. It hurt in the sweetest way, causing me to strain toward him even as I cried out at his rough, rapid strokes. When he reached his climax, he threw me against the headboard and shouted with rapture, his whole body trembling. I clung to him, shaking also, my heart beating fast enough to explode.

After several seconds, Bones unglued me from himself—and the headboard—to lay me back on the bed. "Bloody hell, Kitten, are you all right?"

If I hadn't still been gasping, his concern over my assumed injury would have made me laugh. "Come back here."

I pulled him down from his hover until he was on top of me once more. He balanced his weight, his free hand sliding to my head as I moved lower to suck his nipple.

He tasted like salt, but that was probably from my sweat. His hand tangled in my hair as he pressed me closer, a deep groan coming from his throat.

"I'll be gentler this time, but I need you again now."

I bit him, feeling him shudder. Yeah, he liked that. So did I, and right now I couldn't stop touching him or tasting him.

"Don't be gentle. I love it when you lose control. I want you to lose it again."

I slid lower, tasting the part of him that was salty with something other than sweat. My lips wrapped around him, taking him into my mouth until he overflowed it, then moaning as he twisted position to reciprocate.

Everything blurred into a haze of skin, lips, tongues, and hard flesh. My need grew the more he fed it, and he kept feeding it. After what seemed like an hour, I squinted over his shoulder at the light intruding into the room.

"Did you turn on a lamp?" I gasped, wondering when he would have done that.

Bones craned his neck, squinting also at the new shaft of light coming from the corner.

"That can't be," he muttered.

"What?" I asked as he jumped from the bed.

More light came in when Bones tugged back what I now noticed was a curtain. He turned to me and raised his brow.

"It's the sun."

It couldn't be morning already. But the proof was there with those yellow rays illuminating the front of him.

Bones stared at me before closing the drapes with a snap. "I don't care," he said, getting back into bed. "Now then, where were we?"

†wenty-seven

Yoou *whore*!"
The first punch rocked me back before I even registered who'd thrown it. Another one came, then another. I tried to defend myself, but my arms weren't moving. Neither were my legs. It took me a second to realize why. They were bolted to the floor. Gregor knelt next to me, beating me without mercy.

"You'll be sorry for this," I got out as soon as he paused.

"You threaten me?" A brutal punch to my stomach doubled me over as much as the metal clamps would allow. Goddamn, who ever said you couldn't feel pain in dreams? "I am your husband, even though you don't deserve to call me that, you traitorous bitch!"

Suddenly the punches stopped, and Gregor caressed my cheek. "*Chérie,* why do you do this? Why do you persist in angering me? You know I must punish you for your adultery, but it pains me to do so."

I managed to laugh even through the pain. "Oh sure. This hurts you more than me, huh? You are the world's biggest asshole, Gregor."

"You will do as I say!" That false sweetness was gone. He was back to whacking me with every other word. "You will return to me *right now,* or you will wish you had."

"Go ahead. Show me everything you've got! I've been beaten and tortured before, but with you, it all goes away as soon as I open my eyes. You don't scare me, Gregor."

He seized my hair, yanking it so hard I felt clumps pull out. "If you let him turn you into a vampire," he hissed, "I will make sure you suffer. Do you understand me?"

I stared at him. "When I was sixteen, I used to care about you. When I first got my memory back, a little part of me still did. Now, however, as God is my witness, I swear I will put you in the ground. Do *you* understand *me*?"

He hit me so hard everything went black, but his temper was to my advantage, because it knocked me right back into reality. I heard an anxious voice.

"Kitten, wake up!"

Bones was shaking me. My cheek stung faintly, and I knew it wasn't residual pain from Gregor's fists. Bones had been doing more than shaking me.

"Stop that, I've had enough of being beaten," I muttered, trying to brush his hands away.

He didn't let go, but he did stop shaking me. "He was beating you? You were crying out in your sleep because he was *striking* you?"

I sat up, pulling the covers over me and trying to shake off the remnants of the dream. The phantom pains from it were dissipating with every second. "He was pissed."

Bones growled low in his throat. His whole body was tense. "You only slept 'round an hour, but should you stay up? Or do you still have those pills? I can't bear the thought of him abusing you if you fall asleep again."

"No pills." I grimaced at the memory of how they'd made me feel. "Gregor's never come at me twice in one night—or day, I guess. I think it takes too much power for him to make a first attempt, and he needs time to rest up before his next one.

"He won't get a next one," Bones said in a grim voice.

No, because later tonight, I'd be turned into a vampire. That's why Gregor had been so pissed. He knew he'd lose access to me once that happened. *Bye, bye, Gregor. Hope you sleep tight. I know I will.*

Bones kissed the top of my head. "Then try to go to sleep, luv. Soon this will be over."

No, I thought. *It won't be over until I kill Gregor. And once I'm a vampire, I'll be another step closer to doing that.*

When I woke up again, Bones was gone. The curtains were still drawn, but if I had to guess, I'd say it was well after one. My last morning as a half-human had passed. This could be the earliest I'd be waking up for a few months after I became a new vampire, unless all those years being a half-breed would help shave time off that.

Now that the day had arrived, a twinge of nervousness wormed in me. What if changing over didn't make me stronger but weaker, like I was starting from scratch? God, I'd hate to wake up afterward and find out I was a wimp. Furthermore, what did not breathing feel like? How would I handle never hearing my heart beat again? How long would my new bloodlust last? A few days, a week?

And what would it be like to no longer be the rare half-breed but just be plain old Cat, the newbie vampire? Actually, that thought pleased me. *Nothing unusual to see here, folks. Move along.* Yeah, I'd wanted that my whole life.

The door opened, and Spade strode in. I snatched at the sheet, since I was still naked, and gave him an aggravated look.

"Don't you know how to *knock*?"

"I heard you were awake," Spade replied. "Here. Brought you breakfast, or I suppose lunch, considering the time."

He set a tray down on a nearby table before giving me a wicked grin.

"I see you and Crispin resolved your differences. Indeed, the pair of you kept the whole house up last night."

I closed my eyes. By now I should be over the embarrassment of having anyone with undead ears privy to hearing my intimate moments, but it looked like that still wasn't beyond me.

"Hope I didn't make you lose your beauty sleep, Spade."

The acid in my voice didn't dissuade him. He waved a hand.

"Not at all. Put Crispin in a better mood, I daresay. He's been such a foul-tempered sod lately."

Which brought up a question I'd been wondering. "Where is Bones?"

"Fetching Mencheres. Can't tell you from where, of course, just in case you catch a nap before the big event tonight. He'll be gone for hours."

Oh. I understood, but I wished I'd seen him before he left. With how bad things had been between us, I was greedy for more time with Bones now that they were better.

"Thanks for bringing me breakfast," I said.

"No trouble. Now I'm off to get my own breakfast."

With Spade gone, I debated over what to do with myself for the next few hours. Eating and showering would only take up so much time. Maybe I should notify some people about what I was about to do.

I could call Denise. But then again, Denise didn't need reminders about vampires in her life right now. After Randy's brutal death, it had been too much for Denise to see Spade making a mess out of that man's head at the rodeo bar. I'd tell Denise once it was over. That way she wouldn't have to worry about something going wrong. Giving her one less thing to worry about sounded like the least I could do as her friend.

Next I considered calling my uncle, but then I decided against it. Don's first words wouldn't be congratulations, even though it was something he probably knew was inevitable.

I certainly wasn't going to call my mother. I already knew everything she'd say, and the words "don't do it!" would factor in repeatedly. What was nice was that no matter how much she'd hate this—and she would loathe it to the bone, no question—it wouldn't mean the end of our relationship. I couldn't have said the same years ago.

I should call Vlad and tell him his offer to sire me wasn't needed. Somehow I didn't think that would surprise him. But even as I was about to pick up the phone, I thought of another person I wanted to speak to.

I shut the door and knelt by the bed. *Hi, Lord, it's Catherine. Been a while, I know . . .*

I heard Bones come in the house. He asked Spade where I was, then his long, booted stride headed toward the parlor I'd met him in yesterday. I'd been on the couch reading, not wanting to inadvertently learn my location by watching TV and seeing a local channel. I rose when Bones walked in, taking in his appearance. He wore black pants, a short-sleeved black shirt, and black shoes. Dark colors looked great on him. They made his skin even more incandescent by comparison.

"Very appropriate," I noted, to cover up any butterflies in my stomach. "You look like the perfect Grim Reaper."

He stared at me for so long that I cleared my throat. "Okay, it was a bad joke . . ."

"Are you certain about this, Kitten? It's not too late to change your mind."

"I want this." And I did. I was ready.

Bones walked over to me with a slow, leashed grace, stopping when he was only inches away. He took my hands, bringing them to his lips. His eyes never left mine.

"You decide when. We can wait until later. There's no rush."

I'd been gearing up for this all day. Waiting wouldn't make me more ready, so there was no time like the present.

"Now. Should, ah, we go somewhere else to do this?"

"Here is fine."

I glanced around the room. It didn't look secure to me, considering the humans nearby, but I didn't expect I'd stay long here after . . . well, after dying. I wondered how long I'd be dead. If death would be like dreaming, or if I'd not be aware of anything until my eyes opened again. Only one way to find out.

"All right."

I'd seen people being turned when Bones changed Tate and Juan, so I knew what to expect, but seeing it and being the one it was happening to felt worlds apart. My heart began to thump. Guess that would only help in this case.

Bones's eyes went green, fangs extending from his teeth. He smoothed my hair back, holding me close next to him. I closed my eyes as he leaned down, touching his cheek to mine. His skin was cool. Soon I'd be the same temperature.

"It's normal to be nervous, but there's nothing to be afraid of," Bones whispered. "I've done this many, many times, and at no point will you be going any-where beyond my reach."

The reassurance was helpful. One doesn't stare death in the face and just give it the finger, no matter the circumstances.

"Are you ready, Kitten?"

Asked against my skin as his tongue probed my pulse. Finding the best place to bite.

"Yes . . . wait!"

That instant's pressure of his fangs ceased. I took in a deep breath.

"No live meals, even if you think the person has it coming. Give me bagged blood. I don't want to wake up with a face full of someone's artery."

Bones pulled back to look at me, stroking the nape of my neck. "It's already taken care of. Don't fret. You'll wake up and I'll be there and everything will be fine."

I slid my arms around his neck, glad it was him who would be bringing me to the grave and back instead of anyone else.

"Bones."

"Yes?"

"Make me a vampire."

Certain things I knew I'd always remember. The look in his eye when he lowered his head. That slow, deep piercing of his fangs into me. His hand pressing me closer while the other one curled around mine, lacing our fingers together. That rush of blood spilling into his mouth from a bite far deeper than I'd ever received. The flush of warmth sweeping over me. My heart, beating so fast at first, then gradually, inexorably slowing. Growing sporadic as the life and that warmth began to ebb from me.

My thoughts became chaotic. *The buzzing's not as loud now. Can't see much anymore. Funny, there were lights a moment ago, thousands of tiny little specks. Pretty. Where'd they go? Colder. Where'd that wind come from?*

What was that? Something's pulling me. Where am I now? Can't talk. Am I moving? Can't see. Why can't I see? Why can't I move? Where am I? Where am I? WHERE AM I?

What? I can barely hear you . . . yes! Yes, it's me, I'm here! I can see you now. I'll be right there, I'm coming.

*Wait, don't go away. Come back! Stop, please, I haven't
seen you for so long.*

No, take me back! I need to see them one more time . . .

I was in hell.

The fire that ravaged me burned with a ferocity that
told me the stuff we had on earth was just a tame im-
postor. This fire was pitiless, and it was everywhere.
Burning me without killing me. Tormenting me with
unspeakable agony. I couldn't scream, though I didn't
even know if I had a mouth anymore. The only thing
I could focus on was the pain. *No more stop stop hurts
HURTS HURTS!*

And then—something cool washed over me, slowly
extinguishing the flames. With all the desperation of
the damned, I strained for more of it, since at last the
pain began to lessen. *More, oh God, it still hurts, please
give me more, more, oh please, need more, a little more . . .*

Sound again, like a drumbeat. Light. Voices over
that sluggish, banging drum. So many different
smells.

I opened my eyes and saw not a flaming lake of fire
but plain concrete walls. It took a second to recognize
the people staring at me, then cognition hit. *That's
right, I was at Bones's house, and he'd turned me into a
vampire. I wasn't in hell, I was changed into a vampire, and
everything was okay, because the pain was gone. I could
see, hear, feel, smell, taste, oh God, taste—*

Something delicious was in my mouth. Oh, yes,
that was good. *So good.*

The last lagging bit of reality clicked into place.
Holy shit, I had someone in my arms. I hadn't been
drinking a bag of blood, but a *person.* My mouth
was pressed to their neck and blood dripped from

my fangs—fuck me, I had fangs!—and there was no pulse under my lips.

"Jesus!" I shouted, shoving the person away with a rush of horror. "I told Bones no people! Where is he?"

I looked around for Bones, sickened that he'd let me kill someone, but Spade's expression stopped me. He looked almost dazed.

"You just threw Crispin to the floor."

I looked down. The corpse I'd flung away from me pushed himself into a sitting position and stared up at me with disbelieving brown eyes. A full, untouched bag of blood was in Bones's hand.

That's when I became aware of my second problem.

"Uh, guys . . ." I began hesitantly. "Why do I still have a heartbeat?"

Twenty-eight

THE STEADY DRUMBEAT I'D HEARD BEFORE was coming from my own chest. For a second, I was confused. Didn't it work? Those two new fangs jabbing me in the lip seemed to indicate otherwise, but why was my heart still beating?

"Is it going to stop soon or something?"

Had they forgotten to tell me an important detail? Like, "Oh, you'll hear some *thump thumps* for the first few minutes, but then it'll quit." And from the expressions aimed at me, this wasn't normal.

"Anytime one of you wants to answer me, that'd be great."

"Don't you want the blood?" Spade blurted.

I gave the purplish bag in Bones's hand a cursory glance. "Not really."

Bones got to his feet. He looked at me in the strangest way, then he ripped the end of the blood bag with his teeth and held it out to me.

"Drink."

"I'd rather not."

"Just take a swig out of the bag!" Bones demanded.

Making a face, I put my mouth around the torn edge and took a tentative sip.

Yuck! Like a mouthful of old pennies. I spat it out. "What were you giving me before? That stuff was excellent, but this is crap."

Spade actually whitened. Bones took the bag back and drained it in with a few powerful swallows.

"Not a thing wrong with it," he pronounced. Then he took a knife from his pants and sliced open my arm without warning.

"Ouch! What was that for?"

I clutched my injured arm, but almost at once, the pain turned into only an itching tingle. Bones pulled my hand back, revealing red-stained but unbroken skin underneath. There wasn't a wound anymore. My forearm had healed completely.

In spite of everything, I began to grin. "That'll save me a *world* of grief in a fight."

"Are you aware that you're not breathing?" Bones asked.

He was right. I wasn't—and I hadn't even noticed! How can you miss that you're no longer sucking in air? When you don't need to anymore, that's when!

"Her heartbeat," Mencheres said, speaking the first time since I'd opened my eyes. "Is slowing down."

I looked at my chest, as if that could tell me anything. Sure enough, what had started out as an even pace of *buh-bump, buh-bumps* was winding down to a sluggish *buh . . . buh-bump . . . . buh* with longer intervals in between. It felt . . . well, it felt goddamned weird, is what it did. Like listening to it, I should be panicked or something.

"That's a good thing, right? Maybe it just needed a minute to realize its services were no longer needed."

Bones put an arm around me. "Kitten, how do you feel?"

"Fine. Good, actually. You know, you smell great. Really, really, *nnnghghh.*"

When I came to, it was with more of that wonderful taste in my mouth. This time, however, I was being restrained, with one arm around my waist and the other under my neck. Since I could still see Bones and Spade, it had to be Mencheres who held me.

"What happened?" I asked.

"You bit me," Bones said.

"Huh?"

Spade nodded in confirmation. I was aghast. "I'm sorry, I don't even remember doing that . . ." Then I trailed off, inhaling near Mencheres's arm. *That smell. Mmmm.*

The next thing I knew, Mencheres's wrist was in my mouth and I was shaking it from side to side like a shark. When I realized what I was doing, I spat it out.

"Will somebody tell me what the hell is wrong with me?"

Even as I shouted it, I couldn't quit licking my lips. *That taste. It was so perfect. God, nothing had ever tasted half this good before!*

"You feed on undead blood."

Mencheres made the pronouncement with his usual impenetrable aplomb. Bones arched a brow. Then he came closer, drawing blood from his wrist with a fang and waving it under my nose.

"You want this?"

I lunged forward with a compulsion that I didn't even have time to think about. Mencheres flicked his free hand, and an invisible wall suddenly smacked me in the face.

"Stay still."

I didn't have a choice—I was frozen in midcrouch, with my knees bent, my hands extended, and my mouth open in a rapacious snarl. What was worse was that I didn't care.

"Give me that."

I knew it was my voice, but I didn't recognize the savage sound of it. That pain began to return, the awful one that felt like I was burning from the inside out.

"Give it to me!"

Mencheres let me go. I noticed that only when I saw him standing next to Bones, who retrieved another red-filled bag from a cooler and ripped the end open again. This time, Bones smeared the blood directly on my lips.

"Do you want this?" he asked, holding the bag under my mouth.

I licked the blood from my lips. "No." An angry growl.

The three men exchanged a glance. Then Bones let out a sigh. "Right, then. We'll try it another way."

He swallowed the contents of the bag. I watched the muscles in his throat work the whole time, mesmerized. When he finally came closer, that pain had reached a boiling point, and I had tears running down my face.

"Please. It burns, it burns!"

Bones laid his wrist against my mouth. Later I'd know I tore savagely at it, but at that moment, all I was aware of was the cooling relief from the pain. That wonderful taste running down my throat. How my entire body seemed to sigh with a bliss that felt very close to orgasm.

"You know this is unheard of," Spade was saying. His voice sounded far away. I was still shuddering in delicious rapture from sucking the last few trickles out of Bones's wrist.

"First time for everything," Bones replied. "Just goes to show that when you think you know everything, you don't. Listen. Her heart's stopped now."

That caught my attention. Well, that and his wrist ran dry, which maybe contributed to my noticing my surroundings again.

"Do you think it'll stay stopped?"

They all looked at each other. Finally, with a shrug, Bones removed another blood bag from the cooler and answered me before he drank it.

"Reckon we'll find out."

The small, reinforced basement room was essentially a prison. No windows, only one door, which was locked from the outside. A twin bed against the far wall. Several books, both new and well used. Pen and paper. And, of course, the cooler.

It was filled with blood bags and, to my surprise, bottles of water. Bones explained those would help keep me hydrated while my metabolism went haywire, burning through all the sustenance it received from the blood without sparing any to prevent me from looking, well, dry. I had to drink water for the first week or so. Then, I was told, I only needed to drink a glass a day of any kind of liquid. Gin and tonic topped my list.

The scent of blood was thick in the air. The room was also rich with the scents of Spade, Bones, Mencheres, and others who had been here before us. I was trying to identify all the different smells, but it was hard, considering my limited frame of reference.

Three more times, that overwhelming hunger hit me, and I'd black out only to find myself latched onto Bones like a rampaging leech. Mencheres had let me out of his invisible cement suit after Bones stated that as long as he kept refilling, it didn't matter how many times I drained him. And since I went flat crazy whenever that need took me, there was no reason for anyone else to get chewed on. I also got the distinct impression that they wanted to keep my unusual diet a secret.

"It figures I couldn't even do this the normal way," I said, after licking the last drops from his wrist yet again. A small part of me wondered why I wasn't embarrassed by my behavior. Helplessly sucking on someone's vein was the height of dependence, yet I didn't care. Maybe because I was still riding the euphoria another bellyful of Bones's blood gave me.

"Do what, luv? Become a vampire? Or bite?"

"I'm *biting* wrong, too?"

Bones chuckled, brushing the wild mass of my hair out of my face. "You're biting exactly the way every new vampire bites, which is too hard and messy, but completely normal, and you can't help what you're craving. No one's ever turned a half-breed before. Maybe if they had, the same thing would have happened, then you'd just be eating what you were supposed to eat."

"Thanks for that." Lucidity was making its brief pit stop now that my hunger had been appeased. "Quick thinking on your part."

"Yes, well, comes from practice. Come on, Kitten, let's get you cleaned up."

Bones cracked open another bottle of water and poured some of it onto a towel, then wiped my chin and throat with it. It came back red, of course, and he did it twice more until he was satisfied. There weren't any mirrors, so it's not like I could have checked for myself, and I liked him performing this task for the simple reason that he was touching me. His hands were so strong, but he handled me with the utmost gentleness. Like anything harsher than a caress would leave permanent damage.

Another scent filled my nose. I breathed in the fragrant smell, surprised to find it was coming from me.

Bones inhaled as well, his eyes filling up with green. Now the air began to be flavored with a heady blend of musk, burnt sugar, and spice—Bones's scent, sharper and stronger.

"Can you smell how I want you?"

His voice was deeper. Absent of that reassuring undertone he'd been using for the past few hours while I struggled with my uncontrollable hunger.

I took in another deep breath, absorbing the intoxicating mixture of scents swirling together. "Yes."

My voice was throatier also. Almost a low purr while I felt the fangs that had receded begin to grow once more. Another hunger swept through me. Though it didn't hurt, it felt just as urgent as the ones before it.

I'd been sitting on the floor—how I got there, don't ask me, I'd come to there with his wrist in my mouth—when lust took over. I flattened Bones onto the small bed, putting my legs on either side of his hips.

"Wait," he said, reaching for something on the floor.

I didn't want to. A surge of pure need made me blind to everything else. I'd ripped off my clothes and made short work of his pants when I cried out in frustration at what I found when my hand clasped around him.

Bones let out an amused grunt. "I did say wait for a reason. You drained me, but don't fret. Plenty of blood here."

He pulled another bag of blood out of the cooler, which was conveniently close to the bed, come to notice, and drank it while taking off the last of his clothes. It was a good thing all that liquid flowed to one place, because in the few seconds it took him to do that, my need had turned into a boiling ache.

Bones didn't bother with foreplay. He sheathed himself inside me as soon as the bag was empty. I let out a cry and moved on top of him. Words began spilling out of my mouth. What they were, I had no idea, but I couldn't stop saying them. Bones sat up, gripping my hips, sucking my breasts, biting my nipples, and holding me while he began to move faster.

The smell of our lust was all around us, erotically ripe and intense. I felt drugged from it, but at the same time, I'd never felt so *alive*. Like my entire life before this had occurred while I'd been asleep. Every inch of my skin was hypersensitive, crackling with passion, and humming now with an internal voltage I'd never possessed before. It grew with every new touch, hurtling me toward a pinnacle of pleasure that made our surroundings fall away. There was nothing but this moment, and the orgasm, if such a trivial word could be used to describe what was ripping through me, wasn't limited to my loins. It erupted all through me.

"Yes," Bones groaned, moving faster. "So good, luv. Not much time, stay with me, stay with me . . ."

I had the briefest moment to wonder, *where does he think I'll go?* before everything went black.

Twenty-nine

"Are you ready for this?"
I nodded. "Do it."

Bones sliced a long upward line along his forearm, splitting open his veins. That scrumptious red liquid filled the seam at once. My mouth watered.

Next, Bones smeared his blood onto his fingers and passed them within inches of my lips. I swallowed hard, fighting down my urge to snatch at his hand and suck his fingers—and then his forearm.

Then, Bones pressed those bloodied fingers into my mouth, teasing me with their unbelievable sweetness. I trembled but didn't lick or bite down. *You can do this, Cat. Don't give in.*

Bones handed me a napkin. "Spit it out, Kitten."

I did, giving back those drops that had made my mouth physically ache with wanting. If I still could, I'd have been sweating bullets by then.

"Again."

Bones repeated this tortuous act five more times,

me spitting out what my body was howling at me to keep, until at last Bones smiled at me.

"You did it, luv."

"Well done, Cat," Spade said.

"It's more than well done." Bones kissed my forehead. "Getting control of the thirst inside of three days is extraordinary."

"What time is it?"

" 'Round 12:30," Spade replied.

Less than six hours until dawn. That was the other "side effect" of this transformation. When the sun rose, I conked out. Not just got sleepy, like I'd been accustomed to my whole life, I meant fall down in midsentence *out*. In a way, that was more concerning to me than my bouts of hunger. If I happened to be in a fight when dawn broke, I'd be toast.

I was working on staying conscious when the sun came up. As of now, I could keep my eyes open a few minutes while my body did an excellent impression of a limp rag. It would go away with time, but I worried about how *much* time. Right now, I couldn't even move until noon.

"I want to go out," I said. "Drive somewhere, stare at every street sign I pass, read road maps until I go blind, and get directions from anyone within twenty yards. Oh, but I'm taking a bath first. That tiny shower in the basement only had cold water."

Mencheres strode into the room. As soon as I saw his face, I knew something was horribly wrong.

"It's Gregor, isn't it?" I said before he could speak. "What did he do?"

Mencheres put his hands on my shoulders. "Cat, your mother has disappeared."

"No!"

It burst from me along with a sudden spurt of tears. Bones's arm tightened around my waist.

"How? Was the junkyard attacked?" he asked.

Mencheres shook his head. "Rodney said she disappeared from her room. Her nightclothes were still in her bed."

He'd snatched her from her sleep. Oh God, Gregor had pulled my mother right out of her dreams to kidnap her.

"He said he'd make me suffer," I whispered, hearing Gregor's snarl again from my last dream with him. "I didn't think he'd go after my mother. How could he if he never drank from her?"

My voice trailed off. Gregor could have. I'd assumed he'd used the power in his gaze to compel my mother to tell me that he was an old friend the night I met Gregor. But obviously, he'd taken her blood as well.

"I need to talk to Gregor," I said at once. "Someone has to know how to reach him."

Mencheres dropped his hands from my shoulders. "You know that's what he wants. He'll want to trade, you for her."

"Then I'll do it," I said.

Bones's grip on me turned to steel. "No, you won't."

"What do you expect me to do? Shrug my shoulders and just *hope* Gregor doesn't kill her? I know you don't like her, Bones, but she's my mother. I can't abandon her!"

"He absolutely will not kill her, Kitten," Bones replied, his voice hard. "She's the only advantage he has over you now that you're a vampire and he can't dreamsnatch you again."

Fear, rage, and frustration boiled up in me to form a harsh scent, like burning plastic. *You could go to Gregor, but then Bones could attack once they know where Gregor is. No, Gregor will expect that and have a trap waiting. If Bones brought enough people to get out of a trap, Gregor would know you were double-crossing him and probably kill her out of spite.*

"Mencheres!" I exclaimed, grabbing his shirt. "You could go with me. You imprisoned Gregor once, you could do it again! Or better yet, we'll kill him."

He shook his head. "I imprisoned him before in secret so as to avoid a war between his allies and mine. If Gregor disappears now, everyone would know Bones or I had a hand in it. Gregor's allies would surely attack us in revenge."

I cast around for another alternative. "You could hold Gregor and his men in a vise with just your mind—I've seen you do it. Then I get my mother back and we can escape."

Some of his long black hair spilled over his shoulder from how hard I'd yanked at him, but his gaze was flat—and sad.

"I cannot do that, Cat."

"Why?" I spat.

"Because Gregor has rights to your mother under our laws," Mencheres said quietly. "To attack him for taking one of his own people would bring more than Gregor's allies against us."

"Gregor doesn't have any rights to my mother," I snapped. Then something cold ran over me that had nothing to do with my new temperature.

Yes, he did. Under vampire law, I was Gregor's wife, which meant anyone belonging to me was his, too. And on top of that, Gregor had bitten my mother, making her his property under vampire law if he chose to claim her as such.

Oh, God. No vampire would violate their laws to help me get my mother back, not even Vlad.

"If the laws are so strict, why haven't I been forced back to Gregor?" I asked bitterly. "Why am I free, when she isn't?"

"You haven't admitted in public to being his wife, for one. Even still, some vampires who believe Gregor have advocated your being forced to return to him, Kitten. But most consider it not their business that you've chosen someone else. Attacking Gregor to retrieve your mum would make it their business, however. You know she'd be considered his property one way or the other, so stealing his property opens up the possibility in people's minds that Mencheres and I might try to steal some of their people without cause, too."

"Without cause?" My tone was lethal.

Bones gave me a look. "Cause in their eyes, not ours."

"I can't just abandon her to Gregor, laws or no laws," I stated.

He turned me until we faced each other. "Kitten, neither will I, but we must wait. Once Gregor's dead, your mum will be free. Gregor is expecting you to rush to him with all haste. He won't be prepared for you to use caution. Will you trust me and wait until the timing is right?"

I bit my lip. The blood filling my mouth reminded me that my fangs were out. Amidst everything else, a wave of hunger swept through me. How could I just wait and hope that Gregor wouldn't get impatient and send me parts of my mother as motivation to return to him? And yet how I could just rush into the fray without a plan, or backup? My *damn the torpedoes, full speed ahead* strategy hadn't been working for me lately.

Bones touched my cheek. "I will find him, luv. And I will kill him. *Trust* me."

I swallowed, feeling a tear slide down my face and knowing it would be colored pink.

"All right."

Bones kissed me, quick but tender. Then he turned to Mencheres.

"We will announce her change. A formal gathering is best, so her introduction to vampire society can be done under an all-truce, avoiding the danger of an attack."

"Agreed," Mencheres said. "I'll set it up at once."

"You want to have a party?" I asked, not sure if I was hearing them right. "*That's* your big idea?"

"There are still ghouls who consider you a threat to their species," Bones replied. "One in particular, Apollyon, has made the most noise about you. Showing him and the others that you're a vampire will get rid of that problem. It will also garner goodwill toward us with the other vampires in the community, which we'll need when Gregor has his unfortunate, gruesome demise."

Cold and practical. Those were Bones's strong suits. If I wanted my mother back alive, they'd better become mine as well.

"Good thinking." My smile was bitter. "If I'd listened to you more often, my mother probably wouldn't be in this mess."

Bones grasped my chin. "Don't you dare blame yourself. How many people you've protected in your very young life is nothing short of remarkable. You place too much pressure on yourself. All the answers don't have to come from you, Kitten. You're not alone anymore."

For all but the two years Bones had been in my life, it felt like I'd been alone. No wonder it was such a hard mind-set for me to break.

"Okay, we'll have my undead unveiling party. I'll even suck on a human's vein in public if that helps, since I assume we're still keeping my eating habits under wraps."

Bones shrugged. "I see no reason to alarm anyone over something so trivial, so yes, we'll be keeping that a secret. But there's no need to do something so dramatic. You're clearly a full vampire now. That's all anyone needs to see."

"Where will this coming-out party be held?"

"Here. We've stayed in this house long enough. We'll have the gathering here, then depart for another place afterward. And then, soon, we'll find a way to rescue your mum."

I was looking forward to that. Right now, slicing through Gregor's guards sounded more fulfilling than anything else I could imagine.

But what if I couldn't slice through his guards? I could be as weak as any new vampire now. There hadn't been time to test my physical strength in the past few days. Only my mental fortitude as I got over the hunger insanity.

"Bones. We need to fight."

To my profound relief, I discovered my strength had *not* been reduced to that of an average new vampire. In fact, Bones had been stunned in our first fight when I'd taken advantage of his restrained attack and beaten him. He'd gaped in shock at the knife in his chest—steel, not silver—then tossed back his head and laughed before engaging me in a no-holds-barred assault that left me feeling like I'd been dropped off a cliff—and then run over by a train.

My recovery period was now lightning fast in comparison to what it had been as a half-breed, but there was a price to pay for those upgrades. Everything felt more intense. This was great when it came to bedroom activities, but not when it came to brawling. A broken bone or knife wound might heal in seconds, but those seconds hurt with a mind-numbing intensity. Bones explained it was because my body no longer went into shock. No, it just went right from scorching pain into complete healing, assuming I was fast enough to not get any new injuries before the old ones cleared up.

The other thing I discovered was how different it felt to be cut with silver versus another metal. Never before had I realized how strong vampiric aversion was to silver, or how much my being half-human had shielded me from it. When injured by silver, I had all the blasting pain of my nerve endings going into shock, plus an added burning agony that made a steel-inflicted wound feel like bliss in comparison.

I'd have to learn how to control my instinctive reaction to the new, amped-up levels of pain. Right now, they stumbled me and cost me time. Time I couldn't afford with the looming battle to get my mom back.

Four days passed with no word about my mother. I spent them in constant activity—when I wasn't immobilized from dawn's power over me. I found that the more blood I drank from Bones, the more I could force myself to stay awake as the sun crept over the horizon. I was up to being awake for an hour after dawn. Granted, that hour consisted of being in a state of near paralysis, but it was progress, though there was no meter for me to compare my progress to. I wasn't the world's only known half-breed, but apparently, I was the only one who'd been turned into a vampire. No one knew how long a typical new vampire's weakness to dawn would affect me. I could be doing cartwheels at sunrise in a week—or it might take me a year.

The fifth night was my coming-out party. I was in no mood to stand there, smile, and greet a bunch of people who might have been screaming for my head recently, but that's what I'd be doing. If it prevented more tensions between vampires and ghouls, as well as helping my chances of getting my mother back, I'd do it naked if I had to. Since this was a formal undead gathering, there would be food—all kinds—drinks, dancing, and festivities, while those in power pondered whether or not to slaughter half the people around them.

In other words, like a high-school prom.

I had just finished drying my hair when I heard the downstairs front door slam, then rapid footsteps on the stairs. Bones was back. He'd gone to get me a dress, since for whatever reason, he didn't feel anything in the house was good enough. He came through the door with a garment bag in hand.

"Just in time," I said. "I'm about to curl my hair. So, let's see the dress."

Bones zipped the bag open to reveal a long black dress, spaghetti-strapped, narrowing to a nondefined waist but with crystals embedded in the fabric around the bodice. Those crystals would mold around my breasts, I could tell from the cut, and even in the low light in the room, they sparkled and threw off dazzling colors.

"Beautiful," I said, then smiled wryly. "Can't wear a bra with it, though. I'm sure that was accidental on your part."

He grinned. "Of course."

It really was a beautiful dress. Simple, gothic, yet sparkly. Very appropriate for a vampire coming-out party.

"This'll go great with my fangs," I said, trying for flippancy to cover my nervousness. Even still, I could smell it on me. It was sickly sweet, like an overripe peach. If only there was a way I could cover my tension with the scent of *eau de brass balls* instead.

Bones kissed my bare shoulder, easy to do since I was still only wearing a towel. "It will be fine, Kitten."

I smiled, ignoring the squeeze in my gut that didn't agree. "Of course it will."

The last receiving line I'd stood in had been at Randy's funeral. This one was almost as cheerful. For one, my conversation with Bones was mostly limited to him saying, "This is so-and-so. So-and-so, may I present Cat, the newest member of my line," and I would shake hands with someone who might just as soon roast me over hot coals.

Rodney was here, looking as grim-faced as I felt. He blamed himself for not waking my mother when Gregor stalked her in her sleep. I'd tried to tell Rodney there was no way he could have known what was happening, but my reassurances fell on deaf ears.

Fabian floated around like a transparent maître d',

reporting in when the drinks or hors d'oeuvres ran low. Spade and Ian paid their formal respects in line. About thirty introductions later, Annette was next. She wore a strapless dress that looked poured onto her voluptuous figure. Long black gloves added a classy touch to the gown's sexiness. Next to her, I felt like Carrot Top in drag.

She put her arms around me. Taken aback, I froze. Annette squeezed me once, and whispered, "You made the right decision," and then let me go with a smile.

"Don't you look lovely, Cat? It would seem death becomes you indeed."

I hadn't expected such a warm greeting from her. "Thank you," I managed. "I heard it was all the rage this season."

She laughed, her chuckle holding a sinful under-current. "Dare I hope your heterosexual exclusivity has been buried along with your pulse?"

Now there was the Annette I knew. A voracious shark disguised behind a beautiful woman.

"That hasn't changed," I told her dryly. "Kind of you to inquire, though."

Her eyes sparkled. "Nothing ventured, nothing gained, as they say. Ah, well, must move along. Frightful lot of blokes here to watch you not breathe, after all."

I saw a familiar frame lingering near the front entryway. Dark straight hair with its pronounced widow's peak framed an angular face while coppery green eyes met mine.

"Vlad!"

The tenseness of the past hour had taken its toll on me, making me so glad to see someone I trusted that I left my place to greet him. *He smells like cinnamon and smoke,* I thought when I hugged him. *What an interesting combination of scents.*

Then I became aware that the room had fallen silent. When I looked around, everyone had stopped what they were doing to stare at us—and the look Bones gave me could have freeze-dried steam.

"Kitten," he said. "Would you kindly return . . . *now.*"

Uh-oh. Guess I'd committed a faux pas by greeting a friend out of order.

"I gotta go do this," I muttered to Vlad. "Thanks for coming."

"Of course." His smile changed from the genuine one he'd given me to its usual sardonic curl. "Go greet your fans."

My fans, indeed. I'd never felt more judged or dissected in my life than I had tonight. Forget my lack of heartbeat or breathing; if someone had pried open my mouth and demanded to see my fangs, I wouldn't have been surprised.

"So sorry," I said to Bones. It surprised me that he was rigid, anger wafting from him like he'd been splashed with kerosene.

"Quite," he said, ice warmer than his tone. "Let me introduce you to Malcolme Untare. You'll recognize him by another name. Apollyon."

I almost snatched my hand back from the insipid grip of the man I'd barely glanced at. *This* was the ghoul who'd been spreading the most rumors about me?

Malcolme Untare, or Apollyon, as he'd named himself, was my height if I was in bare feet. He had black hair anybody could see was dyed, and even had one long piece wrapped around his head in that way some men did to fool no one into believing they weren't bald. I resisted a sudden strong urge to tug away that piece and scream *peekaboo!* at his bare crown underneath. Since I just left him standing there after I'd dashed off to welcome Vlad, however, I thought that might be pushing things.

But some things couldn't be helped. "How *do* you do?" I asked, giving him a more-than-firm handshake.

Apollyon let go like touching me had been distasteful. He had flat blue eyes and those smooth baby cheeks seemed at odds with his persona. Somehow I thought he should be covered in warts because he reminded me of a mean, squat toad.

"You are just as I expected you to be," he said with a scornful twist of his lips.

I straightened to my full height. In heels, I had two inches on him. A prick like Apollyon would hate to be looked down on by a woman. "Let me return the compliment."

"Kitten," Bones drew out.

Right, this was supposed to be a "no stones thrown" affair. "Great to meet you, Apollyon, and make sure you save me a dance. I'll just bet you've got on your boogie shoes."

Vlad made no attempt to hide his laughter. Mencheres gave me one of those you're-not-being-prudent glares, and Bones looked like he wanted to throttle me. Well, too bad. Apollyon had tried to incite people to kill me and other vampires, all based on lies and paranoia. Damned if I was going to kiss his ass and say it tasted like candy.

Apollyon moved past me reeking with anger— I was getting good at this scent thing!—and I fixed another false smile on my face as I greeted the next dubious well-wisher.

Thirty

It was after I'd shaken the last person's hand in line that Bones turned to me and spoke through a clenched jaw.

"Why did you invite Tepesh?"

I glanced over at Vlad, who was on the far side of the room talking with a vampire named Lincoln. To my knowledge, it wasn't the same man who'd freed the slaves, but then again, he *was* really tall.

"I didn't."

Bones stared at me as if weighing whether I was telling the truth.

"Ask him yourself if you don't believe me," I said, exasperated. "Not that I mind Vlad being here, but it didn't occur to me to invite him since he wasn't one of the people screaming for my head."

"Keep your voice down," Bones hissed, tugging me none too gently toward an alcove near the front door.

I didn't know what he was so angry about. Had it really been such a big deal for me to leave the line and say hello to Vlad? Frigging vampires and their warped rules.

Though maybe I should rethink that statement, since as a full vampire, I was insulting myself now, too.

"What is your problem?" I asked, keeping my voice very low.

Bones looked at me like I'd grown two heads. "My *problem*, pet, is you leaving my side to greet your former lover as if you'd severely missed him."

Now it was my turn to stare at Bones like he'd morphed into an alien being. "My former lover? Have you lost your mind?"

In my disbelief, my voice wasn't as soft as it had been before. Bones's fingers tightened on my arm. "Do you want to air our business in front of everyone? Just say the word, then."

I forced myself to calm down, because otherwise, I'd get really shrill. "What gave you the idea that I'd had sex with Vlad?" I managed to ask in a whisper.

Bones raised a brow. "Charles telling me about how he'd rung you when you were in bed with Tepesh."

Oh for God's sake, that's right. Spade's phone call that morning when Vlad slept in my room. With everything that had happened, I'd forgotten about how that would have looked.

"You know how you told me I should have *asked* you about what happened in New Orleans, instead of assuming based on appearances? Well, back at you, Bones. If you had asked, I'd have told you I've never had sex with Vlad. I've never even kissed him. We slept together because we were both lonely and needed a friend. Nothing more."

From his face, Bones was wrestling with the information. I tapped my foot. *If I can believe you picked up girl after girl with Cannelle and only drank them to sleep, then you'd* better *be able to believe me about Vlad,* I thought with a glint.

"All right," he said at last. "I believe you, and I should have asked."

"I can't believe you thought I slept with Vlad, yet you decided not to mention it."

"Oh, I would have mentioned it, just not until this situation with your mum was resolved." His voice was rough. "I thought you did it because you believed I'd cast you off and had been shagging multiple women myself. I understood how it could have happened, though I damn sure wasn't going to let it continue."

So that was the other reason Bones challenged Vlad to a death match the night he'd taken me from the Impaler's house. He hadn't just wanted me away from Vlad out of concern over Vlad sacrificing me instead of his people if ghouls attacked.

"You came to get me even though you thought I was cheating on you?"

Bones cupped my face. "You pulled me out of New Orleans even though you believed I'd left you and humiliated you with several other women. That's what vampires do, Kitten. We always come for what's ours, no matter the circumstances."

I was just thinking I'd never been happier to be a vampire when a withering voice crackled the air.

"Take your hands off my wife."

My whole body stiffened as I turned in disbelief. The opened door behind me gave a clear view of Gregor striding up.

Bones pushed himself between me and the advancing vampire. I felt rather than saw Mencheres glide over to us.

"You are not welcome here, Dreamsnatcher," Mencheres said with frightening courtesy.

"Mencheres." Gregor had a cold curl to his lips. "You thought you'd won, taking her memory away and imprisoning me all those years, but you failed. Everyone now knows that Catherine and I are bound, and our laws state that at any formal gathering where one spouse is present, the other can't be refused entry."

Gregor was right. In fact, why hadn't I thought of that? Why hadn't the several-thousand-year-old vampire next to me thought of that? Hell, where was one of Mencheres's famed visions when it would actually be useful?

"I've never been called a more degrading insult than your wife," I ground out. "Where is my mother, Gregor?"

Vlad also moved closer. Between him and Mencheres, if Gregor dared to attack, he'd be immobilized, then deep-fried until crispy.

This might turn out to be a great party after all.

"Your sharp tongue only guarantees you more punishment," Gregor replied as he swept inside the house.

Unexpectedly, Bones smiled, running his hand down my arm in a slow caress.

"Don't care for her tongue, do you? How strange. I find it's one of my favorite parts."

Gregor started forward in a rage—and then stopped. Gave a cagey look at Mencheres and Bones. Then he let out a rich laugh.

"No," he said. "I won't cast the first blow under

an all-truce. You and I will have our day, *chien*, but not today. In fact, I came because I have a present for Catherine."

Rodney elbowed people out of the way, glaring at Gregor with almost as much hatred as I did. Gregor didn't mind. He smiled as he looked behind him at the woman making her way to the house. She was dressed in a red gown with a white fur coat. She had a leash in her hand, another vampire crawling behind her at the end of it.

"You're dead," I said in disbelief.

The auburn-haired woman laughed. "*Oui*, Catherine! You should know, as it was you who killed me. But you made a mistake. You fed me vampire blood just before slaying me, and then you sent me back to Gregor with my head attached. *Merci* for that. He wouldn't have been able to raise me as a ghoul otherwise."

Cannelle smirked the whole time she said it. Meanwhile, I wanted to smack myself. Of course. Cannelle had swallowed some of Ian's blood right before I stabbed her in the heart. Gregor would have known that by filching it from my dreams, same way he'd learned countless other details. Cannelle had wanted to be a vampire, but as it turned out, I'd helped make her a ghoul instead.

Cannelle kicked the vampire near her feet. I glanced down, saw long dark hair hiding a woman's face . . . and my blood ran cold.

"No," I whispered.

The vampire's head came up, her hair falling to the side—and I sprang forward.

"*Mom!*"

Bones snatched me back. I struggled, desperate to

get to her and horrified by the glowing green ringing her previously blue eyes.

"Catherine." Her voice wavered, so unlike its normal, strident tone. "Please. Kill me."

"Bones, let me go!"

He mercilessly tightened his grip and hauled me back instead. Next to me, Spade had Rodney in a similar grip as the ghoul hurled curses at Gregor. Mencheres strode forward and pointed his finger an inch from Gregor's chest.

"What is the meaning of this?"

Gregor threw back his head and laughed. "This is my present to my wife. See how merciful I am? Now Catherine can have her mother forever with her . . . once my loyal Cannelle no longer needs a servant, that is."

Cannelle smiled and delivered a kick to my mother's face. She fell over.

"I will *kill you for this*, Gregor!"

A booming began in my ears. At first I thought it was just the thwacking of my fists against Bones, who was using all of his strength to hold me. But then I realized the noise wasn't coming from that. It was coming from inside of me.

Cannelle's eyes bugged. There were shocked mutters. People all around began to stare. Apollyon pushed his way through the crowd, then glared at me.

"Her heart's beating. What trickery is this?"

I don't know who threw the first punch, but all of a sudden, everyone was brawling. Apollyon and the ghouls surged toward me, shouting.

Bones snapped, "Get her away from here," then handed me to Vlad before jumping into the melee. Vlad held me in a viselike grip, backing away. Mencheres began casting out his power like a net to try to and subdue the violence, but there were too many powerful undead people to freeze them all. Shouts flew through the air, then people, as things got more physical, and at last, there was fire as Vlad decided to make an exit.

A wall of flame appeared around us, protecting us as he elevated straight upward while clutching me. In the next instant, the ceiling blasted over our heads. Then the next one, and the next, until nothing but the night sky was above us.

"Goddammit, I won't leave them!" I shouted, as we vaulted through the ruined roof.

"It's the only way," Vlad muttered, squeezing me so hard I would have puked if I still could.

Boom. Boom. Boom. My heart continued to bang in my chest. It made me dizzy, the sensation amazingly unfamiliar after only a week. A slew of images tormented me as our distance from the house grew. Mom. Oh God, *Mom.* Changed into a vampire. Being dragged and beaten while on a leash. Bones flinging himself into the fray. Gregor laughing at it all.

"Mencheres will settle things down," Vlad said. He had to shout to be heard above the wind as our speed increased. We were even trailing fire like a comet. "But not if you're there with your rage at Gregor and your mystifying heartbeat. You stay, and this won't end until half the people are dead."

I wanted to fling myself out of his arms and go back to the house, but the bitter truth was that Vlad was right. Once again, everyone I cared about would be better off if I was gone.

When my eyes opened, it took me a few seconds to get my bearings. The first thing I knew was that I was in the backseat of a car. Second, it didn't seem to be moving. Third, I had my mouth clamped ferociously on someone's throat, and I knew from the taste that it wasn't Bones.

I flung myself back to reveal it was Vlad I'd just neck-raped. His shirt was ripped open, and I'd had him pressed against the side of the car door.

He straightened to an upright position. "What was that?" he asked calmly.

I cursed myself for forgetting to tell him about a very important detail concerning my eating, even though that had been the last thing on my mind. After our aerial exit from the free-for-all that had once been a party, Vlad kidnapped the first person he came across, green-eyed him, and had us driven to the train station. There, we boarded the next available train. Once on it, I'd insisted on calling Bones, who hadn't answered. Neither had Spade or Mencheres.

Vlad dismissed my concerns, saying they were probably too busy to bother answering their phones. My further attempts to reach them were cut short when the sun rose an hour later, and I passed out in my chair. That was the last thing I remembered.

"Have you heard from Bones?"

"I spoke with him a few hours ago. He should be here soon."

I digested this, noting that my heartbeat, which had precipitated the melee, was silent now. How ironic that we'd had the coming-out party to try and soothe any ghoul concerns. Now the repercussions from last night might give Apollyon more fuel for his paranoid fire. I could only hope that Mencheres and Bones had managed to calm things down, and that my being a weird vampire was less threatening to ghouls than being a half-breed.

Vlad drew the torn edges of his collar together and I brought my attention back to explaining my earlier actions.

"Something strange happened after I was changed. I went straight for any vampire near me instead of drinking human blood. For some reason, vampire blood is what I, ah, crave—and now you already know that sometimes my heart still beats."

Vlad looked as stunned as I'd ever seen him. "Extraordinary," he murmured.

Even as he said it, I couldn't help but lick my lips. Vlad's blood had a different flavor, sure, but it was still delicious.

Vlad watched me doing it, and I stopped. Even though I hadn't been aware when I did it, I felt guilty for munching on my friend.

"Sorry," I mumbled.

His lip curled. "Never let it be said that you're predictable, Cat."

I wished I were. First, I'd been a freak as a half-breed, now I was an even bigger one as a vampire.

And now my mother was a vampire, too. My mother, who'd hated vampires ever since she first found out about them. My mother, who'd begged me to kill her last night.

"You might want to rethink your friendship with me, Vlad, because I'm getting my mother back even if I have to break every vampire law to do it."

Vlad's coppery green gaze was steady. "I wouldn't expect any less from you."

I didn't reply to that, just glanced out the window. The sun was halfway up in the sky. It must be around noon. I'd been unconscious for hours. All vampire laws aside, how I'd make good on my promise to rescue my mother, considering that dawn stole all the strength from me, was the real question. Not to mention I didn't know where the hell Gregor had my mother hidden away. She could be anywhere by now.

"Cat." I looked up to find Vlad still staring at me. "I can't help you with this, you know that."

A small, sad smile twisted my lips. "Yeah, I know." I understood, but oh, I would have liked Vlad as backup.

"Gregor's greatest weakness is his pride," Vlad stated. "Use it against him. He'll fall for it every time."

I felt Bones minutes before I heard the car. Since he'd changed me, I was attuned to him in a way that defied logic. Even now, I could sense his impatience, like sandpaper grating across my subconscious.

I was already out of the car by the time the black Mercedes pulled up next to Vlad. Bones got out, yanking me to him before I could speak. He gave me a hard kiss that would have stolen my breath if I still had any. Then he set me back, tracing my mouth while his eyes turned green.

I knew he could taste Vlad's blood on me. Part of me wanted to apologize while the other argued that out of all people, Bones would understand.

"Bones," I began.

"Don't fret about it," he said, brushing my mouth again. "Let's go. Tepesh." Bones gave Vlad a short nod. "Until the next time."

Vlad leaned against his car with his usual jaded half smile.

"Somehow I think that might be sooner rather than later."

Thirty-one

I WAS SURPRISED TO HEAR THAT ONLY THREE people had been killed last night. Since it was a formal gathering under an all-truce, most of the guests had been unarmed. The three who'd been killed were humans, who couldn't survive a weaponless undead free-for-all the way vampires and ghouls could. As far as the ramifications of breaking an all-truce, no one knew—or would say—who'd started the violence. Mencheres and Bones managed to get people calm enough to leave without wars being declared. Gregor left with my mother and Cannelle in tow. As for how Apollyon and his ghouls would deal with my unprecedented vampiric heartbeat . . . time would tell.

I was less worried about that as I was about hatching a plan to rescue my mother. I brooded over ideas the entire drive and train ride to Bucharest. Don and my old team couldn't help. My uncle had international connections, true, but not of the undead variety. He'd be as out of depth in this scenario as I was. I also stalled calling him because I didn't want to start the whole, "So, I'm a vampire now," conversation. Overcoming my uncle's long-held prejudices was the last thing on my To Do list at the moment.

We arrived at our destination, a mansion that looked straight out of a horror novel, after 3:00 A.M. With dawn in just a few hours, I'd be comatose again soon. Losing morning time was something I'd thought I'd prepped myself for before changing into a vampire, but I hadn't figured on how dire the circumstances would be when it happened. Now every minute I was passed out seemed like a taunt. What was Gregor doing to my mother? God, what was Cannelle doing to her? I'd thought the worst thing Gregor could do was kill my mom. I should have known he wouldn't be that merciful.

Rodney came out to meet us. The ghoul had the same smoldering-furious look in his eyes that I probably did. On impulse, I hugged him, feeling a lump in my throat when he squeezed me back, hard. Bones would walk through fire to get my mom back, if that's what it took, but he'd do it out of love for me. Not out of any affection for her. My mother didn't have many fans, which was her own fault; but right now, it meant more to me than I could articulate to know someone cared for *her*, flaws and all.

"She's tough," Rodney said. His beard rasped my cheek as he leaned back. "If we can get her back, she'll make it. Doesn't matter what she is now or what he's done to her."

"She wanted me to kill her," I whispered. "God, Rodney, she always said she'd rather be dead than be a vampire."

"She'll make it," he repeated. His voice hardened. "You had it hard growing up, but so did she. Justina's shocked and scared now, but she's not a quitter. I'd bet my life on it."

"Rodney, the laws," Bones began.

"Save it." The ghoul let go of me to stare at Bones. "If you don't manage to kill Gregor soon, I'm going after her, laws or no laws—and backup or no backup."

"Don't be a fool, that would be suicide," Bones snapped.

Rodney gave him a cold smile. "You always said no one lives forever."

I was torn between wanting to hug Rodney again and knowing Bones was right. "She'll need you when we get her back," I said, choosing logic for once. "My mother and I, you know we clash. You're the only one she seems to listen to, but you can't help her cope with being a vampire if you're dead."

Rodney flicked his gaze to me, then walked back into the house without another word. I had no idea if that meant he'd wait, or if that was his way of saying he wouldn't.

"This won't last long, Kitten," Bones said, breaking the loaded quiet. "Gregor's run out of tricks. He'll be forced to seek me out soon, because each day he doesn't, people will question why Gregor refuses to face the man who stole his wife and who's daring him to a duel over her."

That snapped my attention away from my mother. "When did you dare him to duel?"

Bones's gaze was dark and steady. "I publicly challenged Gregor as soon as Mencheres told me he was invading your dreams."

I'd known Bones had planned to fight Gregor in New Orleans, but I hadn't known a standing challenge had been thrown down. The realization that at any time

Gregor could accept it, resulting in a fight to the death between him and Bones, filled me with icy fear.

"He's stronger than you are." My voice was barely above a whisper.

Bones snorted. "I know that, luv, but he won't be the first bloke I've shriveled who exceeded me in power. All I need is one mistake from Gregor, and he's mine."

I didn't say aloud the thing that made my heart ache with dread.

But what if Gregor doesn't make a mistake?

Two days passed with no word from Gregor. Rodney and I took turns wearing holes in the carpet pacing. Bones kept cautioning patience. If Rodney was anything like me, he loathed that word by now.

One thing the stress seemed to be good for was forcing myself awake and moving after dawn. I could now even walk through the entire morning hours, though it must look like I was doing an impression of a staggering drunk. Aside from stress being a motivator, I also continued to notice that the more I drank from Bones in the morning, the more I could push off the paralyzing effects of the sun breaking the horizon. Maybe good nutrition really was the key to health, for people or vampires.

Today, I'd marked a personal milestone; making it down the three-story winding staircase to the kitchen and back again. It took me two hours, something that in the afternoon, I'd accomplish in seconds, but I was happy with the progress even as I collapsed, exhausted, on the nearest chair.

"Tomorrow, I'm going outside," I said. Direct sunlight would be even harder on me, but I had to get myself up to speed. Fast. As it was, a human could kick my ass from dawn to noon.

"Do you have any idea how remarkable it is that you're even awake?" Bones said, gesturing to Mencheres. "Tell her. I slept from dawn until dusk for the first two months. It was considered admirable progress for me to be about during daylight at all in my third month. This is only your second week, Kitten."

"It's unprecedented," Mencheres agreed.

His tone made me glance up at him. I caught a flicker of something on his face that quickly smoothed into impassiveness. Bones must have caught Mencheres's tone, too, because he arched a brow.

"Is there something else you'd like to add, Grandsire?"

An unfamiliar vampire coming into the kitchen interrupted whatever Mencheres's reply might have been. Must be another of Mencheres's staff, though he bowed to Bones instead of the Egyptian vampire.

"What it is?" Bones asked.

"Pardon me, but there's someone on the phone who says they have a call for you."

My brows went up. So did Bones's. "There's a call to tell me I have a call?" he asked with heavy skepticism.

The vampire looked uneasy as he held out a cell phone. "It's my friend Lachlan. He called me to say he'd been contacted by Chill, a vampire he knows, who was called by Nathan, who's a member of Kyoko's line, who says a vampire named Rollo contacted him because he met a *ghost* who claims to be yours—"

"Fabian!" I exclaimed, just now realizing I hadn't seen him since the fiasco of the party.

Bones took the cell from the vampire and everything changed.

We waited two miles away from the craggy house in Moldova where Gregor had my mother held captive. Rodney crouched to my right, weighted down with multiple wickedly curved silver blades. Bones hunched to my left, his body so still that he might have been carved from stone. I tried to duplicate that same immobility, but I couldn't. My gaze kept flicking around in impatience. *Where was Fabian? He should be back by now.*

Spade crept up from the brush. He'd been making sure no enemy forces were sneaking up behind us while we waited for Fabian's report. At Spade's nod, we were the only ones stalking others in the chilly surrounding countryside. Wind blew Spade's inky hair back from his face as he set his gaze ahead in the same direction Bones stared.

After what seemed like an eternity, a hazy flash appeared in the trees, and we saw Fabian streaking just above the frost-covered ground.

"Gregor isn't here, but from how Cannelle's acting, he'll be back soon," the ghost said when he reached us. "Right now there are about a dozen guards. More will be with Gregor when he returns."

Bones didn't glance away from whatever he'd been looking at in the distance. "Then now is the best time. Fabian, keep a lookout on the road. At the first sign of Gregor or his men, you come warn us."

The ghost nodded, his see-through features taking on a determined expression. "I won't fail you."

For about the dozenth time today, I wished I could hug Fabian. Never did I expect to be so indebted to a ghost, but I owed Fabian more than I could repay. After the disastrous party, Fabian had the presence of mind to follow Gregor, haunting the trunk of whatever vehicle Gregor drove or hitchhiking on various people who happened to be near Gregor. True to undead prejudice, Gregor hadn't seemed to realize he was being spied on, even if he or one of his people might have glimpsed the ghost. Always pride before a fall.

Fabian's hardest task after finding Gregor's hiding place was to contact us and let us know about it. It's not like a phantom could use a phone, e-mail, or pass on a letter. Factor in the same dismissal of ghosts that had made his spying possible, and Fabian had had a hell of a time getting a vampire ally to listen long enough to start the chain of calls that eventually reached Bones.

Until we arrived, we hadn't even been sure that Gregor would still be in this house. It took a full day and a half from the time Fabian left the vicinity to the time Bones was handed that cell phone from the very bewildered member of Mencheres's staff. Then another several hours to get to Moldova, then a couple hours of reconnaissance to determine this wasn't a trap. Not that I doubted Fabian's loyalty, but there was always the chance that Gregor *had* recognized the ghost and put two and two together. So far, though, it seemed like those in the house had no idea they were about to be attacked.

I gave a worried glance at the sky. All that was good news. The bad news was, dawn was only about half an hour away.

As if hearing my thought, Bones met my gaze. "You should stay back, Kitten."

My first instinct was to argue. Vehemently, and with lots of profanity. That was *my mother* trapped in the house, so I damn well wasn't going to sit back and just hope things went okay.

Then I looked around the faces staring back at me. Everyone here was risking their lives on my mother's behalf, plus breaking undead laws on top of that, and I was the only one susceptible to the dawn. Sure, now I could stay awake and even walk when sunlight hit, but fight? No. Not even if my mother's life—or mine—depended on it.

"I'll stay," I said, seeing Bones's brows go up like those were the last words he expected to hear from me. "Give me the detonator. We might need the diversion if Gregor returns before we have my mom safely away."

Spade nodded, handing over the detonator he'd had located in his belt. Several packs of TNT had been strapped to the trees, as close to the house as we dared to plant them without being seen. In a fight, the explosions wouldn't harm any vampires or ghouls, unless they happened to be right next to the trees when the bombs went off, but they would make a hell of racket. And sometimes, distraction made all the difference between life and death—or escape and capture.

Bones gave me a quick, hard kiss. "I won't return without her," he promised.

"Don't say that." The words were out of my mouth at once. "If something happens, if it's too dangerous to get her now, you come back to me. We'll find another way."

Rodney began crawling through the brush. Spade gave me a somber look and followed. Bones caressed my face once, then left as well. So did Fabian. I stayed where I was, not needing binoculars to watch their progress toward the house. There were four guards outside and, according to Fabian, at least eight more inside, plus Cannelle. The element of surprise would be all the advantage they had, outnumbered four to one, and I doubted Gregor had left weak vampires or ghouls as guards.

Even though the distance was less than two miles, it took the three men over ten minutes to crawl there, barely disturbing the long grass around them. I was almost a wreck by the time they approached the house. A jumble of fear, hope, frustration, and nerves made me feel like I could jump out of my own skin. Did the guards have instructions to kill my mother at once if there was an attack? Could Bones, Spade, or Rodney get to her in time, without getting themselves killed in the process? *Oh God, please, let this work.*

I couldn't help it; I began to crawl closer, promising myself to only get within a mile. Just close enough to really see what was going on. The scattering of trees made for a skewed view of the house.

The ground was free of tall grass within thirty yards of the house, so there was no more coverage for Bones, Rodney, and Spade to sneak up in. Everything in me tensed as I saw the three men rise at the exact same time to charge the house.

Shouts of alarms came from the four guards, but I was savagely pleased to see how fast they were cut off. Bones took two down himself, one from a distance by throwing silver into his chest, and the other by an up-close twist of the same metal through the guard's heart. Spade and Rodney made short work of their two guards, then, from different angles, the three men entered the house.

More shouts came from inside. I crawled faster, keeping low but within eyesight of the house. Gunshots barked in terrifying staccato from what sounded like automatic weapons. A feminine voice rose in a furious, accented screech. *Cannelle.* Remembering her kicking my mother while holding a leash made me want Cannelle dead almost as much as Gregor.

I'd made it to the mile mark when Fabian came streaking toward me, waving his ghostly arms.

"Gregor's returned!" he exclaimed.

Oh shit. "Go tell Bones," I said, taking the detonator out of my belt. I eyed the sky with mounting despair. Definitely too close to dawn for me to risk jumping into the fight, but I could still press some buttons. That much I could do to help.

Fabian disappeared through the structure of the house, not bothering to use one of the smashed front windows as an entry point. I waited, counting off the seconds in a frenzy of tension until he came out, hovering near the roof. It looked like he pointed to my left, which was where the screech of tires had come from. Damn Gregor for being a clever bloodsucker. He wasn't going to drive right up to the house and provide an easier target. No, he'd come through the trees and brush to make his own ambush instead.

I waved at Fabian, careful to stay low, and the ghost dove down and seemed to disappear into the ground. He came up moments later right in front of me, startling me at how he was all of a sudden inches from my face.

"Tell me where they are," I whispered.

Fabian disappeared below the dirt again. I waited, the following seconds like a blowtorch on my nerves.

Then Fabian's ghostly head popped up from the dirt like a hazy gopher.

"They're circling around." His voice was so soft, I could hardly hear him. "They're heading this way, but a little farther up than you are."

I smiled grimly. That would put them right near the TNT strapped to the trees. *Come on, Gregor. Show me where you are.*

My wish came true when I heard the stealthy sounds of movement in the brush not fifty yards from me. I waited, counting off the distance. *Twenty yards. Ten. Almost there. Almost . . .*

I blew the charges right as Gregor and his guards passed the closest to the most-heavily-rigged trees. The explosions went off, one after the other, scattering Gregor and the others with their confusion over what might blow up next. It was also my very loud signal to Bones that they had to pull out, now, whether they had my mom or not. With the dozen guards Gregor had with him, it would be dicey making it out alive ourselves. We couldn't afford to wait any longer.

I glanced at the ever-brightening sky with loathing. If only it were an hour earlier, I could fight! I could help get my mother, or draw off some guards, or just *do* something, other than hide to keep a bad situation from getting far worse by being captured.

A window in the house exploded outward, two forms hurtling through it onto the ground. I recognized them and had a second of cold satisfaction when I saw Bones, his arm locked around Cannelle's throat, give a hard twist, jerking Cannelle's head off. *Adieu, bitch,* I thought, seeing him shove her lifeless body aside. But my moment of victory was short-lived. Gregor shouted an order in French and all twelve of his guards rushed at Bones.

I was already on my feet, forgetting about staying hidden, when Spade burst out of the house. He flung silver knives at the undead horde who'd descended on his best friend, drawing their attention to him instead of only on Bones. *Coward*, I thought viciously, seeing Gregor stay where he was near the far corner of the house. *What will you do, Dreamsnatcher? Will you run while you have a chance, or risk your life to stay and fight?*

The front door was kicked open. I gasped, seeing Rodney come out with my mother in his grip. Her arms were around his neck, and she was moving. *She's alive. Oh, thank God.*

Gregor snarled something and drew out a sword. Rodney paused, swinging around with my mother still in his arms. Gregor's sword seemed to flash in the predawn light as he strode toward them.

Bones and Spade were each battling half a dozen vampires apiece. Neither one of them could help Rodney. I ran, pulling knives from my belt while cursing. Gregor was too far away for me to hit him. God, why couldn't I run any faster?

Rodney set my mother down, caressing her blood-stained cheek for just an instant, then turned to meet Gregor. He only had two knives left in his belt, and Gregor was far stronger than he.

"Gregor," I yelled.

That ash-blond head jerked up as he saw me running flat out toward them. "Catherine," I saw more than heard Gregor say.

In that moment of distraction, Rodney flung one of his knives. It hit Gregor in the chest, but from how quickly Gregor pulled it out, I knew it hadn't pierced his heart. Gregor spun back to face Rodney, his sword slicing the air between them.

Instead of ducking back, Rodney charged. He barreled into Gregor with all of his undead force behind him. Gregor staggered, but didn't go down. The knife Rodney rose to slam into Gregor's chest never made it. Gregor grasped Rodney's wrist with his free hand and flipped him brutally to the ground, using Rodney's own momentum against him. That long sword flashed down in a straight, merciless line.

My mother rushed forward. "Rodney, no!" she cried.

Gregor didn't look up. Not until that blade arced its path all the way through Rodney's neck and came up bloody on the other side. Then Gregor looked right at me. And smiled.

I didn't look away from Gregor's emerald gaze. Not when he kicked Rodney's severed head at my mother, or when he started walking toward me with a measured, unhurried stride.

As if in a dream, I stopped running. Dropped my knives and watched Gregor come. I heard Bones's shout, but it seemed to be from far away. A dull booming began in my chest that I recognized as my heart starting up again, but even that didn't matter. All I could focus on was the unadulterated hatred pouring through my veins, surging in ever-increasing waves, until it felt like I'd explode where I stood.

Which was why it didn't seem unusual to me when the grass around me burst into flames. Through the red haze that dropped over my vision, it made perfect sense. The grass shouldn't exist to be able to soak up Rodney's blood. The house Gregor had used to torture and kill my mother in shouldn't exist, either.

In fact, everything here needed to burn. Every. Last. Thing.

Orange-and-red flames raced up the short grass to lick up the sides of the house, tangling out to cover the roof in a writhing carpet of flame. Then the grass around Gregor became an arena of fire, shooting up his legs. Seeing Gregor's legs on fire pleased me, but it wasn't enough. I wanted to see Gregor's skin crackle and split. See everything around him burned into smoldering ash. And I wanted it now.

The trees next to me exploded, but I didn't glance away from Gregor. *Burn. Burn.* It was all my mind was capable of thinking. Nothing seemed real anymore. Not my mother crying over Rodney's body in great, wracking sobs, or Gregor screaming as flames covered his entire body.

"Catherine, stop!" Gregor yelled.

A part of me was bemused. Why did Gregor think I was responsible for this lovely fire? Spade must have set some new explosives on his way in. Or Bones had. I should get my mother away from here, now that Gregor was occupied with being on fire. But I couldn't make myself move. Those hot, glorious waves of rage pulsing through me had me rooted to the spot. *Burn. Burn.*

"Kitten!"

Bones's voice broke my trance. I looked at him, surprised that he seemed to be colored red and blue. So was everything else. Bones ripped his blade through the vampire in front of him and threw him to the side. With nothing obstructing my view of him, I saw his face tighten with shock.

His gaze was fixed by my waist. I glanced down—and gasped. My arms were blue from the elbow down, covered in pulsating flames that I somehow couldn't even feel. Orange and scarlet shot out of my hands, scorching everything in my path from my feet all the way to the roof of the house.

Bones ran to me, yanking me against him, ignoring the flames that continued to sprout from me.

"Charles, take Justina!" he shouted, then my feet abruptly left the ground. Through the red/blue haze of my vision, I watched Spade snatch my mother and shoot into the air. Gregor and the house still burned below us, but even now, I saw Gregor rolling on the nonburning part of the earth, dousing the old flames fast enough to keep the new ones from consuming him.

Murderer, I thought, that savageness rising in me again. Red smothered my gaze, and Gregor screamed, rolling faster as more flames erupted on him.

Clouds shifted, allowing a beam of sunlight to sear across my face. It hit me like a roundhouse kick to the head, clearing some of the red from my vision. And at the same instant, Bones sank his fangs into my neck, sucking hard.

The last thing I saw was the blazing colors of the dawn, looking like the flames still burning below us on the ground.

Thirty-two

BARE CONCRETE WALLS MET MY VISION WHEN my eyes opened, then a dark head bent over mine.

"All right, Kitten?"

Bones's face, streaked with soot. A heavy scent of smoke hung in the room, in fact. Immediately, I looked at my hands. They rested over my stomach, pale and innocent. *Maybe I'd imagined what happened.*

I sat up so fast, my head banged into Bones's. Mencheres stood a few feet away in the small room that I recognized as a vampire holding cell.

"Easy, luv," Bones said, smoothing his hands down my arms.

I hoped I'd passed out after setting off those detonations and everything after it had been a terrible dream. "My mother? Rodney?"

"She's safe. He's gone." Bones's voice was a rasp.

Rodney's death had been real, which meant the fire was real, too. *The fire. Coming from me.*

I didn't want to believe it, but I remembered—oh, I

remembered!—the exhilaration of letting all my hate and anger surge out of me, then watching it somehow transform into the form of fire.

"I'm pyrokinetic."

I said it out loud, watching Bones's face, hoping somehow, he'd offer another explanation for what had happened. He didn't.

"It seems so."

"But how?" I asked, swinging my legs off the cot only to have them flop like limp rags. There went my idea of pacing. My whole body felt exhausted. "You told me a vampire's individual powers don't emerge for decades—and I thought they were directly related to their sire's powers, too. But you're not a pyro, Bones, unless you've been hiding something from me."

"I haven't been hiding anything from you, and even if your human years were added to the equation, I've never seen a vampire, Master or otherwise, manifest powers like you did so soon after changing."

Bones sounded frustrated. I shot a glance over to Mencheres, meeting the other vampire's cool, charcoal gaze. There was no surprise or confusion in Mencheres's eyes—and all of a sudden, I knew why.

"You bastard," I whispered.

At first Bones thought I'd been talking to him, but then he followed my gaze to the dark-haired vampire, who hadn't spoken.

"He's known all along." My voice started to rise, as did my anger. "He knew Gregor didn't see me in a vision and decide he had to have me because I was a half-breed, or because he was in love with me. He knew Gregor saw me as a *vampire*, lighting things up around me like a Roman candle. *That's* why Gregor's wanted me, so he could control the power through me. But that's what Mencheres wanted, too. That's the other reason why Mencheres took me from Gregor and locked him up all these years. He wanted my power on *his* side. That's what *all* of this has been about!"

Bones didn't ask Mencheres if it was true. His brown eyes turned green as he stared at the man he'd known for over 220 years.

"I should kill you for this." It was almost a growl.

Nothing changed in Mencheres's expression. Glass was more emotive. "Perhaps you will. My visions of the future only went up to this morning, so I assume I'll be dead soon. Now that you're co-ruler of my line, and Cat is as she's meant to be, my people will be protected when I'm gone."

His impenetrable mask dropped, leaving defiance and resolve flowing over Mencheres's features.

"Yes, I took Cat from Gregor twelve years ago in order to have her power for my people instead of his. More than that, it was I who gave you the tip that sent you to that bar in Ohio the night you first met her, Bones. Do you find that too manipulative? I don't. Thousands of people in my line rely on me to protect them, which has to mean more to me than your feeling of betrayal right now. If you survive as long as I have, you'll learn that being cold and manipulative is necessary, even with those you love."

Bones snorted in a manner as bitter as I felt. "You claim to love me? It's obvious I am nothing more than a pawn to you."

Mencheres's dark gaze didn't waver. "I've always loved you. Like a son, in fact."

Bones walked over to Mencheres. He was still wearing the same outfit from earlier, making Bones covered in blood, soot, and dirt . . . and a few remaining silver knives.

Mencheres didn't move or blink, nor did a hint of his tremendous power leak out, even when Bones pulled out a knife.

"Are you so certain of yourself?" Bones said, tracing the tip of the knife on Mencheres's chest. "So convinced you could stop me, before I twisted this blade through your heart?"

I wanted to jump up and stand between them. Not out of concern for Mencheres, but because if Bones attacked and Mencheres decided to defend himself, that knife might end up in Bones's heart. But my legs still wouldn't work.

"I could stop you, but I won't." Mencheres's voice was very weary. "If you must do this to avenge what I did, then do it. I've already lived more than long enough as it is."

"Bones," I whispered, not really knowing if I was urging him to drop the knife—or use it.

Bones's hand tightened on the knife. Mencheres still didn't move. I waited, feeling like I was holding my breath even though I didn't breathe anymore.

His hand flashed and the knife buried back in its slot on his belt. "I deserved death from you once, Mencheres, yet you let me live. Now I'm letting you live, so we're squared. But lie to me, or use me or her again, and that will change."

Bones stepped back. I thought Mencheres sagged a little, in relief or in surprise, I wasn't sure. Then Bones sat next to me, placing a hand on my still-useless leg.

"No more secrets. How does she have this power? She's too young, and she didn't inherit it from me, so how is it possible?"

Mencheres ran a hand through his long dark hair before answering. "Vampires drink human blood to absorb the life from mortals that vampires no longer have. She doesn't drink mortal blood, however, because she isn't really dead."

My mouth dropped. Bones didn't react. "Go on."

"Her heart beats when her emotions run high," Mencheres continued. "Proof that life still clings in her. Because of this life, her body rejects human blood, since she doesn't need the life in it. But what her body does need to exist is power. Just as a dying human absorbs the power in vampire blood to change over, she, being perpetually near death, absorbs undead power every time she feeds from other vampires."

But I'd only fed from Bones—no, wait. *Vlad.*

I'd fed from Vlad, and he was pyrokinetic. Was it truly possible I'd absorbed Vlad's power over fire from drinking his blood? It had to be. Nothing else could explain the fireworks shooting from my hands, and I'd already noticed that every time I fed from Bones, I grew stronger. Far stronger than any new vampire should be.

I gulped. "Does Gregor know how I have this power?"

"Gregor's visions aren't as strong or as frequent as mine. All he saw was your power. He didn't know its source. He probably thought you needed time to grow into it, or he would have changed you into a vampire at sixteen."

Knowing Gregor, I believed that. It also explained why Gregor hadn't been afraid of me using any of these borrowed abilities on him before. He didn't think I'd get them so soon.

"Are these powers permanent? Or will they, you

know, fade, if I don't drink from vampires with special gifts anymore?"

Mencheres glanced away. "I don't know," he said. "I told you; I can't see the future anymore. About you . . . or anyone else."

Since there was nothing more that could be done about my "condition," as I thought of it, I went to see my mother. She'd been through worse than hell in the past two weeks. In order to get over my body's refusal to move, however, I drank from Bones, noting with a sense of unease how quickly it made me feel better. I'd been so proud of my progress, but turns out, none of my progress had really been mine. I'd gone from being a half-breed to being a mostly dead power leech. I felt like a fraud as a vampire, or more accurately, an even bigger freak.

When we didn't go upstairs to see my mother, but continued down a narrow hall under the basement, I was surprised to discover she was in the equivalent of a vampire holding cell.

"Why?" I asked. "Isn't she over her bloodlust for humans yet?"

"It's for her protection," Bones replied in a clipped tone. "She's tried to harm herself. Repeatedly."

Oh no. I tried to brace myself as Bones nodded to the guard outside a steel door, and we were let in.

My mother sat in the corner of the small room. From the looks of her, she hadn't showered or changed clothes, either. Her long brown hair was streaked with blood and dirt, as was the rest of her. She didn't even glance up to see who'd entered the room.

"Mom," I said softly. "It's Catherine."

That picked her head up. I gasped to see brightly

glowing green eyes fixed on me and the hint of fangs under her lip as she spoke.

"If you ever loved me, tell me you're here to kill me, because I *cannot* live like this."

My hands fisted while pain seared its way into my heart. "I'm so sorry for what happened," I began, never feeling more helpless, "but you can—"

"Can what?" her voice lashed out. "Live as a murderer? I killed people, Catherine! I ripped into their throats and *murdered* them while they fought to get away. I can't live with that!"

It was only my rage that kept me from bursting into tears. That bastard Gregor put people in with my mother after he'd changed her, knowing what would happen. No new vampire could keep from drinking someone to death while in the first craze of blood hunger. If Bones hadn't already been dead, I'd have killed him myself several times over when caught in the grips of my own hunger.

"It wasn't your fault," I tried desperately.

She looked away in disgust. "You don't understand."

"I do."

Bones's measured tone made my mother look up. "I understand exactly," he went on. "Ian changed me against my will, drinking me to death while I tried to fight him off. Then I awoke in a burial ground with a young man in my arms, the poor lad's throat chewed open and the most wonderful taste in my mouth. That happened six more times until I controlled my hunger enough not to kill, and believe me, Justina, I hated myself more each time. Yet I survived, and you will, too."

"I don't want to survive," she shot back, standing now. "It's *my* choice, and I refuse to live this way!"

"Rodney believed in you." My voice choked at the memory of my lost friend. "He said if we could get you back, you'd make it. No matter what had happened to you."

"Rodney's *dead*," she replied, pink tears glittering in her eyes.

Before I could blink, Bones hauled my mother up by her shirt, her feet dangling several inches off the ground.

"Rodney was six years old when I found him, orphaned and starving in the streets of Poland. I raised him, loved him, then helped turn him into a ghoul— all a century before you were even born. He died saving you, so you will *not* disrespect his sacrifice by killing yourself. I don't care if you hate what you are every bloody day for the rest of your life, you're going to live because Rodney's earned that. Do you understand me?"

Bones gave her a shake, then dropped her. She staggered as she fell, but I couldn't bring myself to reprimand Bones. The pain in his voice had been too raw, too deep.

The door opened, and Spade came in. He looked as haggard as I felt, his normally teasing tiger-colored gaze bleak and hard.

"Gregor's alive, and he's decided to accept your challenge. He'll be here tomorrow night."

I closed my eyes for a moment. *Why now? Why so soon after this last devastating blow?*

Of course, that was probably why Gregor had done it, hoping to capitalize on Bones's grief over losing his friend. Or maybe Gregor's ego couldn't stand the fact that soon, everyone would know Bones had snatched my mother out from under him in addition to keeping his wife. *Gregor's greatest weakness is his pride*, Vlad had said. Maybe Gregor's pride couldn't handle the repeated blows it had been dealt.

"Tomorrow, then," Bones agreed.

"What's the challenge?" my mother asked.

"A fight to the death," Bones replied shortly.

My mother was still sprawled on the floor, but a different look grew in her glowing, pink-tinged eyes. Anger replaced her previous self-loathing and despair.

"Kill Gregor. If you do, I'll live like this no matter how much I hate it," she growled.

"I'll kill him," Bones replied in that same unflinching tone.

A spasm of fear gripped me. Tomorrow night, either Bones would make good on that vow—or he'd be dead.

Thirty-three

Bones stood in front of me, wearing nothing but a pair of loose-fitting black pants. I tried to choke back my panic, but no matter how bland I kept my expression, the sickly-sour scent permeating from me gave me away.

He squeezed my hands. His were warm from his recent meal. Mine were icy by comparison.

"Maybe I could have burned Gregor to death yesterday, given time," I said, hating what was coming next. "Why did you bite me when you flew us away? You might not have needed to do this if you hadn't sucked so much blood out of me."

A bark of wry laughter came from Bones. "Indeed, but not how you're thinking. You were burning me as I held you, Kitten. It was either let you fry me, or bite you and hope that draining you combined with the power of the sun doused your flames, or drop you. Still critiquing my choice?"

I'd burned *Bones*, too?

"I hope this power goes away," I said, meaning it.

He shrugged. "It might. Vampires only sustain power from human blood for a few days until we need to feed again to replenish our strength. The same dwindling-down effect could hold true for you, and I don't fancy you biting Tepesh again to refresh your fire abilities."

"Never again," I agreed, shuddering at the thought of burning Bones. Who would want power like that if you couldn't control it, and it hurt those you loved?

Spade entered without knocking. "It's time," he said. His face was tight and emotionless, even though I knew he was as wound up as I was.

Bones's dark brown gaze met mine. He smiled, but I couldn't return it if my life depended on it. His power brushed over me like a caress. I could feel it smoothing back my fear, entwining into my subconscious, linking us tighter together.

"Don't fret, luv," he said softly. "Soon this will be over, and Gregor will be dead."

I nodded, not trusting myself to speak. Oh God, if I could trade places with Bones, I would. In a second.

"I'd ask you to stay here," Bones went on, "but I suspect you'd refuse."

I couldn't contain my snort. "As you would say, *right you are.*" I couldn't hide in a room while Bones fought Gregor in a death match, no matter what. "But don't concern yourself with me. You focus on him. I'll be fine."

"Oh, he'll have all my attention, Kitten," Bones said in a grim tone. "Count on that."

I wanted to tell Bones he didn't have to do this, that we could find another way, but I knew how useless that would be. No matter what, Bones wouldn't walk away from this fight, even if Gregor all of a sudden promised to let us alone and my mother decided she was thrilled to be a vampire. Gregor had murdered Rodney. Bones was fighting Gregor for more reasons than me.

Mencheres appeared in the doorway, Ian behind him. I looked at the two vampires, one dark-haired and exotic, the other russet-haired and classically handsome. Both men were responsible for Bones's existence, since Mencheres turned Ian into a vampire, then Ian changed Bones. So many events had led up to this moment.

Bones leaned down, kissing me with the lightest brush of his lips. I traced my fingers over his jaw when he lifted his head, fighting the urge to grab him and refuse to let go.

The harsh scent of my desperation floated around me. Bones held my shoulders, squeezing gently.

"This isn't the first time I've faced death, Kitten, and I don't intend it to be the last. I've chosen to live a very dangerous life, but this is who I am. It's who you are, too, and the same would be true even if we'd never met."

I knew what he was really saying. *If I die, it won't be your fault.* Yes, it was true that Bones and I both would have lived equally dangerous lives even if we'd never met, but the bottom line was that if he died today, it *would* be my fault.

"I love you."

It was all I could say right now. Anything else would just upset him and he needed to be focused in order to beat Gregor.

"I know you do," he whispered. "And I love you. Always."

Then he turned before I could even blink and walked out the door.

It had been decided the duel would take place on Mencheres's back lawn. It was certainly big enough, with its acres of land bordered by high trees. An area the size of a baseball diamond had been cleared of everything but dirt, as the place where Bones and Gregor would square off. I didn't know why so much space was required, but then again, it was my first experience with this sort of thing—and hopefully, my last.

Gregor was already there, standing next to his blond servant, Lucius. I was surprised Lucius was alive since I'd assumed he'd been one of the vampires Bones, Spade, or Rodney had killed inside the house. Lucius's absence yesterday was odd, since every other time I'd seen Gregor, Lucius had been with him. Still, I had bigger concerns aside from wondering why Lucius hadn't been at Gregor's side during the previous ambush.

Gregor and Lucius weren't the only new arrivals at the house. Having a formal duel was apparently an event. There were several Master vampires I didn't recognize. Gregor's allies, Mencheres told me, plus several more members of Bones's line, along with four vampires who were introduced as Law Guardians.

Out of those four, the tall blond female crackled with enough power to make me uneasy. While she looked only eighteen, she felt about five thousand years old, and the three other male Law Guardians with her were mega-Masters as well. Bones, Spade, and I had all broken the law in taking my mother from Gregor. So had Rodney, of course, but he was past any undead judgment. Maybe the rest of us still had penalties coming.

Speaking of my mother, she was present as well. I'd thought she would avoid getting anywhere near Gregor, but she stood on the far edge of the lawn, watching Gregor with her eyes lit up like streetlights. Anyone within a thirty-foot range of her could smell the rage and hatred pouring off her. I didn't even want to imagine what else might have happened to my mother during the time Gregor had her. It filled me with enough fury for me to worry about my hands sparking again.

Bones had avoided me since leaving the room twenty minutes ago. I understood why; he was clearing his mind of everything but the imminent fight. Somehow, he'd even barricaded himself from the connection I'd felt between us ever since I woke up as a vampire. I couldn't sense anything from him now. It was as if a wall had replaced the rub of him inside my subconscious. I felt bereft, like I'd lost a limb. Many times, I'd heard Bones speak of the connection vampires felt to their sires. Only now that it was gone did I truly understand how deep it ran.

Bones was on the perimeter of the battlefield, talking to Spade. I couldn't hear them, either from the background noise of everyone else or because he was keeping his voice too low.

Moonlight glinted off Bones's pale, beautiful skin, and his dark hair appeared highlighted under those alabaster rays. I couldn't stop staring at him, my anxiety mounting as the time ticked ever closer. *Bones couldn't die tonight. He just couldn't.* Fate couldn't be so cruel as to let Gregor win after every awful thing he'd done, right?

I hoped not.

Across the cold red earth, I saw a familiar dark head part through the waiting onlookers. Vlad.

He glanced at me, but then kept walking in the opposite direction. My brows rose when Bones waved him over, the two Law Guardians around Bones stepping back to let Vlad through. Vlad's hair obscured his face as he leaned in, listening to whatever Bones said. I couldn't tell anything from Spade's closed expression, and I couldn't hear a word. Frustrated, I could only watch as Vlad replied, also inaudible, and Bones nodded once. Then Vlad walked away, headed this time in my direction.

"What did he say?" were my first words when he reached me.

Vlad shrugged. "What you might expect him to say."

Ice crept along my spine. Knowing Bones, he would have asked Vlad to look after me if Gregor killed him. Even though he disliked Vlad, that's exactly the sort of thing Bones would do. Was he just being cautious, or did he know there was no way he could beat Gregor? God, had Bones gone into this knowing he'd die but refusing to back down regardless?

I was about to run over to Bones and beg that we call the whole thing off when the tall blond Law Guardian strode into the center of the clearing. "The duel will now begin. As agreed beforehand, it will not end until one of the combatants is dead. Anyone who interferes forfeits their life."

Mencheres gripped my hand. "It's too late to stop it," he said softly, as if he'd guessed what I'd been about to do. "If you interfere now, you die."

I swallowed out of habit, but my mouth was utterly

dry. Vlad put a hand on my shoulder as Bones strode out into the clearing, Spade following him. Gregor did as well, Lucius at his side. I didn't understand until Spade and Lucius handed over a knife to their friends, then backed away to the edge of the irregular circle. *Weapon-bearers*, I realized. Both Spade and Lucius each had carried only three knives, and now they'd given up one of them. When those weapons ran out, there would be no more.

I gulped again.

The Law Guardian left the clearing as well. Only Gregor and Bones stood in it now, facing each other with just a dozen feet between them. Their eyes were green and their fangs extended, power uncurling from them until the air felt charged and heavy. I was tense enough to shatter when the female Law Guardian said, "Begin."

Bones and Gregor flew at each other with a blur of speed, crashing together several feet off the ground. For a second, I couldn't make out who was who in the mad whirl of pale flesh, since Gregor was also shirtless. Then they broke apart, both of them with healing red slashes on their bodies.

I gripped Mencheres's hand despite my anger with him, feeling his answering tight squeeze. In my peripheral vision I saw Annette standing close to Ian, her face white. Ian also looked grim. Another spasm of fear welled up in me. Did they believe this would end in Bones's death? Had everyone known that but me?

Gregor and Bones met together again in a frenzy of violence. This time, I could see silver cutting into flesh, flashing in the moonlight before coming up red as they hacked at each other. Neither of them made a sound, though. No one watching did, either. The silence was somehow more loaded than screams.

Bones rolled away from a downward swipe toward his heart, pushing back from Gregor and coming up dirt-smeared a few feet away. He flung his knife in the next instant, burying it to the hilt in Gregor's sternum—but not before Gregor fired off his own blade, which landed right in Bones's eye.

I choked back my scream, afraid the smallest sound would prove lethally distracting to Bones. He yanked the blade out without pause, countering Gregor's attack as Gregor freed the knife from his chest and came at him with incredible speed. If I hadn't been a vampire, I would have hurled at the sticky red substance on Bones's knife, but he never paused as he fought Gregor while his missing eye slowly grew back.

Gregor feinted left, then dove low, sliding under Bones and coming up on the other side so fast, I hadn't realized what he'd done until I saw Bones arch in pain, the hilt of a knife buried high in his back. Gregor barked out a command to Lucius, catching the silver knife Lucius threw and then charging at Bones as Bones tried to reach the knife in his back. He couldn't do that and hold off Gregor's fresh attack, though.

Gregor increased his speed, somehow seeming to have four arms instead of two as he slashed at Bones, opening up new cuts on Bones's body even as Bones kept that glinting silver knife out of his chest. *Gregor had been holding back before*, I realized, horror and panic welling up in me. He was even faster than he'd first appeared.

Bones was forced back, that other knife still protruding from between his shoulder blades, as Gregor pressed his attack. The only sounds were silver clashing with silver, or the sickening slices of flesh and bone being split apart—until the slow, dull boom began in my chest.

Mencheres squeezed my hand so hard, it was painful, but I couldn't stop the beat of my heart. Each new blow or slash, each new glittering smear of crimson, seemed to add speed to the tempo in my chest. Murmurs broke out in the crowd, mostly from the newcomers, as the cadence inside me became steadier and more audible.

Gregor flicked his gaze to me—and Bones flung himself forward, bashing his skull into Gregor's and ripping his knife into Gregor with a brutal upward swipe that cleaved his ribs. Gregor howled but jerked back fast enough to prevent the blade from climbing higher into his chest. He swept Bones's feet out from under him, leaping on top of him without regard for how it forced the knife buried in his rib cage deeper still.

I didn't understand why until Bones let out a gasp, his face twisting with agony. *The knife in his back.* Their combined weight had thrust it all the way through, its silver tip poking out of the front of Bones's chest, dangerously near his heart. When Bones bucked up, throwing Gregor off, and spun around to meet his next attack, I saw that the end of the hilt was level with his back. *He'll never be able to pull it out now,* I thought, the booming in my chest becoming stronger. *How could Bones beat Gregor with silver burning him up inside? When each thrust and blow forced the knife ever closer to his heart?*

But Bones continued to fight with a speed and ferocity that defied his condition. He forced Gregor back, tripping him with a move too quick to follow, and slashed his knife deep across Gregor's eyes when the other vampire moved to protect his heart. Bones leapt off Gregor in the next instant, avoiding the knife Gregor tried to ram into his back, and kicked dirt into Gregor's face, further blinding him. When Gregor's arm came up to defend himself, Bones hacked through it with a force that left half the limb severed on the dirt.

I yanked free of Mencheres's grip to clasp my hands together in fervent prayer that this would be it for Gregor. But he avoided the next downward swipe of Bones's blade to leap straight up into the air, calling out to Lucius for the third and final knife. Gregor's eyes must have healed enough to see the flash of silver against the night sky as Lucius threw the blade, high enough that Gregor had to reach to catch it.

Bones met him in the air just as Gregor grabbed his blade. The knife Bones had aimed for Gregor's chest drove into his stomach instead as Gregor's downward blow blocked him. Bones ripped his knife sideways, spilling red gore over himself. The two of them tumbled to the ground, Bones twisting to land on his feet, Gregor falling in a heap, clutching the wide wound in his gut.

When Bones charged at Gregor, and the Dreamsnatcher did nothing to protect himself, I felt a moment of triumphant exhilaration. But even as Bones's knife descended on Gregor's unprotected back, right where his heart would be, Gregor's fist shot forward, the knife it gripped stabbing Bones deeply in the stomach.

Pain blasted across my subconscious as the wall

Bones had erected between us fell and his emotions came roaring through. I felt the agony of the silver inside his back and his gut. The latter wound burned much hotter, making me clutch my stomach in instinctive reaction. If this was only a shadow of what Bones was feeling, then the pain must be boiling like acid all through him.

Bones's blade wavered and skidded across Gregor's back instead of burying into his opponent's heart. I watched, appalled, as Bones staggered backward, his hand going to the knife still buried in his stomach. He pulled it out even as Gregor rose to his feet, his arm and the previously disabling slash in his gut healed. Bones continued to back away, his steps wavering. I couldn't hold back my scream as Gregor yanked the knife out of Bones's hand and kicked him hard enough to leave Bones sprawled onto his back.

Rage and anguish washed over me, so tightly interwoven into my emotions that I didn't know if it was mine or Bones's. Even though the silver knife was out of his stomach, his pain there didn't lessen. Unbelievably, I felt it grow with crippling intensity, smashing over me in waves, until only Vlad's arm around my shoulders kept me upright.

Something was wrong. It shouldn't be getting worse; the silver was out. Why couldn't he move? *Get up*, I screamed silently. *Get up!*

Boom. Boom. My heart thundered in my chest as Gregor pounced on top of Bones, who was weaponless. Dimly I heard Annette sob, felt Vlad's hand tighten on my shoulder, but everything else seemed to fade away except the two figures against the dark clay of the earth.

As if in slow motion, I watched Gregor raise the

knife. Saw his knees slam into Bones's arms, holding him down as Bones tried to throw Gregor off. Watched the knife begin its descent toward that blood-smeared chest directly underneath it. Felt Bones's despair, bitter as poison. Saw Gregor's glowing emerald gaze flick through the crowd until he found me. And then Gregor smiled.

It was the same smile he'd given me right after killing Rodney. Satisfied. Triumphant. Merciless. Gregor's blade touched Bones's chest, slicing into his skin, and his smile widened.

My vision went red and a single thought permeated through my whole body: *No.*

Flames shot up Gregor, so fast they covered him before the smile had time to leave his face. I had an instant to smile back—and then Gregor's head exploded. His hands still gripped the knife in Bones's chest, but then his body pitched to the side, nothing but flames left where his head had been.

Next to me, Vlad let out a shocked curse. That's when I became aware that every eye was on me and my hands were engulfed in blue fire.

"She dies," the female Law Guardian said.

†hir†y-four

No one tried to stop the three male Guardians when they strode forward and seized me. To tell the truth, I didn't try to stop them, either. I was too focused on trying to see Bones, now that there were people blocking my view of the clearing. He hadn't moved since the last glimpse I'd had of him. Had Gregor's knife been stopped in time? Or had it bitten too deep?

"Cat, what have you done?" Vlad rasped. He couldn't stop staring at my hands. The flames were dying down, which I supposed the Guardian's appreciated since they held me by the arms.

"Is Bones okay?" I asked, ignoring that. A weird sort of peace settled over me. I hadn't consciously meant to send that deadly fireball at Gregor's head, but I didn't regret it. Even if I hadn't saved Bones in time, this way, it wouldn't be long until I joined him, and killing Gregor meant freedom for my mother. There were far less valuable things to die for.

Mencheres looked as stunned as Vlad did. He really must have lost his visions of the future since his expression said he'd never imagined things would turn out this way.

My mother pushed her way through the people. Her gaze was still lit up with green, and she punched the first Guardian she came into contact with.

"Get your hands off my daughter!" she shouted.

"Vlad," I said, "please . . ."

His face closed off, and he nodded once. Then he grabbed my mother, holding her against his chest in a grip she'd never be able to break. I gave him a grateful smile, knowing he'd agreed to protect her for more than just that moment.

"You're a good friend," I said.

That was all I got out. One of the Guardians closed his arm across my throat, choking off my attempted goodbye to my mother, and I was dragged out into the clearing. The blond female Guardian was already in the middle, a long silver knife in her hand.

Quick with carrying out the punishments, aren't they? I thought, mustering up my courage. I couldn't bring myself to look at where people were gathered around Bones. If he was alive, I didn't want him to see this. I was hoping the Guardians would be *really* quick and it would be over before Bones even realized what was happening.

"*Stop.*"

I recognized Bones's ragged voice, and my heart leapt. He *was* alive. *Please let this be quick, and oh God, don't let him watch.*

"She's broken the law," the blond Guardian snapped. She grabbed me, yanking my head back even as Bones staggered into view.

I met his gaze, trying to tell him in that brief instant that I loved him, and I wasn't afraid, when his next words made the Guardian pause.

"Gregor cheated."

The Guardian let me go so abruptly that I fell. Bones didn't glance at me again. All his attention was on the female who marched over to him.

"If you're lying, you'll join her in death," she bit out.

Bones pointed at his stomach, where an odd dark swirl was visible in his flesh even under the smears of blood.

"Liquid silver," Bones said. He held out Gregor's knife. "Somewhere in this is an injection device. Gregor poisoned me with that last stab, so I'd be slower and weaker while fighting him. Probably reckoned no one would know what he did once I was shriveled."

So that explained the agony I'd felt from Bones—it had been silver spreading through his veins from that single, treacherous stab. I knew the pain had been too debilitating to be caused by a normal wound. How like Gregor to cheat in such a foul way, once he'd realized he couldn't beat Bones in a fair fight.

The Guardian took the knife, looking it over carefully. She squeezed it from every angle, and when her thumb pressed the very tip of the hilt, a gleaming liquid slid along the blade.

"Clever," she murmured. Then her gaze hardened as she looked at me. "She had no way of knowing about this. Thus her punishment is the same for interfering."

"I knew."

The Guardian's head swiveled toward me.

"I felt the silver burning up Bones inside," I continued. "We're connected, since he's my sire as well as my husband. That's how I knew."

Lucius strode up to me. "He's not your husband, Gregor is!"

Bones arched a brow in the direction of Gregor's body. "She's only got one husband now, doesn't she?"

From the expression on the Law Guardian's face, my explanation wasn't good enough. I stiffened. It was one thing to die to save Bones, but if there was a chance to live . . .

"Plus, Gregor had shown me a similar knife when I was a teenager," I added. "It was so long ago, I'd forgotten about it. But when Bones acted so strangely after being stabbed, and I could feel his pain spreading even after the knife was taken out— "

"Liar," Lucius shouted. "Gregor never had a knife like that until I picked it up for him yesterday!"

The Guardian's eyes settled on him. Too late, Lucius realized what he'd done.

"You were part of his cheating," she stated. "Take him."

Two of the male Guardians caught Lucius as he tried to run. From how strong they were, I knew Lucius didn't have a chance of escaping. Then again, neither might I.

The Guardian's knowing green eyes landed on me next, suspicion plain in her gaze. "You swear by your blood that you only interfered in the duel when you realized Gregor had cheated?"

"Yes."

After all, it was mostly true. I'd known something was wrong; I just hadn't known what it was. So in that regard, I hadn't interfered until I realized Gregor was cheating. Besides, if Gregor hadn't cheated in the first place, then there would have been no need for me to interfere, because Bones would have eventually killed him.

The Guardian glared at me for a long moment, but I didn't flinch under her gaze. Then she looked around. Bones was giving her a hard stare, as were Mencheres, Spade, and Vlad. Since there was room for reasonable doubt, if she ruled against me, Bones wouldn't accept it and this would turn into a bloodbath. She had to know that. But would it factor into her decision?

Finally, she shrugged. "I have no way to prove if you're lying, and Gregor's guilt is clear, so you are free to go."

Bones grabbed me in the next instant, holding me in an embrace that would have squeezed all the air out of me, if I'd had any. I held him back just as hard, hearing some of Gregor's allies sputter indignant objections. *There'll be repercussions,* I thought. There would also be repercussions for showing so many people what I could do with fire, even if I didn't know how long I'd have that power, but I pushed those concerns aside for a later day.

"We need to get the silver out of you, Crispin," I heard Spade say over Bones's shoulder.

"Not yet," Bones replied.

I shoved him lightly. "Yes, now. Are you crazy?"

He let out a snort as he released me, intensity lurking in his gaze. "No, luv. You are."

Bones knew I hadn't interfered just because I'd realized Gregor had cheated. *There'll be repercussions for that, too,* I thought, but first things first.

The liquid silver had to be cut out of Bones, I discovered. It was a gruesome, bloody process that made me wish I could kill Gregor a thousand times over.

No wonder something like this was illegal in a duel. I wouldn't use such an insidious weapon against an enemy. Bones had his shields up between us as Spade cut into him, but I didn't need our supernatural connection for it to hurt me as well.

Lucius was executed by the Law Guardians during his process.

When they were done with Lucius, the head Guardian informed us that we owed financial restitution for the theft of a member of Gregor's line—my mother. My mouth dropped at the amount she named, but Bones just nodded and said it would be taken care of. Since Gregor was dead, I wasn't sure who'd get the check, or if it would just go to the Law Guardians, but once again, I filed that away under Future Business.

Mencheres knelt next to us in the bloodstained earth. He held out his hand to Bones, who looked at it for the space of several seconds before he took it.

"You didn't see any of this?" Bones asked Mencheres.

The Egyptian vampire had the faintest smile. "Not a single part. I find I hate not knowing what will come to pass."

Bones snorted. "Welcome to the way the rest of us live."

Spade finished digging out the last of the silver from Bones and sat back with a grunt. "Blimey, Crispin, I hope never to do that again."

Bones let out another snort. "I quite agree, mate."

"Can we get out of here?" Now that Bones no longer had silver inside, poisoning him, I figured it was a good time to leave. Gregor's allies were still giving us very hostile looks, though the Guardians' presence—

and Bones's allies—kept them from acting. Still, no need to press our luck. Between Bones and me, we'd probably run through all our nine lives that night.

"Excellent idea, luv," Bones said, rising. "Where do you want to go?"

An ironic laugh escaped me. "Anywhere but Paris, Bones. Anywhere but there."

Dear Readers,

I'm so excited to introduce an excerpt from the first "spin-off" novel of the Night Huntress series, *First Drop of Crimson*.

After her husband's murder, Denise wants to leave all things paranormal behind, but thanks to an ancestor who made a pact with a demon and then ran off, she's forced back into the vampire world. Spade, a.k.a. Charles, is the powerful Master vampire Denise turns to for help trying to find her demon-dodging relative. If she doesn't succeed, the demonic essence she's been branded with will be permanent. After he lost the woman he loved to a mortal death, Spade has no intention of caring for a human again, especially one who wants nothing more than to return to a normal life. But as the demon brands gain strength inside Denise, she's unable to suppress her attraction for Spade, and his cool detachment toward humans is put to the test.

So turn the page for your first look at this exciting new chapter in the Night Huntress world.

Jeaniene Frost

Y OU'RE SAYING THE MAN JUST . . . DISAPPEARED?"
The police officer couldn't quite keep the disbelief out of his tone. Denise fought the urge to slap him. She didn't know how much more she could take. She'd already had to call her family and tell them this unthinkable news about Paul, grieved with them as they arrived at the hospital, then gave her report to the police. The one they seemed to have such trouble believing.

"As I said, when I looked up, the killer was gone."

"No one at the bar saw anyone out there, ma'am," the officer said for the third time.

Denise's temper snapped. "That's because they were inside when we were attacked. Look, the guy choked my cousin. Doesn't Paul have bruises around his neck?"

The officer glanced away. "No, ma'am. The medical examiner hasn't looked at him yet, but the paramedics didn't see any signs of strangulation. They did say they found evidence of cardiac arrest . . ."

"He's only twenty-five years old!" Denise burst out, ice sliding up her spine. Paul was dead—of an apparent heart attack. Just like Amber and Aunt Rose. Denise knew she hadn't imagined the man who'd been immune to both pepper spray and silver nitrate. The one who'd disappeared in a blink—and the big dog that had come out of nowhere.

Of course, she could relay none of this to the officer. He already looked at her like she was teetering on the crazy end of distraught. It hadn't escaped Denise's notice that when she'd been treated for pepper spray, her blood had also been taken, presumably to check her alcohol level. She'd already been asked multiple times how much she'd drank before leaving the bar. It was clear nothing she said, even leaving out mention of the supernatural, would be taken seriously if the medical examiner ruled that Paul had died of a heart attack.

Well, she knew people who'd believe her enough to investigate, but none of them was in this city, let alone this room.

"Can I go home now?" Denise asked.

A flash of relief crossed the officer's face. It only made Denise want to smack him more. "Sure. I can arrange for a squad car to take you."

"I'll call a cab."

He stood, bobbing his head. "Here's my card if you remember anything else."

Denise took it only because wadding it up and throwing it at him would look questionable. "Thank you."

She waited until she was inside her house before she made the call. No need to have the taxi driver talk about how his latest fare had babbled on about a murder by a man who *might* have turned into a dog. If the police found out she'd said that, she could forget about them following up on any leads she gave them, even if they did figure out this was a murder.

On the third ring, however, an automated voice picked up and intoned that the number she'd dialed had been disconnected. Denise hung up. That's right,

Cat had been moving from place to place because some crazy vampire was stalking her. She obviously changed her number, too. Was Cat still overseas? How long had it been since Denise last spoke to her? Weeks, maybe.

Next Denise tried the number she had listed for Bones, Cat's husband, but it, too, was disconnected. Denise dug around her house until she found an address book with the number for Cat's mother in it. The number was from over a year ago, so no surprise when that was also out of service.

Frustrated, Denise flung the address book on her couch. She'd been avoiding contact with the undead world, but now when she needed someone plugged into it, she didn't have anyone's current number.

There had to be *someone* she could reach. Denise scrolled through the entries in her cell phone, looking for anyone who had connections to Cat. When she was almost at the end, one name leapt out at her.

Spade. That's right, she'd inputted his number in her phone three months ago, because Spade had been the one to pick her up the last time she saw Cat.

Denise pressed "Call," praying she didn't hear that chipper monotone telling her that the number was no longer in service. Three rings, four . . .

"Hallo?"

Denise felt light-headed with relief at hearing Spade's distinctive English accent. "Spade, it's Denise. Cat's friend," she added, thinking of how many Denise's a centuries-old vampire probably knew. "I don't seem to have Cat's number and . . . I'm pretty sure some *thing* murdered my cousin. Maybe both cousins and my aunt, too."

It came out in a babble that sounded nuts, even to

her. She waited, hearing nothing but her breathing during the pause on the other line.

"This *is* Spade, isn't it?" she asked warily. What if she'd hit the wrong number somehow?

His voice flowed back immediately. "Yes, apologies for that. Why don't you tell me what you believe you saw?"

Denise noticed his phrasing, but she was too wired to argue about it. "I saw my cousin murdered by a man who didn't even twitch when I maced him in the face. Then the next thing I saw, a big damn dog was standing where the man had been, but it ran off, and the police think my twenty-five-year-old cousin died of a heart attack instead of being strangled."

Another silence filled the line. Denise could almost picture Spade frowning as he listened. The vampire scared her, but right now, she was more afraid of whatever had killed Paul.

"Are you still in Fort Worth?" he asked at last.

"Yes. Same house as . . . as before." *When you dropped me off after killing a man in cold blood.*

"Right. I'm sorry to inform you that Cat is in New Zealand. I can ring her or give you her number, but it would take a day at least for her to get to you, if not more."

Her friend and expert on all things inhuman was halfway around the world. Great.

". . . but I happen to be in the States," Spade went on. "In fact, I'm in California. I could be there later today, have a look at your cousin's body."

Denise sucked in her breath, torn between wanting to find out what had killed Paul in the quickest way possible, and feeling edgy about it being Spade doing the investigating. Then she shoved that back.

Paul, Amber, and her aunt's death meant more than her being *uncomfortable* about who was helping her.

"I'd appreciate—"

Spade cut her off. "Expect me 'round noon."

She looked at her watch. Less than six hours. She couldn't get from California to Texas that fast if her life depended on it, but if Spade said he'd be there around noon, she believed him.

"Thanks. Can you tell Cat, um, that . . ."

"Perhaps it's best if we don't involve Cat or Crispin just yet," Spade said, calling Bones by his human name as he always did. "They've had an awful time of it recently. No need to fret them if it's something I can handle."

Denise bit back her scoff. She knew what that translated to. *Or if you've just imagined all of this.*

"I'll see you at noon," she replied and hung up.

The house seemed eerily quiet. Denise glanced out the windows with a shiver, telling herself the foreboding sensation she had was a normal reaction to her violent night. Just to be sure, however, she went through each room and checked the windows and doors. All locked. Then she forced herself to shower, trying to block the image of Paul's blue-tinged face from her mind. If she hadn't agreed to go out drinking with him, he might still be alive now. Or what if she'd immediately run into the bar for help, instead of staying in the parking lot? Could she have saved Paul if she'd come out with a bunch of people who could have scared the attacker off? He'd left as soon as people responded to her screams; maybe she *could* have saved Paul if she hadn't stood there uselessly macing his killer.

Denise was so caught up in her thoughts that she

ignored the tapping sounds until they happened a third time. Then she froze. They were coming from her front door.

She pulled her Glock out of her nightstand. It was filled with silver bullets, which might only slow down a vampire but would kill anything human.

What if it was someone trying to pick the lock? Should she call the police or try to see what it was first? If it was just a raccoon nosing around and she called the cops, they'd *really* discount anything she said in the future.

Denise kept the gun pointed toward the sounds as she edged around to the front windows. If she angled her body just so, she could see—

"What?" Denise gasped out loud.

On her porch was a little girl, something red on her outfit. She was tapping on the door in a way that looked hurt or exhausted or both. Now Denise could make out the word "help" coming faintly from her.

Denise set down the gun and yanked open the door. The little girl's face was streaked with tears and her whole frame trembled.

"Daddy's hurt," the child lisped.

She picked her up, looking around for a car or any other indicator of how the little girl had gotten there.

"What happened, sweetie? Where's your daddy?" Denise crooned as she took the child inside.

The little girl smiled. "Daddy's dead," she said, her voice changing to something low and deep.

Denise's arms fell at the instant deluge of weight, horror filling her as she saw the little girl morph into the same man who'd murdered Paul.

"Thanks for letting me in," he said, his hand clapping over Denise's mouth just in time to cut off her scream.

Spade closed his mobile phone, mulling the conversation he'd just had. Denise MacGregor fancied her cousin had been murdered by some sort of weredog—except weredogs or were-anything didn't exist.

The only reason he was making the trip to Texas was on the off chance that there was another explanation. It was possible a vampire murdered her cousin and then tranced Denise into thinking she'd seen him transform into a dog. Human memories were so easy to alter. And if Denise *had* witnessed a vampire attack, the murderer might decide to use more than glamour to make sure she didn't retell the tale. Since Denise was his best mate's friend, he'd go to ensure her safety, if another vampire was involved.

Spade cast a look at his bed with regret. He'd long ago mastered the crippling lethargy that came with sunrise, but that didn't mean he relished a trip to Texas now. Ah, well. It was the least he could do to ensure Crispin and Cat didn't rush back from New Zealand for what was, in all likelihood, just the emotional breakdown of a human who'd snapped from too much grief and stress.

He remembered the look Denise gave him the last time he'd seen her. Specks of blood dotted her clothes, her face had been as pale as Spade's own ivory skin, and her hazel eyes held a mixture of revulsion and fear.

"Why did you have to kill him?" she'd whispered.

"Because of what he intended to do," Spade replied. *"No one deserves to live after that."*

She hadn't understood. Spade did, though. All too

well. Humans might be more forgiving with their punishments, but Spade knew better than to show a rapist, even a potential one, any naïve mercy.

He also remembered the last thing Denise said when he'd dropped her off at her house later that night. *I'm so sick of the violence in your world.* He'd seen that look on many humans' faces, heard the same flat resonance in their voices, and it all ended the same. If Crispin weren't so busy with everything that had happened lately, he'd explain to Cat how the kindest thing to do for her friend was to erase Denise's memory of all things undead. Perhaps Spade would do that himself if Denise had become delusional. Kindness aside, if her grasp on reality *had* slipped, it would also eliminate a liability if everything Denise knew about them was erased from her recall.

Spade filled his satchel with enough clothes for a few days and went downstairs to the garage. Once settled behind the wheel of his Porsche, he put on dark shades and then clicked open the garage door. Bloody sun was already up. Spade gave it a baleful glare as he pulled out into the dawn.

Humans. Aside from tasting delicious, they were usually more trouble than they were worth.

History of Passion ...

Dearest Reader,

Don't be deceived. Behind her demure smile and guarded gaze even the most proper lady has a secret. But what happens when the sting of betrayal, ache of sacrifice, or ghosts of lovers past return, threatening to shake that Mona Lisa smile?

This summer, Avon Books presents four delicious romances about four women who are more than what they seem, and the dangerously handsome heroes who are captivated by them. From bestselling authors Elizabeth Boyle, Loretta Chase, Jeaniene Frost, and a beautifully repackaged edition by Susan Wiggs.

Coming May 2009

Memoirs of a Scandalous Red Dress

by *New York Times* bestselling author

Elizabeth Boyle

Twenty years ago, Pippin betrayed her heart and married another in order to save Captain Thomas Dashwell's life. Now their paths cross again and Pippin is determined not to let a second chance at love slip away. Dash's world stops when he sees her standing aboard his ship but promises himself he'll never again fall for the breathtaking beauty.

$\mathcal{D}$ashwell's nostrils were filled with the scent of newly minted guineas. Enough Yellow Georges to make even the dour Mr. Hardy happy. Nodding in satisfaction, he whistled low and soft like a seabird to the men in the longboat.

They pulled up one man, then another, and cut the bindings that had their arms tied around their backs and tossed the two over the side and into the surf.

That ought to cool their heels a bit, Dashwell mused, as he watched the Englishmen splash their way to shore. His passengers had been none too pleased with him last night when he'd abandoned their delivery in favor of saving his neck and the lives of his crew.

Untying the mule, he led the beast down the shore toward the longboat. It came along well enough until it got down to the waterline, where the waves were coming in and the longboat tossed and crunched against the rocks. Then the animal showed its true nature and began to balk.

The miss who'd caught his eye earlier came over and took hold of the reins, her other hand stroking the beast's muzzle and talking softly to it until it settled down.

"You have a way about you," he said over his shoulder, as he walked back and forth, working alongside his men, who were as anxious as he was to gain their gold and be gone from this precarious rendezvous.

"Do you have a name?" he asked, when he returned for the last sack. This close he could see all too well the modest cut of her gown, her shy glances, and the way she bit her lip as if she didn't know whether to speak to him.

Suddenly it occurred to him who, or rather what she was, and he had only one thought.

What the devil was Josephine doing bringing a lady, one barely out of the schoolroom, into this shady business?

"What? No name?" he pressed, coming closer still, for he'd never met a proper lady—he certainly didn't count Josephine as one, not by the way she swore and gambled and schemed.

As he took another step closer he caught the veriest hint of roses on her. Soft and subtle, but to a man like him it sent a shock of desire through him as he'd never known.

Careful there, Dashwell, he cautioned himself. If the militia didn't shoot him, he had to imagine Josephine would. "Come sweetling, what is your name?"

There was no harm in just asking, now was there?

The wee bit of muslin pursed her lips shut, then glanced over at her companions, as if seeking their help. And when she looked back at him, he smiled at her. The grin that usually got him into trouble.

"Pippin," she whispered, again glancing back over toward where Josephine was haranguing Temple and Clifton for news from the Continent.

"Pippin, eh?" he replied softly, not wanting to frighten her, even as he found himself mesmerized by the soft, uncertain light in her eyes. "I would call you something else. Something befitting such a pretty lady." He tapped his fingers to his lips. "Circe. Yes, that's it. From now on I'll call you my Circe. For you're truly a siren to lure me ashore."

Even in the dark he could see her cheeks brighten with a blush, hear the nervous rattle to her words. "I don't think that is proper."

Proper? He'd fallen into truly deep waters now, for something devilish inside him wanted to make sure this miss never worried about such a ridiculous notion again.

But something else, something entirely foreign to him, urged him to see that she never knew anything else but a safe and proper existence.

A thought he extinguished as quickly as he could. For it was rank with strings and chains and noble notions that had no place in his world.

"Not proper?" He laughed, more to himself than

at her. "Not proper is the fact that this bag feels a bit lighter than the rest." He hoisted it up and jangled it as he turned toward the rest of the party on the beach. "My lady, don't tell me you've cheated me yet again."

For indeed, the bag did feel light.

Lady Josephine winced, but then had the nerve to deny her transgression. "Dash, I'll not pay another guinea into your dishonest hands."

No wonder she'd brought her pair of lovely doves down to the beach. A bit of distraction so he'd not realize he wasn't getting his full price.

"Then I shall take my payment otherwise," he said, and before anyone could imagine what he was about, he caught hold of this tempting little Pippin and pulled her into his arms.

She gasped as he caught hold of her, and for a moment he felt a twinge of conscience.

Thankfully he wasn't a man to stand on such notions for long.

"I've always wanted to kiss a lady," he told her, just before his lips met hers.

At first he'd been about to kiss her as he would any other girl, but there was a moment, just as he looked down at her, with only one thought—to plunder those lips—that he found himself lost.

Her eyes were blue, as azure as the sea off the West Indies, and they caught him with their wide innocence, their trust.

Trust? In him?

Foolish girl, he thought as he drew closer and then kissed her, letting his lips brush over hers. Yet instead of his usual blustering ways, he found himself reining back his desire. This was the girl's first kiss, he knew that with the same surety that he knew how many casks of brandy were in his hold, and ever-so-gently, he ventured past her lips, slowly letting his tongue sweep over hers.

She gasped again, but this time from the very intimacy of it, and Dash suddenly found himself inside a maelstrom.

He tried to stop himself from falling, for that would mean setting her aside. But he couldn't let her go.

This Pippin, this innocent lass, this very proper lady, brought him alive as no other woman ever had.

Mine, he thought, with possessiveness, with passion, with the knowledge that she was his, and always would be.

He wanted to know everything about her, her real name, her secrets, her desires . . . His hands traced her lines, the slight curve of her hips, the soft swell of her breasts.

She shivered beneath his touch, but she didn't stop him, didn't try to shy away. Instead, she kissed him back, innocently, tentatively at first, then eagerly.

Good God, he was holding an angel!

And as if the heavens themselves rang out in protest over his violation of one of their own, a rocket screeched across the sky, and when it exploded, wrenching the night into day with a shower of sparks, Dashwell pulled back from her and looked up.

As another rocket shot upward, he realized two things.

Yes, by God, her eyes were as blue as the sea.

And secondly, the militia wasn't at the local pub bragging about their recent exploits.

Driven by moral code, Lord of the Night, Sandro Cavalli, polices the streets of sixteenth-century Venice bringing malefactors to justice. No one can sway him from his duty until he meets the young and disarming Laura Bandello. But could this innocent beauty be involved in a shocking plot? All Sandro knows is that he'll sacrifice everything for the warmth of her arms.

Laura seated herself, and Sandro took the opposite chair. The fire crackled cheerily in the marble framed grate. "Have you run afoul of the law, madonna?"

"Of course not." She folded her hands demurely in her lap. "My lord, I have information about Daniele Moro."

Her words pounded in Sandro's head. Disbelief made him fierce. "How do you know of Moro?"

"Well." She ran her tongue over her lips. Sandro knew women who spent fortunes to achieve that beautiful shade of crimson, but he saw no trace of rouge on Laura. "I have a confession to make, my lord."

A denial leapt in his throat. No. She could not be involved in the butchery of Moro. Not her. Anyone but her. "Go on," he said thickly.

"I heard you speaking of Moro to Maestro Titian." She leaned forward and hurried on. "Please forgive me, but I was so curious, I couldn't help myself. Besides, this might be for the best. I can help you solve this case, my lord."

He didn't want her help. He didn't want to think of this innocent lamb sneaking in the dark, listening at doorways, hearing of the atrocity that left even him feeling sick and soiled.

Without thinking, he jumped up, grasped her by the shoulders, and drew her to her feet. Although he sensed the silent censure of Jamal, he ignored it and sank his fingers into the soft flesh of her upper arms. He smelled her scent of sea air and jasmine, saw the firelight sparkling in her beautiful, opalescent eyes.

"Damn you for your meddlesome ways," he hissed through his teeth. "You have no business poking your nose into the affairs of the *signori di notte*."

She seemed unperturbed by his temper, unscathed by his rough embrace. She lifted her chin. "I'm well aware of that, my lord, but remember, I did warn you of my inquisitive nature."

"Then I should have warned you that I have no use for women—inquisitive or otherwise."

She lifted her hands to his chest and pressed gently. "Your fingers are bruising me, my lord."

He released her as abruptly as he had snatched her up. "My apologies."

"I wouldn't worry about it, but Maestro Titian will

question me about any bruises when I model for him."

Sandro despised the image of Laura laid out like a feast upon the artist's red couch, lissome and sensual as a goddess, while Titian rendered her beauty on canvas.

"Do you truly have no use for women, my lord?" she asked. "That's unusual, especially in so handsome a man as you."

Sandro ignored her insincere compliment and paused to consider his four mistresses. Barbara, Arnetta, Gioia, and Alicia were as different and yet as alike as the four seasons. For years they had fulfilled his needs with the discretion and decorum he required. In exchange, he housed each in her own luxurious residence.

"It's my choice," he said stuffily, settling back in his chair. He did not need to look at Jamal to know that he was grinning with glee.

"Well, I believe my information could be useful to you." She sent him a sidelong glance. Not even the demure brown dress could conceal her lush curves. "That is, if you're interested, my lord."

As she sank gracefully back into the chair, he stared at the shape of her breasts, ripe beneath their soft cloak of linen. "I'm interested."

She smiled, the open, charming expression that was fast becoming familiar to him. "I happened to mention the murder of Daniele Moro to my friend Yasmin—"

"By God," he snapped, "don't you understand? This is a sensitive matter." He gripped the chair arms to keep himself anchored to his seat. "You can't go airing police business all over the city."

"I didn't." She seemed truly bewildered. "I told only one person."

"You could endanger yourself, madonna. The killer is still at large."

"Oh. I'm not used to having someone worry about my welfare."

"It is my vocation to worry about the welfare of every citizen of the republic."

She shifted impatiently. "Never mind all that. I found someone who saw Daniele Moro on the night he was killed."

Once again, Sandro came out of his chair. *"What?"*

"I'll take you to meet this person, my lord."

"Do that, and I'll think about forgiving you."

Coming July 2009

Don't Tempt Me

by *New York Times* bestselling author

Loretta Chase

Imprisoned in a harem for twelve years, Zoe Lexham knows things no well-bred lady should . . . ruining her for society. Can the wickedly handsome Duke Lucien de Grey use his influence to save her from idle tongues? A simple enough task, if only he can stifle desire long enough to see his seductive charge safely into respectability . . .

Zoe went cold, then hot. She felt dizzy. But it was a wonderful dizziness, the joy of release.

Now at last she stood in the open.

Here I am, she thought. *Home at last, at last. Yes, look at me. Look your fill. I'm not invisible anymore.*

She felt his big, warm hand clasp hers. The warmth rushed into her heart and made it hurry. She was aware of her pulse jumping against her throat and against her wrist, so close to his. The heat spread into her belly and down, to melt her knees.

I'm going to faint, she thought. But she couldn't let

herself swoon merely because a man had touched her. Not now, at any rate. Not here. She made herself look up at him.

Lucien wore the faintest smile—of mockery or amusement she couldn't tell. Behind his shuttered eyes she sensed rather than saw a shadow. She remembered the brief glimpse of pain he'd had when she'd mentioned his brother. It vanished in an instant, but she'd seen it in his first, surprised reaction: the darkness there, bleak and empty and unforgettable.

She gazed longer than she should have into his eyes, those sleepy green eyes that watched her so intently yet shut her out. And at last he let out a short laugh and raised her hand to his mouth, brushing her knuckles against his lips.

Had they been in the harem, she would have sunk onto the pillows and thrown her head back, inviting him. But they were not and he'd declined to make her his wife.

And she was not a man, to let her lust rule her brain. This man was not a good candidate for a spouse. There had been a bond between them once. Not a friendship, really. In childhood, the few years between them was a chasm, as was the difference in their genders. Still, he'd been fond of her once, she thought, in his own fashion. But that was before.

Now he was everything every woman could want, and he knew it.

She desired him the way every other woman desired him. Still, at least she finally felt desire, she told herself. If she could feel it with him, she'd feel it with someone else, someone who wanted her, who'd give his heart to her. For now, she was grateful to be free. She was grateful to stand on this balcony and look out upon the hundreds of people below.

She squeezed his hand in thanks and let her mouth form a slow, genuine smile of gratitude and happiness, though she couldn't help glancing up at him once from under her lashes to seek his reaction.

She glimpsed the heat flickering in the guarded green gaze.

Ah, yes. He felt it, too: the powerful physical awareness crackling between them.

He released her hand. "We've entertained the mob for long enough," he said. "Go inside."

She turned away. The crowd began to stir and people were talking again but more quietly. They'd become a murmuring sea rather than a roaring one.

"You've seen her," he said, and his deep voice easily carried over the sea. "You shall see her again from time to time. Now go away."

After a moment, they began to turn away, and by degrees they drifted out of the square.

Coming August 2009

Destined for an Early Grave

by *New York Times* bestselling author

Jeaniene Frost

Just when Cat is ready for a little rest and relaxation with her sexy vampire boyfriend Bones, she's haunted by dreams from her past—a past she doesn't remember. To unlock these secrets, Cat may have to venture all the way into the grave. But the truth could rock what she knows about herself—and her relationship with Bones.

If he catches me, I'm dead.

I ran as fast as I could, darting around trees, tangled roots, and rocks in the forest. The monster snarled as it chased me, the sound closer than before. I wasn't able to outrun it. The monster was picking up speed while I was getting tired.

The forest thinned ahead of me to reveal a blond vampire on a hill in the distance. I recognized him at once and hope surged through me. If I could reach him, I'd be okay. He loved me; he'd protect me from the monster. Yet I was still so far away.

Fog crept up the hill to surround the vampire, making him appear almost ghost-like. I screamed his name as the monster's footsteps got even closer. Panicked, I lunged forward, narrowly avoiding the grasp of bony hands that would pull me down to the grave. With renewed effort, I sprinted toward the vampire. He urged me on, snarling warnings at the monster that wouldn't stop chasing me.

"Leave me alone," I screamed as a merciless grip seized me from behind. "No!"

"Kitten!"

The shout didn't come from the vampire ahead of me; it came from the monster wrestling me to the ground. I jerked my head toward the vampire in the distance, but his features blurred into nothingness and the fog covered him. Right before he disappeared, I heard his voice.

"He is not your husband, Catherine."

A hard shake evaporated the last of the dream and I woke to find Bones, my vampire lover, hovered over me.

"What is it? Are you hurt?"

An odd question, you would think, since it had only been a nightmare. But with the right power and magic, sometimes nightmares could be turned into weapons. A while back, I'd almost been killed by one. This was different, however. No matter how vivid it felt, it had just been a dream.

"I'll be fine if you quit shaking me."

Bones dropped his hands and let out a noise of relief. "You didn't wake up and you were thrashing on the bed. Brought back rotten memories."

"I'm okay. It was a . . . weird dream."

There was something about the vampire in it that nagged me. Like I should know who he was. That made no sense, however, since he was just a figment of my imagination.

"Odd that I couldn't catch any of your dream," Bones went on. "Normally your dreams are like background music to me."

Bones was a Master vampire, more powerful than most vampires I'd ever met. One of his gifts was the ability to read human minds. Even though I was half-human, half-vampire, there was enough humanity in me that Bones could hear my thoughts, unless I worked to block him. Still, this was news to me.

"You can hear my *dreams*? God, you must never get any quiet. I'd be shooting myself in the head if I were you."

Which wouldn't do much to him, actually. Only silver through the heart or decapitation was lethal to a vampire. Getting shot in the head might take care of *my* ills the permanent way, but it would just give Bones a nasty headache.

He settled himself back onto the pillows. "Don't fret, luv. I said it's like background music, so it's rather soothing. As for quiet, out here on this water, it's as quiet as I've experienced without being half-shriveled in the process."

I lay back down, a shiver going through me at the mention of his near-miss with death. Bones's hair had turned white from how close he'd come to dying, but now it was back to its usual rich brown color.

"Is that why we're drifting on a boat out in the Atlantic? So you could have some peace and quiet?"

"I wanted some time alone with you, Kitten. We've had so little of that lately."

An understatement. Even though I'd quit my job leading the secret branch of Homeland Security that hunted rogue vampires and ghouls, life hadn't been dull. First we'd had to deal with our losses from the war with another Master vampire last year. Several of Bones's friends—and my best friend Denise's husband, Randy—had been murdered. Then there had been months of hunting down the remaining perpetrators of that war so they couldn't live to plot against us another day. Then training my replacement so that my uncle Don had someone else to play bait when his operatives went after the misbehaving members of undead society. Most vampires and ghouls didn't kill when they fed, but there were those who killed for fun. Or stupidity. My uncle made sure those vampires and ghouls were taken care of—and that ordinary citizens weren't aware they existed.

So when Bones told me we were taking a boat trip, I'd assumed there must be some search-and-destroy reason behind it. Going somewhere just for relaxation hadn't happened, well, *ever*, in our relationship.

"This is a weekend getaway?" I couldn't keep the disbelief out of my voice.

He traced his finger on my lower lip. "This is our vacation, Kitten. We can go anywhere in the world and take our time getting there. So tell me, where shall we go?"

"Paris."

I surprised myself saying it. I'd never had a burning desire to visit there before, but for some reason, I did now. Maybe it was because Paris was supposed to be the city of lovers, although just looking at Bones was usually enough to get me in a romantic mood.

He must have caught my thought, because he smiled, making his face more breathtaking, in my opinion. Lying against the navy sheets, his skin almost glowed with a silky alabaster paleness that was too perfect to be human. The sheets were tangled past his stomach, giving me an uninterrupted view of his lean, taut abdomen and hard, muscled chest. Dark brown eyes began to tinge with emerald and fangs peeked under the curve of his mouth, letting me know I wasn't the only one feeling warmer all of a sudden.

"Paris it is, then," he whispered, and flung the sheets off.

THE NIGHT HUNTRESS NOVELS FROM

Jeaniene Frost

✦ HALFWAY TO THE GRAVE ✦

978-0-06-124508-4

Before she can enjoy her newfound status as kick-ass demon hunter, half vampire Cat Crawfield and her sexy mentor, Bones, are pursued by a group of killers. Now Cat will have to choose a side…and Bones is turning out to be as tempting as any man with a heartbeat.

✦ ONE FOOT IN THE GRAVE ✦

978-0-06-124509-1

Cat Crawfield is now a special agent, working for the government to rid the world of the rogue undead. But when she's targeted for assassination she turns to her ex, the sexy and dangerous vampire Bones, to help her.

✦ AT GRAVE'S END ✦

978-0-06-158307-0

Caught in the crosshairs of a vengeful vamp, Cat's about to learn the true meaning of bad blood—just as she and Bones need to stop a lethal magic from being unleashed.

At Avon Books, we know your passion for romance—once you finish one of our novels, you find yourself wanting more.

May we tempt you with . . .

- **Excerpts** from our upcoming releases.

- Entertaining **extras,** including authors' personal photo albums and book lists.

- Behind-the-scenes **scoop** on your favorite characters and series.

- **Sweepstakes** for the chance to win free books, romantic getaways, and other fun prizes.

- Writing **tips** from our authors and editors.

- **Blog** with our authors and find out why they love to write romance.

- **Exclusive content** that's not contained within the pages of our novels.

Join us at
www.avonbooks.com

AVON

An Imprint of HarperCollins*Publishers*
www.avonromance.com

Available wherever books are sold or please call 1-800-331-3761 to order.

FTH 0708